By Don Travis

BJ VINSON MYSTERIES
The Zozobra Incident
The Bisti Business

Published by DSP PUBLICATIONS
www.dsppublications.com

THE BISTI BUSINESS

A **BJ VINSON** MYSTERY

DON TRAVIS

DSP PUBLICATIONS

Published by

DSP PUBLICATIONS

5032 Capital Circle SW, Suite 2, PMB# 279, Tallahassee, FL 32305-7886 USA
www.dsppublications.com

This is a work of fiction. Names, characters, places, and incidents either are the product of author imagination or are used fictitiously, and any resemblance to actual persons, living or dead, business establishments, events, or locales is entirely coincidental.

The Bisti Business
© 2017 Don Travis.

Cover Art
© 2017 Maria Fanning.
Cover content is for illustrative purposes only and any person depicted on the cover is a model.

ISBN: 978-1-63533-112-7
Digital ISBN: 978-1-63533-113-4
Library of Congress Control Number: 2016914509
Published March 2017
v. 2.0
First Edition published by Martin Brown Publishers, LLC, 2013.

Printed in the United States of America
∞
This paper meets the requirements of
ANSI/NISO Z39.48-1992 (Permanence of Paper).

To my family, who sometimes took second place to my writing,
and to all the readers in the world.

Acknowledgments

TO MY critique buddy, Joycelyn Campbell, for her stern eye and steady guidance. And to Wordwrights, the writing class I coteach, for their willing contribution.

THE BISTI BUSINESS

A BJ VINSON MYSTERY

DON TRAVIS

Prologue

Bisti/De-Na-Zin Wilderness, south of Farmington, New Mexico

A HUGE red-tailed hawk soared above the high desert floor, her keen-eyed gaze scouring the panorama unfolding below. The plumed predator dipped a wing and veered eastward, attracted by movement. The huge bird's flitting shadow startled two figures, interrupting a heated argument. Both glanced up quickly.

Taking advantage of the moment, the larger man snaked a belt from his waist and slipped behind the other. He whipped the leather strap over his victim's head and snugged it against his throat, driving the hapless man to the ground with a knee to the buttocks. After a long, desperate struggle, the figure sprawled in the sand ceased to resist. The violent tremors in his extremities passed, and he lay still.

Panting from his exertions, the killer rose and began the hunt for a suitable crevice to hide the body. It wasn't difficult to find one in the unstable terrain of these remote badlands. Satisfied his cairn of loose stones and sandy soil blended well with this weird, otherworldly place, he turned and plodded toward his distant vehicle, ignoring the display of nature's wry humor all around him. Mute, grotesque gargoyles of clay and sandstone; hoodoos masquerading as monumental toadstools; spheroid stones aping gigantic dinosaur eggs; and eroded clay hills with folds like delicate lace drapery.

Chapter 1

THE TELEPHONE jolted me out of my reverie. Hazel Harris, my secretary, aide, and surrogate mother, had left for the day, but the answering service could field the call. Ninety percent of my clients were attorneys, and there weren't many of them working this time of day. But when the phone shrieked a second time, I glanced at the unfamiliar long-distance number on the caller ID and caved in to curiosity.

"B. J. Vinson, Confidential Investigations."

"Who's speaking?"

"B. J. Vinson. What can I do for you?"

"What's this?" a gravelly voice demanded. "Some rinky-dink outfit where the boss answers his own phone?"

Curiosity has its limits. Without another word I dropped the receiver back into its cradle. It usually takes a while to recognize a problem client, but this obnoxious prick had done me a favor by convincing me of it within a couple of sentences.

I swiveled my chair around to return to what I had been doing, savoring the view from the north-facing window of my third-floor office in one of Albuquerque's historic buildings at Fifth and Copper. I often undertook this ritual before heading home. It was my favorite vista at my favorite hour in my least favorite time of year—about three-quarters of the way into evening on a muggy summer's day made uncomfortable by the lingering humidity of an earlier quick-moving thunderstorm. Fortunately a more hospitable autumn hovered just around the corner.

The phone intruded again. Determined to cut this guy off at the pass, I snatched up the receiver, but before I could say anything, a loud laugh threatened to burst my eardrum.

"Short fuse, huh? Okay, I can respect that. Look, I'm in Hawaii on business and lost track of the time difference. Sorry to call so late."

The bastard was pretty good at defusing things.

"Let's start over, shall we? I'm Anthony P. Alfano. I run Alfano Vineyards in Napa Valley. I've got a problem out there in New Mexico, and I think you're the guy who can help me. I got your name off the Internet. I like your website. It's a solid professional layout."

He left me little recourse except to respond gracefully. "Thanks. I assume you checked me out with someone too." I exhaled and tried to ignore the feeling I was being manipulated by an expert. "Okay, what's the problem?"

"My son. He's missing. Probably nothing serious, but I need to locate him."

Orlando Selvanus Alfano—was this family Italian, or what?— twenty-one and a graduate student in history at UCLA, had left on July twenty-second for an extended vacation. He and his traveling companion, another student named Dana Norville, intended to explore the natural wonders of the great Southwest and sample the wares of the local vineyards. Even though they were three days late returning home, the vacationers were still registered at the Albuquerque Sheraton on Menaul and Louisiana across the street from Coronado mall. Repeated phone messages left at the hotel and on Orlando's cell phone had gotten no response. The two were going to miss the first classes of the fall semester if they didn't return immediately.

"I take it the other student—this Dana—is his girlfriend."

Alfano's pregnant pause and terse answer raised my antennae. "It's Dana James Norville. One of those names that can go either way."

So that's the way it was. Alfano needed a gay PI to look for a gay son. "Does he? Go either way, I mean?"

His rage was palpable. "Only *one* way. The wrong way."

"And your son?"

Instead of the expected explosion, Alfano sighed heavily. "You have to understand something—Orlando's not queer. Hell, most of us jerked off with buddies when we were kids. We grew out of it. No harm done. Lando's just a slow developer. He hasn't come out of it yet, but he will."

"How about Norville?"

"That bastard's a dyed-in-the-wool pansy, and he's contaminating my son."

I bit my tongue at the sophomoric outburst. "For your information, Mr. Alfano, I'm pretty 'dyed-in-the-wool' myself. I think you need to call someone else."

"Now wait a minute." Anthony Alfano obviously was not accustomed to getting the brush-off. "I know all about you. And except for that—nonsense—you've got a good reputation. You can move in both the straight world and the gay world. You're the one I want. Find my son, Vinson, and send him home to his mother and me."

"It's *Mr.* Vinson." Might as well set the bigoted SOB straight right at the beginning.

"All right, *Mr.* Vinson, score one for you. Are you sure you're gay? You don't sound it."

"Does your son?"

"No, but—"

"But in your dreams he's not twisted, right? How about Norville? Am I looking for a flaming queen?"

"Of course not. Lando wouldn't hang out with someone like that. No, I've got to admit, looking at Dana Norville, you wouldn't suspect."

"Then how can you be certain?"

"I did a quick background check on Norville when the two of them started bumming around together, and the guy was clean. But when they… uh, got close, I took another look and found the man Norville had been shacking up with before he latched onto my son."

"Very well, Mr. Alfano, I'll look into the matter. I'll do it for Orlando and Dana, but you're going to be footing the bills."

He promised to have his secretary in California call Hazel tomorrow with the credit card information for my retainer and to provide anything else we requested. I asked him to e-mail color photos of the two men. If they were as close as he believed, there would be a few around somewhere. He also gave me his son's cell and pager numbers.

After hanging up, I tapped my desk blotter with a gold-and-onyx letter opener fashioned into a miniature Toledo blade. I sighed aloud. The Alfano case had all the hallmarks of developing into a nightmare. Working for attorneys was easier; they understood the process. Private individuals had a warped idea of what a PI did, which was nothing more or less than gathering information. But I was committed, so I might as well make the best of it.

I returned to the visual meditation of the landscape outside my window. As nature's glow dimmed, man-made lights came alive: amber lampposts, white fluorescents, flamboyant neons, yellow vehicle headlights reflecting off wet pavement, and far in the distance, a tiny spot moving slowly across the sky—one of the aerial trams hauling patrons up Sandia Peak's rugged western escarpment to the restaurant atop the mountain.

By leaning forward, I caught the faint, rosy underbelly of a western cloudbank, the lingering legacy of a dead sunset. Was that what had drawn Orlando and Dana to the Land of Enchantment? Spectacular scenery and surreal sunsets? Or was it our rich heritage of Indian and Hispanic art? The two were history majors, and Albuquerque had a long history. It was approaching its three-hundredth birthday, while Santa Fe and many of the nearby Indian Pueblos had longer lifelines.

Beyond my line of sight, the city's original settlement lay to the west where one- and two-storied adobe shops—some ancient and some merely pretending to be—hearken back to their Spanish colonial roots. Now known as Old Town, it was founded in 1706 by Governor Francisco Cuervo y Valdez as the Villa del Alburqurque—some say Ranchos del Alburqurque. In either case, the Spanish colonial outpost was named in honor of New Spain's viceroy in Mexico City. The second *r* of the duke's name disappeared in 1880 with the coming of the railroad to New Town, located two miles east of Hispanic Old Town, a signal the Anglos had successfully wrested the heart—if not the soul—of the community from its founders.

It seemed as though a similar battle was being waged between Dana Norville and Anthony Alfano for the heart and soul of Orlando. Papa Alfano had given me cell phone *and* pager numbers for his son. He kept his pup on a short leash—or tried to. Not only that, but the old man had checked Norville out at the first signs of a budding friendship between the two. I'd bet Alfano was accustomed to throwing his weight around, railroading or buying whomever he wanted, including his son. My instinctive dislike of the homophobic bully made me wonder how far he would go to "turn his son around." Maybe Orlando went on the run to get out from under the thumb of his tyrannical patriarch.

Spinning back to the desk, I went on the hunt for information over the Internet. According to Dun & Bradstreet, the Alfano Vineyards' net worth was somewhere around $100 million. Although California is notoriously anal-retentive about releasing its criminal records, the superior court websites I searched revealed nothing on Alfano, but that only meant he wasn't a known murderer, rapist, or kidnapper. He would have bought his way out of anything less than that. Orlando, on the other hand, had a sheet in Los Angeles. From the limited information available, it looked to be nothing more than a couple of disturbing the peace charges. Norville's record was about the same, leading me to believe they had been activists in their early university days. Maybe they met while agitating for some cause or the other. Gay rights? Voting rights?

There was no answer at their room in the uptown Sheraton. Well, no surprise there. The call to the kid's cell phone went to a message center. I left a callback on the pager without much hope. Things are never that easy.

I had finished dictating instructions for the Alfano contract and was reaching to snap off my old-fashioned, green-shaded banker's lamp when the telephone rang again. Maybe I'd caught a break. I hadn't, but the sound of Paul Barton's baritone sent my energy level soaring.

"You still at work?" he asked.

"Just finishing up. How about meeting somewhere for a late dinner?"

A deep chuckle. "Meet me at 5229 Post Oak Drive NW."

"You're home?"

"Yep. And I have a surprise for you."

"Let me guess—green chili stew and warm, buttered tortillas. Uh… what's for dessert?"

"I'll leave that to your imagination." He hung up in the middle of a wicked laugh.

Chapter 2

IT TOOK a little effort to get my mental and physical pistons running in sync the next morning. Living with a champion swimmer in his early twenties wasn't always easy for a guy my age—a month shy of thirty-five. Paul can get by on less sleep than I can and has no compunction about waking me in the middle of the night with his not-so-subtle nuzzling. But I wouldn't change a thing.

Despite a night with little sleep, I got into the office at a decent hour. Hazel had Alfano's contract ready and awaiting my approval. I signed with a flourish, handed it back to fax to his secretary, and gave my secretary/office manager/surrogate mother the once-over. This sixty-two-year-old gray-haired model of efficiency was undergoing a transformation. First a feather-cut bobbed style replaced the bun formerly held in place by tortoiseshell combs. Then her black-rimmed spectacles had vanished in favor of gold-framed designer glasses. Today the granny look was replaced by a smart chalk-striped, two-piece business suit and a white blouse with about a yard of frilly lace at the throat hiding at least one of her chins. I smothered a smile. Charlie Weeks, the retired cop who sometimes handled my overflow cases, had been hanging around the office more than usual lately.

"What?" She peered at me through her new lenses.

"Nice suit. New?"

"Not particularly." She lifted her powdered nose enough to make a statement. She had no compunction about poking into my business but resented me meddling in hers.

"Looks good on you." I reached for the telephone as she marched into the outer office.

The Sheraton on Menaul confirmed Alfano and Norville were still registered but refused to divulge any further information. Deciding against driving uptown to try and talk my way into their room, I undertook another approach.

Gene Enriquez, my old partner at APD, had recently made lieutenant, and he sometimes chaffed at the rein the promotion put on his fieldwork. When I called he indulged in some bellyaching about being swamped but agreed to meet for a cup of coffee at Eulalia's in the La Posada on Second and Copper, a short walk for each of us.

The central core of my building opened onto an atrium soaring through all five levels. As the elevator doors parted on the ground floor, my eyes automatically swept the waxed tiles. A year ago a man had died on those hard clay squares when he went over the railing after attacking me on the landing outside of my office on the third level. Sometimes I still saw smears of blood on the floor, but it was an illusion. The blue-black terra-cotta was scrubbed spotless and polished to a high shine.

I exited the building and headed east on Copper, pausing to say hello to the *Sidewalk Society*, nine life-sized bronzes by the Santa Fe–based sculptor, Glenna Goodacre, that were grouped on the corner sidewalk outside the Hyatt Regency. After greeting the cast figures almost daily for the past few years, I had reached a few conclusions about them. The young woman with a briefcase was said to be an up-and-coming CEO, but I'm convinced she was a 1950s lawyer. The construction worker and his foreman, who sported a battered, old-style broad-brimmed hat, represented the thirties or forties. It had taken me some time to tumble to the fact the statues reflected different time periods in Albuquerque's more recent history.

Gene yelled for me to wait for him as he strode briskly across Civic Plaza. "You always talk to statues?" He was a little breathless after running to beat the light change at the intersection. A stocky Hispanic with regular, pleasant features that seem vaguely Polynesian, Gene always appeared slightly frazzled, a consequence of dealing with the Albuquerque Police Department, a wife, and five kids on a daily basis.

I accepted both his hand and his ribbing. "Every time. Get some of my best answers from them."

"I keep expecting one of the rookies to arrest the kid." He motioned to the bronze of a teenager with a skateboard.

We entered the La Posada by the north entrance and stepped into another world. The interior was done in Spanish Territorial with aged wood copings, corbels highlighted in scarlet and turquoise, and heavily carved lintels. *Nichos*, small shelves in the white plastered walls, held carved wooden *santos* and ornate Mexican tinwork. This hotel had once been part of the Hilton chain—Conrad's first in New Mexico, as a matter of fact—but had been recently sold, yet again, and was scheduled for a makeover in the near future.

Gene and I selected a heavy oak table stained ebony by the passage of time, and claimed a pair of sturdy straight-backed chairs padded in green and gold. We spent a few minutes bringing one another up to date on our lives.

After making a brunch of the restaurant's éclairs and a wedge of superb lemon meringue pie dribbled with chocolate, Gene was through chitchatting. "Okay, so what do you want?"

"What makes you think I want something? Can't I call a pal without having an ulterior motive?"

"No."

I pretended to think for a moment. "Okay then, I've got a client looking for his missing son and the kid's traveling companion." In less than two minutes, I'd briefed him on the situation.

"So they're like that, huh?" He wiggled his hand back and forth, a gesture that was supposed to convey something. Gene knew me too well to be sensitive about my sexual orientation.

"You mean are they gay? Yeah, I'd say so."

"And you want to get in their hotel room."

"Seems a logical place to start since one of their fathers hired me to represent the family."

"These two, they're emancipated, right? Adults."

"Both are twenty-one, according to Alfano."

"Hmm. Alfano gonna file a missing person's report?"

"He will if you think it'll help."

"Naw. We've got enough to do without looking for a couple of kids who've run off to play hanky-panky. But if they strayed across the border into Arizona, they might be cooling their heels in some county sheriff's jail as we speak. They take that shit seriously over there."

"Possible, but not likely. They could be in real trouble, Gene. Alfano keeps a tight rein on his boy, and the fact he's looking for him is troubling."

"Maybe the colt got out of the family pasture and is feeling his oats. But okay, have the old man file a report, and I'll see if I can get us inside the hotel room. Unofficially."

I picked up the tab to see what kind of damage Gene had done to my pocketbook. Anthony P. Alfano's pocketbook, actually.

Gene caught me peeking at the check. "Come on, you can afford it."

"Maybe so, but it's not my expense, it's my client's, and I don't know how picky he is."

Gene Enriquez is a good detective and a smooth talker, at least smooth enough to get us access to the room occupied by—or held in the names of—Orlando Alfano and Dana Norville. There was little to see. The pair had taken their traveling bags with them, leaving behind nothing personal except for two bundles of clothing destined for the laundry, the only sign they intended to return. One set of duds was expensive Abercrombie & Fitch, the other bundle was Gap. It wasn't hard to figure which clothes belonged to what dude.

The breast pocket of one shirt held a carefully folded chamber of commerce brochure extolling the virtues of El Moro's Inscription Rock and the Ice Caves near Grants. A rumpled pair of trousers—the expensive ones—gave up a not-so-neatly folded tourist road map of the state.

The bell captain remembered the two men asking his advice about the Enchanted Circle in the Taos area. They had specifically asked about white-water rafting along the Taos Box.

The clerk in the gift shop remembered the pair because, she blushingly admitted, they were both so handsome. Shortly after checking in, they picked up several pamphlets from her, expressing interest in the Turquoise Trail, a fifty-mile National Scenic Byway up Route 14 to Santa Fe studded with quaint, historic villages. Orlando and Dana had been especially curious about Valles Caldera, the thirteen-mile-wide crater of an extinct volcano south of Los Alamos, the Atomic City. Unfortunately, they also asked about Lincoln County and Carlsbad Caverns to the south and east, as well as Mesa Verde and the Bisti badlands in the northwest corner of the state.

As we drove back downtown, Gene agreed to put out a bulletin on Orlando Alfano's Porsche, an orange 2008-model Boxster S, California vanity plate LANDO 06. The kid probably got his undergraduate degree that year.

"A buggy like that's bound to have a navigational system with a GPS satellite signal," Gene said.

"A Magellan 750 Plus. The old man has his attorney contacting the company to get the present coordinates. They're touchy about giving out such information, and Alfano is bound to have more clout than I do. The way I read this guy, he'll have everyone from the governor on up calling the company if he can't buy the data from them."

"You do attract a certain type of client, don't you?"

Chapter 3

Wednesday morning found me trailing an aardvark—a Peterbilt eighteen-wheeler—as she nosed right and rolled sedately down the off-ramp toward a sprawling truck stop. The silver lettering on the butt end of the trailer promised "Tembro Carpets of North Carolina Are the Best." I'd followed the big rig for the last few miles on one of the few downhill slopes since climbing Nine Mile Hill out of Albuquerque on the long westward grind to the Continental Divide. We had driven through a summer rainsquall, and his backwash left my Impala's windshield smeared with gunk.

I parked in front of a squat adobe building sporting a modest green neon sign reading "Tia Maria's Cafe—Home Cooking Like Your Grandma's." A large gas station with service bays to accommodate big rigs sat across a broad stretch of tarmac. What looked to be a small motel with no more than half a dozen rooms abutted the café on the right.

While waiting for Alfano or his attorney to come up with the satellite positioning information for the Porsche, I had decided to follow the only decent lead I had. Four names had been scribbled on the back of that wrinkled and tattered state tourist map in Orlando's laundry. The first three were gay bars and hangouts in Albuquerque. The fourth was simply "Chesty's!!!" The three exclamation points lent that single word importance.

There was no place more likely to capture the imagination of two young gay adventurers than Chesty Westey's Truck Stop on the Continental Divide just off I-40 in western New Mexico. I had experienced the same titillating curiosity about the place in my salad days. Immediately upon hitting the legal age, I had headed due west with pounding heart and high expectations. Frankly, when I arrived, the place scared the living hell out of me. I had heard about eagle bars, and while Chesty's wasn't labeled as such, it was nonetheless an out-and-out bear place filled with bikers and truckers. Now, fourteen years later, I experienced the same trepidation at tackling the place, especially to ask a lot of awkward questions.

I entered the café through a screen door that squeaked just like your grandma's might have. The floor was plain brown tile. A hand-cranked cash register perched on the near end of a long Formica counter running the length of the left side of the room. Behind the counter was an opening for passing orders and receiving dishes from the kitchen. Half a dozen tables occupied the center of the room. Six big and exceptionally sturdy booths lined the outer wall where windows allowed patrons a view of what was going on at the truck stop. Three rigs were presently being serviced, including the black Peterbilt I'd followed off the highway.

I was the only patron at the moment, so I claimed one of the booths and scanned the typed menu, noting the homey dishes: home-cooked pies, home-baked cakes, fresh homemade bread. The heavy, yeasty aroma coming from the kitchen set my stomach to growling. I ordered a bowl of Texas-style chili and a glass of milk as an appetizer and took my chances with a southern trucker's plate. As soon as the waitress—probably Tia Maria—took my order, managing to call me "honey" and "sugar" at least three times, she retreated behind the counter and yelled to someone on the other side of the wall.

My attention turned to the outside where a thick man with no recognizable body definition beyond a head, arms, and legs ambled toward the café, looking like a walking six-six oil drum.

"Tree Trunk!" the woman yelled when the trucker came through the door. "Come in outa the snow."

I blinked. This side of the divide probably hadn't seen snow since last May. Oh, well, truckers and bikers and those who service them have their own language. And her name for the man was more apt than my mental description of him.

"Auntie," he roared back. "Been too long since I've had a decent meal."

"Don't let your wife hear you say that."

They enjoyed a little joshing as he took a seat at a nearby table, ordered, and then spent a minute hand brushing a horseshoe moustache that started thick and blond on his upper lip and finished up thick and red-brown on his chin. The ends were parted by a deep dimple.

My mission was temporarily forgotten when Maria delivered my appetizer. I was raised on New Mexico chili. "Red or Green?" is the state's unofficial question, and green was my preference. But occasionally I like to dig into a good Texas dish. Tia Maria's concoction contained meat ground so finely a toothless octogenarian could handle it without any trouble. A film of grease floated on top. The whole thing smelled so spicy I took a precautionary drink of cold sweet milk to coat my innards before diving in and working my way slowly through the bowl, enjoying the flavor, the aroma, the bite of every delicious spoonful.

I returned from gastronomic nirvana as the waitress brought the trucker the biggest, rawest Kansas City steak I'd ever seen. Nothing else shared the platter except a heaping pile of mashed potatoes smothered in gravy and some green beans. Poor old Tree Trunk had to make do with that simple fare plus a loaf of dark rye bread and a tub of butter—probably home-churned.

After Maria—at five six and one seventy-five, the best advertising for her own cooking—finished another short discourse with Tree Trunk, she brought a plate loaded with fried chicken, more of those mouth-watering potatoes, okra, whole kernel corn, and what I took to be spinach but turned out to be collard greens. A tub of salted butter and corn pone sticks completed the meal. When she departed, I slipped the pepper shaker off my table and hid it on the seat beside me.

"Say, buddy, could I trouble you for some pepper?" I spoke in a low voice so as not to attract the attention of the waitress.

"Why sure," the man called Tree Trunk said.

I thanked him as he handed over a small pepper mill. "I take it from your reception you're a regular here."

"I measure my miles, so I pull in here with enough time to spend the night. The motel ain't much, but the beds are reinforced, and that's all I need—besides lots of Maria's cooking, that is."

"Fudge the log book, do you?" I jokingly referred to the time and mileage log the Department of Transportation required of long-distance truckers. If the rules hadn't changed, they were allowed a ten-hour run for every eight hours of rest.

A frown told me he'd mistaken my intent. "Pure as the driven snow. Do my ten and go down for my eight. I hold to the posted speed limit. No uppers to keep me awake. No downers to make me sleep. I'm righteous."

"Relax, I'm not DOT. Just making conversation."

He cocked an eye at me. "That said, what I claimed is just the facts, man."

I chewed for a couple of minutes, finding it hard to keep my mind on business when the chicken was so good. Maria even made the collards passable, and I hate the things. "I hear there's a bar out back."

"Yep. Big fucker across the arroyo."

"It's a gay bar?" I tried to make it sound as casual as possible, but addressing that particular subject with a three-hundred-pound trucker raised the hair on the back of my neck.

"Queer as they come," he agreed. "I'm heading over soon's I clean up. But it's a bear place. Don't know how you'd fit in."

I held up a hand. "Not looking for a companion, just curious. Who runs the show around here?"

"Chesty Westerfield's boy, Russell, runs this end since his dad passed on. A big hippo named Sweetie runs the bar."

"Friendly?"

"Friendly as it takes. Mean as she wants."

"How about first-timers? She put up with them?"

"Joint would eventually die if they wasn't some of them from time to time. If you go over, just look for the biggest, blackest dude in the joint."

"Dude?"

"Yeah, Sweetie's a he even if he resents the fact." Tree Trunk glanced out the window. "If you decide to go, you can take the footbridge over the arroyo or drive your car around the west end of the truck stop and take the vehicle bridge."

"Thanks."

We concentrated on filling our stomachs after that. He cleaned his plate first and went on his way after paying his bill and planting a big kiss on Maria's cheek. I succumbed to temptation and ordered a slice of dutch apple pie but righteously passed on the dip of ice cream Maria offered.

That done, I left the car where it was and walked across the footbridge spanning a broad, deep gully to a big, ramshackle adobe with a ten-foot neon sign on the roof modestly proclaiming it "The Continental Divide Bar." It staggered the imagination to find a real leather and Levi joint out here in the hinterlands of New Spain, but here was Chesty Westey's notorious sin palace—if you can call a half-acre mud building a palace. They said the Continental gets plenty of uniforms from the Air Force community in Albuquerque and Army boots from Ft. Huachuca over in Arizona, but it was predominately a trucker and biker joint.

The south parking lot was full of animals, presidents, exotic metals, Swiss auto racers, and American industrialists: Cobras, Mustangs, Lincolns, Mercurys, Chevrolets, and Fords. Towering over them all were the big rigs like Tree Trunk's long-nosed aardvark. The north lot was given over to two-wheeled chrome hogs, hog wagons, and choppers. There was no orange Porsche Boxster in either lot.

The atmosphere hit me in the face like a pillow of wet feathers the moment I walked through the door. The air was heavy: smoke-heavy, fart-heavy, beer-heavy, sweat-heavy, with the musk of men on the make permeating everything. After buying a beer, I hauled it around on a tour of the place. The main bar was immense, meandering out of sight in two different directions, one leading to a big patio, the other to a smaller, quieter bar and thence to the back rooms.

There wasn't a stranger around, blind or sighted, who couldn't find the right bathroom in the Continental. A big curved brass penis mounted on the door identified the men's side, and an embossed plaque in the shape of labia marked the women's. Apparently everyone used the phallus as a door handle; it was worn thin, making the engorged head appear outlandishly huge.

The joint undulated like a den of writhing serpents. The clack of billiard balls and thunk of darts and an outclassed, inadequate, old-fashioned jukebox laid down the beat. The talking, laughing, drinking, cussing, spitting customers, and blousy waitresses, almost all of them with bolt-ons, as these people likely called boob jobs, provided a wonderful, discordant rhythm.

Deciding it was time to make my pitch, I claimed a spot at a tiny table opposite a mountainous black man in bib overalls boasting the long, graying beard of an Old Testament patriarch. Tree Trunk had said Sweetie was his handle, but it should have been Sweaty. This guy would have perspired in an icehouse.

"What's new, Sweet?" I went for the personal touch and lost my fist in the grip of a gigantic coal-black paw.

"This ain't your kinda joint," he said in a high-pitched voice as effeminate as any swish-queen I've ever encountered.

"How do you know?"

His big rheumy eyes gave me the once-over. "Honey, you got a waistline, that's how I know. Look around at these bozos. Ain't a one of them even remembers where theirs is at." He paused and read me with shrewd eyes. "'Sides, I been around long enough to know these things." He leaned forward, bringing the odor of sweat with him. "You might like to play, but these ain't your playmates."

"You're probably right. But I'm looking for two who are. Okay if I show you a couple of photos?"

He leaned back, making his reinforced chair creak. "You could be fuzz, but the aura ain't quite right. You believe in auras?"

"Oh, yeah. Auras… energy… whatever you want to call them."

"Yours is yellow. Goes to green sometimes, but mostly yellow. I'd say that makes you an okay dude except I keep getting a flash of tin. You a cop?"

"Used to be. I'm private now. And I'm not looking to jam up these two guys. As far as I'm concerned, they've got a right to live their own lives."

"Amen to that, brother. All right, show me the pictures." The giant's eyes lit up when I handed them over. "Oh, them sweethearts."

"You know them?"

"Why? They in trouble?"

"Missing."

"I seen them. 'Bout three weeks back, it was."

"Three weeks? Can you pin it down any closer?"

"Yeah, it was the first weekend of the month when the guys come in and cash their paychecks. On a Friday night. That's the only time we got trim little asses in this joint. Dancers, you know. Kids wanting to make an extra buck. Got a corporal from Kirtland AFB makes more in one night than he takes home in flyboy pay for a month."

"First weekend," I said with a frown of concentration. "That would make it around the third." Then his words struck me. "These two danced?"

Sweetie laughed with pure joy. "Kinda like a lark for them. I told them they didn't fit in with the clientele unless they wanted to shake their booties to music. Surprised me cross-eyed when they took me up on it. Skinned down to their skivvies and went right up on that stage in the back room. Wasn't very good at it, but they sure was enthusiastic. That made it better somehow. Everbody knew they didn't do it for real. You know, professionally. For the half hour they wiggled their little butts, I thought I was in love. Contemplated losing a hundred pounds and making my move." The belly laugh that followed was all man, nothing feminine about it. "Everbody in the house bought them drinks. They got so pie-eyed we put them up in a room over at the motel. On the house."

"They okay?"

"Sick as dogs the next day, but they took outa here under their own steam in the sweetest-looking bright orange Porsche a girl ever saw."

"Is it possible they were followed?"

"Hell, honeybunch, anything's possible. People go in and outa here all the time. As I recollect, it was pretty close to noon. They wasn't broke when they left here, I can tell you. The fellas musta stuck close to five hundred bucks down their underwear. Got so bad, them two had to pull the bills out and pile them in the corner—paper cuts, you know." He gave his belly-rumbling infectious laugh again.

"You mind if I ask around about them?"

"Have at it, but it's a whole other crowd here tonight. Probably not more'n one or two of this bunch was here then."

"How about the help?"

"Yeah. Some of the same crew's here."

"Thanks, Sweet. Can I buy you one?"

"Right courteous of you, Mr.… uh."

"Just BJ."

"Okay, just BJ, tell the bartender to send over my usual. And good luck. I sure hope you find them sweet babies walking around on their own two feet."

I spent another two hours talking to anyone who would give me the time of day, but I located only one trucker who was at the Continental Divide that Friday night. Three of the staff had also been there. After the four finished fawning over those two "damned fine-looking college kids in their BVDs"—in words more graphic than that—I left the bar to try the other establishments.

Tia Maria recognized the pictures and went maudlin over those "cute kids." She'd tried to plump them up with a man-sized brunch that Saturday, but all they could handle was black coffee. Lots of coffee.

The crew at the truck stop was a little more reticent, or perhaps less observant since Orlando had not tanked up the car. By the time I left, I was convinced the two California men had left Chesty Westey's Continental Divide Truck Stop just the way Sweetie described it—under their own steam. The real question was what happened after that? Could the two have incited one of the big bears at the bar to rape? And possibly murder?

Since Orlando and Dana were still registered at the Sheraton, I took the overpass and picked up eastbound I-40 for the trip home. The truck stop alongside the highway at Acoma Pueblo lured me off the interstate. If the two men had not gassed up at Chesty Westey's, perhaps they stopped here.

The big modern station, seemingly made entirely of extruded aluminum and plate glass, sold every kind of fattening, artery-choking junk food known to man. A single attendant, a smooth-skinned, chubby tribal member of about nineteen or twenty, appeared to be managing everything on her own. Although preoccupied with chewing a mouthful of gum, the girl handled my ten-dollar fill-up efficiently enough. As I received change for a twenty, I handed over my photos and asked if she had seen the men.

She lifted the glasses hanging from a black ribbon around her neck and peered through them.

"Uh-uh." She handed the pictures back to me.

"Does that mean no?"

"Yeah. I mean, no, I haven't seen them."

"They would have been in a bright orange Porsche."

"Oh, wait. An orange car? Saw it the other day. Or one like it. I remember because this other guy asked if I'd seen a really bright orange car."

"What guy?"

"Some guy filling his tank. He was just making conversation. Flirting, I guess."

"Do you remember the two men in the orange car?"

"Let me see those pictures again." After giving them a second look, she wrinkled her nose. "Yeah, I remember them now. It was them in that orange car."

"Would that have been the first Saturday in the month? Around the fourth?"

The wrinkled nose appeared again, this time accompanied by a creased brow. "No, I don't work weekends. This was last week sometime. Or maybe a couple of weeks ago. On a Monday, it was. I think they said they'd been to the ceremonial—you know, the big Gallup Inter Tribal Ceremonial—and were headed back to Albuquerque."

"How did they pay?"

"I don't remember. Who are you, mister? Did those guys do something wrong?"

I shook my head. "No, just trying to locate them for a family member. Tell me about the man asking about the car. What did he look like?"

The girl, who wore a nametag reading Loreen pinned atop a plump breast, shrugged. "Just a man. I don't really remember him except he had a big forehead. Like I say, he was just making conversation. He didn't really ask about *that* car—he was just talking about one on the road bright enough to blind a fellow."

"Was he here when the Porsche was filling up?"

"No, he came in later."

Further questions failed to elicit any additional information, so I pulled back onto I-40 and sped toward Albuquerque. At least I'd learned that Orlando and Dana had made it out of the Continental Divide safely. They'd probably gone straight west to Gallup for the big ceremonial held the first week of August each year. After that they'd headed back to Albuquerque.

Loreen's inability to recall how they paid for the gasoline was a bad break. These days it took a subpoena to pry billing information out of credit card companies, especially if you didn't have the card number. A quick look at his gas receipt, if there was one, would have helped a great deal.

Chapter 4

UPON MY return to the office, Hazel pressed me to sign off on some other cases. My newly renovated guardian angel had a fetish about timely reporting to clients and prompt billing for our services. That was good, but sometimes it got in the way of important things—like pursuing a train of thought while it was still rattling around in my head. Yet what would I have done without her? Performed half of my services for free, most likely.

When I took the pile of signed documents out to her desk, she turned to face me. "If you're going to be tied up in this Alfano case, you might consider bringing Charlie in to cover for you."

"Okay, call him in."

Charlie Weeks again. For a brief second, I tried to imagine that pairing. My sometime associate was a spare man something shy of sixty with blue eyes and thinning gray hair who stood two inches over my six feet. He was easy-going with a spine of steel; Hazel was bossy but a pussycat underneath. Quite a pair. I wished them well. Maybe she'd devote some of her mothering to him and ease off on me.

It was close to five before I was free to take the next step in the case of the missing graduate students. It was only four on the Pacific coast, so I placed a call to the Alfano Vineyards and was promptly transferred to a lady with the improbable name of Gilda Gistafferson who turned out to be Anthony P.'s executive secretary. Given that Alfano was a grizzly, I expected his secretary to reflect his sense of power, but she turned out to be courteous, helpful, and friendly.

"Ms. Gistafferson—" I began.

"It's Gilda, please, Mr. Vinson. I know who you are and appreciate your efforts on Mr. Alfano's behalf. I'm sorry he's not available, but he has instructed me to give you my full cooperation."

"That's good to know, but if I'm going to call you Gilda, you've got to call me BJ."

"Very well… BJ. What can I do for you?"

"A couple of things, actually. Do you know if any progress has been made with the GPS coordinates on Orlando's Porsche?"

"Mr. Brasser—that's Mr. Alfano's attorney—is working on it. We'll let you know as soon as the information becomes available."

"If it becomes available."

"Oh, it will. Mr. Brasser always delivers."

I tried to put a grin in my voice. "It helps to have money, doesn't it?"

"As I understand it, you should know."

So she had seen Alfano's report on me and knew I'd inherited twelve million from my folks. Probably read the thing when she filed it. That's okay. Prudent business on Alfano's part.

"There's money, and then there's money," I said.

"That's certainly true."

"Tell me, Gilda, are Orlando's credit cards personal or through the company?"

"It's Lando. Everyone calls him Lando."

"I gather you and Lando get along."

"Lando's a great kid. He brings the sunshine when he enters a room."

"Okay, so does he get his credit cards through the company?"

"He has a company Amex card, but he only uses it if Mr. Alfano asks him to represent the company at some function. He's very scrupulous about that. Everything else goes on his personal cards."

"Where do the billings for the personal cards go?"

"To his apartment in Los Angeles. Would you like me to get them for you?"

"If you can."

"I think I can lay my hands on them. Have you found any sign of him yet?"

"I've run across his trail, but it went cold." I resisted the temptation to confess that her darling was last seen shaking his booty on Chesty Westey's stage. "The trouble is, he collected brochures for points of interest scattered clear across the state, so I'm not certain where to start looking next."

"He was planning on seeing as much of New Mexico as possible. One thing about Lando, he has the energy to match his curiosity. They are both boundless. He's a live wire."

"How about Norville?" Might as well test the water.

"I don't know him that well, but he seems like a very nice young man."

"Does he come from money as well?"

"No, his father is an electrician. I can send you the report Mr. Alfano has if you wish."

"It wouldn't hurt. Fax it when you have the opportunity. This might be a sensitive subject, but do you know anything about his… uh, living arrangements before he met Lando?"

"Not much. Apparently he was in a two-year relationship with a man named Bruno Wills. Wills is a former student at UCLA. Now, I understand he's a construction foreman for a company in one of the LA suburbs."

"Was it an amicable split?"

"I gather not. Wills is older than Dana by ten years, and he took the breakup hard. At least, that's what Lando told me."

"Did Lando share his travel plans with you?"

"He didn't really have any. He had talked about taking a trip but hadn't mentioned it recently. Then he came in one day and announced he and Dana were leaving on vacation. That very afternoon, in fact."

"Sudden, wasn't it?"

"Yes, it was. Very sudden. Took me by surprise. As far as plans are concerned, the only thing I know is they were to stop in Las Vegas on the way to New Mexico. Lando's not a big gambler, but he does like the slots. Then they were going to stop at the Grand Canyon on the way to Phoenix where they were to see an old classmate for dinner that night. After that, they had no plans beyond heading for your part of the country. He mentioned some of the obvious places. You know, Carlsbad Caverns and Santa Fe and Taos. Beyond that, I don't know what his plans were or even if he had any."

"Mr. Alfano seems to keep his son on a short leash. In fact, I'm surprised Lando is at UCLA. UC Berkeley's a lot closer."

"Yes, it is, and it's quite a good school too. But I think Lando wanted to get away. You know, put a little distance between himself and the family. Mrs. Alfano's been in ill health, and he didn't want to stray too far." She cleared her throat. "He always came back to the Valley during the Christmas and spring breaks. Took a few courses at Berkeley, but mostly he spent the summers here."

"Doing what?"

I sensed she wasn't comfortable discussing personal family matters with a stranger, but she didn't hesitate. "Well, as I said, he took a few courses at Berkeley, although he commuted for those. And he worked off and on for the company."

"Doing what?" I repeated.

"Mostly he worked in the lab. That was the only part of the business he ever showed any interest in. He liked to work with Tom trying out new recipes. Developing new blends… tastes. That sort of thing."

"Tom?"

"Tom Scavo. He runs the Alfano labs."

"Has Lando been in touch with Mr. Scavo?"

"No. I asked Tom about that just this morning. Tom hasn't heard a word from Lando since he left on vacation."

"How else did Lando spend his time? Was he active in any organizations? Sports or civic clubs?"

Her laugh came across the line like a bell. "Country club. He likes to play a little tennis, but he's not avid about it. He isn't on a team or anything like that. He does belong to the Napa Valley Historical Society. History is his passion." She cleared her throat.

"As far as Mr. Alfano keeping him on a short leash, Lando swore he would turn off his phone if his father was going to check up on him all the time. In a compromise, Lando promised to keep in touch."

"With you?"

"Yes, and he did for a while. He'd call once or twice a week. But the last time I spoke with him was on the eighth. He was at some place called Isleta. That must be a casino because I heard slots." She laughed again. "He was complaining about the rain. He didn't expect rain in New Mexico."

"Haven't you heard of the southwestern monsoon system?"

"I don't ever recall hearing the words monsoon and New Mexico in the same breath. Honestly, I've heard something of it, but I never related it to your part of the country."

"It's real. When it behaves and shows up on schedule, we get about half the annual rainfall during July and August."

"Oh, dear. Lando didn't do his homework very well, did he? Planning his trip in the middle of the rainy season."

"Has anyone else spoken to Lando since the eighth?"

"No, and when he didn't call again, Mr. Alfano started to worry."

There was a pause in the conversation before Gilda added, "Lando told me to call him on Dana's cell phone if I really needed to reach him."

"Norville has a cell?" I noticed she didn't volunteer the number. "Have you tried his phone lately?"

"Several times. No one answers or returns my messages."

"You better give me the number, but we'll keep it just between the two of us, okay?"

Gilda gave me the cell number and as many details from her conversations with Lando as she could remember. She was a very precise person, so she recalled a great deal.

After finishing with Gilda, I dialed Norville's phone number and let it ring until a computerized voice invited me to leave a message. Out of an abundance of caution, I declined. This thing was beginning to look like something more complicated than two young men having so much fun they forgot to keep to their original time schedule. Until I knew the lay of the land, I wouldn't leave any more blind messages.

I consulted the notes from my conversation with Gilda and began building an itinerary on a pocket calendar. The two travelers had left the Napa Valley on Sunday, July 22. That meant they probably hit Vegas and remained there overnight. They would have had a good drive to reach Phoenix on the twenty-fourth, especially if they spent any time at the Grand Canyon, but that was apparently what they did. They first checked into the Sheraton in Albuquerque on the following Wednesday. The next day they talked to the gift shop clerk at the hotel and mentioned the Turquoise Trail. They probably drove the back road to Santa Fe that same day. Then they likely spent a few days seeing the local sights, such as Old Town and the gay bars, before taking off again.

According to Gilda, Lando had called her from Carlsbad on the thirty-first. They had visited the Caverns and were going to Billy the Kid country—Lincoln County. My guess was that they also hit the ruins at Abo and Gran Quivira or perhaps swung west and took in the lava beds in the Valley of Fires.

As I worked, Lando Alfano began to rise in my estimation. He lived life the way he saw fit. His relationship with Dana was open and honest and in obvious defiance of his father. He refused to take Alfano's calls while on vacation. The kid had backbone.

What puzzled me was the old man waiting until his son was overdue returning home before contacting a PI to hunt him down. If Gilda's last contact was on the eighth, Alfano had waited twelve days before putting me on Lando's trail. He phoned me the night of August

20, but maybe I wasn't his first choice. Perhaps he had someone else on the job too. That girl at the Acoma truck stop—Noreen or Loreen—said a man asked about an orange car. She thought it was someone just making conversation about a flashy auto he'd seen, but maybe he was pumping her for information. If so, he knew the Porsche had been at Acoma.

Lando and Dana were driving willy-nilly all over the place, and New Mexico is a big state—over 121,000 square miles. They'd passed through Gallup and drove another 130 miles east to Albuquerque. Then they headed west to Gallup again after leaving the Continental Divide Truck Stop. Well, that made sense; the Inter Tribal Ceremonial hadn't kicked off until that weekend. Later they had checked back in at the Sheraton and still held a room there, making it their base of operations in this driving vacation. These two young men were wrapped up in a love affair—a threesome that included an exotic sports car. And as strikingly handsome as the two men were, the orange Porsche was what really caught people's attention.

I quickly forgot the Alfanos and their problems when I returned home that evening to find Paul sitting shirtless on the couch in the den in cutoff denims with his bare feet propped on the coffee table. It took some effort to turn my attention from him to the rerun he was watching on television; a rerun of the Texas Rangers walloping the Baltimore Orioles 30 to 3. August 22, 2007 would go down in baseball history for the record number of runs by a single team in one game. Better headlines than the more usual reporting of the deadly war in Iraq that didn't seem to want to stop.

Chapter 5

THE MORNING'S first sip of scalding, Splenda-sweetened java laced with Coffee-Mate had not yet reached my gullet when the cell phone went off. The number was not familiar, but the California area code meant it was likely connected to my newest case. The deep baritone was likewise unrecognizable.

"Mr. Vinson? I hope I'm not imposing by calling this early on your personal telephone, but my father asked me to contact you. My name is Aggie Alfano."

"Let me guess, you're Orlando's brother."

"That's right, his older brother. We were just contacted by the company monitoring the Magellan GPS device in Lando's Porsche. I have the latest coordinates."

"Pacific Coast time is an hour behind us. Someone's been working late—or early."

"When Carl Brasser gets involved, people tend to forget normal working hours."

"That's good to know. Okay, shoot."

Aggie rattled off a meaningless string of numbers and then brought them into perspective. "That puts him in Taos."

"Great. I'll phone the local police and head right up."

"Good. I'm not far from the airport now. I have my own plane and can be there in about three hours."

"That's not necessary. I'll pick up your brother and deliver him to the family."

There was a brief pause. "Lando can be a handful, especially if he thinks the old man is interfering in his life. I think I'd better come out and give you a hand."

"Your call. Taos is small, but it's a tourist spot, so they have a decent airport."

"I'm familiar with the place. I've landed there before."

"Has Lando?"

"Oh, yes, he's visited several times. He's into art in a big way."

As a lifelong history buff fascinated by New Mexico's small villages and multiple cultures, I knew Taos was awash in galleries. We made arrangements to meet at the police station and terminated the call.

A new wrinkle. An older brother. Alfano had said "my son is missing" when we first spoke. Well, I suppose not everyone draws a family tree right off the bat.

Paul walked into the dinette in the denim cutoffs he wore around the house. His dark brown, almost black, hair was rumpled, and his Hershey-colored eyes still looked fuzzy with sleep. A tiny dragon tattoo on his left pec performed calisthenics as he placed a cup of unsweetened black coffee on the table. I liked watching that tattoo, that pec.

"Business?" he asked.

I nodded. "The missing students from California. Got their GPS coordinates. Taos."

"Good. I hope they're floating down the Rio Grande in the Taos Box having the time of their lives."

"Me too, but I'm beginning to lose faith in the fantasy these are two lovers so wrapped up in one another they lost track of time. I'm going to have to go up there—to Taos."

"I hope you're wrong and they're off somewhere having a ball. Don't be gone long, okay?" Paul glanced across at the kitchen clock and snatched a quick sip of coffee. "Whoops, I gotta hit the shower. I'm gonna be late for class."

He rushed down the hallway, his broad-shouldered, lean-hipped, five-foot-ten frame evoking images of a powerful physique knifing through the water in a race for the finish line. Paul enjoyed soccer and played a mean game of sidewalk basketball, but swimming was his passion. Swimming and dancing. After class—he was a graduate student in journalism at the University of New Mexico—he would go straight to his job as a swimming instructor at the North Valley Country Club, which is where I first met him.

Reluctantly turning back to business, I placed three calls before leaving the house, four if you count the one to the office to let Hazel know I wouldn't be in today. After Gene Enriquez agreed to contact the Taos cops, I dialed a local flying service to arrange for a charter and then phoned the Taos Police Department directly.

Gene had contacted Officer Gilbert Delfino, who was awaiting my call. The Magellan coordinates were not in Taos itself but in the little settlement of El Segundo north of town. Delfino had already asked the Taos County Sheriff's Office to detain the automobile, although he added a caution that the good citizens of Taos and villages in the vicinity were known for a deep-rooted reluctance to cooperate with the law. It was difficult, he noted, to locate someone who did not want to be found in those mountains. Delfino agreed to pick me up at the airport.

Jim Gray and his Cessna Skycatcher were available, but because of the short notice, there was a delay in getting it serviced and ready for flight. Jim, a lanky six-footer with a small beer belly, had been both a fixed-wing and whirlybird jockey in Vietnam and returned from the experience a little traumatized—more from what he observed on the ground than in the air. After leaving the military, he flew with a couple of charter services for a number of years until he saved enough to buy the Cessna and go into business for himself. He was a careful and competent pilot I used for local flights, so I settled comfortably into the right-hand seat of the Cessna—a good hour and a half after talking to Aggie Alfano.

We encountered turbulence as the little plane lifted off from the Double Eagle Airport on the west side of town and headed straight up the Rio Grande. The browns and reds and grays of the desert terrain turned a monotonous dun as we gained altitude, broken only by darker wrinkles of dry washes known as arroyos, the double black ribbons of Interstate 25, and the dull sheen of the river—itself somewhat brown. The Rio is classified as a "dirty river," meaning it carries high concentrations of silt on its way to the Gulf of Mexico. The green-shrouded slopes of the Jemez Mountains to the west provided a splash of color, as did the Sangre de Cristos to the north.

With a maximum range of 470 nautical miles, plus a thirty-minute reserve fuel supply, the Cessna would not need to set down before reaching our destination. Taos is a 132-mile trip by car, and at a cruising speed of 129 mph, we would arrive in something under an hour.

"Quite a view, huh?" Jim asked. "I never get tired of it."

Feeling a kinship with a soaring eagle, I took in the panorama. "Is that weather off to the west going to cause us any heartburn?" Bright bolts of lightning strobed the black sky on the distant horizon.

"I checked before we lifted off. It's moving north-northeast, so I doubt we'll be bothered."

"Feel free to put down somewhere if we are." I glanced down at the river again. "It's really amazing how the Rio Grande changes character. Around Albuquerque it roams around in a broad channel made for a bigger river."

"You can blame that on the dams," Jim observed. "When the Rio Grande was declared a wild and scenic river, it flooded regularly. Then they put in all the dams. The way I look at it, they put an end to the flooding all right, but the river and the Bosque are paying the price. They're both slowly dying." The Bosque was a two-hundred-mile swath of cottonwood forest lining both banks of the Rio.

Above Santa Fe, the water flowing beneath the plane picked up energy, shimmering in the sunlight as it rushed over rocks on its fall from the high country. The farther north we traveled, the wilder the river became. Soon it was white-water rafting country. A few miles below Taos, the true might and determination of the river become apparent as it raced down long boulder gardens to spill out of the black volcanic canyons of the Taos Box. From above, the river appeared to sink, but in reality the terrain rose on its climb north toward Colorado.

Over the eons gravity and friction and the sheer power of water molecules had carved a deep crevasse through the hard basalt of the Taos Plateau. The Rio Grande Gorge Bridge spanned that spectacular canyon ten miles west-northwest of Taos. We circled over the awesome 1,280-foot, cantilevered steel-and-concrete marvel of modern engineering as we lined up for a landing at the town's small strip.

Taos claims a 6,000-year history based on arrowheads, potsherds, and pictographs left by nomadic hunter-gatherers. The town takes its name from the older Taos Pueblo, a massive, multistoried, prehistory apartment complex of Tiwa-speaking Native Americans. Both the town and the Pueblo are cultural as well as tourist draws. Dozens of Hollywood films, documentaries, and television commercials have been filmed there ever since the 1940s.

Jim had radioed the tower well before touching down at the small municipal airport, and Officer Delfino met the plane, as promised. He turned out to be a police officer with more than a touch of the local blood. Standing five foot six in his boots with coarse black hair not quite long enough to wear in the traditional bun but shaggier than most lawmen, he projected a calm competence as we shook hands. It would not be wise to provoke this man. His hatchet face wore an air of serious determination, an impression reinforced by his extraordinarily broad shoulders and deep chest.

"Mr. Vinson, we might have a problem," he said. "The sheriff's people couldn't find the Porsche in El Segundo, but a unit spotted it on the road. There's a cruiser on its tail right now."

"Do you know where it is at the moment?"

"Not far to the west of us, as a matter of fact." He motioned with his chin. "Headed for Agua Amarga… or in that direction, anyway."

"That'll take them over the gorge, right?"

"They'll cross over in a few minutes."

"Maybe they're just going sightseeing. You know, stand on the bridge and toss rocks into the gorge like all tourists do."

His lips pulled into a frown. "Maybe, but somehow I doubt it."

"I expect they're out of your jurisdiction by now."

"The town and the county have a reciprocal arrangement, so I have permission for us to join the chase. If it gets too bad, I expect we'll have to call in Tom Duggin. He's the state police trooper up here."

"Well," I said, "let's get going, unless you think the Cessna might make a good spotter for the sheriff's people."

He eyed the machine with evident interest. "Can't hurt."

He raised the sheriff's department on his cruiser's radio while I prepped Jim. Within minutes we took off with the Taos policeman occupying the right-hand seat while I crammed my carcass into the baggage storage cavity behind the two men. Delfino would have fit much more comfortably in the small space, but he knew the territory and I didn't. He was of more value as a spotter in the front.

The countryside east of the airport is relatively flat and open, so automobile traffic was clearly visible. Almost immediately we saw a county car, lights flashing, on the road ahead of us. Leading the sheriff's cruiser by almost a mile was a blur of color that was undoubtedly Orlando Alfano's orange Boxster. Both vehicles had already crossed the gorge.

"These guys aren't fugitives, are they?" Delfino asked. "I thought we were just locating them for a family matter."

"That's right," I said.

"So why're they running?"

"I don't know. Have two Anglo guys from California had any trouble around Taos in the last few days?"

"There's no record of Alfano or Norville in the area, period. I checked every motel in the vicinity after the Albuquerque police called. If they were here, they didn't leave any tracks."

"Then how did Alfano's car get here?" I asked.

"I don't know, but there it is right down there. Uh-oh," Delfino said, "it turned off the road. Hope our guys see it."

"They're still back around the curve. They won't see the maneuver unless the dust gives the Porsche away."

Delfino asked Jim if he could buzz the cruiser and try to alert them.

"I can do better than that if you know the county frequency." Jim reached for his radio dial.

Within seconds, Delfino was talking to his compadres. By that time, they had passed the point where the Porsche had left the main road. Before the cruiser could reverse direction, the orange car regained the highway, heading back toward Taos.

"You want me to distract them?" Jim asked.

Delfino shook his head. "No, they don't realize we're a spotter. Let's let this play out."

"Here they come." I nodded at the county car now in hot pursuit. "But I doubt they have the muscle to overtake the Porsche."

"Maybe not, but we can keep them in sight from up here," Delfino replied.

The occupants of the fleeing car were obviously aware of the posse on their tail. The vehicle hugged the ground as it took off like it had been goosed in the rear by a hotshot. The erratic way the car raced down the road made me question if an experienced driver was at the wheel.

"We got him now."

Delfino pointed ahead of us. The Porsche rapidly approached the Rio Grande Gorge Bridge where a second sheriff's vehicle sat in the middle of the span, blocking the fugitives' escape. Even from this distance, we saw officers herding tourists off the walkways and observation platforms of the bridge.

"Christ!" Jim muttered. "Those guys better slow down."

Delfino grabbed the radio mike and shouted warnings to the sheriffs' deputies. Belatedly the Porsche tried to stop, but it was traveling too fast. Skidding sideways, the car almost went over. Then it left the roadway short of the bridge, careening through a vacant rest area and sideswiping a stone picnic shelter. Now totally out of control, the Porsche crashed through the fenced area at the brink of the gorge. We let out a collective groan as it hurtled out into space.

Jim banked over the canyon to watch the automobile take flight. It free-fell a couple hundred feet before striking the side of the gorge, tearing out a sizeable chunk of the wall. From our perspective it looked as if the car dropped in slow motion, tumbling over and over before smashing into the bottom of the gorge. There was no dramatic explosion, merely an awful finality as the machine appeared to disintegrate like a toy automobile smashed beneath a child's heel.

Delfino and Jim crossed themselves and muttered a Hail Mary, bringing home the awful, tragic reality of the last few moments. This was no movie stunt. Someone had just died.

Oh, hell! What would I tell Alfano?

Chapter 6

I ELECTED to tell Anthony Alfano nothing for the moment. Although no one could possibly have survived that fall into the canyon, I wanted to confirm the identities of any bodies in the wreckage before informing the man his son was dead. Besides, Lando's older brother was on his way.

The Cessna returned to the airport where we recovered Officer Delfino's cruiser and started for the bridge. We hadn't made it to the highway before a high-winged, dual engine Mitsubishi Marquise lined up for a landing, so I asked Delfino to turn back. We watched the craft touch down in a perfect landing and shudder to a halt with plenty of runway to spare.

"That's a good plane for this airport," Delfino observed. "Good airspeed and can land on a postage stamp. Short takeoff too. My granddaddy said that's the same outfit that built those old World War II planes that dropped bombs on them in the Pacific."

The Mitsubishi taxied up to the terminal and went through its shutdown procedure. Eventually a tall, lean man about my age cracked the hatch and stepped down onto the asphalt. It had to be Aggie Alfano; he resembled the picture of Lando in my pocket—same dark hair, deep eyes, strong chin. I stepped forward.

"Mr. Alfano?"

He turned at the sound of my voice and started toward me. "Mr. Vinson."

"BJ, please."

"BJ, I'm Aggie."

"Someday you'll have to enlighten me as to what 'Aggie' stands for."

The grin was crooked and infectious. "The old man has a wry sense of humor. It's Aquila Felix. Happy Eagle. Do you blame me for answering to Aggie?"

"Hell, no. I'm Burleigh J. Vinson. Blame me for going by BJ? This is Officer Gilbert Delfino of the Taos Police Department."

"Sir." Delfino accepted a handshake and then cleared his throat with a glance at me.

I took the hint. "We've got a situation, and it's serious."

Aggie heard us out and then strode to Delfino's police car. "How fast can we get there?"

"Just a few minutes," Delfino replied. "But there won't be anything to see yet. They'll need to get some rafts in the water upstream. Either that or some climbers and equipment over the rim."

"I'm a climber," Aggie announced. "I'll get to him. I saw the people on the bridge when I came over. I just didn't know they were all looking down at my brother."

"We don't know that," I cautioned.

"It was his car, wasn't it?"

I nodded. "Not much doubt about that."

"Well, nobody else was driving it. That Porsche was his pride and joy. Unless…." He paused with his hand on the door handle of the cruiser. "Yeah, he'd let Dana take it out for a spin." He stared at me like a man clutching a lifeline. "Maybe he's holed up in a motel somewhere waiting for Dana to come back with a six-pack and burgers."

Delfino frowned. "That car wasn't out for beer and burgers. It was hauling ass to outrun the sheriff's deputies. Took evasive action."

"That doesn't sound like Lando. He faces things squarely. If it was something he couldn't handle, he knew the old man would. Although," he admitted, "he doesn't make a habit of relying on Papa's influence. Something's not right."

"Would Norville react the same way?"

Aggie pursed his lips. "Yeah, he'd hide behind my brother if Lando decided to hide behind Anthony P. Unless they had a falling out and Dana took the car, that is. Either way that argues Lando wasn't in the car when it went over the precipice."

With that, Aggie folded his six-two frame into the front passenger's seat of the police cruiser, leaving the back for me. Delfino had the lights and siren going before we were out of the parking lot.

The run to the gorge wasn't far, but by the time we got there, a crowd had collected. Delfino parked and muscled his way to the middle of the bridge with the two of us in tow.

"What's the situation?" he asked a sheriff's deputy wearing sergeant's stripes. Without waiting for an answer, he introduced us to the fair-skinned, sunburned man.

"Good to meet you," Sergeant Hatton said. "Wish it was under better circumstances. Things are still flexible at the moment. We found an unconscious kid over on the other side of the bridge. Looks like he managed to get out of the Porsche before it went over."

"Have you identified him?" Aggie asked.

"Local kid. Neighboring village."

"What does he say?"

"Nothing yet. Knocked out cold. The meat wagon's with him now." Hatton threw a thumb over his shoulder toward the west side of the bridge.

"What about the car?" I asked. "What are the recovery plans?"

"We have a mountain rescue unit, but it's a volunteer outfit. It'll take them a while to assemble their men and equipment. Quickest way is to put rafts in the water at the John Dunn Bridge west of Arroyo Hondo. Some of them may want to tackle the cliff."

"I want to go with the climbers," Aggie said immediately. "I'm qualified. I've been up Hood three times."

"That's up to them. They work as a team. But it's gonna be a couple of hours before anything gets going." He glanced into the gorge and sighed. "A delay's not gonna bother them none. Nobody coulda survived a bounce like that."

"Let's go see what's happening with the kid they found," I suggested.

We picked up a newspaper reporter and photographer on our way across the bridge. Hatton told them where to get off in no uncertain terms, so they resorted to tagging along behind us. Undoubtedly there were already television crews on their way from Colorado and Albuquerque. Such a spectacular event was going to get some publicity, and judging from the information available when I'd googled the Alfano name, things would get worse.

The boy they found rolled up against the fence where the car had gone over the edge was already in the ambulance. Delfino, Aggie, and I took turns crawling inside to take a look at him.

"Do you know him?" I asked Delfino.

"Yeah. Name's Cruz. Family lives in El Segundo where the coordinates from the GPS put the Porsche this morning. He and his brothers are a pain in the butt, but they're not bad kids. Although that probably explains why the Porsche was running. Stolen."

Hatton rejoined us. "Medic says the kid's probably got a fractured skull. No telling when he'll wake up. You recognize him, Gil? He's one of Mateo Cruz's boy's, right?"

"Yeah. The one they call Joe."

"Man, I don't like the way this is turning around," Hatton said. Then he gave an apologetic wave in Aggie's direction. "Sorry, don't mean I hope it's your brother down there, but not too happy it might be locals either." Hatton removed his hat and ran a freckled hand through his thinning reddish hair. "Well, that don't change what's gotta be done."

As the two law enforcement officers discussed the situation, I watched Aggie go over to study the area where the Porsche had breached the fence. A moment later he walked out onto the bridge to stare over the edge, assessing the situation like a rock climber. We tagged along behind. The river far below us looked the same as always—except for the tiny, shattered automobile lying wheels-up at the edge of the water.

"I've got my climbing gear in the plane," Aggie said. "I usually carry it when I fly. I'm gonna get it and go over the edge. If somebody will lend me a walkie-talkie, I can stay in contact."

"I wouldn't advise that, son," Hatton said. "I'm willing to bet you ain't got enough rope for a haul like that one. It's 650 feet to the bottom if it's an inch."

"And that river doesn't look like much from up here, but it's white water down there. Class IV rapids," Delfino added.

"I have enough rope to get me from one pitch to the other—one rock shelf to the next. I'll leave rope and carabiners in the pitons to make coming back up easier. Are there any bolts?" he asked, meaning permanent anchor points drilled into the rock.

"Not around here," Delfino responded. "And you're not gonna be able to bring any… uh, bodies out vertically. Not without a whole S&R team. Too much scree and flakes and too many overhangs."

"The white-water guys will get them out on rafts, Mr. Alfano," Hatton said.

"Okay, but if I get down there, at least we'll know, and I can call the old man. Actually, I'll let you do that, BJ, since I'll be at the bottom of that crack in the ground."

"You'll need someone to belay," I said. "I'll go down with you."

"Have you done any climbing?"

"Some," I hedged.

Delfino sighed. "I'll go. I've been down and back a couple of times. Let's go get your gear. You got enough for me, or do I need to go get my own?"

Aggie took in the short man's broad shoulders, deep chest, and bulging arms and smiled. "Got plenty for both of us. Let's go."

HATTON AND I stationed ourselves at a pedestrian overlook platform in the middle of the bridge where kids liked to heave rocks over the railing to watch the aerial missiles strike the water below. It was a dangerous practice since rafters regularly rode this section of the river.

Aggie and Delfino began the climb from a sit-down start where the Porsche had breached the fence. Aggie went first; Delfino acted as belay slave. I glanced to the west the moment they went over and was relieved to see Jim had been right. The monsoon storm had turned north. Weather wouldn't be a factor in the recovery effort.

After an hour of rappelling and traversing, the climbers had covered less than a third of the distance to the bottom. It was slow and treacherous going, but they worked well as a team. Aggie gave clear, crisp climbing commands, and the cop reacted decisively. So far as we could tell, neither had taken a false step so far.

"You ever go down there?" I watched the climbers through a set of borrowed binoculars.

"Once," Hatton answered, "and that was enough for me. Course, that was fifteen years ago. If I tried it now, I'd likely take the quick way." He adjusted his hat to protect his already burned neck. At this altitude the sun could sneak up on a man and roast him alive before he knew it. "Been through the gorge by raft a couple of times," he added.

"You think those two will reach the site before the rafters make it down the river?"

"Probably. Those boys gotta collect their team and drive up to the bridge at Arroyo Hondo before they can even put rubber in the water." Hatton winced. "Oh shit! Alfano slipped, but Gil's got him."

I watched in horror as Aggie bounced at the end of a dynamic rope—a strong cord with slightly elastic properties to take some of the shock out of a fall. Oh, Lord! Would I have to tell Alfano both of his sons were gone?

But Aggie was an experienced climber; he kept his cool, dead hanging to minimize the strain on Delfino. The powerful little man bowed his back and took his companion's weight. Delfino's muscles bunched as he lowered Aggie hand over hand to a small outcropping. Both Hatton and I let out sighs of relief as their calm voices echoed off the sides of the gorge.

"Sure hope they have enough rope," I said.

Hatton nervously fingered his walkie-talkie but prudently stayed off it. The last thing the two climbers needed was the distraction of a useless call from spectators.

"If not, they'll take the last couple of lengths with them to the bottom." Hatton turned to face me, fanning himself with his hat. "Don't seem like Alfano believes he's gonna find his brother down there. What do you think?"

"Don't have any idea. I don't know the kid. Aggie does. But from the air, it didn't seem like the driver was very experienced. The car was too erratic. There was no good reason for them to go over the cliff. An experienced driver would have started braking a quarter of a mile before he did."

"Drunk. Drugs. Not paying attention. Joyriding," the deputy cited possible explanations.

I couldn't find fault with any of them. Nonetheless, they didn't ring true somehow.

FOUR HOURS later the two climbers were mere specks far below us. It was difficult to see much of them even with the binoculars.

"It won't be long now." Hatton glanced around. "Shoulda waited until morning. We're gonna lose the light pretty soon."

The low-lying sun still bathed the bridge in its waning heat, but the gorge was now in deep shadow. When the two men had begun their descent, we could clearly see the river; now all we caught was white water where the current broke over rocks. Thank goodness both of them carried strong torches. Soon the radio crackled; it was Delfino saying they were at the bottom.

"Had a little trouble there in a couple of places," Hatton joshed.

"Nah, it was a cakewalk. Well, except for a rattler we had to chase outa the way once. Now all we gotta do is get to the car. It's about a hundred yards downstream."

"In the water?" Hatton asked.

"No. On rocks… mostly. Rear end's in the current. Sweet Jesus! This thing's all tore to pieces."

We watched two pinpoints of light move uncertainly to the south. It was obvious when they reached the Porsche; both merged into one. Five minutes later the radio crackled again. This time it was Aggie.

"BJ, it's not them. It's not Lando or Norville. Christ, man, it's hard to tell who they are, but it's not my brother or his friend."

"How do you know?" Hatton demanded.

"Too small. Clothes all wrong. One of them's more or less recognizable. The other one's got a big scar on his left arm. An old one."

There was a click on the other end, and then we heard Delfino's voice again. "Hatton, better go give old Mateo the bad news. I think he just lost half his family. And, Mr. Vinson, Mr. Alfano wants you to phone his father in case this thing goes out over the air waves."

Chapter 7

I CALLED Alfano from the bridge as soon as we knew the identities of the victims, but the conversation was short and unsatisfactory since there was little to tell my client except that although his son's car lay at the bottom of a deep chasm, Lando and Dana were still missing. I hitched a ride with Hatton as far as the airport to rent a car while he went to see the dead boys' family to deliver the tragic news and learn what he could of the Cruz kids' recent acquisition of a very expensive automobile.

I had collected my lend-lease Chevrolet and started to leave the airport when Jim Gray's Skycatcher caught my eye. Although I hadn't noticed him in the crowd at the bridge, he'd apparently hung around for the outcome. I made a detour to the plane and asked him to stay in Taos in case his aircraft was needed. Jim's more of a pilot than a businessman, so he declined my offer to cover his time. We piled into the rental and drove to the takeout spot near the Taos Junction Bridge to wait for the search and rescue recovery team.

After a couple of hours, Hatton's patrol car pulled up. The deputy got out and shook his head. "Didn't learn much. Neighbors say Mateo and his wife went to a family meeting over in Mora. The Cruz clan has a farm in the valley."

All he learned about the Porsche was that Martin and Jaime Cruz, the middle two of four Cruz brothers, had shown up in it two days ago, lovingly washed and rubbed it down, and bragged about their new wheels without divulging where they got them. The two boys took it for short drives with Joe, the youngest, tagging along. The neighbors were unanimous in their opinion the car was pure foolishness; it wasn't practical for this terrain. But none expressed curiosity about where the boys got it, probably because the whole village would know everything once Mateo laid eyes on it. The Cruz brothers weren't considered the most sensible boys around, except maybe the oldest, Pablo, who was over in the Mora Valley with his parents.

That left us with a single source of information about the Porsche: Joe, the unconscious seventeen-year-old who had been medevacked to the hospital in Santa Fe. Ignoring the fact it was after eleven, I called Artie Hartshorn, a detective with the Santa Fe Police Department, an old friend—or at least he was before I hauled him out of bed—and asked him to get someone to bird-dog that situation for us until I could get there tomorrow morning.

It was close to midnight when the search and rescue team's two rubber boats approached the takeout point. The lower Taos Box was a year-round run of white water, so the rafters had had no trouble reaching the wrecked Porsche, but they spent two hours extracting the bodies from the crumpled car and making the last leg of the run in darkness. Something I wouldn't have wanted to attempt.

Drenched, his hair spiked from the wind and water, Aggie ignored us until he and Delfino helped the team load two blanket-shrouded forms into an ambulance. Then he turned to me. Although exhaustion was clearly etched on his face, Aggie seemed pumped by the discovery his brother was not in the shattered automobile at the bottom of the Rio Grande Gorge.

"You get hold of the old man?" he asked.

"Yeah. You're to call him as soon as you can, regardless of the time."

"He'll have to wait. I need to change into dry clothes and get something to eat."

"Okay. I rented a car. Let's go."

We all piled into my rental, and we took Delfino back to his cruiser at the gorge bridge before going in search of a motel.

Now we sat in Aggie's room in the Taos Inn just off the town square while he dialed his father's number. I was pleased he'd chosen this place instead of one of the fancy new hotels. I liked the privacy management gave its guests. In fact, you were left to your own devices to the extent that if you wanted firewood for the hogan-style fireplace in your room, the clerk courteously directed you to the woodpile. The tasks of hauling it to your room and laying the fire were yours. A modest load of logs already rested in my own room just across the way.

"Papa?" Aggie said when his call connected. He paused. "No, it wasn't Lando. No doubt about it. They've identified the two bodies."

After he finished explaining the situation as we knew it, he held the phone out to me. "He wants to talk to you."

Alfano immediately started issuing orders. "Vinson, I want you to stay on this thing. It's more important than ever to find Lando. Something must have happened to him. He wouldn't give up that automobile without a fight. It was a graduation present."

"All right, Alfano. I'm heading to Santa Fe to be on hand when the third kid in the car—the boy who survived—regains consciousness. He's the only one who might know when and where they got the Porsche. In the meantime, the police are putting out a bulletin to locate and hold your son and his companion. I talked to my contacts in Albuquerque and with the state police in Santa Fe, so they are up-to-date on events. There's a possibility the boys have met with—"

"I know." The heavy voice suddenly seemed exhausted. "My boy might be dead. Killed for his car."

"A possibility, but that's leaping to conclusions. The people who know the family tell me the Cruz brothers were irresponsible but not killers. There are at least a couple of layers to this story."

"Do what you have to. I'm flying out in the morning."

"Not a good idea." I sensed the shock on the other end of the line. Probably not many people spoke to Anthony P. Alfano like that.

"Why the hell not?"

"So far we've kept your name out of it. If you come out, the television networks are going to swoop down in droves."

"Maybe we should make the whole damned countryside know my son's missing."

"Let me talk to the boy in the hospital before we go off half-cocked."

We sparred a bit longer before I hung up and turned to Aggie. He had a tired grin on his face.

"What?"

"You called him Alfano. If you knew my dad, you'd know that's kinda ballsy."

"If he knew me, he wouldn't call me Vinson," I snapped. "I warned him about it once."

The grin grew into a broad smile. "I like you, B. J. Vinson."

"And I like you, A. F. Alfano."

"Are you going to try to see the Cruz kid tonight?"

"No, I don't think they'll let me in until he's stabilized and they're certain of his condition. But I'm heading out first thing in the morning. That's why I sent Jim to bed, so he'll be fit for flying at daybreak."

Aggie glanced at his watch. "Daybreak. That's only three hours or so."

"I know, but it's important to see Joe Cruz. And since he's probably going to be charged with car theft, I want to be there before a lawyer gets to him. He's more apt to give me what I want if he hasn't been advised to keep his mouth shut."

"I'll fly you down in the Mitsubishi. It's faster."

"No. I'll take the Cessna. You stay here and work with Delfino. He'll be poking around at this end. If you're nice, he might even let you tag along with him."

"Nice? Hell, we're climbing buddies. He'll take me along."

I HAD been in Santa Fe's old hospital a couple of times, but this was my first visit to the new one. The steel and brick and stucco might be new, but it had the same antiseptic aroma and deceptive air of peace and calm masking death and disease as the original.

Artie Hartshorn stood at the receptionist's desk running a calloused hand through what remained of his once-brown hair. The rough hands were not the product of his service with the SFPD but of his avocation. Artie did woodworking in his spare time and had gotten good at it. I'd bought a pair of scallop-topped maple lamp tables out of his garage a few years back, and they were two of my prized possessions.

Artie turned when I called his name. "There you are. You get me up in the middle of the night and then don't bother to show up."

"Made pretty good time from Taos, I'd say."

He glanced at his watch. "Guess so. Anyway, the Cruz kid's on the fourth floor. They tell me he's awake but not making much sense."

"Who's with him?"

"Aunt of his by the name of Lucinda Cruz de Schwartz. The bad news is she's married to Harvey Schwartz."

"The attorney? Crap. Well, let's go see the kid anyway. Maybe they'll let him say something."

Lucinda Schwartz looked about five generations removed from Hispanic farmers in northern New Mexico. Her lustrous black hair was done in a tight french roll. Her full, sensual lips—Botox, in my opinion—looked pouty. Generous mascara, but not overdone. In fact, nothing about the woman was overdone, except the dangling enameled earrings and black sheath with a slit up to there, which came close. She must have been dressed for an evening out when she got the call about her nephew.

She strolled across the room to block access to Joe Cruz as we approached. She'd obviously done this before, which told me her nephews were likely a pain in the butt to the family.

"Officers," she said without benefit of an introduction, "may I help you?"

"You're partially right, Mrs. Schwartz," I said. "He's carrying a shield. I'm private."

She shrugged. "Birds of a feather."

"Mrs. Schwartz," Artie spoke up, "we need to speak to your nephew."

"Not without my husband present. He represents the family."

"Ma'am," I said, "I'm not interested in any sort of prosecution. My sole interest is locating the owner of the car lying at the bottom of the Rio Grande Gorge. I can probably trace Joe's brothers' movements back and learn what I need to know, but that's going to take time. And we might not have much time. If the man who owned that Porsche is in trouble, the quicker we get to him, the better."

"That may be your interest, Mr.… uh.…"

"Vinson. B. J. Vinson."

"Vinson? Weren't you the PI involved in that Zozobra thing last year?"

"We both were." I indicated Artie. "Detective Hartshorn was the lead detective in the case. If your nephew could just tell me where to start looking, it would help a lot. I don't expect it can do any harm, because I'm pretty sure that boy over there was not involved in taking the car. That was probably his brothers. But anything he knows from hearing them talk could be helpful."

"Why don't you wait out in the hall for a few minutes," she suggested.

As we restlessly paced the polished tiles outside the injured boy's hospital room, I picked up a call from Hazel on my cell phone. According to Gilda Gistafferson, there were no charges on the company credit card Lando carried. Alfano's attorney was making arrangements to get copies of the kid's personal bills from LA. Before hanging up, I asked Hazel to remind them to also pick up statements for Norville's cards, since they likely went to the same address.

If Lando was traveling on a fun trip with a lover Papa Alfano detested, he might be using plastic sparingly. But if the journey called for stealth, why hadn't he disabled the GPS device in the Porsche? Maybe because he intended to ignore his father, not evade him. Or had he even thought that far ahead?

Then Gilbert Delfino called to say he'd learned from friends and neighbors of the Cruz family that the two middle brothers—the ones who died in the canyon—had gone to the Mora Valley with their parents. Joe, the youngest, stayed behind with an aunt. Something about a girlfriend, Delfino surmised. But Martin and Jaime didn't stay with the family. They had headed off on a side excursion to Farmington, a town in the Four Corners area.

"How did they go?" I asked.

"Rode their thumbs."

"Hitched? Did they make it all the way to Farmington?"

"So far as we know. I called the city police up there and asked them to start making inquiries. I also told them you'd probably be in touch. I talked to Sergeant Dixie Lee in their Patrol Division and tried to pave the way for you a little. You know, let them know you were once one of the brotherhood."

"Thanks. Appreciate it. We're waiting to talk to the youngest brother now, but he's represented by counsel. Don't know if he'll cooperate or not."

"Well, good luck. This sure has caused a flap around here. I've had a bellyful. Think I'm gonna become a medicine man and take up smoking peyote."

"Right." I laughed. "Trade one set of problems for another."

"Yeah, but they're different problems. Well, sorta."

Lucinda Schwartz emerged from her nephew's room, so I thanked the Taos policeman-cum-shaman and hung up.

"Gentlemen, on the advice of my husband, I am unable to allow you to question my nephew. However, Mr. Vinson, it might be possible that someone left an expensive automobile unattended and with the keys in the ignition, almost as if he wanted to be rid of the machine."

"And," I added, "it might be possible it was abandoned on some street in Farmington."

Her eyes glinted with amusement. "Harvey said you were sharp. Yes, it's possible such an automobile was abandoned on a road a little south of Farmington. Perhaps at a little clearing with a cottonwood and honeysuckle on one side and a meadow across the road. There might have been a white horse in the meadow, but we're just speculating, you understand."

"The only thing is, that's a lot of speculation from a youngster who wasn't along for the trip. You know, all the detail."

"Let's just say one of my nephews liked to take Polaroid snapshots. And he happened to like horses. Somehow an orange car and a white horse ended up in one of them."

"I don't suppose I could get a copy—"

"I'm afraid not. Not without a lot of paperwork."

"I understand completely. And thank you."

"One more thing." She hesitated dramatically. "It's possible that a car like that would have had a couple of bullet holes in it."

"Bullet holes? Where?"

"My spirit guide was a little fuzzy on that one. In one of the back panels—on the driver's side, perhaps."

"Any blood? A body?"

"Apparently not."

As we left the hospital, I got Aggie on the line and shared everything except the information about the bullet holes.

"Looks like we're headed to Farmington," Aggie sighed.

"Guess so," I agreed.

Chapter 8

AGGIE ALFANO casually operated the controls of the Mitsubishi as he received landing instructions from the tower at the Four Corners Regional Airport. I don't speak "radio" and was always mystified how a pilot made enough sense of the mumbo jumbo to bring his craft safely to ground. He finished his discourse and made an adjustment to a dial.

"You ever landed at Four Corners Regional before?"

"No," I said.

"I have. I've fueled up there on the way to Taos. You're in for a thrill."

My gut tightened. "What does *that* mean?"

"The airport is high, and the runway ends in a cliff. Dicey."

"Dicey? Is that pilot lingo for suicidal?"

He laughed aloud. "No, but I'm glad we're in the Mitsu. Short takeoff, short landing," he explained. "We'll be okay."

A massive fluffy plume boiled up out of a gigantic smokestack and rode the prevailing air currents beneath our wings like one of the malevolent spirits of native folklore, spreading mischief far to the southwest. Plans for a new electric power-generating plant, to be fed by area coal mines, were slowly making their way through the bureaucracy to one day add dollars to the economy and carcinogens to the environment.

"Those emissions look nasty." Aggie reflected my own thoughts. "You know much about Farmington?"

I chuckled. "I'm a history buff, so I know a little about a lot of places, and not a lot about any of them."

Farmington, a small city of just under 50,000, which the early aboriginals called Tótah, or the Meeting Place of Waters, perched on the Colorado Plateau at the conjunction of the San Juan, Animas, and La Plata Rivers. Combined, these three rivers accounted for 25 percent of all the water in the state. The local economy was carbon based: natural gas, coal, and oil.

"There's something that worries me more than that smokestack at the moment," I said. "Farmington's been the target of several civil rights investigations, mostly for hate crimes motivated by racial discrimination. The place is virtually surrounded by Native Americans—the Navajo Nation west of Farmington, the Ute Mountain Reservation to the northwest, and the Southern Ute to the northeast—and that's sparked trouble at times. It's not much of a leap to conclude that a couple of gays might run into the same type of prejudice."

"Lando and Norville don't flaunt their lifestyle," Aggie said. "But they wouldn't hide it if asked if they were gay." He glanced over at me. "Well, here we go."

He aligned the Mitsubishi with the runway and touched a lever that lowered the landing gear. I felt a distinct thump when the wheels locked into place. Although I'm an experienced flier, my sphincter puckered as he dropped toward the runway. The landing wasn't actually scary, but his warning had primed the pump and he knew it. There was a touch of a grin on his lips as the craft shuddered to a halt well short of the end of the runway.

"That wasn't so bad, was it?" he asked.

"No, except for the buildup."

Aggie made arrangements for refueling and a tie-down while I went to find a rental car. He had piloted the plane, so it was only fair I drove the auto. Farmington is spread out over some thirty miles, and I've always had trouble deciding where "downtown" was. Even so, we found the municipal complex easily enough and headed for the police station to ask for a Sergeant Lee. Delfino had apparently cleared the way for us.

Sergeant Dixie Lee turned out to be a voluptuous woman about an inch shorter than I was who regarded the world through two of the bluest eyes I'd ever seen, a lapis blue, set in an attractive, fair face only slightly hardened by all the crap she'd seen in her years on the force. Her voice was scratchy like a smoker's.

"Good to meet you." She gripped my hand firmly and swiveled to face Aggie. "You too, sir. I expect you're not interested in small talk, so let's get right down to it." She picked up a file from the counter where we were standing. "Orlando S. Alfano and Dana J. Norville have already come to our attention."

"How so?" Aggie craned his neck to get a glimpse of the document she held.

"They were involved in an incident in a roadhouse out on the city limits a couple of weeks ago." She consulted the file. "August 11. Saturday night."

"What kind of incident?" I asked.

"Well, we don't have a gay bar here, but the Sidewinder Bar and Grill catches some of that trade."

The name rang a bell. "Wasn't that the place investigated in a civil rights case a few years back?"

"Yes, sir. At least, a couple of their patrons were. They claimed a man made homosexual advances. They took it outside, and the victim—or the perpetrator, depending upon your viewpoint—almost died from his beating."

"Was that what happened to Lando?" Aggie asked.

"Not exactly, but close."

Absently toying with a curl of blond hair that fell to her shoulder, Dix Lee told us Lando and Dana went to the Sidewinder, perhaps under the impression it was a gay bar. Once there, they struck up a conversation with a local identified as Harper Yarborough, an oilfield roustabout better known as Bud. According to the police incident report, Yarborough claimed the two had propositioned him. Offended, he left. When Lando and Dana exited the bar a little later, Yarborough and a couple of friends were waiting in the parking lot, no doubt figuring two pansies would be easy pickings. Lando and Dana proved to be anything but.

The cops at the scene wrote up the incident and sent the parties in separate directions without making any arrests. Orlando was in possession of his Porsche at the time, because the report indicated the two men left in it.

"Nothing after that?" I asked.

"Found where they stayed. Trail's End Motel down on Main."

"How long were they there?" Aggie asked.

"Checked out on Tuesday the fourteenth. Nothing since then."

"I hope you don't mind," I said, "but we're going to be nosing around town. We'll keep you informed of anything interesting we turn up. Or you can assign an officer to escort us if that works better for you."

"Thanks, but we don't have that kind of manpower. Just leave your cell phone numbers, and let us know where you're staying."

"Might as well try the Trail's End, provided they have a couple of vacancies." I gave one of my cards to Aggie, who added his phone number to mine and handed it to Dix Lee.

She nodded. "We'll let you know if they turn up anywhere."

We exited the municipal complex parking lot, hung a left on Auburn Drive, and proceeded south until we picked up Main. The Trail's End was a surprise. It was a two-story, stucco-clad, cinder block motel, typical of those built in the forties. White paint, flat roof, and steel casement windows made it indistinguishable from the one down the street and the one beyond that. It was certainly not a place I'd expect the son of a megamillionaire to select for his base of operations in the area. Nevertheless, we checked in and were given adjoining rooms at the rear, away from the busy commercial street.

After cleaning up a little, I went to the lobby to do some of that nosing around I'd warned Sergeant Lee about. The same young lady who'd seen to our registration was still at the desk. I returned her professional smile and paused to examine some postcards on a revolving rack.

"Your first time in this part of the country?" She moved closer to field the payment for any card that caught my fancy.

"First time in quite a while. What sights would you suggest for a stay of no more than a couple of days?"

"Oh, there's so much to see. All you can do in two days is hit the highlights. There's Navajo Lake and the butte over at Shiprock. Mesa Verde National Park is forty miles to the northwest. Chaco Canyon is only about fifty. Aztec Ruins National Monument and the Salmon Ruins are both old pueblo sites close by. Then there's the Bisti badlands country south of here. If you're into the arts, we have some good galleries."

As she gave me the tourist pitch, I noticed she wasn't as young as she appeared at first glance—probably thirty or so. The brown hair worn in a ponytail contributed to the deception.

"Actually, this is not just a pleasure trip. We're hoping to cross paths with Mr. Alfano's brother who's vacationing out here."

"Oh, the guys in the orange Porsche. I wondered about that name when you registered. You know, the name and the fact the brothers look so much alike." Her gray eyes shifted from her tanned hands folded on the counter to a spot over my head and back again, as if she were distracted. I took a shot in the dark.

"Don't worry, Melissa." I caught her name from her nametag. "Mr. Alfano knows his brother is gay and is here with another young man."

Her features relaxed. "I wasn't sure. Neither of them acted… you know, that way. Boy, they sure did attract a lot of attention. Or that car did, anyway. A day after they checked in, some guy was asking about it."

"Asking about it? How?"

"Well, he started making car talk, you know, quoting the stats on a car like that and speculating about how much it cost. Wondered about the owner. That kind of thing."

"What did he ask about the owner?"

She shrugged. "Nothing, really. Just wondered who'd be able to afford a car like that." She paused before adding. "And why he'd be staying at the Trail's End instead of one of the fancy places."

I smiled. "I have to admit that thought crossed my mind too."

Melissa wrinkled her nose. "I think it's because they liked the freedom. Everybody left them alone. Nobody looking over their shoulders. Close to the highway. That kind of thing."

"Back to the man asking about them."

"About the car," she corrected.

"Okay, about the car. What did he look like?"

"Like a hundred other guys, I guess. Older than you. Maybe bigger than you. The only thing that stood out was his forehead. Domed, I'd call it." She giggled. "Really domed."

"What was he driving?"

"I don't know. He must have parked at the side. He just came through the door and asked for directions to one of the parks around here. Then he made a comment about the car. I remember he spoke a lot better than he looked. I mean, his grammar was okay, but he was sorta tough looking. I had the feeling he was just making conversation. Guys do that sometimes," she added.

"I can believe that."

"They seemed so nice," she blurted. "Lando and Dana, I mean. They laughed and joked and flirted with me like regular guys."

"Did you talk to them much?"

Melissa blushed. "Some. They came back to the motel one day and told me about their trip to the Aztec Ruins. And they liked the Salmon Pueblo too. They asked about the art galleries, and I steered them to the Three Artists' Studio down the street. They must have liked it because Lando told me he bought a John Haley Muller landscape. That's a local artist, and he's not cheap either. There's nothing in the studio under five thousand. He told me he had it shipped directly to California. They really seemed to be enjoying their vacation." As she finished speaking, a frown tugged at her features.

"What changed?"

"The first night they were here, they ran into some trouble out at the Sidewinder. That's a bar at the south end of town. Not sure what it was, but they both had bruises. I asked about it, but they just brushed me off. I heard later the police got called out there."

"Did they seem seriously injured?"

"No. Like I said, just bruises."

"But that's not all, is it?"

She shook her head, her ponytail wagging like a dog's appendage. "No, they shrugged that off okay, I guess. Kept on taking short trips around the area." Her eyes swept the room before continuing. "Then they got in a fight."

"Another one?" I asked.

"Not like that. With each other."

"A fist fight?"

"No, but I thought it was going to come to that before it was over. It got loud enough another guest complained, and I had to go over and ask them to keep it down."

"What was it about, do you know?"

Melissa reddened again, and I realized she had been attracted to one or both of the men. "About a boy."

I made a quick mental connection. "A boy named Cruz?"

She frowned. "I don't know any Cruz. This was a local kid. Jazz Penrod."

"You know anything about him?"

"I know him," she said without any inflection in her voice. "Trouble. Has been since he was thirteen."

"What kind of trouble?"

"Maybe you better go ask somebody else. I don't like gossiping."

"Okay, lend me your phone, and I'll call Sergeant Dix Lee at the FPD and have her come ask the questions."

She opened up right away, rendering all her protestations false. "All right, Jasper Penrod is a mixed-blood kid who's lived here all his life. Here and on the Big Rez." She tossed her head in a westerly direction. "He's about the biggest competition the girls in this town have. He's as pretty as any of them—heck, prettier—and he likes the same thing they do, except he's more aggressive about it."

"He's gay?"

"Most definitely."

"You mean dresses up in women's clothes?"

"Not Jazz. He dresses like a man and acts like a man, but he puts the moves on a man just like a woman. Been more than one guy in trouble for fooling around with Jazz when he was underage."

"How old is he now?"

"About eighteen. He's a good kid, really. By that, I mean, he doesn't get anyone in trouble on purpose. But he wants what he wants and isn't shy about it."

"A kid could get in trouble for that—especially around here, I understand."

"Yeah, a lot of the fellas don't like gay people. And Jazz doesn't make any bones about being that way. But he does it different. Not faggy or flighty or anything like that. And he's just so… so pretty."

"A pretty face sometimes causes bad trouble."

"You're right about that. But his daddy's one mean Indian, and he's got a whole clan to back him up—including Jazz's brother. Half brother, I guess. So the word went out, and nobody in his right mind tackles Jazz. His mom's brother stands up for him too. He's white."

"How about the law?"

"They just try to keep things peaceful. They don't bother Jazz as long as he doesn't do anything outrageous. Outrageously illegal," she amended.

"Jazz. How'd he come by that name?"

"He doesn't like the name Jasper, so he started calling himself Jazz."

"You sound like you know him pretty well."

"I ought to. His mom lives just down the street from our house. I watched the guy grow up."

"Does Jazz go with anybody? Steady, I mean?"

"You want to know if somebody might be jealous enough to make trouble for Lando and Dana?"

"Something like that."

"Jazz has never had a serious relationship so far as I know. So I can't help you there."

"How about the family? The brother or the uncle?"

"Oh, they wouldn't get involved unless Jazz was being threatened or something. They accepted how Jazz is a long time ago."

I pressed the conversation, but the only additional information of value to surface was Jazz Penrod's Farmington address. Melissa had no idea where to find him if he was on the reservation.

"I understand Lando and Dana checked out of the motel better than a week ago. On the fourteenth, I believe."

She nodded. "That sounds about right."

"Did the man asking about the Porsche show up again?"

"Nope."

Aggie came into the lobby, so I thanked Melissa and we left. After filling him in on my conversation with the desk clerk, I called my office to ask Hazel to look into the whereabouts of Bruno Wills, Dana's former lover. Maybe he was the one shadowing the two men. Then we left in the hot pursuit of… absolutely nothing.

"Bud Yarborough, the roustabout Lando and Dana fought with at the Sidewinder, is probably on the job out in the oilfield," I said. "We'll have to catch him this evening. So let's go see if Jazz Penrod is home."

Eunice Penrod and her son lived on the north side of town in a modest residential section that reminded me of the company towns of yesteryear. It was more than the small box houses looking similar. Plenty of developments suffer from that problem, but these were almost exactly alike, as if few of the occupants had an imagination or sought to establish an independent identity. The one-story, porchless clapboard buildings were as depressing as any tenement. To her credit, Jazz's mother had set out trellises of incredibly delicate climbing rose vines on either side of the stoop.

Ms. Penrod, a nervous woman of about forty, was reluctant to talk about her son to two strangers, at least one of whom—Aggie Alfano— was certifiably handsome and hunky. Her guarded attitude confirmed she was aware of her son's lifestyle. How could she not be? The kid had been on the hunt since his early teens if you could believe the desk clerk at the Trail's End.

"He's not home right now," she declared in a well-modulated voice.

"Can you tell us where to find him?" I watched alarm flash across her eyes at the question. "We're looking for Mr. Alfano's brother, and we understand Jazz might be able to point us in the right direction."

"I don't know anything about it." With that she gently but firmly closed the door.

We exchanged glances and returned to the car. Deciding to raise the mother's anxiety level a bit, I sat in front of the house while I dialed Lando's cell phone. As usual it went to his voice mail. I got the same results with Dana's.

"How many times have you called those numbers?" Aggie asked.

"Gave up counting. No one's going to answer, but I'd feel mighty foolish if I later found out one more call would have established contact."

As I pulled away from the curb, Aggie gave an exasperated snort. "Why are we doing this alone? Why aren't the police here with us?"

"Why? No crime's been committed."

"No crime? My brother's car was stolen, and two boys are dead as the result. He's been in a fight, and now he and Dana are missing."

"The fight was dealt with, at least as far as the cops are concerned. There's no real evidence the car was stolen from here. After all, it ended up halfway across the state. Mixed jurisdictions are always tricky."

"And," he added dryly, "the missing guys are both queers. No reason to break a sweat over them, is there?"

"That could be a part of it, but mostly it's because they're both adults. They don't have an obligation to keep you informed of their whereabouts."

"But Lando didn't even report the car stolen. Doesn't that mean anything?"

"To you and me, it does. And I'll warrant Dix Lee did a database search after we talked and has put out a bulletin. She'll probably interview Bud Yarborough again, but that's about it."

"What about this Jazz Penrod?"

"Chances are they don't know about that connection yet. The girl at the Trail's End said the police weren't called when Lando and Dana had their dustup."

"I can't believe it." Aggie shook his head. "I can't believe they had a fight over another guy."

"You never had a fight with your girlfriend over looking at a woman?"

"Yeah, but—" He caught himself. "Okay, I get it. It's the same thing, right?"

"I'd say so. Tell me, Aggie, do you approve of Lando's association with Dana?"

"He's got a right to live his life the way he wants to, and I support him in that."

"Unlike your father."

"Yeah. Papa's old school. He still thinks all gays are queers—you know, fags and flaming queens. I like to believe I'm more understanding than that, but every once in a while, I catch myself hoping the old man might be right. That one day Lando will wake up and put all that behind him."

"That's okay too, if that's what he really wants to do."

Chapter 9

WE WENT to see what Dix Lee knew about Jasper Penrod and found she knew a great deal. The kid had first come to the department's attention the day he turned thirteen when he broke a bottle over his father's head during a drunken domestic brawl. The prosecutors decided he was acting in defense of his mother, so no juvie charges were filed. Within a month he was back in their sights when a cop caught a twenty-two-year-old man in a compromising position with him. Since Jazz was a minor, the entire weight of the law fell upon the adult, who was charged with child sexual abuse. The next time it was a high school senior basketball player who suffered the consequences. The FPD file listed other such incidents over the years, but none in the past few months. I asked about that.

"Nobody believes he's changed his habits," Dix confided, "but before he didn't give a damn if he got caught because he didn't pay the price. That said, he's smart enough to realize we'll come down on him now he's eighteen."

"There's not much here except for sexual liaisons and the beer bottle incident with his father," I said. "Just a shoplifting charge last year that was dismissed."

"Yeah. We looked into it, and it was clear the accusation was payback when Jazz spurned some guy's advances."

"No fighting. Nothing like that," I continued. "That's unusual, especially the lack of fighting. I'd think an obvious gay would be in scrapes all the time around here."

"Probably would be except for his older brother and his uncle. He's got protectors on both sides of the family. Henry Secatero, his half brother, is more of a father than Louie Secatero ever was. Henry's a tough guy, and if anybody plows into Jazz…." Dix faltered, apparently tripping over on her choice of words. "That is, if anybody attacks Jazz, they have him to deal with. Henry's been in trouble more than once over situations like that, but it's never anything serious enough for more than a night in jail."

"How old is Henry?"

"Around twenty-eight or so."

"Native American, I take it," Aggie interjected.

"You take it right."

"You said something about protection from the other side of the family too," I said.

"Yeah. Jazz's mother, Eunice, is sort of a sad case. She's a hard worker but never had any luck with men. Louie Secatero is one good-looking guy—Jazz comes by it honestly—and he sorta swept her off her feet. But he didn't have any interest in her except for the usual, and he made himself scarce when she got pregnant. To his credit he started coming around after Jazz was born and even contributes a little money to the family now and then. He works in the coal mine on the Navajo Reservation.

"Anyway, Eunice's brother, Riley Penrod, looks after her. She lives in his house. He never married, probably because of her dependence on him. He took to Jazz right off the bat. He's the kind of man you'd think would toss a gay kid down a deep well with no rope, but he's always been protective of his nephew. Riley's been in a few fistfights over Jazz too. Not as much and not as violently as Henry but enough so you'd sit up and take notice. So word got around pretty quick not to lean on Jazz."

She did that thing with the curl of hair at her shoulder. "Of course, Jazz does all right on his own. He looks like an angel, but he fights like a devil."

I tapped the folder in her hand. "Nothing about that in there from the quick glance I saw."

"No, he's always been the victim. That is to say, the other guy threw the first punch, but Jazz gets in his quota. You wouldn't think it from looking at the kid. He's long and lanky, but he's got a set of muscles hidden under his shirt. Here, take a look for yourself."

Even the kid's mug shot, taken for the bogus shoplifting charge, was something. A spectacularly handsome adolescent peered out from the image through dark, smoky eyes. Full, blushed lips. High, smooth cheeks. Gracefully arched brows that ended in a slight, upward twist, giving the teen an impish look. Raven hair spilled down on his neck in an ebony halo, slightly wavy and looking silky to the touch. Jazz Penrod was saved from androgyny by an Adam's apple and the defined, definitely male slope of his shoulders. I got the feeling that in person, the kid was graceful, maybe even excessively so, but not a mama's boy. I could understand how he came by his reputation. With those sultry, exotic looks, he'd get plenty of action by just crooking his little finger— or better yet, lifting one of those eyebrows. There was little of his mother in the image. He probably resembled Louis, his father.

"Where can we find him?" I asked.

"Your guess is as good as mine. The kid doesn't have steady work, but he does odd jobs both here and on the reservation. That and the gifts he gets from his admirers keep him in enough money to get by." Dix gave the photo one last look before putting it back in the folder.

"He's a male prostitute?" Aggie asked.

"No, and if he was, we'd run him in. But he doesn't turn down gifts. Despite what I've said, Jazz won't go with just anyone. He's got to be attracted to a man. Not all of the guys who got in trouble over him have had money."

"So we're on our own finding him?" I asked.

"Yeah. There's no reason to put out a bulletin on him. But if a unit happens to see him, I'll give you a call."

"Thanks."

With little to do until people started getting off from work, Aggie and I reported in to Alfano and then took a run out to the Aztec Ruins National Monument to see if we could find a trace of the two missing men on the trip Melissa had mentioned. As usual, the orange Porsche had snagged the attention of some of the monument's attendants, although there was nothing about the behavior of the car's occupants to attract notice.

From there we went to the Salmon Ruins, an ancient Anasazi pueblo, with similar results. Before wheeling out onto Highway 64, I paused and glanced at Aggie. "Lando and Dana exhibited some interest in the Bisti badlands a couple of times. It's a bit farther than these last two we visited. You want to take a swing down there? It's a different sort of attraction, a wilderness area with a bunch of weird-shaped rock formations. Hoodoos, they call them. The last time I checked, Bisti gets very little traffic. There probably won't even be any park people around."

He consulted his watch. "How far?"

"Probably forty miles or so. And then you do a little hiking, if things haven't changed in the five years since I was there last."

Aggie made a point of glancing at his polished loafers. "Let's go back to Farmington. I want to look up this Yarborough bird. If we don't learn anything from him, we'll go tomorrow."

THE SIDEWINDER Bar and Grill occupied a wood-frame building isolated in the middle of a large gravel parking lot at the southern city limits of Farmington. The green paint covering the outside walls reminded me of dried bile. The lot served up a miasma of dust and gas fumes every time a vehicle pulled in or departed. Tonight the place did not appear to be very busy. About a dozen pickup trucks and sports coupes huddled close to the building, leaving the remaining two acres vacant.

I nosed the rented Ford in beside a double cab Dodge Ram. We got out of the car and started for the door. The walk, although short, was rough. How in the hell did drunks and women in high heels—drunk or sober—make it across the parking lot?

Up close the bar was no more appealing. The paint had cracked and fallen away in some places. Pipes poking up from two swamp coolers atop the flat roof led me to believe they were derelict. The lack of a humming motor heightened the impression. Probably steamy as hell inside. On the other hand, this was northern New Mexico, where the nights were usually cool.

A false-front overhang held a painted sign with the bar's name in black letters lighted by a flood at either end. Competing neon signs in red and blue advertised different brands of beer on the building's two front windows. A short concrete ramp led to double doors like the ones found in more pretentious homes, except the wood was as cracked and paint hungry as the rest of the exterior. Obviously the Sidewinder's attraction was not its exterior.

Once through the door, I was proved wrong. The interior temperature was comfortable. Something scrunched beneath my feet. Sawdust. The floor was covered in old-fashioned sawdust. To sop up spilled beer or spilled blood—or both. The decibel level was lower than I expected, giving the place the atmosphere of a corner pub. But it was early yet. The jukebox was modulated and the buzz of conversation, subdued. People— mostly men—clustered in twos and threes around small tables. A couple of bosomy waitresses in short shorts moved among the patrons bringing a steady supply of drinks. A quick glance around the bar revealed a glass or two of the hard stuff, but this was overwhelmingly a suds joint.

Conversation didn't exactly die when we came through the door, but we moved through an odd tunnel of silence as talk faded with our approach and resumed with our passing. I felt the weight of curious eyes as we made our way to the bar.

"What'll it be, gents?" The bartender sported a luxurious black moustache. His professional smile revealed a missing front tooth.

"A draft," I said. Aggie nodded, earning him one of the same.

The beer was good, another surprise. Probably Coors, which was not one of the two brands advertised outside. Aggie and I exchanged glances as we silently sipped our brews. There was a raised dance floor at the east end of a room that seemed bigger than the building housing it. No one was dancing. In accordance with barroom protocol, we inspected the place with our eyes above the heads of the seated patrons, although several of them stared at us boldly.

"Newcomers?" a voice at my side asked.

I turned to find a man of about thirty with a bronzed face and a physique fashioned by hard work. Oilfield worker or open-pit miner, no doubt.

"Yeah, I'm up from Albuquerque. My friend's visiting me from San Francisco. We're trying to decide whether to tackle Navajo Lake or the San Juan tomorrow."

"You already missed the best fishing, but it ain't bad. We was up at the lake last week and pulled out a couple of pike. Best bet's probably the Animas this time of year. Course, depends on what you're fishing for."

"Anything that bites," Aggie said.

"I hear you. My name's Oscar." A strong, work-calloused hand clasped mine.

"Good to meet you, Oscar. I'm BJ, and my friend's Aggie."

"Aggie." Oscar acknowledged my taller companion. "How'd you find the Sidewinder?"

"It's all we've heard about since we got here. Best beer joint in the Four Corners."

"That's the truth. Anything else?"

So that was his game. Two strange males had entered the place, and he was already setting out his bait. What was it Dix Lee had said about the Sidewinder? It wasn't a gay joint, but it attracted some of that trade.

I took another glance at the man. My height and weight but younger. An attractive face if it hadn't been so weather-beaten. But the arms and chest outlined by his tight T-shirt would have attracted anyone halfway leaning toward queer. The huge gold-and-turquoise Western belt buckle at his trim waist pulled one's gaze to his groin. I nudged Aggie's foot, hoping he'd get the message to keep his mouth shut.

I decided to deliberately misunderstand his question about "anything else." "Just that we oughta check out the old Anasazi ruins around here. Walk through the tourist-trap art studios downtown. The usual."

"I meant about the bar," Oscar said.

"No, nothing in particular. Are you saying this is a drug joint?" I glanced around.

"Naw. Well, not so's you'd notice. A few of the boys are probably toting a private stash, but this ain't where you go to get it. That your game?"

"Nope. Don't have a game. Came in for a beer. You have a game, Oscar?"

The broad shoulders lifted and fell. "Everybody has a game, BJ. You did say BJ, didn't you?"

"Yeah, it's BJ. My game is living my life and letting the other guy live his."

"That's a good game."

"But it's not yours," I suggested.

"One of them." He turned coy.

"And the other?"

"Well, I'm always looking for a good time."

"Who isn't? But one man's good time is another man's nightmare."

Oscar's eyes told me he was tired of sparring. He'd either make his move or figure it was a lost cause. Then loud laughter and a booming voice in the corner beyond the dance floor diverted our attention to where four men were crowded into a booth.

"Hell, Bud," someone yelled. "You been playing that same George fer two months now. Time to get some new bills."

I picked Bud Yarborough out of the group by the nasty smile he gave his companions. From this distance he appeared to have a long, thin head. There was nothing attractive about him, but on the other hand, there was nothing unattractive either. He had one of those faces that if you considered each feature—the deep-set eyes; long, thin nose; sunburned cheeks; dimpled chin—nothing was particularly outstanding.

Put together they looked "passable," as my mother used to say. His dingy blond hair was gathered at the back in a ponytail that made me think of Melissa at the Trail's End.

Aggie's reaction to the name, Bud, was obvious—and unfortunate. Our new companion caught it immediately.

"Dollar poker." Oscar leaned against the bar and took a swig from a dark amber bottle. "You know old Bud Yarborough?" The words were casual, but the body language was tense. His shoulders were thrown back, his chest motionless as he held his breath. His eyes swept back and forth between Aggie and me.

"Never met the man," I answered. "Somebody we oughta know?"

Oscar put his elbows on the counter and shook his head. "Just a fella." He stood straight and stared at Aggie. "You look like somebody I oughta know. We ever run into one another before?"

"Not unless you've been to Na… uh, San Francisco," Aggie answered. "Spent a little time over in Taos. Maybe we saw one another over there."

"Uh-uh. Can't place it, but I will."

He probably would; Aggie was a taller, older version of Lando Alfano. This Oscar character was on the hunt for something, and my guess was trouble. It was time to get out of there. I shuffled around in the sawdust as the bartender offered another round.

"No, thanks. Better get some shut-eye if we're gonna go fishing tomorrow."

"Where you guys staying?" Oscar continued to eye Aggie.

"One of the downtown motels. Must be something going on in town. Had to hit a couple of places before we found one with two vacancies."

If Oscar knew that was a lie, he let it pass. His eyes fixed on me. "You'd save a buck or two if you doubled up."

"Not my thing," I said flatly. "I'm here for the fishing, not listening to some big galoot snore all night."

I left a fiver on the counter as a tip and headed outside, sensing Aggie's reluctance as he trailed along behind. He voiced his objections as soon as we were through the door.

"That was the guy we're looking for over in the corner."

"Right, and that was one of his backups in the fight with Lando standing right beside us. The guy was baiting us, Aggie. He was inviting us to make a move on him so his team could swing into action."

"I'm not a lump of coal, BJ. I know what he was up to. Let's go back in there and do what we came to do."

"There were four of them in that booth, and Oscar made five. I'm not afraid of a good fight, but those odds are a little long."

"Hell, Yarborough's gonna be with buddies anytime we see him. I say we tackle him now."

"Aggie, it's important you trust me about this. We're not going to win a fight with a man who's got a whole bar full of buddies. Get in the car. We're going to leave."

He was still grumbling as he slammed the door. "What now?"

"You'll see. Chances are somebody's watching."

I pulled out of the parking lot and headed back toward Main Street and our motel. "Anybody follow us out?"

"Nope. Nobody."

Once out of sight of the Sidewinder, I pulled a U-turn and drove back past the bar. Half a mile south of the building, I found a road that cut back to the east. It meandered through a semirural residential area before turning back north. By trial and error, I finally found a back entrance to the bar's parking lot. A lone sycamore near the highway provided a dark spot to wait.

"Now you'll see how a PI does most of his work. Sitting on his backside."

Chapter 10

AGGIE WASN'T cut out for surveillance. To calm his rising case of the fidgets, I asked if his father had hired another PI to look for his brother.

"No. At least not to my knowledge. But the old man does things his own way, and it's usually the right way. He's been known to hedge his bets. Why do you ask?"

"Before I left Albuquerque, I got a whiff of someone else on the hunt for the orange Porsche." I told him about the casual conversation with the clerk at the Acoma truck stop. "Of course, it could be an innocent comment about a car someone saw on the highway."

I watched him for a moment through the darkness before continuing. "And then there's what the motel clerk told me. Somebody was curious about the car while Lando and Dana were checked in at the Trail's End."

"That bomb always attracted attention."

"And that might be all it was, but I don't like coincidences. So what do you think? Your father's man?"

"In all honesty I don't have the foggiest idea."

"I get the feeling Anthony Alfano is ashamed of Lando."

"No, that's not true. He's proud of Lando. The kid's good-looking, smart, and very good with people. And Papa's convinced this gay thing's a phase. He expects Lando to grow out of it any minute, start going out with girls, and give him a bunch of grandkids. It's an Italian thing."

"It's a human thing," I responded. "Do you think he's right?"

A stray beam of moonlight caught in Aggie's hair as he shook his head. "Naw. Lando's who he is. The old man's usually a realist, but he can't handle one of his sons being gay. He's in denial."

"How do you feel about it?"

"I wish it wasn't so—for Lando's sake. The way I figure it, there are enough obstacles in a man's life. He doesn't need another one that flies in the face of convention. Not one that big, anyway. Lando's life would be just about perfect if… if he wasn't that way. No matter how much he accepts being gay, it makes dealing with most of society that much harder."

"You don't figure he's up to it?"

"Oh, yeah. Lando'll be just fine."

"Except at home."

He turned to glance at me. "I never thought of it that way, but you're right. He runs into more bigotry in the Alfano household than out in the real world."

"Sad."

"Shit!" Aggie shoved the door open. I lunged to cover the dome light with my palm, but for a moment, our location was exposed to anyone watching. He slammed the door and stalked away. I understood he wasn't angry at what I'd said; he was simply coming to grips with the price his brother paid for living life on his own terms.

Although my night vision was impaired, so far as I could determine, no one had taken notice of us. By the time Aggie returned, I had shut off the dome light.

"Sorry. It hit me in the gut, I guess. I started remembering my brother when we were younger. He was a cute little kid. And he grew up to be a cute big kid… man. Why does it happen? I mean, I've known gay guys ever since middle school, and it never bothered me a bit. But this is my brother."

I drew a deep breath. He was asking for my take on things because his father had apparently told him I was gay. Either that or he had good gaydar. "I've read all the books, Aggie. And I've sorted through all the theories and come to the conclusion it's a matter of predisposition… hardwiring, if you prefer. In my case it wasn't anything my parents did or didn't do. I had a normal childhood and a pretty typical adolescence."

"When did they find out?"

"Before I was out of high school. My father was a very shrewd man, and he picked up on it. Probably before I did. Anyway, we talked, and that helped focus things for me."

"So he brought you out… intellectually, I mean."

"I guess that's true. And as a result, I went into the Marines right after graduation to make a point. And learned I was as much a man as any of them."

Aggie sighed. "Lando didn't have the advantage of an understanding father. The old man just went for the jugular, telling the kid he wasn't gay—or queer, as he put it. In spite of that, Lando's a happy-go-lucky guy. Happy with who he is."

"Not everybody agonizes over being different, but given his home environment, I suspect he went through a lot."

"It's like seeing a new brother."

"No, it's like seeing a brother anew."

Bud Yarborough, or someone with a ponytail who looked like him, ambled through the front door of the Sidewinder Bar and Grill followed by three of his pals. The group made for a pair of double-cab, heavy-duty Ford trucks that could have been identical twins.

I kicked over the motor. "We've got to get closer. It's going to be hard to keep the right truck in sight. Watch them and tell me which truck he gets into." I dropped the car into gear and allowed it to coast forward slowly without turning on the lights. Once out of the shadow of the overhanging sycamore, it was almost as light as day. The cloudless sky and bright moon spotlighted us—or so it seemed.

There was no sign we had been observed. The four men shouted good-natured insults and split up into pairs. Yarborough stepped up into the cab of one pickup; Oscar joined him in the passenger's seat. With a blast of horns, the two trucks roared out of the parking lot and turned north toward town.

"You get a fix on them?" I maneuvered my way without benefit of lights.

"Yarborough's in the second truck."

Just before turning out onto the highway, I flipped on the lights. Yarborough was lead-footing it out of sight, so I goosed the rental.

"What's the plan?" Aggie asked.

"Play it by ear. Hopefully he'll drop Oscar by his place and go home alone."

"What if they hit another bar?"

"Then we wait."

In less than a mile, brake lights flashed as the truck directly in front of us slowed for a right turn into a trailer park. The other pickup kept going. I took the turn more cautiously and watched as Bud braked beside a doublewide. Both men got out.

"Either they're roomies or Bud's going in for a Bud," Aggie said.

"Makes you wonder, doesn't it?"

"You think Bud and Oscar…?"

"Dunno, but it's possible. At any rate, it doesn't look like they're going to split, so I guess we get to take on the pair of them. You up for it?"

"Let's do it."

Yarborough had already stripped off his boots and shirt by the time he answered my knock. Work at the oilfield had added muscles to his slender frame. Sun bronzed around his arms and neck, he was a pale ivory from there down, making his dark nipples seem almost obscene. His plain face twisted at the sight of us. The ash-blond ponytail had been released, and his hair flowed over his shoulders.

"Who're you?" Yarborough's voice was like a bass drum.

"Need to talk to you a minute. Can we come in?" I asked courteously.

"I repeat, who the fuck are you?"

"My name's Vinson. I'm a private investigator from Albuquerque. This is—"

He shot a thumb in Aggie's direction. "This is kin to one of them queer sons a bitches tried to put the make on me awhile back."

"And therein lies the rub," I said, stepping up into the trailer.

I halfway expected Yarborough to stop me, but he backed away. Aggie was hard on my heels. Once inside the door, I stepped aside so as not to block him. Oscar came out of the back, also shirtless. Had we interrupted something?

Yarborough emerged from his trance. "Get outa here. I didn't invite you in."

"You backed away and gave us access," I said. "That constitutes consent. Of course, if you insist, we'll have to leave."

"I fucking insist," he snarled.

"Very well, then we'll have to ask our questions at the police station after they invite you down. But then we'll have a couple of other people with us."

"Who?"

"Two… and possibly three others you've baited and assaulted."

"I don't know what—"

"Sure you do. And you know who too. It doesn't take long for word like that to get around. Hell, it was the cops who put us onto you. They'd like to get you out of their hair. So do we leave, or do we talk?"

"About what?"

I motioned toward Aggie. "About Mr. Alfano's brother."

"What about him? The asshole got zonked and grabbed my cock, so I invited him outside and taught him a lesson his brother oughta taught him before he got out of short pants."

Out of the corner of my eye, I saw Aggie's fists ball. I stepped forward, putting myself halfway between him and the idiot standing in front of me.

"That's not what the cops say. You baited those two men and waylaid them when they left the bar. We hear they held their own against three of you. But as much as I'd like to push your face in for that, it's not why we're here. I want to know what happened after that."

"Nothing. The cops sent us on our way. We left, and I guess they did too. Never saw them again."

"That's not true. Mr. Alfano's brother and his friend came back to the Sidewinder later and hooked up with a fellow you felt you had a claim on."

Yarborough's sunburned face turned redder. Even his pallid chest took on a slight hue. "You saying I'm queer, motherfucker?"

"Wouldn't surprise me," I said calmly. "Bullies usually attack what frightens them the most. Throws others off the scent, I guess."

That was too much for him. He lunged at me. But he telegraphed his move. I sidestepped and put a foot between his legs. He went over, banging against the wall of the trailer. The flimsy fiberboard cracked, leaving an impression of his head before he dropped to the floor.

Aggie went by me in a blur and wrenched a baseball bat out of Oscar's hand. The guy just stared at him, openmouthed, as the taller man placed a hand against his face and pushed him back onto the sofa. The couch went over. The cheap carpet didn't do much to cushion his skull.

Yarborough wasn't finished. He rolled into me, almost sending me to the floor, but I backed away and stomped on his wrist as he grabbed for my ankle.

"Ow!" He clutched his injured arm to his chest.

I staggered like I was drunk, but it was only the unstable mobile home swaying beneath our feet. Trailers aren't the place for fistfights and wrestling matches. If we weren't careful, the damned thing would end up on its side like the sofa.

"Look, Yarborough, this isn't necessary. Level with us, and we'll leave," I said into the sudden lull.

"Arright." He rolled to his feet, nursing his sprained wrist. He'd likely lose a couple of days' work. "Seen them two again the next night."

"On Sunday?"

"Guess so." He moved past me and took a chair opposite the overturned couch. Oscar lay as he was, his legs splayed in the air over the edge of the couch as he watched Aggie with a wary eye. Aggie still held the metal bat he'd taken from the man.

"Get the fuck up, Oscar," Yarborough snarled. "And turn the couch upright."

Oscar didn't move until Aggie backed away. Nobody said a word as the furniture was put back in place. Aggie moved forward, and Oscar promptly sat down.

"So what happened Sunday?"

"Nothing. They came back, but they kept their distance from us. And then that kid came in. First thing I know, he's sitting at their booth, and they're laughing and talking and carrying on."

"What kid?"

"The Penrod kid. Jazz. The town queer."

"I hear he's the town vamp," I said. That earned a blank stare. "Never mind. So what happened?"

"They got in a fight."

"With Penrod?"

"Naw. Nobody ever fights Jazz. They fight over him. Those two qu—uh, guys got to arguing over something. Maybe over Jazz. And he did what he always does, sat there and smiled, waiting to see who'd come out on top. The little shit."

A note of longing haunted his voice, but there was no profit in baiting Bud Yarborough. "What happened after that?"

"They left. Penrod too. Piled in the car with both of them. That was some car, man."

"And then?"

"And then we never saw them again."

I came at him again and again with the same questions asked in different ways, but Yarborough stuck to his story. Finally I nodded at Aggie. It was time to go, but Lando's brother wanted to get his dig in first.

"Tell me, Oscar," he said, tossing the bat contemptuously on the sofa beside the man. "Who fucks who in this household? Or does it go both ways?"

I mentally rolled my eyes, but neither of the two roustabouts said a word. Their gazes met briefly, and then each man studied the floor in front of him. Answer enough in my book.

Aggie was quiet after we left the trailer park. At length he spoke. "Fucking bullies. They always turn out to be cowards when you face them down—unless they can gang up on you."

"Not always. I've met a few who weren't all bluff. Taken a beating or two in my life."

"You believe Yarborough?"

"I don't believe or disbelieve. He's given us a little something, and now it's up to us to confirm it and find out what happened next."

"Like that old game of Clue. What's next?"

"Tomorrow we'll go see Dix Lee and talk some more about Bud Yarborough. Tonight we'll see if we can find Jazz Penrod."

Aggie checked the luminous dial on his watch. "Kinda late. Midnight."

"It's not late for a guy like Penrod. This is when he comes alive. The only problem is finding out where he does it. Let's swing by his mom's place again. See if she can tell us where her darling is."

"I don't understand something. I thought the legal drinking age in this state was twenty-one. If I remember right, Dix Lee said the Penrod kid is eighteen. So how does he get in the bars around here?"

"Same way you did when you were underage. Learned which ones will let him in on the sly. The Sidewinder's at the edge of town, so they probably turn a blind eye. If some of the gay trade comes there, he's probably a draw for them."

"Okay, another question. If the management at the Sidewinder puts up with gay trade, why do they let bullies like Bud and Oscar in?"

"The Four Corners is a place of contradictions. Given the makeup of the population, Native Americans, hard-hat miners, and oilfield workers, it's predisposed to conflict. So long as the patrons take their disputes outside, management will let them all in and count their money. In a perverse way, that reputation probably draws more people than it repels."

"Weird."

"And Castro Street isn't?"

"Point taken."

Darkness cloaked the Penrods' small home, making it seem less shabby. Foliage blurred the boxy outlines of the house. A light burning over the stoop cast a golden glow, turning the ivory trellis roses into faint gray splotches in the darkness. A Dodge Ram pickup in the circular drive almost blocked the house from view.

"Bet that's her brother's. Jazz would want something sportier," I said.

As if in confirmation of my guess, a man I took to be Riley Penrod answered my knock. A big man, he made an intimidating silhouette in the doorway.

"Help you?" His tone indicated he wasn't willing to go very far in the pursuit of that goal.

"We're looking for Jazz. Is he home?"

Penrod stepped out into the night and closed the door behind him. I pegged him at six two and around two twenty or better. He carried a beer belly, but no one in his right mind would consider the man flabby.

"You got a lot of balls looking for the kid at his mama's front door this time of night. Ain't you guys got no shame? Who are you, anyway?"

I made the introductions, confining it to names and the fact I was a PI wanting to talk to Jazz as a possible witness to an incident at the Sidewinder on Sunday the twelfth.

"Jazz ain't here, and I don't know where he is. Probably out on the Big Rez. If he's there, good luck finding him."

Beyond leaving my name and asking that Jazz call me at the Trail's End, there wasn't much else we could do.

"This is taking a lot of time," Aggie observed as we pulled away from the curb in the rental. "And I've got a feeling Lando and Dana don't have much time."

Unfortunately I agreed with his assessment.

Chapter 11

AGGIE AND I located Jazz Penrod the next morning, but not because of any clever sleuthing on my part. Just as we pulled out of the Trail's End headed for the police station to see if Dix Lee was working on a Saturday morning, a tall, slender young man strolling down the sidewalk on the south side of Main caught my eye. I immediately threw the car into reverse and eased back into a parking spot at the motel.

"Forget something?" Aggie asked.

"Look across the street. The kid walking west."

"It's him. It's the Penrod kid, isn't it?"

"Think so, but I can't be sure."

"Let's go talk to him."

I pulled out and turned back toward our rooms. "We will. But I don't want to spook him."

"What are you going to do?"

"The kid's gay. He's receptive to the attention of presentable men, so—"

"Hell, we're presentable. Let's go."

"Not we. Me. You look too much like your brother. You wait in my room while I try to pick him up. If I can, I'll bring him back for a chat."

"Sounds like a plan."

I let Aggie into my room and drove onto Main. For a moment I thought I'd lost Penrod, but then I spotted him far down the street. That long-legged gait ate up the distance.

I drove past, confirming it was Jazz. Pulling a U in full view of him, I approached at a crawl. His stride shortened as he eyed the car. I halted ten paces in front of him and leaned across the seat so he could get a good look at me.

The "stare" is a standard move for a lot of gays on the make, but in New Mexico it is a complicated maneuver. Many Native American cultures have an eye-avoidance custom, considering it rude. Gangbangers take it as dissing, a challenge to their *machismo*. A lot of straights feel it's an invasion of their space. It makes them uncomfortable. Jazz Penrod didn't have a problem with it. His gaze locked onto mine.

"Morning."

"Morning." His smile displayed a row of straight, sparkling white teeth. "Can I help you?"

"Maybe you can. I'm new in town. Just here for a couple of days. You look like a fellow who can tell me where the action is."

"Depends on what kind of action you're looking for."

"Why don't you get in the car and we'll discuss it. Maybe we can go back to my motel room to talk at leisure."

"Where you staying?"

I motioned with my head. "Down the street. Trail's End."

He did a half turn and looked toward the motel. "Don't see why not." He stepped off the curb, grasped the door handle, and slid into the passenger's seat. "My name's Jazz."

I accepted the handshake, noting the strength of his grip, which argued Jazz Penrod worked for his living, although exactly what kind of work seemed to be a mystery.

"BJ. Up from Albuquerque for a visit."

"BJ. Like the initials?"

I nodded.

"Here on business?"

"In a way."

As I pulled out onto the street, his eyes raked me. "Go in the back way," he directed. "I know the girl who works in the office there."

"You mean Melissa? She seems like a decent sort."

"She is, but…." He left the rest unsaid.

I turned away from the office and circled around behind the building in order to reach my room. Jazz got out of the car and waited until I unlocked the door. As I moved aside, he stepped into the room where he abruptly halted.

"What is this?" He backed up, bumping into me. "I don't do threesomes."

"Not asking you to." I applied pressure to his broad shoulders. "Just want to talk to you for a few minutes."

"No, thanks. I gotta be someplace."

I managed to close the door and lean against it, blocking his way. "Hear me out, and then you can leave if you want. Won't take but a minute."

Jazz stepped forward, giving me some room. He motioned toward Aggie sitting on the edge of the bed. "I know you. Well, I mean…."

"Looks just like his brother, doesn't he?"

"You're Lando's brother?"

"I'm Aggie Alfano."

"Look, man, Lando and Dana came on to me. I didn't—"

"Nobody's pissed, Jazz," I assured him. "We just need some answers. Dana and Lando are missing, and we're trying to find out what happened to them."

"Missing?"

"Yes, and their car went over the Rio Grande Gorge near Taos the other day, although neither of them was in it."

"No shit? That Porsche? Man, that was a bitchin' ride."

"Sit down." I indicated one of the two chairs at a small table. "Let's see if we can figure out a couple of things."

I examined the young man as he strolled to the table and settled into a seat. Although the photo Dix Lee had shown us looked vaguely androgynous, the flesh and blood Jazz Penrod exuded a powerful masculinity. But there was something else at work too. Some sense of vulnerability, approachability. This guy could probably raise the pulse rate of half the men and women in town. He tossed his head, throwing his shoulder-length hair back. Seductive as hell, and he wasn't even trying.

"When did you meet Lando and Dana?" I asked.

"I don't remember the exact date, but I know it was a Sunday night a couple of weeks ago." His voice was a light baritone with a husky quality. The inflection on some of his words was different—he almost swallowed the final syllables. Yet he came across loud and clear.

I took out the calendar I'd worked up for Lando's trip and made a notation. "That would have been August 12, right?"

He shrugged. "I guess. I know they'd gone to the Aztec Ruins that day because they talked about it."

"You met them at the Sidewinder?"

"Yeah. We got to talking, and they bought me a drink or two."

"We understand Lando and Dana got into an argument at the bar. Was that over you?"

Jazz smiled. "Nope. They were arguing about where to go the next day. Lando wanted to go see the Bisti badlands, but Dana wanted to try the Salmon Ruins."

"That was it? That caused an argument?"

"Not really an argument, but—" Jazz cut his eyes to where Aggie sat on the bed. "—Lando did this Italian thing. You know, getting earnest when he talked."

Aggie chuckled aloud. "You got him down pat, Jazz. That's my brother. Italian."

"So did you go back to the motel with them when they left the bar?" I asked.

Jazz shook his head. "No."

"Look, we need the truth, okay?"

"Uh-uh, I didn't go to the motel with them, but they gave me a ride back to town and dropped me off at my place. It was their decision, not mine," he added. "They were pretty much into each other—that night, anyway."

"But you saw them again and decided to get between them."

"Not exactly. I mean, I saw them again. I went to the Salmon Ruins with them the next day, but I wasn't trying to cause trouble."

"But that's the way it turned out, right?" I asked. The skin around those expressive black eyes tightened. I recognized stubbornness when I saw it. "Jazz, those guys might be in real trouble. We need to know everything that happened. Some trivial little detail might turn out to be important. You caused some trouble between them—right or wrong?"

"Okay. Yeah, Lando caught me flirting with Dana at the pueblo. Pissed him off, but he got mad at Dana, not me."

I decided to push. "Come on, Lando was a good-looking guy. He owned the car, and he was the guy with the money."

Jazz came halfway out of his seat. "Hey, man, I'm no whore. I only go with guys I like."

I nodded at Aggie. "What's not to like? And from the picture I've seen, Lando's even better looking than his brother."

"Yeah," the kid said, settling back in his chair again. "He was fucking beautiful. But Dana was too. And I like guys who don't look like me. You know, with the same dark hair, dark eyes—like me." With a sideways look at Aggie, he gave a grin. "I'd go for you before him. That's cool hair. Brown, but not really brown either. Reminds me of coffee with cream in it. And I like green eyes—you know, like emeralds."

"Thanks for the compliment. I understand how it went now. So Lando got steamed?"

"Yeah. They got in an argument—a real one this time. I guess I shoulda felt bad, but I didn't."

"You like two good-looking guys fighting over you?"

"Well, yeah. Who wouldn't? But it wasn't like that. Lando didn't get his nose outa joint because I didn't come on to him. He just didn't want Dana to get with me. They argued all the way back to town. But you know, after a while I got the feeling they weren't really arguing about me. Something was bothering them all right, but it wasn't me."

"They never said what it was?" He shook his head. "But you went back to the motel with them, didn't you?" I said.

"Yeah. I got out in front of the motel to walk home, but I heard Lando say he was going down the street to take care of some business at a gallery. Something about a painting he wanted to buy."

"And he left you alone with Dana."

"Not really. Like I said, I got out in front of the motel and started up the street, but when Lando pulled out alone, I went back—you know, to apologize to Dana. He invited me inside."

"So you got together with Dana?" Aggie's voice held a trace of anger.

The insolent grin returned. "Yeah, we did it."

"And Lando caught you?" Aggie pressed.

"No, but it took longer than we planned, and I was just walking up the street when the Porsche came back. Lando might have seen me on the sidewalk, but I'm not really sure."

Aggie and I exchanged glances. That explained the fight that almost came to blows Melissa described.

"Did you see either one of them again?"

Jazz shook his head. "Nope. I came by once, but the car wasn't there, so I didn't stop."

"Tell us about Bud Yarborough," I said.

A spot of color touched Jazz's cheeks. "That trailer trash likes to bait gays and beat up on them. Him and his buddies. But you know what? I think him and his roomie get it on after they beat up on queers. Gets them hot."

"I think you're right," I agreed. "He had a run-in with Lando and Dana, didn't he?"

"I wasn't at the Sidewinder that night, but I heard about it. Bud tried to bait Lando and Dana. They wouldn't bite, but that didn't stop

Bud and his buddies from waylaying them when they left the bar. Heard some fists got tossed.”

“Cops were called, weren’t they?”

“They get called out there all the time. They just usually separate the two sides and send them home. Too lazy to throw anybody in jail— takes too much paperwork. The Sidewinder’s right on the city limits, and sometimes it’s the cops and sometimes it’s the sheriff’s department. Anyway, I heard Lando and Dana did okay. Held their own against Bud and two of his friends.”

“When was that?”

“The night before I met them, so it must have been Saturday. That’s why I went over and talked to them. You know, because people said they did okay against the bullies and had the balls to come back the next night.”

“Surprised the bouncer let them in,” I said.

“Naw. So long as you take your problems outside, anybody’s welcome at the Sidewinder. Now if they’d tore up the joint, that woulda been different.”

“You figure Bud’s capable of tracking them down and getting his revenge later?”

“Be the first time if he did. His attention span’s about as long as his dick. But he can hold a grudge sometimes. I guess if he ran across Lando or Dana with his buddies at his back, he might mix it up again, but I can’t see him plotting against them.”

“Now the questions get harder,” I warned. “Did your uncle Riley ever meet either Lando or Dana?”

“Riley? You know about Riley? No, he never met them. Not that I know of, anyway. Why?”

“We understand he watches your back sometimes. Maybe he got the wrong idea.”

“Nah.” Jazz shook his head firmly. “Riley’s cool. Besides, I never talked about those guys to him.”

“Maybe not, but he goes to the Sidewinder too, doesn’t he?”

“Sometimes. But they weren’t giving me any flack, so Riley wouldn’t have been involved.”

“Does he like the same things you do?” Aggie asked.

Jazz made a face. “No, he likes his women. Man, does he like his women.”

"But he's been known to break a few heads for you now and then," Aggie persisted.

"Yeah, but he had no call to take on Lando or Dana."

"And your brother?" I asked.

"Man, you're a real private eye, aren't you?"

"That's what it says on my license, except the state cleans it up a little. It says Private Investigator."

"Henry never laid eyes on either one of them." The kid paused. "But I did tell him about them. Me liking guys pisses Henry off, so I tease him about it sometimes. You know, tell him about a prime cut now and then."

"How did he react?"

"Like he always does. Blew some steam at me and then dropped it. He never gets involved if it's a fair fight, but he won't stand for them ganging up on me. So far as I know, he didn't even come off the reservation that weekend."

"Would you know if he did?"

"Might not until later when he went to talking about some girl he banged." Jazz put a long forefinger to his lower lip. "But I'll tell you somebody they did worry about."

"Who's that?"

"Dana's ex-boyfriend. Bruno somebody or the other."

"Bruno Wills," Aggie said when I looked in his direction. "His name is Bruno Wills."

"Lando told Dana to shut off his cell phone because the dude was calling. You know, that might be what they were arguing about—that Bruno guy."

I already knew a little about Wills. As soon as Melissa'd told me about the curious stranger asking after the orange Porsche, I had Hazel check out Dana's former boyfriend. She'd given me a preliminary report this morning before I left my motel room. Aggie's take on the man might add something. When I asked what he knew about Wills, he shook his head.

"Not much. He's older than Dana, but they met at school when they took some classes together. They supposedly had a thing going until Dana met Lando. Word was the guy took the breakup hard."

"Who is he?"

"Construction foreman in LA last I heard. Think he's got some kind of engineering degree."

"He come from money?"

"Comfortable, but not...." Aggie trailed off.

"Not like your old man," I supplied.

"You could say that."

Aggie's information fit what I already knew. I turned to Jazz. "Did they say if Bruno was here in the Four Corners?"

"I don't have any idea."

"What were they going to do the next day?" I asked. "Before they argued, that is."

"Lando still wanted to see the Bisti badlands. He'd heard about all the weird shapes and spooky things down there. I told them they oughta go late in the afternoon so they could stay and see it at night. Some of those hoodoos blow your mind at night."

"Did they go?"

Jazz pursed his lips and shook his head. "Dunno. I never saw either one of them again."

AFTER JAZZ left, Aggie smiled and shook his head. The kid had made an impression on him. I understood. Jazz Penrod was what my mom used to call "a presence."

Next I phoned my client. The sessions with Anthony Alfano were tedious affairs. This one was no exception. He heard me out and then started in on me.

"This is taking too long, Vinson."

"You can always fire me, Alfano," I shot back. We had long ago dropped the customary "mister" but hadn't graduated to first names… and probably never would. "Or"—I dug at him a little—"send in that other guy you hired."

"What other guy?"

"The one you hired before you dumped on me."

"I didn't hire anyone else. What makes you think I did?"

"Figured that was your style. Cover your ass. And besides, there's some indication another guy was chasing Lando's orange rocket ship."

"Why am I just now hearing about this? That could be significant."

"Because there's nothing certain about it. Someone commented on the Porsche. But that car attracted attention. There's no evidence it was the same man both times."

"Did you get a description?"

"Mr. Everyman with a high forehead and thinning hair. His approach was so low-key, neither clerk I talked to took note of the guy. It was in two different parts of the state, and like I say, very casual."

"Wills," Alfano snorted. "That queer's sugar daddy is following them. It was probably a setup all along. I'll get somebody down in LA to run him to ground."

"If you mean Norville's former roommate, don't bother. My Albuquerque office got someone in LA on it a few days ago. Wills has been on the job every day except for the weekend. They're trying to account for that time as we speak. But if you hired someone else, I need to know about it right now."

"I already told you I didn't. If that's it, I need to speak to Aggie. Is he around?"

I traded phones with my companion and used his to call Hazel to see if she'd had another update from the PI we'd hired to look into Bruno Wills. She hadn't, but she took the opportunity to bring me up to date on a couple of other cases. Charlie had determined the insurance company's client had indeed committed suicide, closed out the investigation, and sent off our bill. We had one new case, which Hazel had accepted in my absence, checking out an officer of the Central Avenue National Bank who was suspected of fraud. The bank's executive committee wanted to gather a few more facts before reporting the man to the feds. Charlie, Hazel informed me, was handling the bank job since he had completed the insurance case.

Aggie was engaged in some of that "Italian thing" when I hung up. The old man's voice was audible even though they weren't on the speakerphone. Aggie didn't bother to modulate his tone either. He'd obviously learned years ago how to hold his ground with his father.

After hanging up he said, "I have a problem. The old man's hell-bent on buying another company, another vineyard. He's insisting I come back and help him work on it."

"But you're looking for his missing son."

Aggie sighed. "Apparently he's got a lot of confidence in you. Anyway, I told him I was going to stay another few days."

"Can I gather from your attitude you're against the purchase?"

"He bought another company less than a year ago. We need to digest that one before we move on to another one. Besides, I'm not sure I want to be left with the chore of assimilating a new business if something happened to him."

"You? How about Lando?"

"Lando has no interest in vineyards. The only time he gets involved is when Papa needs him to show up at a function and wave the Alfano flag." Aggie grinned. "We have one, you know. Our own Alfano flag. A purple standard with a grape cluster in a circle of white."

"Even if your father has confidence in me, I'm having trouble with the fact he wants you to come back right now. If it were me, I'd want someone who knew Lando out here looking for him."

"Normally he would, but this De Falco Fine Wines buyout has a deadline, and I've been fighting him hard. I think he wants to wear me down."

The whole thing struck me as odd, but maybe Alfano knew he had his bases covered even without Aggie on the scene—that other investigator asking about the Porsche. If, indeed, he was Alfano's man.

We traded cell phones again, and since it had been at least twenty-four hours since I tried Lando's number, I dialed. As usual it went to voice mail. I tried Dana's and got a surprise.

"'Lo."

"Hello." I lifted a hand to attract Aggie's attention. "Dana?"

"Who? Who you callin', man?"

"My name's Vinson. Who is this?"

The telephone went dead. I stared at the thing a minute before checking the number-dialed function. It was the correct number. Someone had answered Dana Norville's phone, but I was willing to bet it wasn't Dana. The voice I'd heard over the little instrument had the same clipped tones and swallowed syllables I associated with the speech patterns of some Native Americans—similar to Jazz Penrod's manner of speaking. But that had not been Penrod's voice.

"Dana answered?" Aggie's voice held a hopeful note.

"No, somebody answered Dana's phone."

"Maybe you misdialed."

I shook my head. "No. I checked the number. I dialed right, and some stranger answered. It was a young voice. Sounded like a teenager." I hit Redial and held the phone to my ear. It rang several times before it went to voice mail. But the recording wasn't Norville. I quickly hit the Speakerphone button and held out the phone so Aggie could hear.

"*Heh.* You got it, man. But Honcho ain't available. He's out making time with some chick. Talk to him, and he'll get back to you."

"That definitely was not Dana Norville," Aggie said. "Try it again."

"We need to get to Dix Lee right away. We'll try it from her office."

We were in luck; Dix was on duty this weekend. She heard our rushed explanation and then called across the room. A lean, dusky man with slick black hair and a proud nose looked up. A Navajo cop, I guessed as he walked over to her desk, a smile of pleasure stretching his lips.

"This is Detective Lonzo Joe," Dix said. "He used to be one of ours, but he deserted and went over to the San Juan County Sheriff's Office for thirty pieces of silver—actually it was a gold shield. But he still hides out in our station when he doesn't feel like working."

"Now, Dix." The man's smile grew broader. He turned his black-eyed gaze on us and explained. "I'm the Sheriff's Department detective assigned to the crime lab we share. I spend more time here than I do in my own office over in Aztec. But I get out of the shop sometimes. Today I'm on the trail of some real mean hombres."

Dix laughed aloud. "Yeah, right. A dog-fighting ring, I hear." After feeding him our names, she asked him to listen to the voice mail recording.

"Sure." He leaned over her desk and supported his weight on bony knuckles.

I hit the Redial button once again and punched Speakerphone. We all listened to the call go to the message center and heard the recorded message.

"What do you think, Lonzo?" Dix asked.

"Kid on the reservation would be my guess. The first word, that *heh*, that's short for *ya-tah-heh*, a common Navajo greeting. Young, I'd say. Probably eighteen or less, but trying to sound older."

"Honcho is a name?" Aggie asked.

"Nickname most likely."

Dix Lee frowned at us. "This is not good unless your brother's friend is so rich he goes around giving away his possessions. We'll try to trace the thing down, although I'm not too hopeful. There's only one tower over there, so we already more or less know the area the signal's coming from."

"Let me try something." I hit Redial again. When the recorded message finished, I spoke. "Honcho, my name is B. J. Vinson. This phone belonged to a friend of mine, and I'm trying to locate him. If you'll help us out, I'll make it worth your while. And you're not in trouble over the phone. You can keep it as far as I'm concerned. Tell you what I'm going to do. I'm here at the Farmington PD with Sergeant Dix Lee and Sheriff's Detective Lonzo Joe. I'm going to hand Detective Joe $500. If you'll give us the details of how and where you got the phone, that money's yours. You can tell us in person or phone me on my cell. I'm sure Detective Joe will get the money to you, right?"

"Right," the Indian cop said aloud. "I can leave it at your chapter house, no strings attached, just as soon as Mr. Vinson says it's okay." I knew that chapter houses spread across the Big Rez functioned as combination county governments and social gathering places. Then Detective Joe added something in Navajo, a reassurance, I assumed.

"What do you think?" I asked my companions after citing my phone number twice and hanging up.

"Five hundred's a lot of money to a kid on the reservation," Joe observed.

"A kid anywhere," Dix Lee put in. "He ought to bite."

"Aggie, how much do you have on you?" I turned to my companion. "I've got about three fifty in cash."

"I'll handle it." He reached for his wallet, and I didn't discourage him.

Chapter 12

MY CELL phone rang the next morning as I was finishing a short stack, light on Mrs. Butterworth's, and a side of ham at a café across the street from the motel. Aggie was attacking a blue-collar meal of eggs over easy, hash browns, link sausage, and biscuits slathered with unsalted butter. A young male voice hesitantly answered my "Hello."

"Is… is this the guy that said he'd give money for this phone?"

"Yes, this is B. J. Vinson. I left that message on the phone yesterday afternoon."

"Is it still good? The five hundred, I mean?"

"You give me what I want, and you get the money. And you're not in trouble over the phone. That is, unless you hit somebody in the head and stole it."

Aggie's silverware clattered on his plate as he realized who I was talking to. His eyebrows climbed, asking a silent question. I nodded.

"Naw, nothing like that," the voice on the phone answered.

"Where did you get it?"

"Where's my money."

"Handed it over to Sheriff's Detective Joe, just like I said on the phone message. You deliver what I need, and he leaves it at your chapter house."

"How I know that?" the kid demanded.

"Ask him about Lando," Aggie whispered.

I held up a hand to fend off his questions. "Look, Honcho—that's your name, right?—I'll do this however you want. I'll come to the chapter house alone or with Detective Joe, your choice. I'll meet you wherever you say, but it's got to be fast. The man whose phone you found might be in trouble. You know anything about it?"

"Uh-uh. Just found the phone laying right there on the ground."

"Where?"

The voice on the other end hesitated, and I could imagine thoughts of entrapment racing through his mind.

"Look, I need more than just the where. I need the phone to check his recent calls. So tell me where you found it."

"Bisti. Bisti badlands."

"Just lying on the ground?" I watched Aggie, his meal completely forgotten, struggling to contain himself.

"Uh-huh. Right in the dirt."

"Was anyone around? Did you see any sign of *anybody*?"

"Nah, didn't see nobody. Just the phone on the ground."

"When was that?"

"Last week sometime."

"Exactly what day last week. It's important, Honcho."

"Dunno. Tuesday, Wednesday. Something like that."

"Okay, here's what I'm going to do. I'm going to buy you a cool new telephone with a camera and a couple of hundred minutes on it. We'll meet and trade the new phone for the one you found. Then you show me where you found it. That's important, Honcho. You have to show me exactly where you found the cell phone. You do that, and the five hundred's yours. Deal?"

"Okay, but be sure and bring the dough."

"Nope, that goes to the chapter house. You tell me which one and who to leave it with, and I'll meet you where you found the phone. You can use your new cell to call and confirm the money's there. That sound okay?"

"Guess so," he replied and gave me the name of the chapter house.

It was like pulling teeth, slow and painful, but eventually Honcho agreed to meet us at the Bisti badlands near a formation called the Cracked Eggs at noon. I phoned Dix and brought her up to date. Lonzo Joe was in the building and agreed to leave the money with a receptionist named Kaylee at the kid's chapter house. Joe knew the woman and promised to come away with the identity of the cautious kid with Dana's cell phone.

"You familiar with the Bisti country?" Dix asked.

"Haven't been there in five years."

"The Cracked Eggs formation is in the Wilderness. That's the smaller piece of the two tracts that make up the Bisti/De-Na-Zin Wilderness area. It's Bureau of Land Management land, so I better call somebody over there. You want to tag along, Lonzo?"

"Can't," I heard Lonzo Joe's deep voice answer. "I've got to get this money over to the chapter house, and then I'm heading north of town on the trail of those dog fighters."

"Don't let them get the drop on you," Dix said dryly.

ABOUT FORTY miles south of Farmington, Aggie and I turned off Highway 371 onto a gravel road, which looped back north. Six miles later we parked on a stretch of ground that faintly resembled a parking lot near a bunch of tumbledown, rotting buildings. There were no other vehicles in sight. In fact, we appeared to be the only two people on the planet.

"You sure this is the right place?" Aggie climbed out of the car and looked around.

I nodded to a modest sign and what looked to be a register for tourists. "According to that, it is."

"Man, this place is deserted."

"Yeah, they don't get much traffic out here."

"Hope we can find our way to the right place."

Forewarned by Dix Lee and Lonzo Joe, we hoisted packs stuffed with water bottles, energy bars, and a compass. Feeling like I was provisioned for a week in the wilds, I clapped a broad-brimmed floppy hat on my head as protection against the sun and glanced at Aggie. He looked a good deal more comfortable with the situation than I was, but then he would be. He hiked and climbed mountains and conquered deserts more or less as a matter of course.

We set off across the rocky ground, following the map Dix had sketched for us. She was supposed to be trailing along behind with someone from the Farmington BLM office. Almost immediately we were swallowed up in a fantastic landscape—not magnificent like the Grand Canyon, but spooky. Weird. Like a moonscape. Mysterious, as if some omnipotent sculptor had capriciously balanced massive, flat sandstone rocks atop slender necks of eroding clay in order to see how long they would stand. I wished Paul were here to share this with me. He'd be blown away by the pure craziness of the landscape.

"Damn," Aggie said in a near whisper. "I've never seen anyplace like this. What the hell's keeping those damned rocks from toppling over?" He indicated one of the distant capped pink-and-gray striated clay towers wearing what looked to be an outlandish stone beret at a rakish angle. "I wonder what the Good Lord was thinking when he did all of this?"

"Probably did it to watch all of us stand around with our mouths open."

We were almost diverted from the gravity of our task by the multicolored stones, petrified stumps, washes filled with wacky shapes, and the silent menacing hoodoos towering uncertainly over us. In one moment our surroundings were whimsical, in another, ominous. The Navajo considered this sacred ground, and I could understand why. We trod forbidden territory, or at least that's the way it felt. There were no footprints in the dry washes or anywhere on the stony ground we traveled, and I felt ours would disappear with our passing, as if we walked an alien planet subject to different natural laws. I glanced behind me to check and took false comfort when I saw my shoe prints still existed.

We had barely started our trek, and already sweat was staining my shirt. Following Dix's hand-sketched map, we plodded on, taking frequent gulps of rapidly warming water, barely able to resist rushing off to explore some fascinating structural gem: thin spires of sandstone rising toward the sky like frozen tongues of flame; piles of mudstone carved by wind and water into ugly, fascinating gargoyles; specks of amber crystal winking in the hot sun; and those endless columns of sculpted, gravity-defying capped rock.

Eventually we reached our target, a broad wash holding clusters of flattened, broken round rocks streaked with wind- and water-carved wrinkles. I'd seen color prints of the Cracked Eggs, but the startling reality was greater than the image. The stones appeared to be gigantic dinosaur eggs broken open and abandoned to the elements—dozens and dozens of them. They weren't, of course; they were merely clay and stone fashioned by that same capricious Hand. In the photos they'd appeared in a dazzling array of color, influenced by the time of day, the intensity of the light, the influence of the clouds. Now, as the sun beat straight down upon us, they were a flat gray with rosy highlights.

Aggie looked around. "Don't see anyone with a cell phone for sale."

I glanced at my watch. "It's early yet. Didn't take us as long to find the place as we thought."

"Uh-oh." Aggie nodded over my shoulder.

I turned as four young men walked over a small rise and headed our direction. They fanned out, putting some distance between themselves as they neared. I'd seen gang members perform this maneuver a hundred times. It was designed to intimidate more than anything else. This crew looked deceptively unthreatening despite the fierce scowls. Young, sixteen at the most—and one looked to be no more than twelve. Three were slender, one stocky. All were Native American. Navajo, probably. They halted as a single unit ten feet away from us.

"Yo, you Vinson?" That was the stocky one.

"That's me." I stepped over to offer a hand. "You Honcho?"

"Yeah." He leaned forward at the waist to accept my shake. He kept his fingers straight, allowing me to do all the gripping. It's a clasp I find repulsive. There's no warmth, no return of camaraderie. "You got my money?"

"I've got your phone. The money's at the chapter house as we agreed. You have Dana's phone?"

"Dana. That the dude lost the phone?"

"He's the one."

Since Honcho obviously held little trust in or love for strangers, I tossed him the package I'd been carrying. He tore it open.

"Cool. A Razr." He held it up for his companions to admire. Then he reached into his shirt pocket and pitched a small silver fold-up cell to me. "Deal's a deal," he declared.

"Show me where you found it."

"Right over yonder." He pointed to the west. "Bottom of that hoodoo. It was just laying in the sand. Almost stepped on it."

"Was it still working?"

"Naw. Battery was flat. My buddy's got a whatcha call it—a charger—and we got it going again."

I turned the cell phone over in my hand. "Are any of the original messages left?"

"Dunno. I didn't do nothing to them. Just started using the phone, man."

Hopefully some of Dana's messages still remained in the phone's memory chip to give us a clue as to what happened. It all depended upon how busy Honcho and his pals had been; these phones had a finite storage capacity.

"Okay," I said, "show me exactly where you found the phone."

Honcho led us a hundred yards over rocky terrain and pointed to the spot where he claimed to have found the telephone. He'd done a little thinking and figured he'd stumbled across it the previous Tuesday. I took out my calendar and noted the fact under August 21.

I held up Dana's phone. "I've been calling this number every day for a couple of weeks. How come you didn't answer it until yesterday?"

"Already told you, man. Battery was dead. Just got it juiced up when you called."

There was enough power in the new battery for Honcho to call the chapter house, and I dutifully instructed the woman on the other end to give the youngster his money when he came for it. The four kids took their leave, vanishing behind the nearest rock formation the moment Dix Lee showed up with a man in tow.

I nodded in the direction of the retreating teens. "Where did they come from? They're not headed for the parking lot—unless there's another one I don't know about."

"No," Dix answered. "There are two or three private Navajo holdings inside the Wilderness. They probably belong to one of those. They're within walking distance."

"And that's why they stumbled on Dana's phone?" I took another slug of water as she spoke and offered her some. She declined with a shake of her head. I wiped a sheen of sweat from my face with a sodden handkerchief.

"Probably." She turned to the man with her. Blond and blue-eyed and handsome in a chiseled features way, he was J. Edgar Hoover's ideal FBI agent—except that he was a Bureau of Land Management man. "BJ, this is Larry Plainer, a Special Agent for the BLM. As I told you, they administer the Bisti Wilderness."

"Nice to meet you," I said and introduced him to Aggie.

I knew that the BLM had its own law enforcement arm, but didn't know exactly how they worked. Some rangers regularly carried firearms and handled criminal cases such as vandalism, theft, and the like. A special agent was new to me. Perhaps they handled the "heavier" crimes. Plainer's fair features labeled him an inside man, not a working ranger. Despite the heat, he wore navy dress pants and a pale blue, long-sleeved shirt, although he had foregone a coat and tie. A black baseball cap with BLM stenciled on it was all that protected him from the sun. It made me wonder how he'd walked the same route I had without staining his clothing with sweat.

I brought Dix and Plainer up to date on the situation while Aggie wandered off somewhere on his own. A few minutes later, a shout attracted my attention.

"BJ, over here!" Aggie yelled.

I hurried over to a hoodoo, one of those sculpted toadstool formations that threatened to collapse momentarily. Aggie slowly walked the rocky ground around the base, as if searching for something.

"What is it?"

"You smell anything?" he asked.

And then I caught a whiff of it—the faint, cloying, unmistakable stink of death.

Chapter 13

IT TOOK only minutes to find the source of the odor, a rubble-filled hollow on the south side of the hoodoo. Aggie was on the verge of open rebellion when Plainer insisted on notifying the San Juan County Sheriff's Office before probing what was obviously a grave.

"He's right," Dix weighed in. "The sheriff has jurisdiction over all homicides on BLM land."

"With our assistance, of course," Plainer added.

Aggie tried an end run. "We don't even know this is a homicide. Might be some animal buried down there."

Plainer leaned back, leveled his blue eyes at my companion, and indicated the grave, if that's what it was. "Long enough for a man. Wide enough for a man. Somebody went to the trouble of digging it and covering it up. Chances are good it's a homicide."

If Dix and Plainer hadn't restrained him, Aggie would have excavated the pit with his bare hands. I didn't blame him; it could be his brother rotting away beneath those rocks. Had Aggie chosen to defy authority at that point, I'd have supported him.

He didn't, so the four of us beat a hasty retreat to the shade of a towering stone phallus while Dix and Plainer both got on their phones. Our water and energy bars, which we shared with the two law officers, were almost exhausted by the time Lonzo Joe made his appearance.

"Hey, I see you got the call," Dix said. There was an obvious bond between the two.

"Yeah. My dog-fighting investigation got put on hold again. You don't suppose the fact one of our undersheriff's cousins runs one of them has anything to do with that, do you?"

We led the county detective to the suspected grave.

"Oohee," he said, breathing through his mouth. "The crime scene boys are on their way, and there's not much we can do until they get here. We notified the medical investigator, but no telling when he'll show up."

Lonzo got on the phone and asked the Navajo reservation police to detain Honcho and his buddies when they showed up at the chapter house to collect his $500. After that we waited—again.

The crime lab technicians arrived shortly thereafter and ordered Aggie and me off the property, or at least banished us from the immediate vicinity. Without being told, Dix joined us in the shade; Plainer stayed with Lonzo and the technicians. The three of us watched from afar as they shot several rolls of film. They had finished opening the gravesite by the time the medical investigator showed up. A heavyset man with a graying beard got down on his hands and knees and did something we could not see.

As the medic got to his feet, Aggie started forward, but Lonzo intercepted him and remained at his side while the CS specialists shot some more film. At last the doc gave the okay, and the team removed a body from the shallow depression at the base of the towering hoodoo. A few minutes later, Lonzo led us forward. Aggie's carefully composed features began to crack as he approached the body bag on a gurney.

"Too short," he muttered when we were within a dozen feet. "Not tall enough to be Lando."

Rational conclusion or rationalization? Rationalization. The black bag hid the proportions of the thing it contained. Aggie nodded when Lonzo asked if he was ready to view the body. He swayed unsteadily as the face was revealed.

Rocks covering the victim had prevented major damage from predators. The wilderness is a dry, hot area, so decomposition was not too bad. Nevertheless, the viewing was not easy.

"It's not my brother," he said.

"Are you sure?" Plainer asked. "Sometimes it's hard to be sure. They change, you know."

"Let me see the clothes," Aggie said in a clipped tone.

A medic unzipped the bag to expose a shirt.

"Hands," Aggie said. "If there's a small tattoo of a Greek delta on the back of the right hand, it's Dana. If not, then it… it might be my brother." He shook his head as the man opened the bag all the way. "No, hair's too light."

A moment later he gave a shuddering sigh as a faded tattoo on the back of one hand came into view. I noticed something else. There was a watch on the body's left wrist and a small diamond on its right ring finger. This man hadn't been killed in a robbery. Lonzo rummaged around in the filthy clothing and came up with a slender wallet.

"Dana James Norville," he confirmed. "So it's not your brother."

"It's his friend. The man he was traveling with."

"We'll need to talk to you and BJ in the office. Dix, can we use your facilities?"

"You can use ours," the BLM special agent said.

"Okay. Can you tell me where your brother is, Aggie?"

"No. I haven't seen or heard from him since he left California on vacation."

"Agent Plainer will ride back to Farmington with you, Mr. Vinson. Mr. Alfano can ride with me. Sergeant Lee, you need transportation?"

"Uh-uh. My unit's in the parking lot."

Lonzo had gone formal all of a sudden. Understandable, under the circumstances.

I knew what to expect, but Aggie was about to be blindsided. I would have warned him, but Detective Joe split us up before I had a chance.

THE BLM'S Farmington field office was located in a two-storied stucco building the color of desert sand on the La Plata Highway. The place was virtually deserted, reminding me this was Sunday, as Plainer led us through a maze of cubicles and walled offices. The interrogation room could have been lifted out of APD back home—small and uncomfortable and filled with cast-off government furniture. I was apparently a minor player because the BLM agent handled my end of things while Lonzo Joe talked to Aggie elsewhere.

Plainer was pedantic. He asked every question he could think of in about three different ways—all of them unimaginative—in a virtual monotone. It was probably by design, his form of water torture. When he finally left the room with orders for me to sit still, I settled back for a lengthy wait. He would organize his notes and huddle with Lonzo before returning to me. I wouldn't miss him. Half an hour later, Plainer returned to lead me to a marginally larger interrogation room where a red-faced Aggie Alfano was about to blow.

"BJ," he sputtered as I entered the room. "They think Lando killed Dana. They claim it was a lover's quarrel."

"It's a logical place to start, Aggie." I watched Lonzo lean back in his chair with his hands clasped behind his head, no doubt intrigued by my line of reasoning.

Aggie came up out of his seat. "Wait a minute!"

"Settle down. I said it's a *logical* place to start. That doesn't mean it happened that way, but these fellows are professionals." It never hurts to stroke the official ego. "They're going to eliminate the obvious before they go charging off in all directions. Besides, at this point, it's to our advantage for them to pursue that line of reasoning."

"Why?"

"They're going to be as interested in finding Lando as we are. And once they do, we'll all learn what happened. Give them all the cooperation you can, Aggie. It'll benefit your brother in the long run. Unless…." I let the word hang.

"No way," Aggie interjected. "Lando's not a killer."

"Very smooth, BJ." Lonzo returned to informality for the moment. A good sign?

"Look, right now we all want to find Orlando as quickly as possible. The only thing we don't want to do is panic him and push him into a corner. That would benefit none of us."

"I don't intend to do that. If Lando Alfano is not the killer, his disappearance could mean he's being held hostage. I understand his father is quite wealthy. Has there been a ransom demand?"

"As of early this morning, there had not been. Or at least," I added, "I haven't heard of it."

"How about you?" Lonzo turned to Aggie. "Are you aware of any ransom demand?"

"No. And my father would have called me if there had been one."

I shrugged my shoulders to relieve tense muscles. My shirt clung to me uncomfortably. The sweat had dried, but I needed a shower. I also experienced a powerful need to talk to Paul. I missed my partner terribly right at the moment. But that wasn't convenient, so I merely asked if Mr. Alfano had been advised of Dana Norville's death. "Has the man's family been notified?" I added.

"Not yet," Plainer answered. "We want to collect all the information we can before word of this gets out. My Los Angeles office will notify his family tomorrow."

"Fine, but I suggest you advise Anthony Alfano of events as soon as possible."

"Why?" Plainer asked.

"Because it's the prudent thing to do," I said.

His flat blue eyes signaled he'd decided not to pursue the matter. "He's your client. You do as you see fit."

Lonzo spoke up. "I'd like to go over things again to see if either of you can recall anything new."

And go over them he did. With our statements side-by-side on the table in front of him, he reviewed everything line by line, asking additional questions as he went. The man was no slacker. His quiet, friendly demeanor masked a keen intelligence. He showed particular interest in the car crash in the Rio Grande Gorge.

When he brought up the bullet holes in the car, I caught Aggie's start of surprise. I hated to spring it on him like that, but I'd had no option but to tell Plainer about it since either he or Lonzo Joe would doubtless talk to Lucinda Schwartz and wonder why I withheld the information.

At length, Lonzo straightened up in his chair and told us we were free to go, but asked us to let him know when we decided to leave the area.

IT WAS dark when we headed for the rental car in the BLM parking lot. Aggie held his tongue, but I could see he was seething inside. He let go as soon as we were in the car.

"Why didn't you tell me about the bullet holes?"

"Because I didn't have the lay of the land at the time I found out about them. I'd just met you, remember? You were getting over the trauma of believing your brother had died in the gorge, and I didn't want to raise your fears again. If I'd found anything significant about those holes, I would have told you."

"Does Papa know?"

"No. And I'm not going to tell him either. Not until we know more."

Aggie sighed heavily. "All right."

"Are we okay?" We were going to be joined at the hip for the immediate future, and things would be stressful enough without bad blood between us.

"Is there anything else you're hiding?"

I shook my head. "I don't hold out on the law, and you heard my statement. There's nothing else."

"Yeah, we're okay."

The words were right, but there wasn't a lot of conviction behind them. Even so, it was the best I could hope for at the moment.

"What happens next?" he asked.

"They'll put out a bulletin on Lando, and we'll be marginalized. Lonzo may decide to keep us in the loop or not. He seems like a decent guy. Thank God, Plainer's not in charge of the investigation. Dix might be good for some information. At least she might give us the results of the OMI's autopsy when it's available. In the meantime, we try to find where the Porsche was abandoned. Right now let's go back to the motel. We haven't eaten anything since breakfast except some power bars."

"I couldn't keep anything down," Aggie replied, running a hand over his stomach.

"Then get some sleep."

"I don't think I can."

"Take something. You need to keep up your strength."

When we got back to the motel, we spoke to Alfano over the speakerphone on my cell, laying out the whole thing in minute detail, except for the bullet holes in the Porsche. He remained gruff but calm. The calculating business mind at work, probably. Once all of his questions were out of the way, there wasn't much else to say, so we closed the conversation.

I looked at Aggie's drawn, haggard features. "Sure you don't want something to eat?" He shook his head. "Get some rest. We need to start moving early in the morning."

After Aggie returned to his room, I sat on the bed to make two calls. First I dialed Artie Hartshorn in Santa Fe—at home again, which would endear me further—and asked him to tackle Harvey Schwartz and get him to loosen Joe Cruz's muzzle.

The second call was to the Taos Police Department. While the dispatcher ran down Delfino for me, I made a quick trip to the all-night service station nearby and picked up a desiccated, prefabricated ham and cheese sandwich. When he called back a few minutes later, Delfino heard me out, grunted a couple of times in appropriate places, and agreed to contact the Cruz family to see if he could develop any more information on the theft of the Porsche.

Then I took a long, soaking shower, put on my robe, and plugged in my charging unit. The cell phone battery was getting low, and I wanted this conversation to be long and slow. Paul answered our home phone.

"Hi, guy." My exhaustion melted like magic at the sound of his voice.

"I was beginning to think you forgot all about me."

"Only for about ten minutes at a time. Gets in the way of my sleuthing sometimes."

He snorted. "Yeah, I'll bet."

"You keeping busy?"

"Between work and school, what do you think?"

"Not getting in any line dancing with some cute little cowgirl at the C&W?"

The C&W Palace was a big barn—no, that's an understatement, a *massive* barn—where cowboys and would-be cowboys boot-stomped until the early hours of the morning. Paul was a good dancer and looked sexy as hell in the tight denims, colored T-shirts, and leather half vests he habitually wore with snakeskin boots and a curled-brim Stetson. As easy as we both were with our sexual identity, neither of us frequented gay bars. Since dancing together in a straight place like the C&W would get us tossed out on our ear, Paul indulged his passion by escorting one of several coeds from school. That caused some heartburn until I figured he simply saw them as acceptable dancing partners.

"Saturday night they had a good band," he said, "and I enjoyed myself. Would have sooner spent it with you."

"That's the risk you run hooking up with a PI. Fortunately I don't work out of town often."

"So long as I've got this beat-up ex-cop who can put up with me, I'll handle his eccentricities okay. Which reminds me, are you behaving yourself?"

"Yeah, but temptation reared its ugly head the other day."

"How's that?"

So I told him about Jazz but downplayed the kid's spectacular looks—didn't hide them, just didn't dwell on what a stunner he was. When I finished, there was a decided pause.

"So you took him back to your motel room to question him?"

"True. We needed privacy to question him."

"We?"

"Aggie Alfano. I told you about him, remember?"

"I remember." He paused. "Hurry up and come home, Vince. Please." Since the rest of the world called me by my initials, he'd settled on Vince as his pet name.

"As fast as I can, but the San Juan County Sheriff's got a good man on the job here. I need to lend him a hand, if I can."

"The sheriff?" Worry edged his voice.

I started to explain, but he cut me off.

"You aren't in any trouble with them, are you? The law, I mean."

"No. In fact, they might help me find the Alfano kid. Get me home sooner."

"Then go, San Juan County," he said.

When I finally hung up, I missed him more than before. It shouldn't work that way, but it did—at least for me. I went to bed, trying to ignore the empty feeling in my chest. That didn't work, so I pretended I was a teenager again and masturbated.

Chapter 14

THE NEXT morning I learned Artie Hartshorn ran into a brick wall with Harvey Schwartz, the attorney for the Cruz family, but Delfino fared a little better. The Taos cop had approached Mateo Cruz as a shaman instead of a policeman. The dead boys' father either had Indian blood in his veins or considered a Taos medicine man a worthy *curandero*. Even so, all Delfino could contribute was that the two Cruz boys had intended to look up a young lady by the name of Maria Martinez on their excursion to Farmington. As a matter of fact, she was the reason for the trip.

"That doesn't help us find where the Porsche was stolen," Aggie said as we roared out of the Trail's End parking lot later.

"No, it doesn't. Let's see if Dix Lee can narrow things down a little."

Dix was out on a call. While we waited for her, Lonzo Joe walked out of the crime lab and moseyed over to say hello.

"Sorry about your brother's friend, Aggie. Any news of him… your brother?"

"No. We talked to my father last night and confirmed there hasn't been a ransom demand. He's heard nothing. But we're hopeful."

"What are you guys up to, anyway?"

"Thought Dix might help us find where Lando's Porsche was stolen."

"If you learn anything, you let me know, okay?" He glanced up, looking past us. "Here's Dix now."

Dixie Lee walked like a woman in sensible shoes—her uniform oxfords—but she looked totally feminine as she slid behind her desk and did that unconscious blond tress-curling thing with the forefinger of her left hand. "Thought I might see you boys again."

"Can't keep away. Lonzo wants us to stay in town for the moment, so might as well have the pleasure of some good company."

She laughed. "Can it, Vinson. I checked. You're a three-dollar bill, and he's married."

"True. I'm found out."

"Turned out is more like it, but from what I hear, you've never been in the closet. So what is it you really want?"

"Have either of you heard the results of the autopsy?"

"I don't think it's finished yet," Lonzo said, "but the doc thinks the guy was strangled."

"How?"

"With a belt, rope, sash—something like that."

"Any guess as to when?"

"Somewhere around two weeks."

I thought for a second. "I can account for the two men's movements up through Monday the thirteenth. They were at Salmon Ruins that day. Lando and Dana got in a hassle over Jazz or something that evening, but before their spat they were talking about going to Bisti. My guess is they went the fourteenth or fifteenth. And Dana never left there."

Dix consulted her desk calendar. "So on a Tuesday or Wednesday, huh?"

"My best guess."

"If they were going to Bisti together, that makes it look bad for the Alfano kid." She cast an eye toward Aggie.

"Yeah, that makes him a logical suspect," I acknowledged. "Neither of us believe he killed Dana, but it would look that way to some."

Dix tipped her head in Lonzo's direction. "Like to the San Juan County Sheriff's Office, for instance. He put out a bulletin on the kid."

"And that's good," I said. "We need to find Lando to make sure he's safe, and I think you can help." I told the two of them about the Cruz brothers hitching out here to visit Maria Martinez.

Dix snorted. "You don't happen to know *which* of the hundred or so Maria Martinezes in the county, do you?"

"No, but I suspect she lives south of town. Probably somewhere in the vicinity of the Sidewinder."

"That doesn't help much."

"The car was supposedly parked on a dirt or gravel road in a rural area near the city limits." I consulted my notes. "There was a big cottonwood and a row of what was probably honeysuckle draped over a fence."

"This is where three rivers come together. There are cottonwoods all along the riverbeds."

"Yeah, I hear you. There was a white horse in a pasture across the road from the honeysuckle. The source said it was a stallion, but I'm not too sure of that part."

"All I can do is point you in a likely direction," Dix said. "But I don't see how finding where the car was abandoned helps you."

"Maybe it won't, but it's better than sitting around waiting."

"Right," Dix said. "Okay, you take the highway south to the Sidewinder. Just before you reach the bar, the country turns rural. The landscape opens up on the west side of the highway, so chances are the road you're looking for is somewhere to the left. East of the highway has a good bit of tree cover. Not the real big ones like down on the riverbanks, but at least they're trees."

She turned to Lonzo. "What's the name of that Martinez kid on the south side that's always giving us trouble? You remember, the one you had a couple of run-ins with while you were still with FPD. Phillip, Peter… one of those saints."

"Oh, yeah. Pete Martinez. The one they call Petey."

"He have a sister named Maria?"

Lonzo chuckled. "If there are girls in the family, odds are one of them's named Maria. And I know for a fact there's girls in that family."

"They have any connection to Taos?" I asked.

"Yeah, moved here from Taos. The area, anyway. One of those little towns nearby."

"El Segundo, maybe?"

"That's it. El Segundo."

I turned to Aggie. "We found our Maria." I looked at Lonzo Joe. "You have a problem with us poking around a little?"

"Be my guest," he said.

THE MATTHEW Martinez home was clapboard with fresh white paint, well-kept grounds, and what appeared to be brand-new asbestos shingles on a pitched roof. The house was an old-fashioned double shotgun structure with a covered walkway between the two halves. That presented a problem in figuring out which of the two front doors was for receiving guests. Reasoning that people gravitate to the kitchen, I opted for the one cluttered with bikes and trikes.

I suspected the kid who answered our knock was Petey. Lonzo had said the guy didn't have a serious rap sheet—yet. Some fights, a couple of shoplifting complaints that weren't pursued, and a drunk and disorderly. Just enough trouble to bring him to the department's attention.

A slender, five-foot-seven male with wide, bare shoulders thrusting out of a white, sleeveless undershirt stared at us from behind a closed screen door. He had a lean, dark, sulky appearance and was probably around seventeen.

"Yeah?"

"Is Maria home?" I asked.

"Who wants to know?"

"Me, for one." I threw a thumb over my shoulder "And him for another. Now stop screwing around and answer the question." I pulled the screen door open, startling him. Manners weren't going to get us anywhere with someone nursing an attitude. Brass might not either, but it was worth a try.

The kid's eyes went flat, and I spoke quickly. "Look, you can let us talk to her about a visit she had from some Taos friends a few weeks back, or we can put in a call for Sergeant Dix Lee down at FPD and she can do the asking. I only have questions for Maria, but Dix and County Sheriff's Detective Lonzo Joe might have some for somebody named Petey."

Stubbornness and hostility wrestled with self-preservation on his smooth brown features. Self-preservation won. "The Cruz brothers?" I nodded, and he shouted back into the house. "Maria, coupla cops wanna talk to you about your boyfriend."

"Just to keep things straight," I said, "we aren't cops. I'm a private investigator working for this man's family. We're looking for his missing brother."

"Don't know nothing about no brother."

"No, but Martin Cruz did. He died in the missing man's car."

Thick black eyebrows shot up. "Marty's dead?"

"He and his brother Jaime went over the side of the Taos Gorge in a car. Joe managed to get out before it took flight."

"No shit! Jaime too?" He yelled for Maria again. "Was it that bitchin' orange Porsche?"

I nodded and dug an elbow into Aggie's side as he started to say something.

"Man, that was some ride. Told him it was trouble. Guess it was. The Big Trouble." The kid crossed himself quickly.

A female version of Petey appeared behind him. The effect was startling, like two identical heads on one body. Same black hair, full but not long. Similar jeans and white cotton shirt, except she filled hers out differently when she elbowed her brother aside. Twins.

"What is it?" she asked. "Who are you?"

"Hey, sis, Marty's dead. *Muerto*. Jaime too."

"What are you talking about?"

Aggie and I didn't exist for those two at the moment. Brother and sister conducted their own conversation. "Drove off a cliff and ended up in the Rio Grande."

"In that car? I *told* you that was bad business. I warned you to leave it alone."

"Excuse me, miss," I interrupted. "That's what we want to talk to you about. That car belonged to this man's missing brother. We need to know where and how it was found."

The girl grimaced and indicated her brother. "Ask him."

"It was just there, man. Sitting right out there on Halmstead Road. Been there two days."

"Can you show us where? It's important."

"Sure, I guess so."

Taking me by surprise, he barged through the door, shot down the drive, and turned east on the road running in front of his place. Petey Martinez was hyper; he walked with everything he had, reminding me of a lizard scurrying over rocks.

A quarter-mile walk brought us to a setting almost exactly as described by Lucinda Schwartz. Heavy tendrils of honeysuckle—you could still catch the scent—almost obscured a wire fence. Overhead, the branches of an old cottonwood in a decades-long process of dying threw a thin shadow across a convenient turnout that was probably used by local kids as a make-out spot. A pasture opened up on the other side of the road. In the distance a white horse stood over a water trough watching us carefully.

Petey Martinez stopped and turned. "Right here. It was parked right here."

"For how long?" I asked.

"I dunno. At least a couple of days. When Marty and his brother showed up out of the blue, I took them to see it. They didn't leave until the next day, so that was at least two days."

"You didn't notice it before that?"

"Well, yeah. I seen it parked here. How else would I know to show Cruz?"

"No, I mean did you see someone drive it in. Did you see a stranger on the road—afoot or in a car?"

"Naw. I didn't see nobody. But I heard something the night before."

"What?" Aggie asked.

"Sounded like a shot."

"Did you investigate?" I asked.

"Naw. You hear gunshots out here all the time—usually a .22 rifle. You know, somebody hunting rabbits or squirrels. So I didn't think nothing of it. Not 'til I saw a couple of bullet holes in the rear quarter of the Porsche. Man, that was a bitchin' car. And Marty tore it up going over the gorge, huh?"

"It's in little pieces rusting away at the bottom right now. Do you have any idea what night that was?"

"Naw. Just a few nights back."

"Petey, you come up with the date and time, and that ought to be worth a twenty. Anything additional might be worth more. But no bullshit, you hear?"

You could almost see the kid put on his thinking cap. His forehead wrinkled, the corners of his mouth turned down, and a forefinger came up to stroke his upper lip. One day he'd probably have a lush moustache there, but right now it wouldn't support one.

"Maybe Thursday," he said at last. "I remember I had a date, but she had to go to work the next day, so I took her home right after the early movie. Musta got back home around nine or so."

"Was the car parked there when you went to pick up your date?"

"I left the house the other direction. You know, by the highway. Didn't pass this spot, but when I came home, I came in the back way, and that's when I saw it."

"How long after you got home did you hear the shot—or shots?"

"The ten o'clock news was on the TV."

"One shot or two?" I asked. He shrugged. "Could you tell the caliber of the weapon?"

"Naw, but it wasn't big. I mean it wasn't a shotgun. Not even a rifle. A pistol, I figure. Anyway, the next morning that orange car was still parked here. I saw the two bullet holes and figured somebody used it for target practice."

"Were those holes there the first time you saw the car? Or did they look new?"

He answered with another shrug.

"Why didn't you report it to the police?" Aggie asked.

"What am I, a cop?"

"You don't get along with Farmington's finest?"

Petey's brown eyes narrowed. "Let's just say me and Lonzo Joe don't get along."

"When did Martin Cruz decide to steal the Porsche?"

"When he saw the keys in the ignition, I guess. I told him he better let it alone. A car like that cost a big hunk of change, and they gonna come down hard on any homeboy boosting it."

"Guess he didn't pay any attention to you," I said.

"Don't put that on me. I didn't even know for sure he took it. He left that Saturday, and when I checked it out on Sunday, it was gone. Hey, I remember Cruz left on Saturday, so I was right. I heard that gunshot on Thursday. Does that tie it down close enough for you?"

I agreed it did and handed over a twenty. As we started walking back to the Martinez place, I thought of something else.

"Where does this road lead?" I looked back toward the turnout.

"Nowhere. It goes on for a couple more miles, and then it loops back to the north and joins up with the highway again. There's just a few houses along the way."

"Then how come you took it to return home?"

"It meets the highway before a big curve to the east, so you knock off a quarter mile or so. But the highway's faster, and that's usually the way I go."

"You heard anything about a stranger hanging around?"

"No, but somebody stole a pie from old lady Ingfield the other day." Petey snickered. "It was like that old cartoon my granddaddy used to read us. You know, the Katzen-Something-or-Other Kids. Stealing pies out of the kitchen window while they cooled. That's what happened to her. And she makes good apple pies."

"She find out who took it?"

"Kids, she told my mom."

I looked east down Halmstead Road. "Petey, if you wanted to get out of the area on foot without being seen, how would you do it?"

"Show you." He took off in a quick gait back down the road.

An arroyo began about twenty feet beyond where the Porsche had been parked and ran south through a line of scraggly trees and brush, growing deeper as it snaked south. Then, according to Petey, it curved to the west and made its way beneath the highway and on toward the Animas River. Anyone walking that route would not be visible from the road.

After donating another twenty to Petey Martinez, Aggie and I walked the arroyo until it cut under the highway. Finding nothing useful, we retraced our steps to take a closer look at where the Porsche had been parked. Except for a few marks in the sandy soil and our own footprints, we found nothing.

Mrs. Ingfield, the pie maker, had turned philosophical by now and shrugged off the loss of the pastry, commenting she hoped the miscreant—her actual word—enjoyed his meal.

As we headed back downtown to look up Dix Lee, I sighed. "Well, we know one thing for sure."

"What's that?" Aggie asked.

"The Porsche sat there a couple of days after the Martinez kid heard the shot or shots."

"That's not good news."

"Afraid not. It was probably someone trying to prevent Lando from getting to his automobile."

"Lord, this doesn't look good."

"No, it doesn't." I wheeled into the FPD parking lot.

After hearing our report, Dix got on the horn to a couple of officers who patrolled that end of town, but they had nothing to add. The two cops had not even seen the Porsche before the Cruz boys took it.

It was time to clue Lonzo in to what we had learned. We stepped outside, and I used the speakerphone again so both of us could listen in on the conversation. It took a few minutes to run him down and get connected.

"Thanks, BJ," he said after hearing us out. "We'll talk to the Martinez family, and I'll get our technician out to the car site."

"Nothing to see except our prints. The Porsche was parked in a relatively clear area, and the wind took care of any tire or footprint evidence."

"Still, maybe they can pick up something. It's worth a try. You think those kids held anything back?"

"Nothing except failing to report the Cruz boys stole the car. You come up with anything?"

"Nothing in the motel room, but we didn't expect anything. Been too many people in and out since those guys were there. Alfano checked out of the Trail's End on the fourteenth. I figure they were headed back to Albuquerque since you said they were still registered at the Sheraton. But they drove to Bisti first, and Norville died shortly thereafter."

Lonzo hesitated before apparently deciding to contribute more. "We found a Giant station not far from the motel where he filled up the gas tank. Probably the last sighting of the guy before he went on the run."

"Or was abducted," Aggie put in. "My brother's not on the run."

"Or was abducted," Lonzo conceded.

"When was that?" I asked.

"The fifteenth."

"He must have abandoned or been taken from the car that evening or early the next morning. Petey Martinez said the car was sitting out on Halmstead Road for at least two days before the Cruz brothers heisted it on the eighteenth."

I switched the cell phone to the other hand. "What's the report on Norville's body?"

"Strangled, just like we thought. Probably with a belt or a strap similar to a belt."

"Any DNA on the body?" I asked.

The speakerphone hummed hollowly. "Lots," he said finally. "The kid had had sex not long before he died. I know the two were boyfriends, but this looked like rape. There was considerable damage to the anal region."

"Aw, shit." Aggie turned away.

"That argues a third party committed the act," I said.

"I'd feel better about that if they hadn't just had a fight," Lonzo responded. "Over another guy, apparently."

"A fellow named Jasper Penrod. He goes by the name of Jazz."

"Yeah, I know Jazz. That matches my information. Have you talked to him?"

"Yes, but that was before Norville's body was discovered. What else did the body tell you?" I asked.

"It pretty well told us how the murder happened. The killer approached him from behind, looped a belt or strap over Norville's head, put a knee to the kid's back and forced him to the ground. Then he just held the guy down and waited. There was the beginning of a bruise where the killer put his knee."

"So he was probably a big man. Was there any sign of a struggle? Let me clarify that," I said. "Any sign of a fight between the two?"

"No. The only fight Norville put up was against the strap or belt."

"Anything under the fingernails?"

"Little flakes of leather he skinned off the weapon that killed him."

"He didn't get a piece of the killer?"

"Not under his nails."

"Meaning you're left with the sperm in the body." He didn't answer, so I continued. "Any hits on your bulletin?"

"Not a thing. Orlando Alfano's still in the wind."

"What in the hell could have happened to him?" Aggie asked.

I decided to be as cooperative as Lonzo had been and gave him the credit card numbers Gilda Gistafferson had provided for Lando and Dana. They were relatively useless to me, but perhaps he had the muscle to get cooperation from the companies. As we left the police parking lot in our rental, I caught Aggie's sidelong look.

"The information I gave him might help Lonzo locate your brother," I explained. "And right now, that's our primary objective. And if he was kidnapped, he might help catch the person who took him."

"Yeah, I know." His breath caught in his throat. He looked away suddenly.

Chapter 15

Sam Dunkard, the old crab who managed the Giant service station on Main a few blocks from the Trail's End, rightly assumed he didn't need to talk to us because he'd already told everything he knew to the "effing" sheriff's office. To make matters worse from his standpoint, Plainer had been by to ask his own questions. The attendant, somewhere in his midfifties, got as much out of his five-four frame as possible by standing ramrod straight in scuffed high-heeled cowboy boots. Thumbs hooked in old-fashioned yellow suspenders gave him an air of defiance. It took some patience on my part and some pleading by Aggie to get him to give us the time of day.

"I dunno why I gotta go to the trouble of doing this three times. Twice oughta be one too many." But he was weakening.

"Because this man's brother is missing and may be in trouble. The sheriff is looking for him, but Mr. Alfano would appreciate anything we can learn on our own."

"Told them two law dogs the only reason I recall the guy is because of that flashy car. A fella could spot it coming a mile off even if it was dirty as hell."

"Dirty?"

"You know, dusty. Kinda like the kid driving it. His eyeballs matched his car. You know, orange. Looked like he'd been driving all night. Figured he drove ten… twelve hours straight from somewhere or the other."

"But he looked okay? I mean, he wasn't hurt or anything?" Aggie fished around in his pocket. "I've got a picture of him. Could you confirm he was the driver?"

"Don't need it," Dunkard said. "Looked a whole lot like you. Like a clone that didn't grow up as big as you." Finally the man glanced at the picture. "Yep, that's him."

"And this was when?" I asked.

"Fifteenth," he said after thinking it over. "My brother-in-law spells me at noon on Wednesdays, so I recollect what day it was."

"What time?"

"Early morning. Maybe eight… nine."

"And he was alone?"

"Yep. All by himself." Sam Dunkard studied us a moment. "Nervous as hell, he was. Kept looking over his shoulder. Made me think it mighta had something to do with the fella asking about him a little later."

"Asking about my brother?" Aggie said.

"Asking about the car. He wanted to know if I'd seen an orange Porsche."

"What did you tell him?"

"Said sure. Not more'n an hour ago. Man claimed he was supposed to meet his friend but got held up by a detour on the way down from Colorado. I never heard of no detour. Course, coulda been up the road apiece, I suppose."

"What did this man look like? Blond, around the same age as the driver?" I fed him a vague description of Norville.

"Naw. Older. Hard-looking customer. Don't recall him too much, but think he was sandy-haired. Thinning. Probably somewhere around forty. Stocky."

"What was he driving?" I asked.

"Don't remember. Something bland. Brown Ford or something."

"Any nicks, dings, dents, decals—anything that stood out?"

"Naw. It was just a plain manila envelope."

"I don't suppose you noticed his license plate?" I said.

"Sure did. It was a New Mexico plate. And he claimed he drove down from Colorado way." Sam Dunkard frowned. "Could of, I guess, if he was on a trip."

"How can you be so sure about the license plate?" Aggie asked. "You aren't even sure what kind of car it was."

"License plates is my hobby, son. Cars ain't. Be surprised how many of these United States I can count every day."

"Do you remember the plate number?" I asked.

"Hell no. That ain't part of the game."

"Did you tell Detective Joe about this man?"

"Sure did. Told Lonzo all of it." He gave a sour look. "Maybe I held out on that other fella, that BLM man. Too smooth by half."

By the time we got back into our rental, Aggie looked ten years older than when we had met a few days back. He was silent, and I left him alone.

I made a quick trip to FPD but learned the brown car hadn't come to their attention. I wanted to talk to Jazz Penrod again to see if he noticed a car following them, but he proved hard to find. His nervous mother said he wasn't home. We drove to the Sidewinder, which was a wasted trip, so we returned to wait outside his house. It was dusk before our stakeout bore fruit. The kid breezed out of the door dressed in black Levi's, a purple golf shirt that fit him tight around the chest and loose around the slim hips. His sneakers appeared to be as black as the shock of hair crowning his head.

We let him get halfway down the block before pulling alongside and offering a ride. If he was surprised to see us again, he hid it well. He nodded and hopped into the backseat.

"Where to?" I asked.

"Sidewinder. Where else?"

"Sidewinder it is."

"I heard about Dana. Man, that was a bummer. He was a cool dude. There was a whole bunch of good in him."

"Yeah," I said over my shoulder. "He didn't deserve what he got."

"Anything new on Lando? He show up okay?"

"No," Aggie answered. "What do you think about that?"

"If you're asking me if Lando did it, then no. Those guys were into each other big time. I don't care if Dana did make it with me. He and Lando made a good team. I could see that even when they were arguing." He paused. "I'm sorry I got in between them like I did."

"Jazz, I've got to ask you a personal question." I eased to a stop in a strip mall and twisted in the seat to face him. "When you made it with Dana, were you top or bottom?"

"Top, man. I'm always top." Then he gave that slow grin. "Well, almost always. I make exceptions now and then."

"Okay." I turned away and adjusted the rearview mirror so I could see him without breaking my neck. "If I understand what you told us before, that was the day you went with them to the Salmon Ruins, right?"

"Yep."

"That would have been Monday, the thirteenth. Did you use protection?"

"I always use protection. I'm not into suicide."

"Okay. We figure they went to Bisti the next day."

"Where Dana died," he said.

"Did you go with them on that trip?"

"Uh-uh. Last time I saw them was the day Dana and me got it on. Like I said, I dropped by the motel once, but the car wasn't there. Then I had a job out on the rez on Tuesday. My brother picked me up Monday night, and I stayed with him most of the rest of the week."

"Okay. One more thing. Did you happen to notice anything while you were with them Monday?"

"Like what?"

"Like a car following the Porsche. Like somebody keeping an eye on the three of you at the ruins. Anything like that."

"I don't wanna sound like I got a swelled head or nothing, but guys watch me all the time. Lots of them hide it—you know, watch out of the corner of the eyes or something—but some stare right back at me. Like you did when you picked me up on Main."

"I was trying to attract your attention. This guy would have been hiding his interest."

A wrinkle creased his smooth brow for a moment. "No, nobody in particular. Wait a minute. You must mean Chrome Dome. What did the dude look like?"

"Around forty. Thinning sandy hair. Stocky."

"Did he have a scar on his chin?"

"Possibly. Why did you call him Chrome Dome?"

"That big old forehead. The guy I saw getting out of his car in the parking lot at Salmon had a big forehead. I mean, a really big forehead, and shiny like, so I called him Chrome Dome. He was kinda pudgy, but not soft. Sorta hard-looking, matter of fact. Didn't see him again, though."

Jazz Penrod's penchant for noticing men paid off. "What do you mean by hard-looking? Shaggy? Unshaven? What?"

"No, he was clean enough, but he'd come up hard, if you know what I mean. Wasn't raised on the soccer fields, more like in boxing rings."

"Got you. Was his car still there when you left?"

"Think so, but I'm not sure."

"Describe it."

Jazz gave a loose-limbed shrug. "Just a car. Nothing stood out about it. Just a brown, four-door Ford. Taurus, I think. A buddy of mine has one that looks a lot like it."

"What year?"

"Late model."

"Any bumper stickers or anything else you noticed about it?"

"Not a thing. Sorry."

"Thanks, Jazz. You've been a big help."

"I don't see how, but you're welcome. Now let me ask you a question. You're one of us, aren't you?"

"Absolutely."

"Interested?"

"Committed."

"He must be one hell of a dude."

LATER THAT night I phoned Paul. I needed him, and if I couldn't have the physical Paul, at least I could enjoy the sound of his voice, even if it was over a tinny little instrument that did not do justice to the bass notes in his deep baritone. He caught the quiet desperation in my voice, so we talked for an hour about anything and everything.

Chapter 16

TO MY mind there was ample evidence Chrome Dome had followed Lando and Dana from the Acoma Pueblo Truck Stop all the way to Farmington. If the man had come from somewhere else for the job—say California, for instance—there was a distinct possibility he'd rented that Ford at the Albuquerque Sunport.

Gene Enriquez usually arrived at APD early, and he didn't disappoint me the next day when I called at 7:00 a.m. He heard me out and agreed to check the local car rentals for a Ford four-door, maybe brown and maybe an '08 model, to see if he could find one that might fit. My old partner asked some questions about the case and expressed the opinion things didn't look too good for Orlando Alfano. Either he was a murderer on the run from the police or innocent and on the run from the killer—or worse.

Next I dialed Hazel, and after offering some suggestions on an assignment involving a runaway teenaged girl, which was beginning to look like an elopement with an older boyfriend, I asked her to contact Gilda to see if she'd been able to lay hands on any of Lando's personal credit card statements. I also asked Hazel to confirm that Dana's ex, Bruno Wills, was still in the LA area.

I hung up and delayed a breakfast meeting with Aggie to do some thinking. Larry Plainer had already concluded Lando had killed his lover in a fight over a sexy teenager. Lonzo Joe was a more seasoned and careful investigator, but he had to be thinking along the same lines. That was okay—for the moment—because it motivated them to find Lando.

Personally I didn't subscribe to the theory the kid was Dana's killer. My conclusion was based on reasoning, not emotions or a bogus sense of loyalty to the client. Three things pointed to his innocence. Lando was still in the vicinity of Farmington the day after Norville's murder, and if he were the killer, he would have headed for home and daddy's protection as fast as that fancy automobile would take him. Second, he abandoned a car he loved, something Aggie was convinced he would never willingly do. And third, someone was stalking the two young men and was likely the person who had put two slugs in the Porsche, possibly on the night it was abandoned on Halmstead Road, maybe to keep him from escaping in it.

Any rational person could poke holes in my reasoning, but put together, it made the case Lando was on the run from Dana's killer. He'd been forced to abandon the car when his pursuer opened fire on him. I didn't buy that he was dead or in the hands of his stalker either. Mrs. Ingfield's missing pie argued he was still in the area the day after the car was abandoned. Despite the fact the kid had half the money in the world, he was hungry enough to steal from others—and frightened enough to avoid them.

But that went straight to the heart of the situation. If Lando was free and moving under his own steam, why hadn't he called his father and yelled for help? Even if he lost his cell phone somewhere along the way, there were other ways to communicate. He'd have been better off asking Mrs. Ingfield for her telephone than swiping her pie. For some reason, he was shying away from the family. Why? Did the danger emanate from someone connected to the Alfanos?

Could Aggie be the one Lando was avoiding? It wouldn't be the first case of sibling rivalry among the superrich. Aggie seemed reconciled to his younger brother's sexual orientation, but it could be a sham. Maybe homosexuality was as deeply offensive to him as it was to Anthony Alfano. He didn't appear to be bigoted on the issue like his father, but he *was* a twig off the same tree.

Aggie was not the man trailing Lando and Dana. Still, he could have hired someone for the job. Of course, that was true of anyone, including the elder Alfano. But it was Aggie who flew out at a moment's notice and attached himself to me when the Porsche was located in Taos. During last night's phone report to Alfano, the old man had pressured him to come home to address the buyout they were tussling over. Aggie had resisted. Was he hanging on here out of concern for his brother or to cover his own butt?

When I caught up with him at the café a few minutes later, he was already digging into a man-sized breakfast.

"I waited for you."

"I can see. Sorry, but I had a couple of phone calls to make."

A waiter approached, but I waved away the menu and ordered lox and bagel with reduced-fat cream cheese and a cup of coffee.

"Give me your honest opinion of the mess we're in," he said.

"The best we can hope for is that the Sheriff's Office picks Lando up quickly and without trouble."

"He wouldn't cause trouble. I mean, he wouldn't resist arrest or anything. The reason I asked is I have to go back to California this morning. I've stalled as long as I can. Papa's dragging Mama to a board meeting, and that means he's going to try an end run. I've got no option but to attend and protect my position, but I'll get back as fast as I can."

"Take your time. It's all grunt work from here on in. I'll stay here and keep an eye on things." Mindful of my dark thoughts of a few minutes earlier, I chose my words carefully. "I'll sniff around and find his trail—hopefully before the cops do. But I'll tell you one thing, Aggie. I don't believe he's dead. I think he's hiding."

"Then why doesn't he call for help?"

"That's a very good question."

I must have put some kind of inflection into my voice because his dark eyes came up from his plate and fixed on mine. "You think he's afraid of his own family?"

I shook my head. "No, I think he's confused. Or he might be hurt and lost somewhere out there."

"Jesus, don't say that."

"I don't necessarily believe it, but it needed to be said."

Aggie tried to muster a smile. "I think that was payback for me raising your anxiety level when we landed at Four Corners. Damn, that seems like a lifetime ago." He pressed thumbs to his eyes. "Do you need any money or anything before I take off?"

"No, I'm fine. Go take care of business." I accepted my order and added a little sweetener to the coffee. "Your father's taking this better than I expected."

"Don't bet on it. He developed a damned good poker face a long time ago. Besides, he has a lot of confidence in you."

"That's thanks to you, I suspect. I'll try not to let you down." I paused to run a hand through my hair. "Aggie, you asked a very perspicacious question a moment ago. Why hasn't Lando called for help? I'm confident there's a reasonable answer, but I've learned one thing in investigative work: Don't leave any stone unturned, no matter how small. Describe the Alfano organization to me. Let's lay that question to rest so I can go on to the next thing."

Over the next fifteen minutes, I sipped coffee and munched my bagel as Aggie gave me a condensed history of the organization known today as Alfano Vineyards. Born as the A and B Winery in the late 1930s somewhere north of Napa Valley, it was a partnership between two refugees from the old country seeking to escape the Fascists and the gathering war clouds over Europe. Giuseppe Alfano and Paolo Baratta were lifelong friends who grew up in the Tuscany wine country where they learned their craft. Relying on the fruit of other people's vineyards, they developed a line of wines, which grew into a brand. As the two partners aged, their interests diverged: Giuseppe remained obsessed with the grape while Paolo became interested in the movie industry, which was in its heyday at the time.

Giuseppe bought most of Paolo's interests in the business, and A and B became Alfano Vineyards. He acquired some acreage and moved the winery south into the Napa Valley. Although his business prospered, he was not entirely successful in escaping the storm he fled. He lost two of his three sons in the European theater of World War II. When the eldest, Anthony, returned from service in the US Army, he proved to be an even more astute and aggressive businessman than his father— although some considered him simply ruthless. Upon the elder Alfano's death, Anthony became chairman and CEO.

Paolo Baratta's son, Franco, who had found the film business boring, was now a vice president of Alfano Vineyards, overseeing sales. Of an age, he and Anthony were often on the opposite sides of issues, but the Baratta family's strong minority stockholder position guaranteed him a place in the company.

Aggie was vice president in charge of the winemaking. This, he explained, was the basis of his objection to the proposed acquisition of another vineyard in the northern part of the valley. They were the wrong kind of grapes. Working with a new grape entailed a whole new educational process, even if the acquisition brought experienced people with it.

A Swiss Jew named Ariel Gonda was treasurer of the company. He was about fifteen years older than Aggie and was the only true outsider in a senior executive position. Tom Scavo, the present head of the company's labs, inherited his position from his father, Tomas. At thirty-eight, Scavo was a maverick. He liked to tinker around with the wines and was always experimenting with different tastes. He was, I gathered, a thorn in the side to Aggie, who took a more traditional approach to winemaking.

Aggie lifted his head from his recently refreshed cup of coffee and looked at me. "Maybe it's my imagination, but I always thought Tom was…." His voice died. He took another sip.

"Tom was what?" I pressed.

"Lando grew up around Tom. My brother worked in the lab all the way through high school. It was the only part of the business that held any interest for him—that and the history of winemaking. He and Tom were… friendly."

"Friendly, how?"

"I always thought Tom liked Lando too much, if you know what I mean?"

"Is Scavo gay?"

Aggie shrugged and eased back in his chair. "I don't think so. He's married and has a couple of kids. His Mary Lynn and my Irena get along great. So do Tom and I, as a matter of fact, except when he goes off on a tangent looking for a new 'aroma.' But it seemed to me he was always touching Lando. Not inappropriately," he rushed on, "but too many hands on the shoulder, mussing the kid's hair. That kind of thing."

"You think there was something between them?"

Aggie sighed his frustration. "I honestly don't know. I never even thought about it until I learned Lando was gay. Tom's a good-looking guy. I keep remembering what that kid, Jazz, said. You know, about preferring you to me because he didn't want somebody who looked like himself. If Lando felt the same way, then there was nothing between them. Hell, they could be brothers." He snorted. "We all could. Maybe if we look into the old man's background, we'll find we share a common gene pool. My father's no saint."

"How did your dad find out Lando is gay?"

"When Lando was home for Christmas in his freshman year of college, he announced he had a boyfriend. I think the old man already suspected because he continually pressed Lando about the girls he was meeting. Finally Lando got fed up and announced he'd already met someone—a man."

"Norville? Does Alfano blame Dana for bringing his son out?"

"No, it was someone else. Frankly I'm halfway convinced Lando made him up. You know, for shock value. My brother didn't meet Norville until about a year ago."

"Your father believes Lando is going through a phase of immaturity, but you seem to have accepted his homosexuality. Why?"

"Because I know him better than Papa. He sees Lando as he wants him to be, as he fits into the Alfano family tree. I see my brother as a human being."

PERHAPS IT was my imagination, but Aggie seemed to be a different man on the drive to the airport. He had already morphed back into a high-powered businessman delegating the problem of finding a missing brother to me.

Once the Mitsubishi was safely aloft, I headed back downtown to check out another possibility. Since Lando had lost his means of transportation, maybe he found another. I probably duplicated steps Lonzo Joe was taking, but I contacted every one of the local rental agencies. Dix Lee agreed to check on reports of stolen automobiles while I hit all of the new and used car lots in town.

By the end of the day, I knew Lando Alfano had not purchased a car of any type in Farmington through any legitimate dealership. Tomorrow I would visit the local newspaper and search out autos listed for sale by owners. In the meantime I cruised the streets of the town with an eye out for that elusive brown Ford. The only positive development of the day came when Melissa, the desk clerk at the Trail's End, confirmed Jazz Penrod's description of the man inquiring about the orange Porsche. No question about it; Lando and Dana had been stalked.

GENE RAISED me on the cell phone midmorning the next day as I sat in the newspaper morgue going through car ads. He had located a lease of possible interest. One Hugo Santillanes with an address in Los Angeles had rented a brown Ford four-door on Thursday, August 2. A quick glance at my calendar showed that was the day before the two boys' trip to Chesty Westey's. Ever the cop, Gene took the next logical step and determined Santillanes was a licensed private investigator in the state of California. I then called Charlie Weeks and asked him to find out all he could about the California PI, including where he was at the moment.

As it turned out, he was here in Farmington—or at least in the vicinity. Armed with his name and license plate number, Dix found the motel where he was registered within an hour. A drive past the plain, cinderblock motel two blocks east of the Trail's End revealed no sign of a brown Ford, so I stopped by the office to ask for his room number. The clerk, a virtual twin of Melissa, informed me that Mr. Santillanes had not been around for over a week, although he was still registered. With a little pressing, I learned they had packed up his suitcase and were holding it in the baggage area. After warning them the County Sheriff might be interested in looking at it, I phoned Lonzo.

He was out of the crime lab—off chasing that despicable dog-fighting ring probably—so I detailed my information to a sergeant and asked him to relay it to Lonzo right away. Frustrated at not being able to speak directly to the detective, I called Alfano's office and listened to dead air in my cell phone while Gilda searched for him. Finally, Alfano's rough voice boomed over the line.

"Don't have a lot of time right now, Vinson. Have you found my boy?"

"No," I replied, nettled by the man's attitude. What could be more important than locating a missing son? "But I found out who's been bird-dogging his steps. Does the name Hugo Santillanes mean anything to you?"

"No, should it?"

"He's a PI out of LA. Did you hire him to find Lando?"

"We've had this conversation before. No, I did not hire the man. Never heard of him. If he comes out of LA, you ought to talk to Bruno Wills. I hear he didn't take kindly to his lover boy leaving him. I'll tell you what, Vinson, you tell me Wills is behind all of this, and I'll take care of it from here on in. Understood?"

"Alfano," I said, "I have no idea who's behind Dana's murder and Lando's disappearance, so don't you go off half-cocked. I've informed the San Juan County Sheriff's Office of what I know, so they're going to be right in the middle of things. If you get out of line, somebody will come down on you hard."

"Are you threatening me?"

"Nope, I'm warning you. You hired me, so that makes me your agent. In that capacity, I owe you the best advice I can give. And right now, that's to let me do my job. But if you lie to me, I no longer owe you any loyalty."

I expected him to come at me over the telephone, but he fooled me again. "Why do you think I lied to you?"

"I don't think it, but I believe you're capable of it if it serves your interests. I'm merely trying to sort things out, and to do that, I have to know you're up-front with me."

"For the last time, I didn't hire this Santillanes fellow. If I had, why would I need you?"

"Good enough," I said.

I snapped the cell shut. Why *did* I suspect he was lying to me? Because he was the kind of man who left nothing to chance. He would have no compunction about doubling up on his options and keeping one party in the dark about the other.

Lando had warned his father he wasn't going to accept any interference on the trip, and Santillanes was on his son's trail shortly after leaving on his fateful vacation. It wasn't a stretch to figure Alfano would put a shadow on his wayward son. From his point of view, it might even be a prudent thing to do. A minder—a guardian—made a certain, perverted kind of sense for a megabucks daddy worried about a son who was passing through a "difficult phase."

That begged the other question—the one he asked me himself. If Santillanes was his man, why would he have hired me?

Chapter 17

Jazz Penrod phoned early the next morning asking for a meet. When I picked him up on the sidewalk in front of his mom's house, he was dressed in denim cut-offs so tight he'd had to split the seam up the outside of the thigh in order to sit down. A thin T-shirt with straps—what my mom had called an undershirt—exposed his broad, red-brown shoulders and sheathed his torso like original skin. He wore open sandals, more like shower clogs than shoes, without socks. He grinned and shoved a black-billed cap with a red Captain Morgan logo back on his head.

"Mr. Vinson," he said.

I popped the lock, and he flowed into the passenger's seat like liquid mercury. "Morning, Jazz. What can I do for you?"

"Maybe it's what I can do for you," he countered, and then laughed aloud at my quick frown. "No, not that. I picked up a rumor. Thought you'd want to know."

"Fine. How about some breakfast?"

"Okay by me."

After we gave our order to a waiter in a nearby café, Jazz threw a long arm over the back of the chair next to him. As a trained investigator, I believe I notice things others do not, but I would have erroneously described him as skinny. Not so. He was slender, yes, but buffed with defined muscles—corded muscles. That thin shirt stretching over his torso clearly outlined a six-pack.

"Okay, now tell me about that rumor."

"My brother—you know, Henry Secatero—he called me last night. He was over at the chapter house to meet this girl. I'd told him about those missing guys and one turning up dead, so when he heard there'd been outsiders on the rez where they didn't have any business, he thought of Lando and Dana."

"Did he get any details?"

"Well, there's a car, somebody said. Supposed to have been parked out on the rim of Black Hole Canyon. Been there a few days."

"Where is Black Hole Canyon?"

"Sort of a rugged area not too far off the highway. It's not really a canyon, just a big-assed arroyo. But Henry said the car's not in it, just pulled up under an overhang where it's kinda out of sight."

My coffee and french toast and Jazz's bacon and eggs and hash browns with a side of ham arrived. He stopped talking and dug in, eating rapidly while I munched and mulled over what he told me. I was tempted to dismiss the incident. There was nothing to directly tie this to Lando, but I was looking for a car, and Henry had found one. It was worth checking out.

Jazz put down his knife and fork after his last bite of ham and drained his glass of orange juice. "You wanna go take a look?"

"Jazz, you're not out to put your mark on me, are you?" I felt like a fool. There were more attractive fish in the ocean than me, but every look, every gesture seemed to be bait—chum for the sharks.

"I wouldn't mind," he admitted, "but I heard you when you said you were taken. Look, I liked Dana and respected Lando. If I can help them out, I'd like to do it."

"Fair enough. If you're finished, let's go."

"Let's rumble, but first I gotta go home and change. I'd burn up out there in the sun dressed like this."

Fifteen minutes later we headed west out of town toward Shiprock with Jazz now clad in a pair of baggy dungarees, a worn, long-sleeved cotton shirt, and walking boots.

This is not really the red-rock part of New Mexico, but the massive, wind-carved sandstone shelves—some the remnants of ancient barrier reefs—glowed red and orange, striated with layers of black and yellow and brown and white. I identified feldspar and hematite, quartz and dark brown calcite, degraded coal and gypsum embedded in the host rock, all deposited eons ago when the shallow marine sea retreated with the upheaval of mountains in what is now southwestern Colorado. Volcanic eruptions had spewed fire and ash over the entire area. As the water retreated, sand dunes consolidated into cross-bedded Entrada Sandstone. Over the ensuing ages, the ceaseless battle between wind and rock and water chopped the terrain to pieces, creating the present landscape.

The Shiprock monolith, which lay in the distance ahead of us, was the throat of a volcano that had died long ago. The terrain around it eroded and washed away, leaving a 450-foot pile of black basalt towering over the Navajo Nation.

Long before we reached Shiprock, Jazz had me turn south on a rocky dirt road. As we began climbing, I threw the car into low gear to make it up the steep inclines of the washboard landscape. The rental sedan wasn't made for this kind of country, and I was about to give it up as a bad venture when he pointed left.

"Take that road there."

"What road?"

He laughed. "It's a road down into Black Hole Canyon. Or at least a track. The car's not far now if I understood Henry right. If it's still there, that is."

With more than a little trepidation, I followed his directions. My stomach fell along with the road as the earth dropped sharply. To our left there was nothing but open air. The narrow ledge supporting us hugged the wall of the canyon—and it *was* a canyon, not a big-assed arroyo. We dropped farther down the uncertain trail while tons of mudstone leaned outward above the car, threatening to shove us into the abyss. My knuckles turned white on the steering wheel.

"This is the worst part," Jazz said. "The trail curves to the right just ahead, and there's an overhang. That's where Henry said the car was parked."

"Like someone wanted to hide it," I rasped, desperate for the sound of my voice one last time before we ran out of road and pitched over into oblivion.

"Yeah, like that. Me and Henry used to come out here when we were kids and hunt jackrabbits and rattlesnakes."

I grunted. It was supposed to be a laugh but didn't come out that way. "I thought you Native Americans were into preserving the environment, not killing anything that moved."

"I'm half white. I guess that part of me's a killer."

The cryptic remark would have earned him a glance if I hadn't been concentrating on keeping the car on this pitiful excuse of a scree-littered burro trail. "Your brother doesn't have white blood, does he?"

"No, but the family ate the jackrabbits. Guess they ate a little snake now and then too."

We inched around the curve. I tapped the brake. A car blocked our progress—a brown four-door Ford sedan.

We didn't need to get out of the car to know what had happened, but we did it anyway. The stench was overpowering. Something—or somebody—was dead. Without touching a thing, I peered through the windows and determined no one was in the passenger compartment. The odor seemed to come from the rear of the vehicle, so the body was in the trunk. Was it a confidential investigator called Hugo Santillanes or a kid named Lando Alfano?

"We've got to get out of here. Right now."

Jazz objected. "Let's see who it is. I can force the trunk, no problem."

"Can't. This is a crime scene. As soon as we get to solid ground, I'll call it in—if I can get a signal."

"Oughta be able to. There's a tower at Shiprock. You back out. I'll give directions."

"You just don't want to be in the car when it goes over the side."

"You got it, kemosabe."

It took a lot longer to make our way back to the rim of the canyon traveling in reverse than it had coming in, but, strangely, it wasn't as frightening. That was probably because I had my eyes glued to Jazz's hand signals in the rearview mirror. Nonetheless, every time the tires shifted on loose rock, my gut clenched. I was drenched in sweat by the time we reached the top. I pulled over onto solid terrain and parked. Now that we were back on level ground, my queasiness abated; my uneasiness did not.

I probably should have dialed the Navajo Police, but I knew the FBI handled serious crimes on the reservation, so I asked the 911 operator to connect me with that agency. I was dismayed to learn the Farmington resident special agent was actually located in Gallup, approximately ninety miles south of us as the crow flies. The FBI operator advised, however, there was an agent named John Gaines in the vicinity and promised to contact him.

I hung up and studied something in the distance. "Jazz, is this part of the reservation used for anything? I mean, do they graze sheep or cows or look for oil or coal?"

"Nope. There's no water up here. There's water in the canyon—not much, but a little. Sometimes people camp down there."

"What the hell for?"

"To get away from other people. Like maybe they want to smoke a little weed or snort something without being bothered."

I looked around the desolate landscape. "Lord, everywhere's away from other people."

"You'd be surprised. There are hogans and huts scattered all around the countryside. Somebody might be watching us right now, and we'd never know it."

At that moment my cell phone rang. It was Gaines. He heard me out and instructed us to stay put until he got there.

I hung up and again eyed the dark splotch barely discernable in the distance. "Anything else go on out here? I'm not looking to put the law on anyone, but it might be important to Lando."

"Well," he said uneasily, "people say this is a place where outsiders bring in things they don't want anybody to know about. You know, it's close to Shiprock, and it's not that far from Farmington. Hell, it's not that far from Colorado or Utah, for that matter."

"So they bring drugs in here?"

"That's what I hear."

"Stay here," I said before walking off to the south. Of course, Jazz ignored me and trailed along in my wake, too curious to remain behind. "Walk in my tracks," I cautioned.

Within a hundred yards, I saw what looked to be tire markings of some sort, although they were so windblown, it was impossible to say what kind of vehicle laid them down. When I came to what had caught my eye, the first in a line of dark smudges, I halted. Jazz almost ran up my back.

"Any reports of planes setting down around here? At night, for instance?"

He shrugged. "Maybe."

I sighed. My shoulders sagged as I realized my last lead had gone up in thin air—literally.

We returned to the car and baked in a hot, late summer sun because I didn't dare burn up gasoline by running the motor so we could have air conditioning. Gaines arrived about an hour later, trailed by a forensics team, the same one that had handled the Bisti business. Apparently they served multiple law enforcement jurisdictions, both federal and local. Before they could get out of their vehicles, a Navajo Police cruiser pulled up. I watched as Gaines unfolded himself from the black SUV he drove and paused to consult with the other officers. He was a tall, gaunt

Ichabod Crane caricature with a craggy horse face. His voice, when he came forth to greet me, sounded like it came from a well.

During my two-minute explanation of the situation and the reason for our interest in it, another vehicle pulled up and disgorged Larry Plainer. Why? So far as I knew, the BLM had no jurisdiction over Indian trust lands. Apparently he and Gaines knew one another.

"Heard the call and decided to come out and see if this murder ties into the one down at Bisti," the fair-haired man explained. "I told Detective Joe I was coming," he added, as if that carried any weight with Uncle Sam.

Gaines grunted but voiced no objection.

This time we walked down to the brown Ford—for which I gave silent thanks. I wasn't about to tempt fate by tackling that rocky ledge in a vehicle again for the FBI or anybody else. As soon as the car came into sight, the leader of the crime scene technicians team had us identify our own tracks and then shooed us away while they took pictures of the car and the entire area around it. We had not retreated far enough to please Plainer; he escorted us back to the top of the rim even though I suspected he didn't have the authority to do so. Nonetheless, I put up no fuss.

"Who do you think they're gonna find in that trunk?" Jazz asked when the BLM agent left us up on top.

"We'll just have to wait and see."

"Man, that's cold. It might be Lando in there."

"Might be, but there's nothing we can do to hurry things along. We'll know soon enough."

Jazz shifted his weight a couple of times. "Why don't they just pop the trunk and find out?"

"They probably already have, but in this state you can't move a body without the Office of the Medical Investigator's okay, and he isn't on the scene yet. They'll take a bunch of pictures of everything and measure distances—tire-track widths, positions of footprints, that kind of thing. But nobody's going to move the car or the body until OMI arrives."

"Weird way of doing things," he said.

A grim-faced Gaines walked up the road to join us. Realizing he wouldn't tell us what was going on until he was ready, I pointed out what I thought was a primitive landing strip with burnt-out bonfires for night landings.

"Whoever killed Hugo Santillanes—" I started.

Gaines turned his long-nosed, narrow visage on me. "How do you know it's Santillanes?"

"Agent Gaines, you're probably a by-the-book kind of guy, but even so, you wouldn't withhold the fact it's my client's son in the trunk of that car. You obviously don't believe it's Lando Alfano. And since that car matches the description of the one I've been hunting, that leaves Santillanes."

He handed over a Polaroid, and Jazz crowded in to catch a look.

"Ugh!" the kid exclaimed.

I didn't blame him. The body was in pretty poor condition. Nonetheless, the dead man matched the description of Santillanes. "What do you think?" I asked Jazz.

"I don't recognize nothing but the forehead. That dude had one big forehead. Yeah, that's Chrome Dome. You know, the guy I saw at Salmon Ruins."

I explained the domed forehead description to Gaines and then continued with my original thought. "Whoever killed him left the area in a small plane. Something like a Piper Cub."

"Or a Mitsubishi."

That took me by surprise. He'd managed to learn a lot in a short period of time. He had obviously been fully briefed by Lonzo Joe. Better not underestimate this guy.

"Could be," I agreed. "It's a short-takeoff, short-landing craft, but look here." I pointed to a thin scratch on the rocky ground. "I'm no expert, but that looks like a tail dragger. The Mitsu has a nose wheel. I'd say a much smaller plane landed here. And if you're suggesting Aggie Alfano, I think you're wrong."

"Why? It fits. Lando Alfano kills his lover and calls on his brother to save his ass. A. F...." He paused to consult his notes. "Uh, Aggie Alfano already has a PI on Orlando and has the guy pick up his brother. Santillanes knows Orlando killed Norville, so the Alfanos take care of him and fly out."

Mentally calling up the calendar I had created of Lando's movements, I nodded. "It's possible, but I don't think so."

"Why not?"

With my own suspicions of Aggie in the forefront of my mind, I had trouble answering. "If you're right about Lando killing Dana Norville, he would have headed straight for California in the Porsche. Abandoning his vehicle across town and hanging around on the desert hardpan waiting for his brother to come for him makes no sense. And I'm sure Detective Joe told you there were bullet holes in the Porsche."

"As I understand it, that car sat on a back road for at least two days, Vinson. Kids could have done that out of mischief. It happens all the time. Well, occasionally," he amended. "And Alfano could have abandoned the car to cast doubt on his involvement in Norville's killing. It worked for you. What's a hundred-thousand-dollar car to a rich kid?"

"Maybe it's because I never hire out to anyone except solid citizens," I said with a sarcasm apparently lost on FBI agents. "But I read it another way. Somebody, probably Santillanes, was stalking Lando and Dana. He caught up with them down in Bisti. For some reason he confronted the two men, killing one of them. Lando got away with Santillanes hot on his tail."

"That doesn't hold water, and you know it. Whoever killed Norville took the time to hide the body in a natural cavity and cover him with rocks and dirt, not to mention getting down and dirty with him before or after strangling him to death."

"Maybe there were two of them," I said.

"Two of them? You mean someone with Santillanes? In two different cars?"

"Not necessarily. Maybe one left the other behind to hide the body and came back later to pick up his partner after he took care of Lando."

"Took care of? You mean killed?" Gaines, his big hands jammed deep into his pockets, drew random marks in the sand with the toe of a size twelve cowboy boot.

I shook my head. "No, I think there's evidence Lando was alive after the car was abandoned."

"The stolen pie? You sure paint an elaborate picture with a little dab of paint."

Man, this guy had a grasp of the smallest details. He rose another notch or two in my estimation. "I'll admit it's thin. It could be the way you say, but I don't believe it. I think he's out there and needs our help."

"Then why hasn't the kid made contact?"

"He could be hurt. Or seeing his friend killed might have sent him around the bend."

Gaines stretched his long torso as if his back was giving him trouble. "Either way, we need to find him. I take it you're going to keep looking."

"Right. I'll keep you posted. Appreciate it if you'd give me the same courtesy. I'd like to know how and when Santillanes died."

"I think we can share that information with you."

"Thanks."

Gaines passed two Navajo cops walking up out of the canyon as he headed back down to the crime scene. Jazz moseyed over to the two policemen to exchange a few words before they got into the cruiser and pulled away.

"They don't know anything," Jazz said as he rejoined me. "They kinda get their noses out of joint when the FBI treats them like intruders. They say Gaines isn't as bad as some of the agents, but they still feel froze out. But they did say the guy in the trunk had been shot."

"Thanks."

The EMTs beat the OMI to the site by about thirty seconds—which must have set some sort of time record. Hard on their heels, a wrecker arrived from Farmington. Another half hour passed before they winched the Ford back up onto the rim of the canyon. Jazz and I watched as the medics lifted the body out of the trunk, laid it on a gurney, and took more pictures. We were a little distance removed, but I clearly heard the doctor give a preliminary opinion, which confirmed what the Navajo cops had told Jazz. The victim had been shot in the head, probably by a handgun.

Eventually Gaines beckoned us over and lifted a wallet in his gloved hand. "Looks like you were right, Vinson. The California driver's and PI licenses say it's Santillanes. You'll come in and give a statement, right? Both of you."

I agreed and headed for my rental car before he decided to take us in for questioning that very minute. Jazz was quiet most of the way back to town, but at length he spoke.

"Heavy, huh? I never saw a rotten dead guy before. I mean, I been to funerals, but those guys sure didn't look like that dude."

"No, but it didn't bother Santillanes any more than it bothered those corpses being cleaned up for the mourners."

"Man, you sure have weird thoughts."

I laughed. "You're not the first one to tell me that. Thanks for your tip, Jazz. If you hadn't called me, the body might not have been discovered for weeks."

"Yeah, sure. What're you gonna do now?"

"Keep looking for Lando."

"How come you don't think he's the killer? You don't think gay guys can be killers?"

"Sure they can, but everything I've learned about Orlando Alfano says he's not a murderer."

"And you're not ever wrong?"

"You got me there. I'm wrong a lot."

Chapter 18

WHEN I dropped Jazz off at his house, I asked him to phone me the next morning. Then I returned to the motel to check in with my office and figure out how much to tell my client about the events of the day.

Hazel had received Lando's credit card statements from Gilda Gistafferson, but there was little of interest in them. The last charges were for the room at the Trail's End. When we were through discussing Alfano, she filled me in on the status of our other cases and rather hastily slid over a new one she had accepted. It was a domestic case for a woman who lived a couple of doors down the street from her. Hazel knew we didn't take that type of job, but I didn't have the heart to argue with her for helping out a neighbor with an errant husband. Besides, there was a familiar quiver to her voice clearly signaling she was loaded for bear and just waiting for me to object. I held my tongue, and she put Charlie on the line.

"How's it going?" His calm voice was as soothing as a balm.

"Slowly. I'm getting frustrated on this end."

"We're not doing much better here. The LA PI we hired tells me Bruno Wills has been in LA for the past two weeks."

"He's sure of his information?"

"He's a good man, BJ. He's got it documented. There are a couple of holes, but they aren't big enough for the guy to have made it out here to New Mexico and back."

"That doesn't mean he didn't hire someone."

"No, it doesn't."

I updated Charlie on everything that happened and asked him to see if he could learn who hired Hugo Santillanes. I also asked him to trace Aggie Alfano's movements in the days before he showed up in Taos.

"Might as well go the rest of the way," I added. "See if anyone knows where Alfano Sr. was. He called me from Hawaii, so he should have left a trail over there."

"Our own client?"

"Why not? Yeah, I know, it's his son that's missing, but it's also his son's gay lover who was killed at the Bisti badlands. I don't have any real reason to believe he or any of the family is involved, but let's be as thorough as we can without making waves."

"Tall order there," he said. "A family like the Alfanos has eyes and ears all over the place."

"I know, but do the best you can."

"Okay, here's something else for you to chew on since you brought up the Alfanos. According to our LA investigator, Anthony Alfano's wife is the former Mona Masterson. Her grandfather, Titus Sabelito, was into booze in a big way back in the old days. Sabelito Distributors. Made a lot of money during Prohibition, they say, and a bunch more after it ended."

"How much money?"

"Not sure yet, but enough to make Alfano look penny ante, they say."

"Now that's interesting."

"Yep. They also say Mona Alfano's health isn't that good. She had breast cancer a few years back. They got it, but some of the stuff keeps showing up in other places."

"That would be a windfall for Alfano. I assume he inherits under California law."

"He can't touch a penny of it. Old man Sabelito put it all in a trust long before he died in '92—at age ninety-two, as a matter of fact."

"Who's the beneficiary under the trust?"

"His granddaughter, Mona. Anthony's wife. From her it follows the bloodline, thereby skipping Anthony Alfano."

"Was she married to anyone else before she met Alfano?"

"Nope. At least there's no record of a marriage."

"I know she and Anthony have two sons, Aggie and Lando, and I've heard Aggie mention a sister."

"Victoria. Named after the great-grandmother, I guess. According to the scuttlebutt, she's the eldest of the Alfano brood and made in the old man's mold."

"How old is she?"

"A year older than Aggie."

"That would make her about thirty-five. She married?"

"Yeah, to William Vitrillo. He's some sort of broker in LA. Stock broker, I take it."

"See what else you can find about the Sabelito trust. Anything else I should know?"

"Nope. That's all I got. Oh, yeah. Hazel wants to know if she can hire somebody to give us a hand. Just till you get back. We kinda got our hands full here right now."

"Sure. You have anyone in mind?"

"I was thinking about Tim Fuller. You remember him? An old sergeant outa downtown. He took his papers about five years ago, but he's got a PI license he doesn't do much with."

"Have at it. It looks like I might be tied up for a while. My best lead's dead, but somehow, I don't think the Alfano kid is. He's out there somewhere."

I hung up and thought about what Charlie told me. There was no rational reason for believing Lando was alive and still in the area. Chances were good he had been in the plane that took off from the makeshift strip on the rim of Black Hole Canyon. I likewise had nothing to indicate any member of the Alfano family had a hand in the death of Dana Norville. Maybe it *had* been a gay lover's quarrel out there in the Bisti Wilderness, but my gut told me otherwise, and that kept me on the ground here in Farmington. Well, my gut and instructions from San Juan County Sheriff's Detective Lonzo Joe. And Gaines had made that same "suggestion." Had Aggie cleared his departure with anyone? I hadn't seen or talked to Lonzo since he took off, so the deputy might not be aware Aggie was in California.

I dialed Alfano's office. It was time to take my client's temperature.

Worry edged Gilda's voice when the operator transferred my call. "Oh, BJ, that's terrible news about Dana. He was such a sweet boy. Well, man, really. I have to stop thinking of those two as youngsters. Is there any news of Lando? I'm so afraid for him."

It all came out in a rush and seemed genuine. If someone had spirited Lando out of New Mexico, Alfano's private secretary wasn't aware of it.

"I think he's alive, Gilda. I have no proof of it, but that's my belief."

"Then why hasn't he contacted us? It makes no sense."

"He may be hurt. Or he may be wary about contacting the family."

"For heaven's sake, why?" Her voice rose.

I scrambled to cover my blunder. "Because that's the first place anyone would look. I think he's in serious danger, and he's trying to keep that danger away from the people he loves."

"That would be so like him," she said in a calmer tone. "But he knows there's no place where he would be safer than here."

"I need to warn you to expect a visit from the FBI."

"They've already been here, and Mr. Alfano was terribly upset by the time they left. Something about a murder out on an Indian reservation. I was so afraid it was Lando."

"They didn't waste any time," I said, more to myself than to Gilda. "No, it wasn't Lando, but they think he might be involved. Is your boss available?"

"Let me check. Can you hold for a moment?"

Sixty seconds later, Alfano picked up the phone, but his voice was not the authoritative blast of prior conversations. "Have you learned anything?"

"Nothing about Lando, I'm afraid. I understand you've had visitors."

"Visitors? You mean the FBI? Yeah, they wasted a couple hours of my time. What could Lando have to do with a dead private investigator?"

"You remember me asking if you'd hired a PI named Hugo Santillanes. The man followed Lando and Dana halfway across New Mexico. That's how Lando's connected to him. I'm the one who found him shot dead out at an unimproved landing strip on the Navajo Reservation."

"Who shot him? It wasn't Lando."

"I agree, but I don't know who it was. He was stuffed in the trunk of his car a couple of weeks ago, and he wasn't a pretty sight. Around forty, husky, thinning blond hair. A scar on his chin. Pronounced forehead. Any of that sound familiar?"

"No, I told you I didn't—"

"Look, I'm going to level with you. My best lead died with that PI. My office is working through another investigator in LA to see what we can find out about him, and I believe whoever killed him immediately left the area in a private plane. Nonetheless, a couple of small things make me believe Lando might still be around here—maybe hurt, most certainly confused, and possibly even dead. The odds of finding him are not good. I have an idea I want to try, but I need directions from you. Do you want me on the job? After all, the FBI is on the case now, and it's your money I'm spending."

"You're damned right I want you to stay on it. And don't worry about money. Or the FBI. Do what you need to do. I want my son found.

And if they're going to fuck around and waste time questioning me, that's not going to happen. Find him, Vinson, before they do. Aggie tells me you're a good investigator and an honest man. Now, what do you have in mind?"

I told him I wanted to hire a local who knew the area and had better contacts than I did. I neglected to tell him my choice was an eighteen-year-old mixed-blood gay kid with a dazzling smile and a smoky, seductive look.

Jazz met me for breakfast the next morning dressed in baggy Levi's and a pearl-button shirt. At least he didn't wear his britches with the crotch down around his knees like so many of the kids nowadays. As soon as we ordered, I turned to business.

"Jazz, I'd like you to nose around to see if you can pick up any sign of a recluse, an injured man, anything that's out of the ordinary. I'll make it worth your while."

"You're hiring me to work for you?"

I hesitated a moment. "Yeah, I guess I am. But you're not a licensed investigator, so all I want you to do is keep your ear to the ground and ask around a little. Remember, two men have been killed, and although I'm confident the killer left the area from that strip out at Black Hole Canyon, I don't want you doing anything to put yourself at risk."

"Cool. A junior PI."

"Dammit, don't go off half-cocked. Just ask around and listen. Like you did when you picked up on the abandoned car."

He smiled. "That was something, huh? Turned up a murder." A calculating look replaced the smile, but he waited until the waiter delivered our chile rellenos—and a short stack of pancakes for him—to ask the question hanging on his face. "What kinda 'making it worth my while' are we talking about?"

"I was thinking maybe you could spend a week nosing around, and I'd come up with five hundred or so."

He cocked his head. "I'll need some wheels."

"You seem to do okay without them. I understand you get around town and out to the reservation any time you want."

"Yeah, but it's a hassle fitting my schedule to somebody going my way. Make you a deal. There's this Jeep Wrangler a buddy of mine is trying to unload. It's old but in good shape. I got it covered, all but about six hundred bucks. You pony that up, and it'll make things easier. You know, get me around to lots more places."

"You have a driver's license?"

"Sure. Wanna see it?"

"No, your word's good." I paused to consider the pros and cons of the thing. "Okay, it's a deal. Let's go take care of it."

In the end he talked me out of a down payment on an insurance policy, which is mandatory in this state, and some driving-around money. I also got him a prepaid mobile phone. It added up to more than I had intended to invest, but it was worth the expense. People who wouldn't give me the time of day would open up to him.

As soon as I was certain Jazz understood what I needed and his butt was comfortably seated in his new—at least to him—Wrangler, I headed for the airport. I wasn't certain about the wisdom of leaving after turning Jazz Penrod loose on the town, but the kid had a good sense of self-preservation and my cell number in case he needed help or found something interesting. The Labor Day holiday weekend loomed in front of me, and I wanted to spend it with Paul. But first I needed a face-to-face meeting with Hazel and Charlie and a few minutes with Gene. Those three had a way of grounding me, and that's what I needed. Almost more than I needed Paul.

I called both Gaines and Lonzo Joe from the terminal to let them know I was temporarily leaving town and to ask if there was any new information on Santillanes. Gaines confirmed he'd been shot once in the head, probably with a .38, but said it was too early for any additional forensic information. However, he confirmed Santillanes's belt had been ruled out as the weapon used to strangle Dana Norville to death.

I CALLED Paul, and he wrangled some time off from work to meet me at the Albuquerque Sunport. Trying to keep my heart from bursting free of my chest as I spotted him waiting curbside, I slipped into his old purple Plymouth, and we exchanged big, loopy grins.

"Let's get out of here," I said.

Nodding, he sped across town to the Double Eagle Airport to recover my own vehicle, and then we ignored the speed limit in our race for home.

The house on Post Oak Drive in the North Valley had never looked so good—although the white trim on the red brick, cross-gabled house needed repainting. But I lost that train of thought the moment the door closed behind us. Judging from the joyful fierceness of his coupling, Paul must have missed me as much as I missed him.

Chapter 19

I WENT to the office that afternoon expecting to take Hazel and Charlie by surprise, but somehow they'd found out I was back in town. Sometimes Hazel was a better PI than I was. At any rate, she was ready for me, insisting on taking care of a multitude of small tasks to clear a couple of cases off the books so she could render the clients a final billing—including the peep job she'd accepted from her neighbor. Instead of sneaking around on his wife, it seems the husband had been getting treatments for a prostrate problem on the sly. Case closed. Satisfied client, embarrassed husband.

When Hazel was finished with all of that, Charlie joined us in my office to discuss the Alfano case. Hazel had contacted the last half-dozen places Lando had charged items on his credit cards but learned nothing we did not already know. Charlie had better luck. He was ready with the details of the estate of Mona Masterson Alfano's grandfather.

"How did you come up with this so fast? We only talked about it yesterday."

"The Sabelito-Masterson-Alfano saga is common gossip from the Bay to points north."

"North—meaning Napa Valley."

"Meaning Napa Valley. Mona Alfano's mother died when the girl was only about two years old. Since Titus Sabelito didn't approve of Mona's father, Dwight Masterson, the canny old bastard had put all of his daughter's assets in a trust as a means of keeping money out of the hands of her widower. Then he gave Masterson a position in Sabelito Distributors and a lifetime income from a smaller separate trust set up for him in exchange for signed legal permission for the old man to raise the granddaughter."

"Give me the background."

"Titus Sabelito was a contemporary of Alfano's father." Charlie consulted his notes. "Giuseppe Alfano came from the same part of Tuscany. These old-world guys usually have large families, but Titus survived all his kin except for his granddaughter, even though he was almost two decades older than his wife, who died of TB back in the fifties.

"The word is the old man didn't care for Mona's choice of mate any more than he did his daughter's. Apparently there was something between the Sabelito and Alfano families from the old days when both were establishing themselves. But by the time Anthony got his claws into Mona, Sabelito was in his late sixties and didn't put up much of a fight. Probably because he knew he could keep a finger on things from beyond the grave through the primary trust."

"How much money are we talking about?"

"Somewhere around a billion dollars."

"Wow! That does make Alfano seem like a piker. So who controls the money?"

"There's a trust committee of bankers, lawyers, accountants, and the like, but Mona has the final say—within the limits established by the trust documents, of course. There's talk about a money struggle going on right now. Something about Alfano buying a vineyard at the north end of the valley."

"Using Sabelito money?"

"That's the talk."

Aggie's sudden trip back home began to make more sense. "Who's objecting to using the trust?"

"Some of the bankers, I guess. And the Alfano boys. Aggie is apparently a little more cautious than the old man. Nobody knows why the younger boy, Orlando, objects to the new acquisition, but the speculation is he doesn't like using his mother's money to finance it."

"But if it's Mona Alfano's decision, who cares what the boys think?" My question brought another thought with it. "And what is Victoria's position on the thing?"

"Well, that's where it gets interesting. It seems the Alfano daughter's husband, William Vitrillo, is in line for a big commission if the sale goes through. So Victoria supports the buyout."

Hazel looked at Charlie. "I thought you said Vitrillo was a stockbroker, not a real estate broker."

"He is. Actually, he's an investment banker with his own small outfit. And the seller—" Charlie stopped to leaf through his notes again. "Uh, De Falco Fine Wines is listed as a business, not as real estate, so Vitrillo is legally qualified to handle the sale."

"What's the price tag?"

"Fifty million."

"A 5 percent commission would net Vitrillo two and a half million," I said. "Nice deal. But that purchase price is half of Alfano's net worth. That explains why he needs his wife's money for the deal."

"As far as who cares what the younger kid thinks," Charlie said, "everyone agrees Lando is his mother's favorite. He has a lot of clout with her."

"So we have Mona holding the purse strings with her husband and daughter on one side and her two sons on the other. Interesting."

"Not so fast," Charlie said with a grin. "You know how the rumor mill is. Nothing is as clean cut as it appears. Some people say Lando was about to change his mind and side with his father."

"Which would put him at odds with his brother," Hazel said.

"But"—Charlie's grin widened as though he was enjoying this byplay—"others are just as sure he had already convinced his mother this was not a good move for the Alfano company, or more properly, the Sabelito money."

"So anyone on either side of the equation could have had it in for Lando." I reconsidered. "Or either side could have been trying to win him over. The kid's sudden New Mexico vacation and his refusal to accept his father's phone calls now make more sense."

"And so does the shadow," Charlie said. "Somebody wanted to know where to get ahold of the kid on short notice."

"Once again, it could be anyone on either side of the acquisition."

"Like Alfano himself," Hazel suggested. "Or the De Falco people."

"Or his brother-in-law," Charlie added to the list. "You can't count him out. Not with two and a half mil riding on the kid."

"We're going to need more horses for this thing." I picked up my miniature Toledo blade letter opener and tapped the point against the desk blotter. They waited me out, aware I was thinking or was pissed about something. Finally I made up my mind.

"I'm going to turn this information over to the FBI. Our task is to find Lando Alfano. The rest belongs to the feds."

Charlie nodded. "Makes sense. So you want me to back off on poking around in California? Call off the LA investigator?"

"No, let him stay on the job, and while he's at it, he can look at the Vitrillos. Nothing specific. Just general information. Charlie, I want to know who hired that PI, Santillanes."

"Our man in LA says Santillanes was an independent, a one-man shop. Probably not much in the way of records. But whatever they are, the FBI will have them by now. You think they'll share?"

I shook my head. "Not that information. That would put us right in the middle of their murder. Gaines won't give that up."

"Too bad," Charlie said. "So what's our next move?"

I glanced at my watch. "I want to try and catch Gene before he leaves the station. But I'd like to pick this up later. I might not get back until closing time. You mind staying late?"

They both shook their heads.

GENE CLAIMED he only wanted a drink, saying it was way too early for dinner. But I knew he'd order an appetizer, and that would soon be followed by a full-course meal, so I agreed to meet him at the original Garduño's on North Fourth. He was waiting for me at a corner table, already munching on a serving of extra spicy nachos. I ordered a Coors Light from the waitress and took the chair across from him.

"Glad you thought of this place," he said. "The newer ones uptown are fancier, but I like the atmosphere here."

"And the food," I suggested.

"And the food. You think Bush's surge is going to work over there in Iraq?" he asked out of the blue, causing me to remember a couple of his boys were old enough for military service.

"Haven't had a lot of time to keep up with the news, but from what I can tell, things seemed to be getting a little better over there. Not so many caskets coming home."

"Yeah. Wooing of the Sunnis has helped. What do they call it? The Sunni Awakening?" Apparently that was all he wanted on that subject. "How you doing, buddy?" he asked.

"Frustrated."

"So this is going to be a therapy session." He grabbed a nacho and popped it into his mouth, its crunch only slightly dulled by melted cheese.

I pulsed air through my lips. "I'd rather work for a lawyer than a private citizen any day. I keep running into little signals that the man I'm working for—or at least his family—is somehow involved in all of this."

"Okay, this looks like a long session, so let's order something to eat."

After the waitress left with our order of steak fajitas with black beans, rice, and sopapillas, I ran through everything I had on the Alfano case while Gene devoured his cheesy snacks and went through two bottles of Coors. When I finished, he wiped his lips with a napkin.

"Could be you're right about your client double-teaming you, but it doesn't have to be the Alfano family. I'd say the De Falco organization would be as interested in Lando's position as anyone. Fifty million is a lot of motive. Looks like a bigger motivator for that side of the equation than the other."

"That's true, but I don't keep stumbling over their people."

"You work for the Alfanos. They're going to be all over your case. But this Santillanes fellow, you don't know who he worked for. He could have been a minder for Alfano, but he could just as well have belonged to De Falco."

I listened to a few other thoughts he had on the case while we ate. I wasn't really hungry, but he hadn't wanted to eat alone, so he ended up with a couple of good-sized doggy bags to take home.

I had no new insights as I headed back downtown after leaving the restaurant, but Gene had said one thing that stuck in my mind. He'd complimented me on using a "local resource" as he termed Jazz Penrod. PIs gather information from locals every day of the week. Were there others out there I could tap?

I SPENT a few minutes on the Internet researching small aircraft after I got back to the office. When I had suggested to Gaines the plane on the rim of Black Hole Canyon might have been a Piper Cub, it was simply because that name had popped into my mind. I'd seen many World War II posters of the heroic little Army Air Force craft running patrols and ferrying passengers. But after my search, I believed the airplane *had* been a Piper, or one very much like it.

The Piper J-3, which had been produced throughout the war and for a short while thereafter, was a tail-dragging aircraft. It was small and relatively quiet—standing only eighty inches high and twenty-two feet long with a wingspan slightly over thirty-five feet. The original craft had a twelve-gallon tank, which gave it a 190-mile range at a speed of 80 mph. The plane was made for a primitive strip like the one at Black Hole, and there were still plenty of them around.

When Hazel and Charlie joined me at my small conference table in the corner of my office a few minutes later, I asked Hazel to search the Federal Aviation Administration's web page for any aircraft owned by the known parties, including the corporations.

"You can search registrations by N-Number, name, make/model, dealer, or territory," I explained. "You'll have to go by name."

"N-Numbers?" Hazel asked.

"Those are the letters displayed on the tail fin or fuselage of all fixed-wing aircraft. The first letter *N* identifies a plane registered in the US. The letters and numbers that follow designate not only the specific plane but also serve as the radio call sign for that craft."

"I assume you want all aircraft registered to our interested parties, not just Pipers."

"Right. Charlie, you get on the horn and call any local landing fields you can find in the Four Corners area and everything west back toward California. You're looking for a small plane with one or two men who would have refueled somewhere between August 18 and August 21. If you locate anything that fits, get a description of the plane, the N-Number, and the pilot and any passengers.

"Start with the small, out-of-the-way fields, those with a windsock and no control tower. The pilot had to use part of his fuel to fly to the reservation, so initially stick to fields within a hundred miles or so of Farmington. If you locate the craft, then try and trace it west... or wherever."

"You're sure banking on this mystery plane being from California," Charlie said.

Before I could respond, my cell phone went off. It was Jazz. He sounded excited.

"Think I'm onto something. I just wanted you to know I'm heading out to the rez so you might not be able to get hold of me. Phone service is spotty where I'm going. When are you coming back?"

"Monday morning. What have you found?"

"Might not be anything, but I'll know by the time you get here."

The phone went dead before I had a chance to ask questions. My callback went to voice mail.

The call worried me. Had Jazz phoned to let me know he was on the job, or did he really have something and was concerned I'd be unable to reach him? Was he biting off more than he could chew?

I turned to my two companions. "Okay, you have your assignments. Paul and I are taking two days to play golf, and then I'm heading back to Farmington Monday morning."

"Monday's a holiday," Hazel said. "Why not go back Tuesday? You need a rest."

"Two days are more than I usually take. No, I need to go back Monday and start looking for Lando. My instinct tells me to stick close to where he was last seen. I just pray the kid is okay."

Chapter 20

I NORMALLY get charged up over my cases, and while I *was* wrapped up in the mystery of Lando Alfano's disappearance, the prospect of two entire days with Paul took the Alfanos and their problems right out of my mind. If Jazz developed something from his trip to the rez, he'd let me know. In that case, I'd have to leave my loving companion and return to the job. I took the selfish approach and hoped that the phone didn't ring. Fate was with me. It didn't. Two days of easy companionship with the most wonderful man on the planet and three nights of coupling passionately with the one person I loved drained me physically but restored me emotionally and intellectually. Admittedly I would have enjoyed it a bit more had I been able to reach Jazz. But he'd warned me he was heading into country where cell phone service was spotty.

Monday raced around all too quickly, and leaving Paul that morning was difficult for both of us. My travels in this Bisti murder business was our first significant separation since his kidnapping a year ago. While he's no pasty-faced weakling, I knew he still occasionally suffered flashbacks, and I wanted to be there for support. Nonetheless, we both knew I had a job to do. He offered to take me to the Double Eagle Airport, but I figured it would be easier on both of us for me to drive myself.

Jim Gray's Cessna was available, so I chartered it for my 190-mile return trip to Farmington. After drinking my fill of the ever-changing panorama passing below the wings, I took advantage of Jim's experience as a pilot to test my theory about a small plane landing and taking off from the hardpan beside Black Hole Canyon. He agreed a Piper J-3 was a logical candidate for that sort of strip and suggested I contact the Piper Club, an organization of Piper aircraft owners and admirers. Many of them knew one another and might be able to help locate the mysterious plane.

Then he proceeded to throw cold water on my theory by naming a number of other fixed-wing aircraft capable of utilizing the same rough field. His own Skycatcher, for example, needed only 420 feet of ground roll for landing and 770 for takeoff. And why a fixed wing? According to Jim, a helicopter would be ideal for such a maneuver, although he did admit those birds made an entirely different noise that somehow attracted more attention than the buzz of small planes.

When we reached the Farmington area, Jim swung west to take a look at the Black Hole Canyon strip. I had trouble finding the place from the air, but once I got us in the general vicinity, he located the strip quickly. Jim buzzed it a couple of times and decided he would not hesitate to set down there. He also pointed out a couple of other nearby spots that had been used by aircraft recently. Jazz was probably right; this was an area for importing contraband.

I drove a clone of the vehicle I'd rented a few days ago from the Four Corners Regional Airport and went straight to the Trail's End. As soon as I'd settled in and freshened up, I tried dialing Jazz to let him know I was back. Mindful of his warning Friday, I was surprised when he answered.

"Glad you called. Think I've found something." He sounded a million miles away, as his voice went in and out. I had a mental image of a huge flock of geese flying between our phones and interrupting the signal. Of course that's not the way things worked, but that's what flashed through my mind.

"What is it?"

"Can I meet you tonight when I get back to Farmington? Can't hear too good right now."

"What time will that be?"

Even through the tinny, uncertain reception, I sensed the smile in his voice. "About dinnertime."

"Right. I should have guessed. Where?"

"How about the Sidewinder?"

"That dump?"

"They got good food."

"All right, but I won't buy you booze. What time?"

We settled on a time, and then I reported my return to Special Agent John Gaines. Apparently Santillanes's murder was keeping him in Farmington, and I wasn't too sure he was happy about that. He listened to my information on the Alfano/Sabelito seesaw without enthusiasm but asked me to put it in writing. I had foreseen the request and had Hazel's neatly typed narrative ready to deliver, with a second copy for

Lonzo Joe. The agent's lack of a reaction was hard to read. It could mean anything from he already knew about it to he didn't want to admit a private investigator had beaten the feds to the punch.

"Any leads on Lando Alfano's whereabouts?" I asked.

"Nothing."

"Not even a whiff?"

"Not even a whiff. How about you?"

"Nothing." I fed him his own answer.

"Would you tell me if you did have anything?"

"Absolutely. I want the kid found. I think he's in danger." I asked if he knew anything about the Norville murder. He didn't have jurisdiction on that one, but it obviously tied into his case.

He had been in communication with both the San Juan County Sheriff's Office and the BLM and condescended to share what he knew of Dana Norville's autopsy report.

"Did the coroner confirm the kid was raped?" I asked when he finished.

"He confirmed the sexual activity and said the penetration had been unusually traumatic. Yeah, he termed it rape."

"Which makes it unlikely Lando was the killer."

"Maybe yes and maybe no. If they had a falling out over the Penrod kid, Alfano could have forced himself on Norville after a fight. If they were steady lovers, chances are good they wouldn't use protection."

"Yes, but it's more likely the rapist was the killer." I thought for a minute. "It could have been some of the local citizens exercising their well-documented objections to people who are *different*."

"That's a possibility," Gaines admitted. "Although my money's still on Alfano."

"Don't forget about Santillanes. Did his DNA match the semen on Norville?"

"Dunno. Norville's Detective Joe's case."

"Yes, it is, but the cases overlap."

"True, and we're cooperating."

"What did Santillanes's autopsy tell you?"

The coroner had confirmed the man was killed by a single gunshot wound to the right temple from a .38 caliber handgun but found little else of interest. But the doctor had ruled out Santillanes's belt as Dana's murder weapon. The LA PI had run a sloppy shop, so the FBI had not been able to determine who hired him. A numbers dump on the man's cell phone showed he had been in constant contact with a throwaway cellular phone with an LA number. That didn't mean much except that it had been bought in the city. Gaines could identify the general area where the calls went by the routing, but that would take time.

"Have you had any luck in tracing Aggie's movements prior to the murder?" I asked.

The response was prompt and firm. "I'm not prepared to discuss that subject. What are you going to do now?"

"Nose around and see if I can find any trace of a stranger wandering the area."

"You can probably come up with a couple of dozen, but I doubt any of them will be Orlando Alfano."

My string had run out; mutual cooperation seemed to be at an impasse for the moment. We closed our conversation, and I headed for the Crime Lab at FPD where Lonzo Joe had an office. He wasn't in, but I dropped off a copy of the report I'd given to Gaines.

Dix Lee was working this holiday. She sat at a desk managing to look delicate in her uniform—well, not delicate maybe, but pretty. She had a couple of John Doe vagrants in lockup and agreed to give me a look at both. Since the FPD doesn't have its own jail, we got in her unit and dropped down to the Bloomfield Highway heading east. A few miles later, she turned north on Andrea Drive and parked in a lot beside a sprawling dark brown building boasting the flag pole and xeriscaping that seemed to be required of government buildings in high desert climes.

The San Juan County Adult Detention Center was a 1,000-bed facility that housed inmates for a maximum of 364 days for all of the Four Corners law enforcement authorities, including federal. It took only minutes to determine neither of her John Does was my client's son, and not much longer to rule out any John Doe inmates placed there by other jurisdictions.

I was impressed with the center. The place was so new it had not yet acquired the atmosphere of despair and suppressed violence evident in most jails and prisons, although there were the ceaseless noise of rumbling conversations, yelled instructions from the guards, and the clang of metal doors. Those come the moment the first inmates enter the facility. The despair and cruelty and violence would quickly follow.

As soon as we got back to the FPD parking lot, I thanked Dix and returned to the motel room to wash up and get ready to meet Jazz. My phone buzzed just before I walked out the door. It was Anthony Alfano—the old Anthony Alfano from our first phone call.

"What the hell are you doing, Vinson?" he bellowed.

"Looking for your son, Alfano," I answered in a calm voice.

"By investigating me?"

Oh, hell. Well, Charlie had given me fair warning.

"Why do you think I'm investigating you? You said the FBI had already been around. They always investigate the family in situations like this."

"The fuck you say. It's a private investigator doing the poking around. Last time I heard, the FBI didn't hire private investigators in Los Angeles. But I know somebody who said he did. I'm paying a sleazebag to investigate myself?"

"Whoa there, buster. I'm no sleazebag, and I don't hire sleazebags. Maybe it never occurred to you that someone in your own organization might be responsible for what happened to your son, but it did to me. I hear there's a power struggle going on over your wife's money with several people's fortunes riding on the outcome."

"Lando's not in the company," Alfano shot back at me. "He opted out. Maybe someday, but right now he's in school."

"Don't try to snow me. He's not in the company hierarchy, but he's sure as hell in the family. I hear his position on the De Falco acquisition is key to the outcome. And before you leap to conclusions, Aggie never said a word about any of this, which pisses me off too. Being up-front would have saved a lot of time and expense. And if you don't like the way I'm doing things, fire me."

The phone went silent a moment. When he spoke again, I heard the worried father, not the indignant wine mogul. "No, keep on it. Looks to me like you're learning more than the feds at this point. And who knows what the sheriff's people are doing? By God, if you find out anyone of mine had a hand in this, I'll kill him myself."

"There are other people involved in the acquisition of De Falco besides members of your immediate family. I don't know how desperate the owners are to sell, and I don't know the situation with your son-in-law. He stands to make a sizeable commission, doesn't he?"

"Yes, and he's desperate for it." Alfano's tone let me know he did not particularly care for his daughter's husband. Did the Alfano and Sabelito offspring go out of their way to piss off their elders in the choice of mates?

I PULLED into the Sidewinder's parking lot late that afternoon just as the sun was pulling everything off its easel and slinging it across the sky in an ostentatious display of color. I desperately hoped Lando Alfano, wherever he was, was enjoying the show, but my faith was getting shaky. I glanced around the crowded lot to see if Bud Yarborough's truck was there. There were a couple that could have been his, but I wasn't certain. As I stepped through the door, the feel of sawdust beneath my shoes took me by surprise once again. Not many bars used the stuff anymore. The place was packed with holiday blue-collar revelers.

The hulking form of Riley Penrod straddled a stool at the bar, and I wondered if he was there to defend against Bud and his bunkmate, Oscar. Jazz stood and motioned me back to the same rear booth Yarborough and his three pals had occupied when Aggie and I last paid the joint a visit. There was someone else sharing the kid's bench seat.

Jazz grasped my hand, unleashed his killer smile, and nodded at the man beside him. "This is my brother, Henry Secatero. Henry, this is Mr. Vinson."

The Lord made them good in the Secatero and Penrod families. The strong hand that reached out and took mine was attached to a brawny forearm covered with tight, glossy skin that reminded me of a newly minted copper penny. The man's biceps rippled with the minimal effort of our handshake. His chest threatened to tear the seams from a T-shirt with a Red Power logo. Jazz was "sleek-handsome," his half brother was "rough trade–handsome." A menacing air rode his wide shoulders like a cloak, but I did not get the feeling he was a ruffian, merely a cautious man always on the lookout for a racial slight. I judged him to be about ten years older than his brother. Gene's comment about "local resources" ran through my mind. Was this another one?

"Mr. Vinson." His voice came up out of his nether regions. If this guy sang, he would be a bass—or a basso. That conjured a vision of Henry in full regalia banging on a huge buffalo-skin drum and chanting a war song, whipping a clan of dog soldiers into a killing frenzy. His coal black eyes studied me intently, no doubt calculating how much of a risk to his baby brother I represented.

"Glad you can join us, Henry. Thanks for tipping Jazz off to the parked car. You uncovered a murder."

"Yeah, that's what I hear. Bad stuff."

I motioned toward the bar. "I see you brought your uncle as backup, Jazz. Something got you worried?"

"Naw. I just didn't want Yarborough and his crew interrupting us."

"You want something to eat?"

"Always," the kid answered. His brother grunted.

After we ordered and instructed the waiter to give Riley whatever he wanted, I leaned back in the booth, which was amazingly uncomfortable for a business establishment that prospered when its patrons lingered. "So what do you have for me?"

Without a word, Henry pulled a black nylon tote from the seat between them. It was a carry-on bag commonly used for airline travel, one with straps to be used as a lightweight backpack. It was an expensive piece.

"Whoa, where did that come from?" I asked without touching it.

"That came from old One-Eye Begay's hogan," Henry growled. "This came from a pawnshop in Shiprock." He placed a soft leather toilet kit with the initials "OSA" embossed in gold on the table.

There was not much doubt what those initials stood for—Orlando Selvanus Alfano.

Chapter 21

JAZZ LEANED back in the Sidewinder booth and laughed aloud, clearly getting a kick out of my reaction. "There's probably more of Lando's stuff spread all over the reservation, but this is what we've found so far. Good work, huh?"

"Damned good work, but I wish you'd left them where you found them so we could let the FBI recover them."

"Those guys?" Henry snorted. "They'd just send the tribal police to get them—if they ever found out about them."

"What's the story?" I asked.

Henry nodded at the black nylon bag. "One-Eye's a superstitious old goat. Claims he found this in an arroyo south of his place. Says a shape-shifter's been hanging around, but a witch doesn't leave stuff like this laying in the sand. What he saw was a flesh and blood human. Maybe this Lando dude."

"So he took the bag home with him? What did he intend doing with it?"

"Says he found stuff scattered around in the sand. He put it back in the bag and took it home. It was all shirts and pants, you know, clothes. One of the shirts has that Alfano guy's initials on the pocket, so we figured it was his bag. Anyway, some of the duds looked like they'd fit one of One-Eye's great-grandsons, so he sent word to the chapter house for his kinfolks to come by. That's how I heard about it. When Jazz came putzing around, I took him down to see the old man."

"Cost us forty bucks to get it," Jazz said.

"Okay, I'll reimburse you. Don't suppose you got a receipt."

Jazz held up a tattered scrap of lined tablet paper. The writing was clearly not that of an old man, but the barely legible "BEGAY" at the bottom was. More a narrative than a mere receipt, it set out—presumably in One-Eye's own words—how and where the bag was found and stated he'd turned it over to Jasper Penrod for forty dollars.

"It cost us to ransom the shaving kit too," Jazz added. "The pawnshop guy wanted a hundred, but we got him down to sixty. Got a receipt for that one too. Old Lando had some good stuff. The electric razor in there musta cost him a couple of hundred bucks."

As I sat staring at the items, Jazz grew impatient. "Aren't you gonna go through them. You know, looking for clues?"

I shook my head. "No. I'm going to call Agent Gaines and let him do the looking. So many people have touched them already they're probably not going to tell us anything, but we should at least let the lab try."

"Hey, man," Henry objected. "My fingerprints are all over those things. Inside and out. Both of ours. We looked through the stuff."

"That's okay. You're the guys who recovered the items. You'll have to tell your story, but that's probably the end of it."

Henry stirred uncomfortably, the muscles in his torso roiling like angry water currents beneath his shirt. "Didn't intend to get mixed up with those guys. They're bad news."

"You have any reason to be worried, Henry? Let's lay the cards on the table. Did you find these items the way you said?"

Both men nodded.

"Did you keep anything from either bag?" They shook their heads and I continued. "Are the feds looking at either one of you for anything, whether or not it's connected to the Alfano disappearance?"

In response to an "uh-uh" and a "no way," respectively, I relaxed. "Then there's no problem. This might even earn you some brownie points with the local FBI agent."

"I just don't like being on their radar screen, man," Jazz's brother muttered.

The waiter interrupted with our meal. Jazz had ordered a Sidewinder Gut-Buster, a massive cheeseburger with spicy nachos on the side. Henry had gone practical and ordered a sirloin with baked potato. I settled for a bowl of green chili stew and flour tortillas. I don't know what Riley Penrod had because he continued to sit across the room at the bar. Jazz said his uncle was expecting a lady friend.

We ate in relative silence, except for some personal joshing back and forth between the half brothers. It was almost comical the way Henry periodically swept the room with a hostile scowl on the lookout for predators. At the end of each of these glances, that pensive gaze always ended up on me. It was all I could do to keep from verbally renouncing all prurient interest in Jazz, but the Bard's warning about protesting too much put a rein on my tongue.

After finishing our meal, we adjourned to my car to take care of the financial details. Flashing a wad of money in a place like the Sidewinder was as risky as propositioning one of the roustabouts. I replaced what they'd spent on redeeming Lando's bags and then hired Jazz for another week. For good measure I made the same deal with Henry. After asking them to try to find other articles belonging to Lando, I cautioned that the FBI would be all over the place looking for the missing man, but I wanted to get to him first.

They assured me they'd get on it right away, and then we went our separate ways. Henry roared out of the parking lot on a new Harley, making me wonder if he worked at one of the coal mines on the reservation. Those were said to be good jobs.

Before following Jazz's Wrangler out onto the highway, I phoned the FBI office. It was closed, of course, but I left a detailed message telling Gaines of the objects I now had in my possession and how they were obtained. Then I drove back to the motel wondering if I had the self-discipline to keep from going through the contents of the bags. I didn't, of course, but I used my knuckles to root around in it so as not to leave fingerprints. I didn't worry about the ones on the handles. The absence of prints there would have raised suspicions. I found only clothing and personal items, nothing to help locate the missing man.

I left Lonzo a message saying I intended to turn the recovered articles over to the FBI. Then in the middle of considering whether to call Alfano and report the find of his son's clothing or wait until I had something more substantial, Aggie phoned.

"I'm flying out tomorrow and ought to be there around three," he said. "Will you be able to pick me up, or should I rent a car?"

"I'll pick you up. The big acquisition's all taken care of?" I asked.

"No, it's on hold."

"My guess is your mother won't consider the financing while she's worried about Lando." If I expected surprise, I was disappointed.

"The old man said you were on top of things. Yeah, she's digging in her heels until she knows Lando's okay."

"Which is probably good news for you."

"The only thing better would be to find Lando alive and well."

"Even if he backs the purchase of De Falco?"

"He won't." Aggie's response was delivered in a flat, even tone.

I spent five minutes telling him about the tote and the toilet kit, but after hanging up and turning out the light, I lay in the darkness worrying about whether I'd made a mistake. It was hard to know who to trust in this situation. Paranoia is a silent partner in my business.

GAINES CALLED while I was at breakfast the next morning and invited me to visit him at his office. I took my time finishing the meal before driving over. He had company. Lonzo Joe and Larry Plainer were both there waiting for me too. I dropped the Trail's End laundry bags containing Lando's recovered items on the desk.

Gaines just looked at the bags without touching anything. "Want to tell us about it?"

"I told everything to the telephone last night so you'd have a recording of it. Don't have much to add, but if you have questions, ask away."

"You bet we've got questions," Plainer started but leaned back in his chair when Gaines raised a hand.

"That was smart using the Penrod kid and his brother out on the reservation," Gaines said. "What made you think of it?"

"Isn't it obvious? They're the ones who found Santillanes."

"Yeah, but Santillanes was out there because that's where the landing strip is. The Alfano kid's Porsche was found south of Farmington, nowhere near the reservation."

"True, but that didn't mean there wasn't a reservation connection. Besides, Jazz Penrod gets around town while his brother listens for gossip on the reservation. It seemed a natural to me."

Gaines gazed at me steadily. "We'll have to talk to them, you know."

"Already told them to expect a call from you."

He nodded at the laundry bags. "Did anything in there tell you something you didn't already know?"

I hedged. "The kids went through it, as did the old man who found the nylon bag—and probably the pawnbroker who bought the toilet kit—so who knows what's been taken out of them. Penrod and Secatero say they didn't remove anything but admitted looking through the bags to see if they could find a clue to Lando's whereabouts."

"Not much doubt about the toilet kit being Alfano's. It's got his initials embossed on it, but why do you think the black bag is his?" Lonzo asked.

"An initialed shirt pocket. And it's the kind of clothing he wears. Yeah, I unzipped it and took a look inside without disturbing anything. And it's expensive. I'm certain it belongs to my client's son."

"Have you talked to the pawnbroker over in Shiprock?"

"No. Figured we'd do that together."

"You leave that to us."

"Agent Gaines, my job is to find Orlando Alfano, and I intend to do my job. I am well aware you will grill the moneylender in Shiprock, but I'm going to speak to him too. I just figured it would be simpler to do it together."

His eyes studied me coolly for a moment before he stood. "Let's go."

I almost laughed aloud at the dismay painted on Plainer's face, but the BLM agent had been reined in once, so he kept his comments to himself. Lonzo smiled quietly and gave an almost imperceptible shake of his head.

I rode with Gaines, while Lonzo followed in a county unit with Plainer as his passenger. Gaines did not seem inclined to talk, so I concentrated on the view outside the window. The trip wasn't long, but it was interesting. We stayed on State Highway 64, bypassing the town of Kirtland, founded in the 1880s by the Latter-Day Saints and presently boasting a population of around 6,000—and Fruitland. I didn't know much about Fruitland, but Upper Fruitland across the San Juan River was predominately a Navajo town. One of these days, I was going to visit both.

Before long the huge volcanic plug called Shiprock hove into view like a massive, oceangoing vessel improbably landlocked on the high desert plain. A bustling commercial center bearing the same name sprawled across the mesa about seven miles short of the monolith.

The Shiprock Pawnshop was right on the highway, housed in a one-story cinderblock building with two display windows crammed full of Native American jewelry and crafts. A weathered, oak coup stick festooned with eagle feathers on a beaded leather band was the centerpiece of one display; a short lance similarly adorned dominated the other. I took a closer look. Hawk feathers, not eagle.

Lonzo caught my double take and muttered, "Replicas. Tourist junk."

Abe Novich, the owner, was a small brown man with a lean face and a jutting nose. His eyes sat well back in his head, which gave him a sly, crafty appearance. Given the trade he had adopted, the look likely reflected who he was. Pawnshop owners often have reputations as cheats, but in truth both sides of the pawn game sought the upper hand. Unless they were sharp, the lenders were victims as often as they dealt a bad hand to others. A long-time pawnbroker friend in Albuquerque was one of the most knowledgeable men I knew. His expertise covered an astounding range of subjects. He could spot a fake Anasazi pot as quickly as he could pick out a genuine Han Dynasty urn.

Gaines greeted the man by name—apparently they'd had dealings before—and then introduced me. The shop owner gave Lonzo a glare, which likely meant they'd crossed paths, and then fixed me with a fishy eye without saying a word. Plainer, the shopkeeper totally ignored. People skills were not included in his résumé.

The FBI agent laid Lando's toilet kit on the counter, and Novich's face revealed he'd known all along the thing would prove to be trouble. In response to questions, he shuffled back to his office and started leafing through small pieces of paper. The computer age had not reached this store. Eventually he came back and uttered his first complete sentence since we entered.

"Old man Hernandez brought it in. Crespido Hernandez," he clarified. "Claimed he picked it up in a flea market down in Albuquerque."

Gaines took Novich over his story several times. I gathered from the tone of the conversation Shiprock Pawn had had a few problems with its tickets over the years. We learned nothing beyond the original statement that Mr. Hernandez had brought in the kit.

As we left the pawnshop, Lonzo got a call on his radio and had to take his leave. Plainer opted to go with Gaines and me. We stopped by the closest chapter house and prevailed upon someone named Atcitty to take us out to see Hernandez, who lived in a traditional hogan with rough timber sides and a sod roof located ten miles from nowhere. The single door to the one-room dwelling faced due east.

Gaines, who apparently knew nothing about Navajo etiquette, parked, got out of the vehicle, and marched up to the hogan. If he'd read Tony Hillerman's popular Leaphorn and Chee mystery series, he would have known to wait in the vehicle until the occupant signaled he was ready to receive visitors. The agent banged on the door aggressively, announcing in a loud voice he was a representative of the Federal Bureau of Investigation. Hernandez demonstrated his opinion of the mighty FBI by taking his own sweet time answering the call.

A stocky, mahogany-hued man, who must have been in his sixties yet looked in the prime of life, eventually stepped outside. His broad, heavy-featured face showed neither surprise nor curiosity. The small, sharp eyes moved restlessly over the three of us and settled on our Navajo guide.

"*Yah-tah-heh*," Hernandez said in a deep voice.

"*Heh.*" Our guide was considerably younger and less formal than his elder. After an awkward pause, Atcitty spoke to Hernandez a full minute in his native tongue. By the end of the monologue, I suspected Hernandez had known our mission all along. Then Atcitty turned to Gaines. "Okay. You ask, and I'll put it to him."

Plainer frowned. "He doesn't speak English?"

"Not much. Better if you ask me."

Under these circumstances the interview was something less than ideal. The old man eventually invited us inside to search for other articles that might have belonged to Lando Alfano. We found nothing. Hernandez agreed to take us to where he had picked up the leather kit, but he refused to get into the car. Instead the old man threw a blanket over a bony pinto in a brush corral at the side of the hogan and set off on horseback across the desert hardpan. Atcitty elected to remain in the brush shelter as the rest of us piled into the SUV. It wasn't long before we came to a long, narrow ditch that rendered the SUV incapable of proceeding any farther—as I suspected both this old curmudgeon and Atcitty had known would happen. Reluctantly we got out and plodded along in the heat. The sun had an extra bite in the high plateau country.

Hernandez, who had pulled up while we got out of the car, wheeled his mount, leaving us to scramble along afoot in his wake, dodging fist-sized rocks and the pinto's horse apples. He led us over the lip of an arroyo that ran in a generally east-west direction and turned his pony up the sandy bottom. After about a mile, he halted and dismounted.

"Here," he announced. I was pretty sure a smile hid behind those dark eyes as he watched the three of us struggle up the bottom of the dry wash.

"Was there any sign of whoever left it?" Gaines asked.

The old man paused but finally admitted he understood English by answering. "No. No sign. Nobody. Wasn't no man."

Plainer had had his fill of the games. "If it wasn't a man, what was it?"

I am absolutely certain the corners of the man's thick lips curled as he answered. "Witch. They was green lightning night before." The thick shoulders rose and fell. "Witch."

"What the hell are you talking about?" Plainer demanded.

"How long have you been out here in the Four Corners area, Agent?" I asked.

"About six months."

"Let me guess. Your last assignment was back east somewhere."

"New Jersey."

"That figures. There's a southwestern phenomenon known as green ball lightning. Nobody's quite sure what it is, but the best guess is it's a small meteorite containing copper, which burns green. Some of the Native Americans believe that's not the case at all. They figure it's the way witches travel around."

The old man grunted at my explanation.

"Mr. Hernandez, were there any footprints? Anything at all?" Gaines asked.

"Here." He stopped before a scraggly piñon. "Maybe where somebody set down to rest."

"Did you look for anything else he… uh…." Gaines tripped over his tongue in an effort to avoid offending the old man again. "I mean, anything it might have left behind?"

The Indian hesitated a minute before waving a broad hand up and down the wash. "Nothing else. Look maybe a mile."

I was unable to remain on the sidelines as an observer any longer. "Have any strangers been hanging around, Mr. Hernandez?" Gaines gave me a look but didn't say anything.

"Old One-Eye's shape-shifter."

"Did you see him too?" I asked.

"Uh-uh."

There was little more to see, although we split up and walked the arroyo for a distance in either direction. All Plainer and I turned up was a cranky little sidewinder, which we gave a wide berth. They are aggressive little creatures, more so than the larger rattlers.

As we reassembled to begin the trek back to the hogan, Plainer looked at the steep sides of the arroyo and groaned aloud. I knew how he felt; my knees were already complaining. The old gunshot wound in my right thigh throbbed from the exertion. Street shoes are not made for soft sand or loose rocks or steep, crumbling clay walls. The pinto, with Hernandez aboard, had little trouble getting out of the gulch and was almost out of sight by the time we topped the gully. Sweat-drenched, we recovered the car and paused at the hogan long enough to pick up our guide. Gaines cranked up the air-conditioning, and we were all thoroughly chilled by the time we arrived at the Begay hogan.

That interview was a virtual rerun of the previous, except One-Eye spoke not a word of English and dwelt a great deal more on shape-shifters—talk that made Atcitty noticeably nervous—without coming up with a good reason why a witch would have any use for a costly nylon bag with dirty laundry—albeit expensive dirty laundry.

The only real surprise was that One-Eye wasn't one-eyed at all. He merely talked with a habitual squint, which made his right eye virtually disappear behind folds of chestnut-colored flesh.

Chapter 22

THE SPECK in the New Mexico sky gradually morphing into a white Mitsubishi Marquise stirred mixed emotions. Aggie Alfano was likeable, cultured, and had a good sense of humor; he was easy to be around. Yet I harbored a growing belief that the two murders had their origins inside the Alfano sphere of influence—if not within the family itself. At the very least, they somehow tied back into the Sabelito money and Alfano's bid for De Falco Fine Wines. That kind of suspicion tended to poison a relationship.

Aggie made a faultless landing and nosed the Mitsu over to a tie-down. I watched as he emerged to give instructions to a lineman on the care and feeding of his mechanical baby. Then he turned and approached with outstretched hand.

"BJ, good to see you. Anything new?" he asked, smiling.

"Not much." I accepted his shake and pulled him toward the parking lot. "Let's talk in the car."

As we drove to the motel, I sketched the events of the last few days, and he gave me the developments on his end.

The De Falco purchase was stalled because his mother, worried over her younger son, claimed she was too ill and in no shape to deal with the transaction. Alfano was furious; De Falco was impatient and threatening to withdraw the offer of sale. His brother-in-law was about to blow a fuse. William Vitrillo, Aggie made clear, was not on the best of terms with most of the Alfano clan. Aggie considered him a boorish opportunist, which made me wonder why his sister married the guy in the first place. But there's no accounting for taste in that clan, especially in the matter of mates.

A lot of people in the Alfano organization stood to gain or lose on the De Falco deal. Frank Baratta, old Paolo's son, wanted the transaction to proceed because it would double his sales staff and enhance his importance to the organization. Ariel Gonda, the treasurer, opposed the purchase, claiming the acquisition was too big to digest so soon after their last buyout. Tom Scavo, who headed the labs, was eager for the opportunity to begin experimenting with the De Falco recipes. The motives of the De Falco people were less clear, except for the dollars that would flow their way.

"Does your sister support her husband's position?"

"All the way. She gets a healthy income from the Sabelito Trust, but she's anxious for Bill to make it on his own. Frankly, the man goes through money like so much confetti. He always seems to be strapped."

I had reserved a room for Aggie, and Melissa checked him in efficiently and effusively. Women reacted to Aggie Alfano the way men did to Jazz Penrod.

While he freshened up, I phoned the office from my room. Hazel had located two aircraft in the Alfano name. One, a Gulfstream executive jet, was under Alfano Vineyards. The second was Aggie's plane, which was his own despite the Alfano business logo painted on the tail fin. The De Falco organization also owned a jet, but it was too large to have utilized the primitive field at Black Hole. Hazel said the N-Numbers and plane specifications were already in my email, a not-so-subtle reminder to check my laptop occasionally.

Charlie had contacted two-dozen remote airfields and turned up a couple of possibilities. A single-engine, two-seater aircraft had landed at a small field in southeastern Utah with no passengers. The pilot, whose name meant nothing to me, said he was headed to Salt Lake City. Charlie was confident he could trace the plane back to its point of origin.

The second was a larger craft with two men aboard that set down in northern Arizona, fueled up, and took off for Phoenix. Charlie was on that one as well.

"BJ, there's a hundred little private fields out there. Some of them's cow pastures with a homemade sock and nothing more. They store gas in cans with hand pumps and probably refuel drug and other contraband runners. We're not going to get anything out of them."

"Probably not, but keep looking. Anything else?"

"Yeah, they say the De Falco buyout's on hold."

"That's what Aggie told me."

"The story about the missing Alfano kid broke in California two days ago, and the whole valley's gaga over what's going on. Some claim the pressure on the kid got so bad he ran away with his boyfriend. Others say the old man chased him off because of the boyfriend. The rest just mutter about dark and dirty deeds. This Alfano clan's got a rough history, especially a couple of generations back when they came over from the mother country. So far, nobody's mentioned the murders. I guess the press hasn't found out about them yet."

I asked how he and Hazel were doing, and he said they were handling things okay. Was he purposefully misunderstanding me, or was my question too oblique? I let it go.

AGGIE HAD changed into dark blue walking shorts with all sorts of buttoned and Velcroed pockets, presumably his climbing attire, topped by a burgundy knit pullover. His black leather ankle boots were obviously hand fashioned, most likely in Italy. The outfit heightened his resemblance to his younger brother. I tossed him a beer from the room's tiny refrigerator, and we sat down at the table beside the bed. I filled him in on every detail, inferring—but not outright proclaiming—my suspicion that the danger came from the west.

"The man who hocked Lando's shaving kit didn't see anyone around his place?" Aggie asked.

"Hernandez—his name is Crespido Hernandez—claims he didn't see anyone. He took us to where he found the kit, and there was no sign anyone had been there."

"Why wasn't it in the traveling bag the other fellow found?"

"Maybe Lando was using it when something interrupted him. Of course, it's possible the kit was left there by someone else."

He sat for a long time with a frown creasing his brow and then chose to ignore my last remark. "That 'shape-changer'? Do you think it was Lando that fellow saw?"

"Who knows what One-Eye Begay saw?"

"I just don't understand why Lando would abandon his stuff."

I sipped my diet cola. "Could be a number of reasons. Exhaustion. Dehydration. He could have been halfway out of his head from wandering around the desert. Or maybe he's hurt and not physically able to carry the bag—although it wasn't heavy."

"Or he was running from someone and had to abandon the bag. Which was found first, the tote bag or the shaving gear?"

"That's a little hard to pin down. Both men are vague about dates. We know the pawn was made August 28. That was a Tuesday."

"Was that before or after Santillanes was murdered?"

"After, but that doesn't tell us anything. It could have been found before he was killed."

"You say there's an airfield out where you found him?"

"Looks like one. A primitive one."

Aggie sat up straight. "Take me out there. I want to see it."

"Okay, but there's not much to see. The wind does a hell of a job sweeping away evidence."

"I don't care. Take me, BJ. Please."

We headed west toward Shiprock in my rental. I watched Aggie out of the corner of my eye as we turned off the highway and started up the rough grade leading to the lip of Black Hole Canyon. When we arrived he got out of the car and took off toward the nearest pile of charred ashes. I leaned against the fender and watched as he went from one dead signal fire to the next. He walked with his head down and his hands in his pockets, kneeling occasionally to study the ground more closely. A quarter of a mile in the distance, he stood staring off to the south for a long time. What was going through his mind? Fear for his brother or fear of exposure?

He turned and started back, motioning me forward as he walked. I met him halfway up the makeshift airfield.

"You're right. This is a drag-tail marking." He indicated a faint scratch in the hardpan. "There's not much left, but from what I see, it was probably a Piper like you thought."

"What other type of plane can land and take off here?"

"A number. It could handle anything up to the size of my Mitsu, but I wouldn't want to try it at night with only bonfires for light. A pilot needs to see where he's going and when he's approaching touchdown."

"Wouldn't the instruments tell him that?"

"The altitude out here's close to a mile above sea level, but yeah, you could make an instrument landing. Personally I'd want eyeball contact on a rough field like this."

He stood observing barely discernable scratches in the dirt, obviously fretting over his brother. I gave him a few minutes to himself before interrupting his thoughts.

"Have you ever heard your father—or anyone else, for that matter—mention Hugo Santillanes?" I nodded toward the lip of Black

Hole Canyon. "Could the PI who was killed out here be an associate of your brother-in-law, Vitrillo?"

"Until he got himself killed, I'd never heard of him. He could be Vitrillo's. He could be De Falco's. Hell, he could even be Papa's, for that matter. I'm not privy to all the old man's connections."

"He says Santillanes wasn't his."

"My father isn't into full disclosure."

"You're saying he doesn't always play straight."

His confirmation of my supposition was interrupted by a call from Jazz on my cell phone. He wanted another meet.

AGGIE AND I rendezvoused with Jazz at a café on the extreme western edge of Farmington. Henry, who was taking vacation time from his job to play detective, was with his brother. A few minutes after being introduced to Aggie, he flexed his shoulders and relaxed, signaling he had decided this new guy was okay.

Jazz barely waited to order his steak and potatoes before getting down to business. "I think we got two sightings, boss."

"Of Lando?" Aggie asked quickly.

"They're *could-be*'s. You know, *maybe*'s. Not actual identifications. Trouble is they're two different guys."

"Did you see either one of them?" I knew Jazz would recognize Lando.

"Uh-uh. We've been nosing around and came up with these possibilities. Funny thing, neither one of them was on the rez. They're in Farmington."

"Where in Farmington?"

"There's a viaduct west of town. Homeless guys hang out underneath there. You know, sleep and eat and talk. We hear there are two guys who match Lando's description—more or less."

"What do you mean, more or less?" I asked.

"Unshaven. Dirty. Ragged. But either one could be Lando."

Aggie popped up from his seat. "Let's go."

"Too early," Henry said. "They won't start gathering until later in the evening. They're out scrounging something to eat right now. And… uh, well, we think one of them took off already."

"A couple of men came around, and the dude we talked to said they made one of the guys real nervous," Jazz explained. "Claims he took off for Utah."

So the FBI and the Sheriff's Department were on the job after all. "This contact's sure the man was headed for Utah?"

"That's what he claims," Henry said.

"Who is this source?"

"The guy we talk to down there's called Shifty," Jazz said. "He's a vet that got messed up in some war and then got fed up with the military docs. Took off to make it on his own. Most of the time he gives you the straight stuff, but sometimes he goes off his rocker. You can usually tell when he's that way."

"And this is your hot lead?" Aggie scoffed.

Henry leveled a look at him. "How many leads do *you* have?"

"And he was okay when you spoke to him?" I asked Jazz. "This Shifty, I mean?"

"Yeah. He was lucid."

"What about the other lead? Same source?"

"Uh-huh, Shifty again. I showed him the picture you gave me, and he told us about the two guys that might be Lando. Like I said, one of them took off for Utah or somewhere, but the second Lando's still around, so far as Shifty knows. Although he hasn't seen the guy in a day or two."

We took time to eat, although Aggie didn't touch much of his plate. I understood he was anxious to be off. So was I, but Henry's assessment was right on target. We needed patience for the moment.

Chapter 23

EVENING WAS descending as Aggie and I trailed Jazz's Wrangler south on a side street that dipped down to skirt a large arroyo. There were already half a dozen homeless men and women sitting in the shadow of a gray concrete bridge that soared overhead. The windswept sage and rabbit bush appeared lush in the twilight—an illusion. A campfire danced in a ring of stones at one end of a bare patch of ground littered with trash. The air, still oppressive, was softening as the sun retired over the horizon.

Jazz and Henry bailed out of the Jeep and stood waiting for us. The half-dozen vagrants seemed to accept the two of them okay, but Aggie and I caused some agitation as we approached. Two of the group hastily vanished into the scrub on the opposite side of the arroyo. One of them was clearly a woman despite the dungarees and man's shirt camouflaging her figure; the other looked to be considerably older than Lando.

"Hey, Shifty," Jazz greeted a balding man with a florid complexion sitting cross-legged by himself, well away from the fire. The shoulders had probably been beefy back when he was doing calisthenics and marching over rugged mountain trails. Now they were thin and knobby with bone. Pale, delicate hands did not match the rest of him. Eyes like steel balls hid in a mass of wrinkles in an otherwise youngish face. Too old for the Iraq war. I pegged him as a Desert Storm veteran suffering from Gulf War syndrome.

"What's going down, Jazz? Who's that with you? You know I don't like outsiders."

"They're friends." Jazz squatted beside the man, his clean jeans and T-shirt a sharp contrast to Shifty's tattered olive-green field jacket and ragged desert camos. "They're all right. They're looking for that guy."

"Hello, Henry," Shifty said as if just noticing Jazz's companion. "What's up?"

"Like Jazz said, we're looking for that guy."

"What guy?"

"The one we talked to you about," Jazz said patiently. "You feeling okay? Need anything to eat? I got a chocolate bar."

The ball bearing eyes, almost hidden by lazy lids, turned greedy. "A big one?"

"Giant size," Jazz assured him, handing over a Kit Kat.

We lost Shifty for a couple of minutes while he clawed open the wrapping and stuffed his mouth, gulping the candy as if afraid someone stronger or hungrier might take it away from him. His head whipped from side to side, on guard for the enemy. When one of the other vagrants started for us, Jazz lifted his hands to show they were empty.

"I got no more, man. That's all there is."

Muttering to himself, the interloper, younger and healthier-looking than Shifty, turned away.

Our homeless vet cleaned his lips with the sleeve of a grimy jacket and licked his fingers before facing us again. "You ain't got nothing to drink, do you?" His expression at the shake of Jazz's head said he hadn't really expected one.

"This man wants to ask you some questions." Jazz motioned me forward. "His name is Mr. Vinson, and he's a friend of the guy who's missing. He thinks his friend is in trouble. You understand?"

Shifty flinched at my approach, but Jazz's hand on his arm seemed to suppress the man's flight response. Cautiously I held out the picture of Lando, but the homeless man didn't bother to look at it.

"You pulling my leg, Jazz?" Shifty asked. "That fella you looking for's standing right behind you. Where'd you get yourself all cleaned up, Young'un? They give you them new duds?"

Encouraged by Shifty's mistake, I said, "No, that's not the missing man. That's his brother. When did you see him last? Your friend, I mean."

"Young'un keeps to hisself. Don't talk to nobody. I tried to be sociable, but he wasn't having none of it. Ever notice how some fellas is suspicious of everbody? Well, that's him."

Aggie stepped forward and started to speak, but I held up my hand. It wouldn't take much to spook the guy, and we needed every bit of information he had.

"Tell me, Shifty, does this fellow have a name? Lando, maybe?"

"Never heard of no Lando. Never heard his name, neither. I just call him Young'un on account of that's the way he is. You know, young. You could tell he don't belong out here."

"Where does Young'un sleep?" I asked.

Shifty licked his lips with a thick tongue, searching for a residual taste of chocolate. "Right over yonder by that concrete support." He reinforced the statement with a nod of his head.

I caught Henry's eyes, and he quietly moved away in that direction. Aggie followed him a moment later.

"When did you see him last?"

"Been a coupla days. Maybe three."

"Do you know where he would go? Is there another place where people congregate?"

"Couple. But he'd be more likely to go off by hisself somewhere. He got jumpy."

"Of what?" Jazz asked.

"Them guys asking questions?"

When I asked if he knew who the men were, Shifty snorted. "Everbody knows those guys. One was wearing a suit." Shifty leaned close and lowered his voice. I was grateful for the waft of chocolate veiling the odors that came with him. "Spies."

"Spies? Spies for who?"

"The government, course. CIA. Seen a lot of them over in the desert. Mean bastards. Them first two claimed they was just lawmen, but they didn't fool me. That other one, he was better at it, but he was the same."

"What other one? How many men have been around asking questions?"

"Three that I seen. But with spies, you don't never know. Hell, you could be spies too." With that thought, he leaned back to give me a hard look.

"No, we're Young'un's friends and family, and we're worried about him."

Henry and Aggie returned, shaking their heads. They had found nothing. I turned back to Shifty, who was getting more nervous by the moment. Before long he would break. I managed to extract the information that Young'un had been hurt. He had a crusted scab on his face from a fall or a beating, and Shifty figured it for a beating. He didn't think the wound was serious, but allowed as to how that might have been why the kid was acting screwy.

"Shifty, just to be clear, this Young'un was the one who resembled this man standing here, right? You told Jazz about another man too. Remember?"

"What other'n? You mean Young'un?"

"No, we just talked about Young'un. I mean the other man."

Shifty's features twisted. "That's what I'm saying. Young'un."

I tumbled. "You called him Young'un too?"

Shifty cackled. "That's good. Young'un Two."

I accepted his misunderstanding of my words. "Yes, Young'un Two." I reached back and tugged Aggie's arm until he moved up beside me. "Concentrate now, Shifty. Which one of them resembled this man—Young'un One or Young'un Two?"

But Shifty was off on his own tangent. "Didn't like him. Wasn't friendly. That Young'un Two was hiding something." He gave his rooster crow again. "Ain't we all? But he was different."

"Where did this Young'un sleep?"

"All around. Never went to the same place twice. Moved around and kept his nose to the air. Always sniffing like he was smelling trouble in the wind."

"You said he went to Utah. How do you know if he wasn't friendly?" I asked.

"Heard him mumbling to hisself about Salt Lake City a coupla times. That's in Utah, ain't it? And when that last man showed up asking questions, he like to of blowed a gasket. He was scared, he was. Snuck off with his tail between his legs before the man got out of his car."

"Okay, but think, Shifty. Which one resembled my friend here?"

It was hopeless. We spent fifteen minutes squeezing a few more tidbits out of the addled man before giving up and retreating to Jazz's Wrangler.

The "suit" had obviously been Gaines. The second man, Lonzo Joe. But was the third man Santillanes, or was he someone on the trail of this other Young'un? Of course, he could also have been BLM Agent Plainer doing some snooping on his own. After discussing the possibilities, we decided that even though Shifty's facts were open to question, we had to run down both leads. Since the second fugitive might have been headed for Salt Lake, Aggie reluctantly agreed to fly up the next morning and see if he could find anything at that end. I used the cell phone to call a PI I knew up there who agreed to help Aggie search the homeless hangouts in the area. Jazz and I would start the search for the first Young'un in town while Henry would put his nose to the ground on the reservation.

Rather than dump money on Shifty, which he would probably spend on booze or drugs, we decided Jazz and Henry would take him to a cheap motel and pay for a week's lodging. Shifty would probably shower and wash his clothes and maybe stay a night or two, but sooner or later, his fears—real or imaginary—would prevail and send him fleeing back beneath the viaduct where he felt safe from the society that had first used and then failed him.

My nerve ends crackled when the man asked a plaintive question as Jazz and Henry took him firmly by the arms and loaded him into the Wrangler.

"You turning me over to the CIA? Please, man, I don't want nothing to do with them bad asses. They do awful things to a man."

Chapter 24

AFTER DELIVERING Aggie to the Four Corners Regional Airport the next morning for his run up to Salt Lake City, I stopped by the local FBI office. Gaines surprised me; he was in.

"Vinson," he said in his mortician's voice when I entered his august quarters. "I was thinking about calling you."

"What's up?"

"You first. What's on your mind?"

His face remained impassive as I described the recent conversation with Shifty, although his eyes flickered, confirming we had gotten a lot more out of the man than he had. But then Shifty thought he was CIA looking for an excuse to throw him into a bottomless pit.

"Maybe I ought to alert the Salt Lake office," he said when I finished. "You know, to give Mr. Alfano a hand in locating this fugitive who might or might not be his brother."

"Your call. I gave him the name of a good PI who can take him to the right places. Now, what do you have for me?"

"We found Orlando Alfano's billfold."

"Where?"

"In the back pocket of a local punk."

Gaines had put out an alert on Lando's credit cards and got a hit on a charge two days ago. Unfortunately it was at a small service station without surveillance cameras, so all he got was a description of the young man who had filled up his tank with Lando's Visa. The cashier's description didn't even come close to Lando. This morning, Gaines got another call, and this time the mercantile store had a good picture of "Orlando Alfano." He turned out to be a petty thief with dishwater-blond hair and sky-blue eyes named Shirttail Bob Hawkins, who claimed he found the wallet in a back alley.

"But that's not the truth, is it?"

"No," Gaines replied. "Shirttail rolled what he thought was a homeless derelict. The head wound this Shifty character mentioned could be from a beating this punk gave Alfano."

"Shirttail. How'd he get that name?"

"No idea, but that's what he answers to. He's been picked up by FPD several times for petty theft, fighting, and things like that."

"So that means Alfano's alive and still in the area. Unless Hawkins killed him for his wallet."

"Shirttail's a rat, but I understand he's not a killer. Anyway, to make that conclusion is a leap of faith. Maybe Shirttail took the wallet off of somebody who'd already rolled Alfano. Or took it off his body. You know, a case of the loot walking up the food chain. We can't quite pin down when the guy was rolled. I suspect it took a couple of days for that idiot to work up the courage to use the cards."

"You could be right, but I'm going with the most logical conclusion—this Shirttail character took the wallet from Lando. If so, that means he didn't leave on a plane out at Black Hole Canyon. He's not running away."

"If your assumption is right, then it doesn't look like it," Gaines admitted.

"Can I have a go at this Shirttail fellow?"

"Sorry, can't do that. He's in federal custody."

"Why? Wouldn't rolling Lando be a state offence?"

"We've got temporary custody because of the federal warrant on Alfano. Probably turn him over to the city cops when we're through with him. Or maybe Detective Joe will want him in connection with the Norville killing."

"Can I at least take a look at him?"

"Why?"

"To see if he's somebody I've run across in the investigation so far."

"San Juan County's housing him for us. I'll call over and approve your taking a look at him, but you can't question him. Clear?"

"Clear. Thanks."

There probably wasn't much to be gained from simply viewing Shirttail Bob through iron bars, but sometimes investigations hinge on weird things, so I called the crime lab at FPD, and they located Lonzo, who agreed to meet me at the San Juan County Adult Detention Center. If Hawkins was a troublemaker, Lonzo would probably know more about the man than Gaines did. I cooled my heels for half an hour in the parking lot watching the human traffic flow in and out of the place before Lonzo showed up to escort me inside.

When we located Shirttail Bob playing pinochle—a major jail pastime—Lonzo shook his head and muttered, "Shirttail, you piece of shit."

Although the man could not possibly have heard the comment, his eyes flicked in our direction and his demeanor changed. His studied nonchalance was now infused with tension. He continued to josh with his card mates, but his body language said he knew we were observing him.

"I take it you know him," I said.

"Oh, yeah. I know him. He's one of FPD's regulars and a constant burr under the county's saddle. Steals anything not bolted to the floor. Picks on younger kids. Roughs them up. The thing is, his family's as decent a bunch as you'll find around here. Sister in college. Brother plays basketball, baseball, soccer… any game with a ball in it. And then there's Shirttail."

"How'd he get that street name?"

Lonzo chuckled. "It's not a street name. His daddy hung it on him when he was a kid. His shirttail was always hanging out, so that's what the family called him. It stuck, and he's been Shirttail ever since."

"Who does he run with?"

"He's been best friends with a kid named Felipe Levy ever since they were toddlers. You see one, you generally see the other."

"I wonder if you're holding him too?"

"I'll check."

I studied the man through the bars while Lonzo was gone. If Shirttail hadn't had a crafty look, he would have been a decent-looking man in his early twenties, but the broad mouth had a cruel twist, and the pale eyes moved restlessly back and forth. Judging from the jiggling foot and sidelong glances, my presence was getting to him. Sweating the information I needed out of him would not have been hard.

Lonzo appeared at my side again. "Nope. Either the feds aren't looking for Felipe—or Phil, as everyone calls him—or else they haven't found him yet."

I nodded toward the card table. "Can I have a shot at that one?"

"Sorry. If he were mine, I'd lock the two of you in a room with no windows and let you have at it. But the detention brass said Gaines made it clear you can see, but no direct contact."

"Would you like to ask my questions for me?"

Lonzo's smile let me know he would like that very much. "Sorry, again. It's strictly against policy to question federal prisoners."

"Okay," I said, giving up. "This Felipe Levy, you know where to look for him?"

"Home probably. He sure as hell isn't gonna be working. Hasn't had gainful employment for as long as I've known him. He's probably lost without his buddy to lead him around by the nose. Phil doesn't have enough ambition to get into trouble on his own. He leaves that to Shirttail."

"Okay, give me his address."

After I parted ways with Lonzo in the parking lot, I called Anthony Alfano and tipped off Gilda that Lando was still with us—somewhere—before she turned me over to her boss. Alfano heard me out, asked a few blunt questions, and told me to go find his son.

I also dialed Aggie's cell phone but got his voice mail. I warned him the Salt Lake City FBI office would probably be looking for him, although I decided not to say anything about Shirttail.

My third call was to Jazz, who answered his phone promptly. Apparently he'd entered my number in his telephone because he greeted me by name. I told him I had a hot lead for Henry to check out.

"Is he still taking time off from work to look for Lando?"

"Till the end of next week. Why do you need him?"

"I'm looking for a guy named Felipe—or Phil—Levy. When I find him, I might need to lean on him some, and your brother looks like he's leaning even when he isn't."

He chuckled after I explained why I was looking for Levy. "Don't need Henry. Not for Phil Levy."

"You know him?"

"Yep. He's older'n me, but I went to school with him. I can handle him. And he won't be home, not if somebody's looking for him."

"You know where he will be?"

"Probably."

"I want to be there when you find him. Swing by the motel and pick me up."

I drove to the Trail's End, parked the car in front of my room, and leaned against the fender until Jazz's Wrangler pulled up. He had removed all the canvas except for a roof tarp to provide protection from the sun. As we tore out of the parking lot, the rush of the wind made my eyes water. I slipped on a pair of shades as Jazz headed east on Main and zigzagged down to the Bloomfield Highway. Just before the road crossed the Animas River, he turned north toward a stand of trees.

"There's a little lean-to in that cottonwood grove where the kids go to party," he said. "Phil and his asshole buddy, Shirttail Hawkins, go there to drink. I'm betting he's there now. And I'll lay odds Phil had a hand in whatever landed Shirttail in jail."

"I want to know everything about the incident. When. Where. How badly Lando was hurt. Everything."

"He'll talk."

"He's not as tough as Shirttail?"

"Not by half." He slowed and pointed off to the left where the tail end of an old Dodge coupe poked out of the bushes. "He's here. That's his car."

"All right, let's do it."

"Phil will talk to us, but you'll have to let me talk to him alone first."

Jazz spoke with such certainty that I decided to trust his judgment. He pulled to a halt short of the tree line and asked me to remain in the Jeep, but as soon as he was out of sight, I quietly trailed along behind.

Although it was still late summer, some leaves had already fallen, making it impossible to walk without raising a ruckus. I watched as Jazz stopped in front of a pudgy figure sitting on a log, scratching at the ground with a stick. Their voices were not loud enough for me to hear, but I understood Jazz's confidence when the young man reached out and touched him on the thigh. I discreetly withdrew and returned to the Wrangler. A few minutes later, Jazz emerged from the grove and motioned me forward. Without saying a word, he led me to where Phil Levy stood in front of a rude lean-to of dried branches. The cottonwood canopy overhead rustled in a gentle wind. It was ten degrees cooler in the grove.

"Mr. Vinson, this is Phil Levy. He's ready to tell you what happened, but he'll only tell you, not the cops. And he doesn't want any witnesses, so I'll wait for you in the Jeep."

So this was Shirttail Bob Hawkins's running mate. The kid was flushed and nervous. He had probably been muscular during his high school days, but he was running to fat now. He refused to meet my eyes.

"All right, Phil," I said, "this is just between us. Tell me about roughing up that derelict and taking his wallet."

"It was Shirttail," he protested. "His idea. I told him to leave the guy alone."

"Okay, we've got that straight. Now tell me about it. Where did it happen?"

"In the alley behind the Corner Market on Twentieth, out near the golf course."

"What time?"

"Ten… ten thirty. The store was closed."

It took some prodding, but eventually he told me he and Shirttail had pulled into a Fast Gas station to get five gallons, all they could afford by pooling every nickel they had. When they went inside to pay, this guy walked past them fumbling to open a quart of milk. He was dirty and unshaven and wouldn't have been worth a second look if he hadn't dropped his milk and his money on the floor—a lot of money, according to Phil Levy. Maybe a dozen or so bills, mostly tens and twenties.

Phil claimed they were only curious where a guy like that would get so much money, although they probably hatched their plot on the spot. But by the time they paid for their gas, he had disappeared into the night. Later, Shirttail got the bright idea of checking the hobo jungle under the viaduct, and sure enough the dude was there, sitting off by himself at the edge of the campground. But they spooked him somehow, and he moved over to join some other men around a fire.

The guy stayed clear of the viaduct after that, but a day or so later Shirttail and Phil spotted him in another convenience store and followed him into an alley. He was sitting in an empty refrigerator crate eating chips and drinking a soda when Shirttail—at least in Phil's self-serving version—attacked the man and took his billfold and money.

"Describe him," I said.

"Thin. Dirty as hell. Scraggly beard."

"Fair, dark, what?"

"Dark. Black hair. Never saw his eyes. Not enough light in the alley, but they looked dark."

"Height. Weight?"

"My height. Probably hundred fifty. Not big. But he put up a fight. It took both of us—" He bit off his words.

"How badly did you hurt him?"

"Wouldn't of, if he hadn't fought us," Phil muttered.

"How bad?"

"We… uh, Shirttail punched him. He punched back. We got him down, and Shirt kicked him in the head. I wanted to dump him at the hospital, but Shirt said no."

"And, of course, you do whatever Shirttail says."

"That guy wasn't right in the head anyway. Ever time we saw him, he was muttering to himself."

"Muttering what?"

"He didn't make sense."

"Do you remember any of the words?"

"He just kept saying this girl's name."

"What name?"

"Sounded like Diana or something like that."

I had intended to give the kid something for his information, but by the time I left the cottonwood grove, I was so disgusted I forgot about it.

Jazz turned the ignition in the Jeep as soon as I scooted into the seat. "Did he deliver?"

"Yeah, but it was all I could do to keep from busting him upside the head. He made my skin crawl."

"Yeah. Uh… I saw you watching from the trees."

"I didn't stay."

"I know. Mr. Vinson, don't get the wrong idea. I wouldn't get with a shit bag like that. I just flirted with him."

"Whatever. It worked." I related what I'd learned from Phil Levy. When I finished, he asked what I was going to do about him.

"Nothing. Sooner or later, Shirttail will give him up, and then he's the FBI's problem—or the County Sheriff's."

"That's what I figure too." Jazz sped up a bit. "What's our next move?"

"We know Lando's probably still in the area, so we search for him. If Henry's got the next week off from work, give him a call and have him give us a hand. I need to find Lando before the FBI does."

"And then what?"

"And then… I don't know. Not yet. There are some things I don't understand about this situation. But I know one thing. Lando's in bad shape. Levy said every time they saw him, he was muttering a name."

"What name?"

"Levy thought it was Diana."

"Dana."

"Yes. He's either mourning Dana or looking for him."

Shifty had mentioned Young'un One's head wound, so that meant Lando, if it was Lando, had returned to the hobo jungle after he had been rolled. He was probably looking for safety in numbers. But that failed to explain why he had not reached out to the best safety net of all—his family. Was he so far around the bend he didn't know who he was? That made no sense. Until Shirttail and Phil came along, he had a wallet with picture ID, credit cards, and money. Even if Lando was suffering from some form of amnesia, he would have taken advantage of the clues in the billfold.

No, something else was keeping him from reaching out to those who should have been his first line of defense, and I intended to find out what it was. Maybe I was overstepping the bounds of the contract, but I didn't care. I wanted an answer, and that was why I needed to find Lando before the FBI did.

You could argue this did not put the interests of my client—and I now considered Lando my client, morally if not legally—first. He would undoubtedly be safer in Gaines's custody than on the streets, but then my access to him would be limited if not cut off completely. That's why I had to find him first. So I offered Jazz and Henry a thousand dollars apiece to locate Lando, a move not without some risk for all of us.

Although I had not seen a federal wanted bulletin on Lando, Gaines had confirmed one had been issued. The agent and Lonzo Joe were aware Jazz and Henry were helping me look for Lando, but there was a slight risk some overzealous law enforcement officer might press aiding and abetting charges if we were caught in the company of a wanted fugitive. I failed to point this out in order to give them the shield of ignorance— which is, of course, no shield at all. The old saying "ignorance is no excuse" is absolutely true. I would have to take the heat for them if things went bad. I'd worry about that later.

AFTER I turned my army of two loose on Farmington, the next morning I booted up the laptop and had almost finished updating the case log when Charlie Weeks called.

"What're you doing up there that's got the FBI all fired up?"

"Come again?"

"They showed up this afternoon and started asking questions. Wanted to go through your office, but I told them they'd need a search warrant for that."

"Good. Have they come back with one?"

"Nope. They haven't gone through the hassle it takes for that—yet. They just separated Hazel and me and asked a bunch of questions. All of them leading back to the Alfano case. So what's going on? What're you doing to stir up the local feds?"

"I have no idea, Charlie. All I'm doing is trying to find Lando—hopefully in one piece. I know he's alive, or at least he was a few days ago. And I've turned over everything I know to the feds and the sheriff's office. In order to get a search warrant, they'd have to involve their Chief Counsel Division in El Paso and the US attorney. They haven't had time for that. Wonder how they knew you'd be in the office on the weekend."

"We've been hitting it hard lately. Hazel and I've been coming in pretty regular on Saturday, and I guess they knew it. That means they've been watching us. Like as not they tried the same trick out at your house."

"Oh, shit. What's Paul going to think? I'd better call him."

"Hazel already has. He wasn't home. At school, I think. But she got him on his cell and warned him he's under no obligation to tell them anything."

"Okay, please let him know I'll call just as soon as I find out what's happening."

"I got ahold of Del Dahlman at home before I phoned you. I figured we might need legal counsel, and he owes you big time."

Charlie was right. My ex, Del Dahlman, was a well-known Albuquerque attorney who was indebted to me for saving his ass last year when he was being blackmailed.

"So what was his reaction?" I asked.

"He's on his way over to talk to Hazel and me. He wants to know everything they asked while it's fresh in our minds. Hazel's putting together a memo right now."

"Good job, Charlie. You and Hazel did the right thing. Let me know what Del thinks, but in the meantime, I'm going straight to the source—a special agent named John Gaines right up here in Farmington."

Gaines was no longer at the office and did not return my repeated calls. Seething, I was forced to wait out the weekend. I considered calling their regional office but decided against it. I didn't want to appear anxious.

Chapter 25

I SPOTTED the tail Monday morning when I took a sudden left turn after almost overshooting the intersection leading to the FBI building. The car behind me had a difficult time making the maneuver, and his squealing tires refocused my attention away from the coming confrontation with Gaines and onto the street. The other driver recognized his mistake, turned into an alleyway, and sped off as I applied my brakes. Traffic prevented me from backing up and giving chase, so I whipped around a couple of corners but saw no sign of the car. From the quick glimpse I got, it was a gray Toyota or Nissan. All I could say about the driver was he appeared to be a large man. At least, his bulk pretty well filled up the front seat.

I cruised the streets in the immediate vicinity, spotting three cars that could have been the one I was looking for, but two were parked and vacant while a woman was behind the wheel of the third. Giving it up as a lost cause, I proceeded to the FBI office, where Gaines appeared to be expecting me.

He waved me into his office. "I thought I might be hearing from you this morning, Vinson."

"You knew damned well you would. Why are you prying into my personal affairs?"

"You have anything to hide?" He slipped behind his desk and sat down, motioning me to a chair opposite him. It was obvious the room was a temporary office for visiting agents. There was nothing personal in it. No art on the walls, just the two obligatory framed photos of the president and the director. The metal desk was bare except for a single file centered in the middle. The effect was cold—even chilling.

"Not like you mean. You ever hear of privacy? It's something we're all guaranteed under the constitution."

"Not a single reference to it, actually. That was the thinking in the old days, maybe, but not so much anymore."

"What are you going to use for probable cause to get a search warrant? That's what comes next, isn't it?"

"Sometimes," he hedged. "But how about consorting with known drug dealers?"

"What in the hell are you talking about?"

"If you don't like that one, then maybe crossing state lines for immoral purposes."

"What state line did I cross for what immoral purpose?"

"You didn't cross a state line, but Alfano and Norville are gay and they did. I hear you're that way too. Were you meeting for a rendezvous? A threesome? Or was the Penrod kid going to make it an even quartet?"

Only the fact that I knew he was deliberately provoking me allowed me to hold on to my temper. I took a deep breath and leaned back in the uncomfortable chair.

"Okay, Agent Gaines, you can stop playing games now. This is serious business."

"Yes, it is, isn't it?" He bounced the eraser end of a pencil on the metal desktop, making a hollow thump. "You're a wealthy man, Vinson. I didn't know police and private investigative work paid so well."

"You're still playing games. You must be aware what I have was inherited from my parents."

"That only moves the question back a generation. I didn't know school teachers made that kind of money either."

That was out of bounds. My jaws clenched. My teeth ground audibly. "You know full well my father put some money in a small Albuquerque business that became Microsoft. He died a wealthy man."

"Around $12 million, I understand."

"And if you ever get a warrant, your bean counters will find that's still what it amounts to plus a reasonable return on the investments. Now let's get down to business. So why do you have a hard-on for me? I've cooperated and passed on every bit of information I've come up with. What brought all of this on?"

He pushed his chair back and swiveled to a beat-up credenza to pick up a sheet of paper in a glassine envelope. "It's about $100,000."

"What hundred thousand?"

He handed over the document. It was a Bank of America statement for Dana Norville's account. The transaction that had caught his attention leapt out at me. All of the entries were four figures or less—mostly less. The prior ending balance was $5.65. The balance as of August 27 was $100,105.50. The large deposit in question was made on the seventeenth.

"Where did it come from?" I asked.

"A wire transfer from a bank in the Caribbean."

"I thought Dana died somewhere around the fourteenth or fifteenth."

"That's what the medical report said. But that doesn't mean the deal wasn't already set up."

"Deal. What deal?"

"This whole vacation was a cover for a drug transaction."

"Let's see if I understand this. Orlando Alfano, the son of a megamillionaire father and a billionaire mother, decides he needs to deal drugs for pocket change. And—"

Gaines interrupted me. "Dana Norville didn't come from money. He's the one who put the deal together."

"You find any drugs on him? In the Porsche on the floor of the Rio Grande Gorge? Anywhere?"

"Small amount of pot in his apartment, as a matter of fact."

"Recreational," I scoffed. "And they weren't going to haul $100,000-worth of marijuana around in the trunk of the Porsche. Besides, California is self-sufficient when it comes to the production of pot. And if they were going to buy some Mexican weed, Tijuana is a hell of a lot closer. You're grasping at straws, Gaines. Haven't you got this backwards, anyway? If, and I stress if, Norville was in a drug deal, he'd be buying, not selling. The $100,000 wouldn't be in his bank account— it'd be in someone else's."

"You're right about one thing. It wasn't pot. It was probably cocaine. Heroin maybe, but that's less likely. And maybe he hadn't had time to pay up before he was killed. In fact, that may be why he was killed. He didn't have the money at the time."

I shook my head in disbelief.

Gaines rubbed his eyes wearily. "The way I figure it, somebody fronted the money to buy drugs. Using the Alfano heir as cover, Norville arranged a meet somewhere in New Mexico."

"This is too far north," I objected.

"They were in Carlsbad. That's close to the border. And besides, deliveries are made in Chicago, Minneapolis, hell, Trenton, New Jersey, all the time. The border doesn't mean much anymore when it comes to narcotics. At any rate, Norville arranged for the purchase on behalf of some third party who put up the money."

"Same argument—Tijuana's a lot closer."

"Three of the four major abused drugs come to the States through Mexico—marijuana, heroin, and methamphetamines. That's the heavy traffic through Southern California. But it's a different cartel in control of Juárez. We've heard rumors they're getting some cocaine through. That's why I think coke's the drug they were buying. Anyway, they took possession, stashed it somewhere, and failed to pay. Santillanes was bird-dogging them because he represented the seller. When Norville couldn't pay, he killed the kid to pressure Alfano into telling him where they hid the stuff. Maybe he figured Norville came from a tougher neighborhood and Alfano would be easier to crack. But Alfano got the drop on him, or more likely called in help. So Santillanes ended up dead."

"But why is Alfano still in the area? Why wouldn't he have left in that plane out on the rim of Black Hole Canyon?"

Gaines waved my question away. "There's no real evidence there was a plane out there at the time Santillanes was killed. And if there was one, it probably had nothing to do with Alfano and Norville. That strip's an obvious contraband delivery area. But even if you're right about it, maybe Alfano was double-crossed. He gave up the drugs, and they abandoned him out on the mesa."

I sighed in amazement. "You once said I concocted an elaborate story out of very little material. Frankly I think you've got me beat by a mile. And how do you think I figure into this if it was a drug deal?"

"Are you looking for a missing Alfano heir or missing cocaine?"

"I'm willing to show you the Alfano contract so you can see who my client is and what I agreed to do for him. But if any whisper the FBI is questioning me or my people as accomplices in a drug deal reaches the street, I'll see you in court, Gaines. I'll fuck up your investigation so bad you'll wish you never passed through my door."

It was an empty threat, and a rash one to boot. Nonetheless, it made me feel better. Gaines's expression didn't change.

"Look," I said more reasonably, "ask me what you want, and I'll answer what I can."

"Why don't we go into the interview room?"

He had at me for the better part of two hours, mostly plowing tilled ground since I'd been pretty conscientious about keeping him up-to-date. As he asked his questions in a dry, funereal voice, I probably learned more from the session than he did. He was clearly serious about this mythical drug connection. I also inferred from a couple of questions that he had found no previous drug history in Norville's background. I wondered how serious an effort the FBI had made to trace the suspect wire transfer. Probably no more than to trace it back to the bank of origin, and in my experience, offshore transactions typically go through at least two banks to mask the identity of the sender.

When he finished, I shifted in my hard seat. "Satisfied?"

"Sounds on the up and up. We'll look into a couple of things, but you're probably in the clear. I'm satisfied you didn't know anything about the drugs."

"There are no drugs. You're on the wrong track. And if you're 90 percent convinced I'm who I say I am, doing what I said I do, you can call off your tail now."

Gaines stared at me blankly. "Tail? I don't have a tail on you."

I was tempted to believe the denial, but on the other hand, you'd expect him to disclaim surveillance. "Okay. Am I free to go now?"

He held up a long, thin hand. "Wait a minute. What about this tail?"

"Probably my imagination. I took a corner too fast on the way over here, and that put the car behind me in a bind."

"Describe the car."

"Gray foreign make. Probably a Toyota. It darted into the alley too fast for me to be sure."

"How many in the car?"

"Just the driver, but I didn't get a good enough look at him for a description."

Del Dahlman phoned me at the motel that evening sounding tired. He got down to business without much preamble.

"The feds were just fishing. They asked a bunch of questions about your relationship with this Napa Valley wine mogul. What's going on?"

I told him the FBI in all their wisdom had decided this was a drug case and expressed my opinion they were on the wrong track. The $100,000 deposit was a red herring to make us think exactly what Gaines believed.

"Not just anybody can throw away a hundred grand," Del said in his familiar, husky voice.

I briefly explained the pending De Falco Wines buyout. "People who are trying to consummate a $50-million purchase might consider it just a reasonable cost of doing business."

"And this kid holds the key to whether it happens or not?"

"He influences the decision, at any rate."

"What do you think happens if he turns up dead?"

"I don't think his mother would be too interested in transacting business. Probably not for a very long time."

"You may have just put your finger on why he's still alive."

I massaged the sore spot on my back the straight chair in the FBI interrogation room had rubbed wrong. "It could also be the reason why he didn't reach out to the family when trouble came looking for him."

"Because someone in his own family's after him?"

"Because he's smart enough to understand why he's being bird-dogged but hasn't figured out who it is yet."

"That must be some family. Who do you think killed Norville and that PI, Santillanes?"

"I don't have a clue. But as of this afternoon, someone's following me, and he's probably on the payroll of whoever did it."

"Be careful, Vince," he said, calling me by his private name.

"I will."

I hung up and immediately dialed Paul. He answered on the second ring. "What the hell's going on, Vince? Hazel said the FBI might come by." I smiled, pleased that Paul's pet name for me was the same as Del's.

"Sorry, but it's nothing to lose sleep over. I've talked to the agent up here and satisfied him, I think. They probably won't be around to bother you." I paused and suppressed a sigh. "Seems like you get mixed up in my cases one way or the other. I know my line of work makes you nervous. After this is over, I'll consider going into something else."

There were a few seconds of silence on his end. "Thanks, but no. What you do is part of what makes you so exciting. Don't change a thing."

After hanging up, I threw on a windbreaker and headed out the door. There was no sign of my tail as I pulled out of the Trail's End parking lot. Of course, he didn't have to stay close if he had planted a GPS tracking device. I pulled into a service station and let the automatic pump fill my tank while I went through the motions of checking my tires. Actually I was searching for an electronic bug. I found it in the rear wheel well on the driver's side. Leaving it in place, I went inside to sign the credit card slip and buy a few items.

I returned to the motel and backed into the parking space in front of my room. On my way inside, I snagged the nasty little bug from the fender and dropped it in the gutter where it would not be crushed by a car's tires. The area was poorly lit, so chances were good my action was not observed, but anyone watching would see my bag of goodies and hopefully conclude I had a sweet tooth in need of feeding.

Since the opposition was into electronic snooping, I tore through the room looking for some sort of listening device but found nothing. To convince my minder I was in for the night, I spent an hour reviewing my case notes and updating my expense log. Then I grabbed a fistful of flyers the local Kinko's had made for me that afternoon. They contained Lando's photo and name and a request to contact me on my cell with any information. The kid took a good picture, and the posed portrait Gilda had provided reproduced well.

I rooted around in my travel bag until I found the Smith & Wesson 9mm semiautomatic I'd carried since my cop days, two extra magazines, and a heavy flashlight. Grabbing the bag of snacks, I slipped through the door, got into the car, and eased out of the parking lot with my lights off. Now I was ready for the real grunt work—physically searching for Orlando Alfano.

The bug was not going to betray me; it was still lying up against the curb.

Chapter 26

JUST TO be safe, I took a roundabout route to the homeless hangout under the viaduct where we had talked to Shifty. Parking well short of the area, I walked down to the clearing. Although it was nearly eleven, most of the homeless inhabitants of the camp were still awake, sitting singly or in pairs or groups around small fires. The night was chilly, and an erratic brisk breeze did nothing to make things more comfortable. I toured the place by the light of a heavy flashlight, drawing frightened stares and angry mutters when I pulled newspapers, blanket scraps, or foul-smelling coats from those already asleep. Lando was not there.

Shifty and a buddy sat across the way, watching every move I made. I strolled over to them with my small bag of goodies in hand.

"Shifty, how's it going?"

"I know you?"

"Sure you do. Jazz and Henry brought me over."

"Oh, yeah. You was looking for Young'un."

I tossed the paper bag to him; he caught it deftly, tearing open the sack and rooting around in its contents. He came up with a giant Mr. Goodbar.

"With peanuts. That's the kind I like."

"Good. You and your friend are welcome. Either of you seen Young'un since I was here last?"

"Who's Young'un?" a dumpy figure asked. Surprised at the young-old female voice, I turned the torch on her. Big blue eyes blinked against the glare, and a grimy hand came up to shadow the face. I turned off the flashlight.

Shifty nodded toward the bridge abutment. "You know, the kid that sleeps over yonder. One with the bruise on his head."

"Oh, him. The good-looking one. Or he used to be, anyway. His name's Dana, but I just call him Cutie."

That gave me a start. "Dana? How do you know that's his name?"

"He's always saying it. Like he's trying to remember it. Don't think he's all there."

"Have you seen him tonight?"

"Not in a coupla days." In the uncertain moonlight, she appeared to be in her early twenties. She probably cleaned up pretty well, but the thick torso was too heavy for her heart-shaped face.

"Any idea where he hangs out when he's not here?"

"Nope." Shifty had wolfed down the candy bar and now munched a mouthful of peanut butter smeared on cheese crackers.

"There's a coupla places," she said. "I seen him there from time to time." She went on to tell me about other homeless hangouts.

"You ever talk to him?" I asked the woman.

It was as if I had pushed the wrong button. "I mind my own business." The woman-child closed up: her eyes flashed; the muscles in her face froze; her voice grew hard. "Who are you, mister?" She yanked on Shifty's sleeve. "You know this guy? Is he one of them?"

"Dunno," Shifty answered, totally engrossed in finishing off the foodstuffs I'd brought. "Probably is. They always coming around. CIA, you know."

The woman scrambled to her feet and fled, clutching the bag of potato chips Shifty had generously given her.

"You shouldn't play with them like that," I said.

He sat with his legs drawn up under him. "Why not? 'Sides, you could be CIA."

"Jazz vouched for me."

"Jazz could be too. They send all kinds a people out to fuck with us, you know."

Exasperated, I turned away to go find the other two locations the woman had told me about. I finally found one, smaller and with fewer people. As I walked over a hill, a birdcall sounded. The trouble was, it was some kind of tropical bird that didn't live in these parts. Somebody needed a better signal.

Or not. Half a dozen figures immediately scurried into the trees, leaving three men standing together in the center of a small clearing staring up at me. Apparently this was prime territory because the inhabitants were more aggressive in the defense of their ground.

The man in front of the other two looked to be in his forties, or so it seemed in the faint light. He was heavyset, although the ankle-length coat they called a "duster" in Clint Eastwood movies probably made him appear bigger. It was ripped in several places and ragged in all the others.

Long, stringy hair of an indeterminate color covered his ears and fell in strands across his face, which glistened in the moonlight with an excess of natural oils. I was suddenly grateful for the heavy flashlight in my hand and the S&W tucked into the belt at my back.

"Get outa here," he snarled. "We full up. Ain't room for nobody else."

Showing fear or hesitation would get me nowhere with this bunch. I walked down the side of the hill toward the three. The night grew quiet. Not even the sound of traffic reached my ears. I could have been in the middle of one of those vast Northwestern forests facing down a trio of Sasquatch.

"Not interested in intruding on your privacy. Just looking to take my nephew home."

"Maybe he don't wanna go home. Where's that, anyway?"

"California."

The man asked a question over his shoulder. "He look like a California dude to you, Bugs?"

"Shit no. He looks like local meat. Sounds like it too."

"I can show you some ID," I bluffed.

"Who's your nephew?"

"Kid named Orlando. He goes by Lando on the street."

"Don't know no Lando. He ain't here."

"Do you know everyone who hangs out here?"

"You bet your ass. This is my place. Nobody here I don't want. And that includes you 'n' this fella Lando."

"He's not quite right. Got hit in a fight and might be injured. Goes around asking for his friend, Dana." I failed to mention Dana was a dude; somehow I didn't think an alternative lifestyle would go over well with this group.

"That shit pile," the trio's leader growled. "He come around, and I tossed him out on his ass. Don't need no more loonies. We got enough of that our own selves, don't we, boys?"

A ragged laugh acknowledged the man's witticism. A few shadowy figures drifted back into the clearing. I sort of appreciated this homeless man's attitude. Although he doubtless bullied the people around him, he provided a measure of protection as well.

"I hear you, man, but when I find him, I'm taking him away. So when did you see him?"

"Who's asking?"

"Me."

"Me, huh. That's all I get?"

"Except for a ten spot for valid information."

"Ten spot? I'll tell you which way he headed, but not for no ten spot. Make it twenty."

"You make it worth twenty, and it's a deal."

"Told him he belonged with them other loony toons down on the Animas."

"Where's that?"

"Under the bridge where 64 crosses the Animas. You know, down at the south end."

"When was this?"

"Not more'n a day or so ago."

"Okay, you earned the twenty, but I want to make you another deal. My name's Vinson, and I'm staying at a motel on Main. You find this guy, Lando, and it's worth five hundred if you can deliver him within twenty-four hours. The price goes down after that. In fact, I'll probably leave town, and he won't be worth anything. You bring him to me unharmed, able to stand on his own two feet, and you get the cash, no questions asked."

"How we supposed to find you?"

I handed over a flyer. "There's a phone number on there, but it's an Albuquerque cell phone, so it'll be a long-distance call. You better hold out enough of that twenty to pay the toll because these cells don't take collect calls."

"Nephews oughta be worth more'n five hundred. 'Sides, I ain't so sure he's your nephew."

"Think what you want, but five hundred's what I'm offering. We have a deal?"

"We got one when I get my twenty."

After handing the man his money, I gave his two pals ten each. Then I faced the big fellow in the duster and held out my palm.

"I want to shake on it."

He hesitated a moment and then engulfed my hand in a big, rough fist. "Name's Gunner."

"Good to meet you, Gunner. You picked up that tag in the military, didn't you?"

He nodded. "Yes sir, the Corps. Copter gunships mostly."

"Should have recognized it. That was my service too."

"Officer material," he said flatly.

"I had my silver bar."

Gunner straightened his spine and came to attention. "We'll find this fella for you, Lieutenant."

"When you do, protect him, okay? Somebody else may be after him."

"Official?"

I considered the question for a moment and then answered honestly. A man's entitled to know what he's getting into. "The FBI and the County Sheriff are looking for him."

"Them's the two guys that was here a few days back. They didn't learn nothing."

"And there's somebody else too. Don't know exactly who, but I'm not sure he wants my man in good health."

So help me, Gunner saluted. I returned it automatically. It was exactly the right thing to do. *Semper Fi.*

I left the area and set about finding the "loony toons" camp along the Animas River Gunner told me about. It was after midnight by this time, so most of the camp inhabitants were already wrapped in blankets, newspapers, cardboard, or whatever else they could find to conserve body heat against the brisk night air. Some of them didn't stir when I flashed a light in their direction; too drunk or stoned to react. The remainder cursed or fled into the brush. I made a complete round of the small camp without coming up with Lando or anyone who remotely resembled him. Discouraged, I returned to the motel.

I cut my headlamps as I turned into the Trail's End and drove by using the ambient light from the lot's lampposts. The parking spot I had vacated was still open, so I backed into it, hoping my watcher, when he checked, would figure I never left.

Before going inside, I plucked the magnetic bug from the gutter and reattached it to my wheel well. While I do not use electronic tracking devices in my cases, if I did, I'd check the vehicle sometime during the night to make sure my bug was still in place.

I felt good about having Jazz and Henry on the lookout for Lando, and now the rather rowdy-looking homeless vets were also on the prowl for him—more of the local assets. If they happened to find him, I just hoped they wouldn't rough him up too much. Maybe I should have made more of a point of that.

Chapter 27

MY CELLULAR telephone roused me early the next morning, and the gruff voice on the line brought me wide-awake.

"Lieutenant? I get you outa the sack?"

"Gunner? Yeah, but that's okay. Hold on a minute, will you?" While I had taken a quick look through the place yesterday, I wasn't equipped to perform a bug sweep. Whoever was dogging our footsteps had planted a GPS device on my car, so he might have installed something in the room as well. I rushed into the bathroom and turned on the faucet. "Okay, go ahead."

"Mission accomplished, sir. The package is a little busted up, but it ain't because of us. What you want me to do with him?"

"You sure it's the right package?"

"Spitting image of your handout with some dirt and bruises and whiskers added. It's him."

"Any trouble?"

"No, sir. No sign of hostiles. It was a plum assignment."

"Where are you?"

"Outside of Walmart on West Main."

"Okay, sit tight. I've got some arrangements to make."

"He's a little panicked, so you better get a move on. He raises a ruckus, we'll have to lay him out. You know, for his own good."

"Stay by the phone. I'll call you back. Your number's in my recent calls list."

"Uh, I guess we earned our pay, right?"

"That you did, Sergeant." I probably promoted him by a couple of stripes.

I hung up and called Jazz, who came on the line complaining about a lack of sleep. Like me, he'd been out looking for Lando the night before, but he perked up when I told him our quarry had been run to ground.

"Look, I've got a minder on my tail, so I don't want to pick up Lando. Can you and Henry go get him?"

"Yeah, sure. Henry stayed in town with a girl last night. If he's not all worn out, he'll give me a hand."

"Tell him the deal still goes if you take care of Lando for a little while. Someplace safe."

"Great. What do you want me to tell him—Lando, that is?"

"As little as possible until I get a chance to talk to him. Right now, pick me up at the Farmington National. I've got to get some cash and give you instructions. Have Henry meet us at that little park west of the bank."

"Okay. Give me thirty minutes. Uh, better make that forty-five."

I didn't argue because that gave me time to take care of business at the bank. I hung up and had a quick shower and shave. Then, unwilling to attract my tail's interest by moving the car, I hiked to the bank. The nut I had to handle this morning was sizeable, so I made a cash withdrawal on my credit card.

Jazz pulled the Wrangler to the curb as I walked out of the bank and slowed down enough for me to hop in. Henry, looking a little less virile than usual, was waiting in the park when we arrived. I handed over the money I had promised the two of them, plus $1,000 in twenties sealed in an envelope for Gunner and his crew. They'd earned a bonus for accomplishing in less than twelve hours what the FBI and I had not been able to do in a week. I ran over the situation with Jazz and Henry twice to make sure we were all on the same wavelength.

"Have you come up with a safe place to stash Lando until I can lose my shadow?"

Jazz glanced at his brother, who answered my question. "Yeah. There's this old hogan where Grandpa Secatero used to live. It's abandoned now, but it's way off the regular path. Ought to be safe enough. You know the one I'm talking about, Jazz?"

"Yeah. Good choice."

"Okay, Henry, draw me a map before you guys go pick up Lando. Jazz, he knows you, so you calm him down. Tell him about me, but don't say anything about his father hiring me. Give him any story you like, but it's important that you do not mention his father or any of the family until I've had a chance to talk to him. And don't talk about Dana. If he brings him up, change the subject fast." I didn't want a confession putting these two in a box if this thing came to trial. "Are we clear?"

Jazz spoke for the two of them. "Got it."

"One more thing. The FBI and the sheriff are both looking for Lando, so technically, you're breaking the law by not turning him in. After I get a chance to debrief… uh, talk to him, I'll turn him over to Gaines myself. Is that a problem for you guys?"

Both men shook their heads.

"Okay, you take off for Walmart. You know who you're looking for, right?" Even though they assured me they did, I repeated a description of Gunner. "As soon as you leave, I'll call and let him know you're on your way."

"Good enough," Jazz said. "You need a lift anywhere?"

"No, I'll walk back to the motel. I don't want anyone to see us together."

"Maybe somebody's got an eye on us right now," Henry said.

"Don't think so. I've been keeping a watch for a tail. He's relying on that bug on the car to let him know when I move. When I figure out how to give him the slip without alerting him, I'll head out to the reservation."

I watched Jazz's Wrangler and Henry's bike out of sight before pulling out my cell and dialing the number Gunner called from earlier. He answered on the first ring. I filled him in on the plan, described Jazz and Henry, and let him know they had an envelope full of greenbacks for him. He grunted in satisfaction.

"Good doing business with you, Lieutenant. Anything else you need, you know where to find me."

"Thanks. Just out of curiosity, where did you locate Lando?"

"I asked around and heard about this guy living off by himself down in an arroyo on the Animas. Sure enough, it was him."

"Good job, Sergeant."

I scanned the area for anyone taking too much interest in me before leaving the park. I decided to skip breakfast and stopped at a gas station mini-mart for a big Styrofoam cup of coffee in case I was observed returning to the room.

I had no sooner closed the door behind me than the phone rang.

"Where are you?" Aggie asked.

"Still in my room." That sounded a little lame, so I added, "I was out late last night looking for Lando."

"Any luck?"

"Found a place he'd been, but he'd cleared out by the time I got there. How about you?"

"Your PI friend and I found the guy Shifty called Young'un Two, but it wasn't Lando. Of course, that was no surprise. We were just covering the bases, weren't we?"

"Right. Let me know when to expect you back."

"I'm already here. I'm at the Four Corners airport right now."

I didn't need this. I had to get to Lando as soon as possible, but I couldn't just blow Aggie off. I needed to come up with something to keep him busy while I slipped off to the hogan. In the meantime, I'd have to trust Jazz and Henry to keep Lando on ice.

"Hold on, and I'll come get you," I said.

"I'd rather have my own set of wheels. I'll rent a car. You still at the Trail's End?"

"Yep." Why did he want his own car? But maybe that was good… mine was bugged.

"Had breakfast yet? Or lunch?" he asked.

"Just coffee."

"Good. I'm starved. I'll meet you at the usual place after I rent a car. About thirty minutes, I'd guess." Our usual place was a café down the street called the Bean Bowl.

I phoned Buster Orville, the Salt Lake PI, and received a report on the hunt for Young'un Two. Despite what Gaines said—or at least implied—nobody from the Salt Lake FBI office had contacted them. Before hanging up, I asked his opinion of Aggie.

"He's aces, BJ. You'd expect a fellow with his money and background to sit on his fanny and let the hired help do all the work. Not him. He was right there beating the bushes with me every step of the way."

As I walked down Main Street toward the restaurant, I dialed Del's number, updated him on this morning's development, and asked him to come up. He agreed to clear his calendar and see if Jim Gray's Cessna was available. He called back five minutes later confirming it was.

I hung up feeling marginally better. Although I wished Aggie was still prowling the homeless camps in Salt Lake City, he was another pair of eyes, and I'd make use of those eyes, even if I didn't totally trust them. Maybe he could divert attention away from me—unless, of course, the bird dog I was trying to elude was his.

I arrived at the restaurant before Aggie and selected a corner table that promised a little privacy. The Bean Bowl had two separate dining areas, one of which was closed due to the early hour. The other abutted a side room filled with games to occupy restless children. The eight-year-old twins darting back and forth between their parents' table and their two older siblings playing a noisy electronic game grated on my nerves.

The dining room was probably fifty-by-fifty with whitewashed walls almost totally obscured by an eclectic display of artwork and artifacts. Miners' picks shared space with oilfield tools and framed black-and-white and color photographs of various local carbon-based activities. The amateurish landscapes and still lifes by local artists in varying styles and mediums, each with a small label in the lower right corner to let the patrons know it was for sale, would normally have drawn me to the wall where they hung. I like art, even bad art. I try to imagine the craftsmen laying down each brush stroke and wonder if they believe they're this century's Rembrandt or Picasso. On some level I shared their struggle to make each picture better than the last. Today I was unmoved.

Aggie showed up with dark bags beneath his eyes and pupils shot with red. The stress was taking a toll on him. But was he worried about his brother or about me or the law finding Lando before he did? His clean-cut, earnest face triggered a pang of guilt that I managed to shake off. Paranoia goes hand in hand with this job.

Despite his evident distress, he greeted me with an enthusiastic handshake and a tired grin. "Any news?"

My conscience sonar pinged as I shook my head. "Not much."

He accepted my spare comment, and we picked up menus with a hand-drawn picture of a steaming bowl of soup—presumably bean soup. The Bean Bowl was grossly misnamed; it boasted a broad menu of surprisingly good food.

After we ordered, he launched into a narrative of his trip to Salt Lake City. When he finished the story of his hunt for Young'un Two, Aggie sat back and leveled a gaze at me, one that was hard to read.

The arrival of our food took the heat off me for a minute. By the time our waitress sorted out the orders and set the plates in front of us, I'd decided Aggie was entitled to something. So I sketched the events of the last couple of days, including Shirttail Bob and Phil rolling his brother in an alley.

"That means he's alive."

I was impressed. He had focused on what was important instead of getting twisted up in the assault. "Yes, he is."

Aggie worked halfheartedly on a rare steak—and he'd claimed he was starving—as I gave him a few other details, going so far as to let him know of my contact with the homeless vets, but withholding the fact they had delivered—literally. Between sentences I bolted down my liver and onions. I like calves' liver, although I rarely indulge myself. This morning I felt in need of the iron.

As I finished the last bite and prepared to make my escape, Aggie pushed his platter away, leaving half of the steak uneaten. "You said you didn't have much to report, but that sounded like a lot. BJ, what's going on?"

His question made me wonder if he was picking up on my impatience. If so, maybe I could turn it to my benefit.

"What's going on is someone besides us is still after your brother, and it's not the FBI."

"What are you talking about? Who?"

"Probably whoever killed Dana. Someone sent Santillanes looking for Lando. And now his replacement is on the job. Somebody's been tailing me. Planted a bug on my rental."

"Who?" he repeated.

"I don't know, but I intend to find out—regardless of where that takes me."

"Regardless?" He stared hard at me.

Crap. Why did I say that? Now I'd have to take the time to explain my way out of that unfortunate slip. "Think about it. It doesn't have to be one of your family, but it's sure as hell somebody interested in the De Falco acquisition."

His dark eyebrows climbed. "That doesn't make any sense. Why would anyone kill Dana if that's what he's interested in?"

"Any number of reasons. Maybe Dana was trying to protect Lando and got killed for his efforts. Look, your brother was opposing the acquisition, wasn't he? Or more to the point, he was opposing the use of your mother's trust to finance the buyout."

I took a surreptitious peek at my wristwatch. Two hours. Jazz and Henry had gone for Lando almost two hours ago. They were probably at the hogan by now. I should have told Jazz to phone me when they were safe.

"That's true." Aggie rubbed his eyes as if that would help clear his brain.

"It's likely that someone just wanted to get control of Lando, and Dana was in the way."

"But if that's what happened, it would have to be someone in favor of the acquisition, and… and that's my father."

"He's not the only one. Your brother-in-law, for example. And any number of people on the De Falco side. On the other hand, the FBI doesn't think this has anything to do with the acquisition."

Aggie waited for me to explain while I silently willed Jazz to take the initiative and call me.

"A $100,000 deposit showed up in Dana's bank account. Gaines thinks it was money for a drug buy, but—"

"Lando and Dana buying drugs? Bullshit!" Outrage flared in Aggie's eyes.

"That's what Gaines believes, but it could have been deposited to make it *look* like they were dealing."

"Lando hated drugs. Loathed drug dealers. He wouldn't put up with it if Dana wanted to deal. He'd have walked away. No, that money was a false lead to divert the FBI. Has to be."

"That means somebody is willing to spend a large amount of money to lay a phony trail, which brings us back to the big money issue on the table."

"The acquisition."

"And there's another possible explanation," I said. "What if someone was paying Dana to influence Lando's decision on the buyout?"

Aggie's reaction was surprisingly bland. "You're talking about my father again."

I tried out some of the Napa Valley gossip Charlie had dropped on me back in Albuquerque. "Not necessarily. Despite what we said about Lando opposing the buyout, there was talk he had changed his mind and was going to lend his support."

"That's nonsense." Then Aggie seemed to reconsider. "If that's true—and I don't believe it—you're saying it could be someone opposed to the purchase. Someone like me. So it could be anyone on either side, provided the acquisition's the motive."

"Exactly. Lando suspecting someone paid Dana to influence him could have endangered the entire deal."

"And Dana's benefactor had to take care of him before he spilled the beans."

"That's one theory, anyway."

He took a deep breath. "This is taking too long. What can we do to speed things up? We need to find Lando and get him to California."

"That kind of talk is dangerous. There are probably outstanding federal and local warrants for Lando's arrest in connection with two murders. I know, I know—it's wrongheaded, but that doesn't alter the facts. We have to turn him over, not spirit him out of the state."

"No way."

"It's the only way. It's best for him, Aggie. But when we do, we'll need a good lawyer standing by."

"Talk to Papa. He has the best."

"There's already one on the way up from Albuquerque."

"You have a lawyer on his way up? Why? What am I missing?"

Damn, what was the matter with my tongue today? I'd put my foot in a cow pie again, and Aggie picked up on it. There was only one thing to do. Lie.

"I didn't call him. He called the office for me, and Hazel told him I was in Farmington. Apparently that was good news because he has a case up here he needs help with. His name's Del Dahlman. He's not a criminal attorney, but he's a damned good lawyer. He'll be on hand for a few days, so he can take care of the preliminaries if we locate Lando. Or if the FBI does. He should be here around six, and I need you to meet him at the airport in my car."

"Why?"

"My car's bugged, and I want to throw my minder off my tail."

"I see." Doubt shadowed his eyes.

"Jim Gray's flying him up, and you know Jim. He was the pilot at Taos. Del will be the only passenger. Tall, blond."

Aggie chewed his lower lip. "What have you told Papa?"

"Just that I'm sure his son's alive, and we are close to finding him."

I dug a key ring out of my pocket. "Time to go meet the vets I recruited. I don't want anyone who might be watching over my shoulder to know about them, so I need your help. Give me your keys. I want you to be the bait for whoever's following the bug on my rental." I handed over my set. "The car's parked right in front of my room at the motel. Get in the vehicle as quickly as possible and hightail it out of the parking lot so there's less chance of you being identified."

"Where do you want me to go?"

"Cruise around town. Make a trip to the bank. Drive down to Bisti. Anything that will keep you on the move and occupy someone's attention. But stay in the car as much as you can to make it harder for anyone to notice we've switched."

"I was hoping to be a little more helpful than just being a diversion."

"There's nothing more important at the moment than giving me some freedom. I need to meet with those vets, and then I want to check in with Lonzo Joe and John Gaines to see if there were any developments overnight. You and I can hook up again later."

"Okay. I'll do it."

I stood up from the table, silently urging Aggie to get a move on. He got up and dropped money for a tip on the table.

"Papa called me late last night before I left Salt Lake City wanting to know what was happening. I told him what I could, which wasn't much. He wasn't very happy."

"He didn't call me."

He stared a moment and then began to move. To speed things along, I told him I'd take care of the check, almost kicking off an argument over who would pay. Damnation. I needed to know Lando was safe.

Chapter 28

As Aggie headed out the door and started hiking to the motel, I dialed Jazz while the Bean Bowl cashier handled my credit card payment. I let the phone ring until an automated voice stated the obvious—the cell holder wasn't answering—and invited me to leave a message. I hung up and called the Trail's End to reserve a room for Del Dahlman. Melissa said there was one available next to mine and cheerfully agreed to bill the cost of his lodgings to my Visa. Then I tried Jazz again with the same results. This time I left a voice mail message.

Aggie's rental car would not have been my first choice as a ride, especially to navigate the back roads of the Navajo Reservation. The dark green Jaguar was a little too ostentatious for my taste, not exactly the low profile I needed. I kicked over the motor and got close enough to the Trail's End to see my rental pull out of the driveway and head west. I waited until Aggie led me by three blocks before tagging along behind.

No one appeared to be tailing him as he passed the municipal complex. When he turned right to make a sweep of the downtown area, I found a parking space and tried Jazz's number again. Still no answer. What the hell was going on?

The liver and onions I'd just devoured sat on my stomach like a lump of lead as a host of disastrous possibilities scrolled through my mind. Maybe someone *had* been watching us at the park this morning and followed Jazz and Henry to the Walmart. In that case, he would have witnessed the transfer of Lando from a bunch of vets to two Indian kids. Even though one of them looked as tough as any two of the homeless men, the odds would seem better to a stalker. So he could have followed them to the reservation. Maybe they were all lying in a ditch somewhere riddled with bullets. I shook my head to clear away that image.

Gunner might have decided to see if the FBI was paying a reward— something I hadn't bothered to check—and found it amounted to a hell of a lot more than $500. He wouldn't have known I kicked in another five hundred as a bonus. But I would have heard from Jazz if he and his brother had been unable to pick up Lando.

Or maybe Gaines had caught the whole bunch of them in a net. I'd never even considered the possibility the bug on my car was placed there by the FBI. Jazz and Henry and Lando could all be in custody right now.

There was another possibility, one that made me cringe. Jazz and Henry might have collected Lando and taken him directly to the FBI. After all, I'd warned them he was a wanted man. They could have decided that betraying me made more sense than risking arrest for harboring a fugitive. And it was possible the feds had placed a healthy reward on Lando's head. Had I made a mistake wasting all that time placating Aggie instead of taking care of urgent business?

After trying Jazz's number again without success, I headed straight for the reservation. Within a block I pulled over and took out my cell to find out if the authorities were already holding Lando here in Farmington. I was reluctant to go directly to Gaines because if he didn't have Lando, he might ask awkward questions. But Dix Lee seemed like a cop who kept her ear to the ground, and because the case didn't belong to the FPD, she'd be a little less interested in collecting information.

The operator had a little trouble running her down, but when Dix came on the line, she had no hard information. She put me on hold and made a quick phone call to the detention center. I drummed on the steering wheel and checked my watch three times before she came back to report neither the feds nor the sheriff had logged Lando in. She snickered as she repeated the latest scuttlebutt; the feds were closing in on the fugitive and expected an arrest soon. Of course, that was always the scuttlebutt, promoted by the FBI itself. That probably meant they didn't have Lando, although Gaines could be questioning the kid at the local FBI office without anyone being the wiser. Still, word usually got around pretty fast, even if the details were sometimes wrong. But there wasn't a ripple of excitement over the apprehension of a double killer.

I thanked Dix before she started asking questions and dialed Jazz again as I pulled out onto the street and started rolling. To my surprise and relief, he answered right away. Judging from the background noise, he was on the road.

"I was getting worried. I tried you several times and got no answer."

It was hard to understand him over the rush of wind. "Aw, sorry. Phone battery ran down. I made a run into town to pick up Henry's cell. He left it at his girl's house this morning. Didn't even think about switching his battery to my phone until I realized you didn't have his number."

"Where are you?"

"What do you mean?" he shouted. "That's not you on my tail?"

"What are you talking about?"

"There's a cloud of dust in my rearview mirror. I figured it was you."

"Listen to me, Jazz, I'm still in Farmington. Turn off somewhere. Don't lead that other car to Lando and Henry."

I heard his motor rev as he fed it gas. "Too late, man! The hogan's dead ahead. Shit, it's that guy, isn't it? That guy looking for Lando."

"That's my guess." The sharp, crisp beep of the Jeep's horn sounded several times; Jazz was trying to warn Henry. "Head out over the desert," I yelled. "He's probably in a sedan and can't follow."

"No, but he can drive straight to Lando. I've gotta hang up now. I'm gonna try something."

"Don't be foolish, Jazz. Don't—"

Too late, the connection was broken. Clutching Henry's map in one hand and the steering wheel in the other, I stomped on the accelerator, praying the vehicle behind Jazz was full of FBI agents. Once off the main highway, I took a wrong turn but discovered it within half a mile and backtracked to pick up the right road. I dropped the map on the seat and tried calling Jazz, but there was no answer. It was a good half hour before the stunted cottonwood grove sheltering the hogan came into view.

I slowed at the sight of Jazz's Wrangler half off the road, listing drunkenly to the left with a front wheel in a runoff ditch. The driver's door hung wide open. I ground to a halt just short of the vehicle and scrambled out of the rental when I saw a long, slender leg sticking up out of the ditch with its boot still on the Jeep's floorboard.

"Jazz!" I slid down the shallow embankment.

He lay sprawled on his back, arms akimbo. His eyes were closed; blood soaked into the sand beneath his head. Jazz moaned and tried to fight me off when I felt his neck for a pulse.

"Lie still," I ordered. "Something might be broken."

"Nuh," he groaned, putting a hand to his head. "Fell out. Hit head… rock."

"What happened?"

"Tried to block road. SOB shot at me. Ow!" he yelped as he tried to move his head. "Bastard put… round through the windshield. Right by my head. Swerved… ow!" he cried again and slid a hand behind his neck. "Hit ditch. Tried to bail. Fell."

"You were lucky. What happened then?"

"Dunno. Went out." His eyes widened suddenly. "Henry. Lando." Jazz, in obvious pain, struggled to rise; I pushed him back.

"Stay here and call for help." I handed him a cell from the front floorboard of the crippled Wrangler. "I'm going to check things out."

I approached the cottonwood grove with my 9mm in hand. I saw no car, but the tree cover was heavy enough to hide one. A fresh set of tire tracks went in and came out again, so the bastard was probably gone, but I wasn't about to take a chance. I abandoned the sandy track leading to the hogan and approached from an oblique angle over the desert hardpan.

A whirlwind gathered dust off to my left and swept overhead, blinding me. I blinked and swiped my eyes. My right leg ached, as it always did when I faced danger—the legacy of a gunshot wound to the thigh while I was at APD. My shirt was suddenly damp with sweat.

The miniature twister reached the grove, shaking the dry, thirsty treetops violently. I crept forward, nervously anticipating the flash of gunfire. I reached the tree line and took shelter behind the bole of a cottonwood. Now I had as good cover as the gunman. Easing my way through the thicket tree by tree, I almost blundered into the little building. The hogan blended perfectly with its surroundings. I circled the place three times, searching the grove thoroughly. Nobody. Nothing.

I hugged the log wall of the old shelter and inched my way toward the door on the east side—it was always the east side in a traditional Navajo dwelling. The entryway was a gaping black hole. The scrap of blanket that had hung as a door covering lay crumpled in the dirt. Mouth dry, I stiffened my spine and held the S&W in a two-handed grip as I rushed the door, rolling through the opening on my back. Barrel held high to avoid clogging it with dirt, I regained my feet. My tongue was thick and tasted like brass. My eyesight gradually adjusted to the sudden gloom. Empty. I gave a shaky laugh before it hit me. The shooter wasn't there—but neither were Henry and Lando. I called aloud. No one answered.

I rushed outside, freezing against the side of the log shelter at the sound of someone approaching. I held the pistol at arm's length, still in a two-handed grip, but jerked it up as Jazz reeled into sight. He put one foot in front of the other uncertainly, using any available tree as support.

"I told you to stay where you were," I said angrily.

"Couldn't. Had to… check on my… brother."

"He's not here. Nobody's here."

"Bike," Jazz mumbled. He pointed to where I was standing. "Was right there."

My spirits lifted. "If the motorcycle's gone, that means they got away."

"Yeah." He motioned with a palsied hand to narrow tire tracks leading around the hogan. "Took Lando out. Back way."

"No car could follow him over that hardpan. Unless…."

"Uh-uh. Sedan. Not four-wheeler."

"Did you call for help?"

"Tribal police." He sagged against the wall beside me. "Man, I feel woozy."

"We need to get you to a doctor."

"Nah. I'm okay."

"Don't argue. You need a doctor."

Jazz flared. "No way. Gotta see 'bout Henry."

"You know where he'd go?"

He gave a loose-necked, floppy nod of his head. "Yeah, we had a backup. Case something happened. 'Nother abandoned shack."

"All right. You take me there first, and then I'll haul you to a doctor. No argument. And if you start getting sleepy, we're heading straight for the hospital."

"Sleepy?"

"It's a sign of a concussion. Let's go."

We made it no farther than my car parked near Jazz's stranded Jeep. The tribal police cruiser rolling slowly down the road blocked our exit.

"Shouldn't a called them. Whada I tell them?"

"Simple, you ran off the road and needed help."

"Uh-uh. Windshield shot out."

"Then it must be a case of mistaken identity. Somebody shooting at you by mistake. You have gangs around here, don't you? Blame it on one of them."

Two burly officers, who looked to be peas from the same pod, got out of their unit. Round faces, coarse black hair, dark wary eyes. To me they looked more like Pueblos than Navajos. Jazz stepped forward and greeted one by name. I was proud of the kid. He handled it like a pro—and I think that's what the two tribal cops believed he was. I could read their collective minds as they eyed me. They thought Jazz brought me out to the hogan for a good time, and he didn't discourage that impression. I acquiesced to his superior knowledge of the way things worked around here and kept my mouth shut. Let them think whatever the hell they wanted.

They soon turned their attention to the stranded Jeep with its starred windshield and flat front driver's tire. The discovery of my firearm caused a bit of a flap until they satisfied themselves it had not been fired recently. Nonetheless, they examined my driver's and PI licenses and carrier's permit with extra care. If it was illegal to carry a firearm onto the reservation—as I believed it was—the two cops chose to ignore it. One of them ambled back to the cruiser with a rolling, mariner's gait, making me wonder where the tribe kept its navy. He was probably going to check my bona fides. That presented a potential problem if he touched base with the FBI, who had jurisdiction on Indian trust lands.

Our statements signed, we were finally free to "take Jazz to the doctor." Actually we dawdled until they were out of sight and then headed deeper onto the reservation. I kept a close eye on my companion, but he seemed to be recovering okay.

I periodically studied the rearview mirror, but there was no evidence of a tail as we tore west down Highway 64. We passed Twin Mountain and took the turnoff to Kirtland, whizzing through the old Mormon town on the approach to Upper Fruitland. Short of there, Jazz directed me south.

"Did you see who was shooting at you?" I asked.

"Naw. Happened too fast. Guy never got out of his car."

"What kind of car was it?"

Jazz flopped back against the headrest and winced. "Just a sedan. Dark, I think. Man, as a junior PI, I suck."

"No, you risked your own neck to give Henry and Lando time to get away. I'd say that was pretty productive work."

He rubbed his neck gingerly. "Don't understand. How'd they find us?"

"Maybe they picked you up when you went back for the phone." We hit a bumpy patch, and my voice vibrated with each shock. Jazz groaned aloud. "Whoever was following me saw us together at some point. He must have discovered Aggie and I switched cars and knew he'd lost me. When he saw your Wrangler, he latched onto you as the next best target." I didn't mention another possibility: the tail was Aggie's man.

"My fault."

"Don't beat yourself up. I should have thought to get you a charger for the Jeep."

We fell silent while I concentrated on getting the low-slung sedan over a faint wagon track made out of rough rocks laced with razor edges. Eventually I spotted a small, isolated hut in the middle of nowhere. As we neared, it turned into a log hogan. There was not a shrub within shouting distance big enough to provide even a smidgen of relief from the weather. This country was searing hot in the summer and bitter cold in the winter. A figure stepped through the darkened doorway of the hut and watched a moment before bolting back inside.

"Stop!" Jazz yelled. "Henry won't recognize this car. He's got a rifle. Let me walk up."

"You sure you're up to it?"

"Yeah. Be okay."

I braked slowly, allowing the car to coast as close to the structure as I dared. Then I shut off the motor. The Jag's heat gauge registered alarmingly high. Jazz, moving like an old man, crawled out of the vehicle.

"Henry," he called, adding something with a lot of glottals in a language I didn't understand.

Henry came back out into the open cradling a rifle in his arms. He reminded me of an old photo of Geronimo's renegade warriors in their last, defiant days of freedom. I know—wrong tribe, wrong time, wrong circumstance.

"*Ya-tah-heh*," he returned Jazz's greeting in Navajo.

After a brief exchange, Jazz glanced over his shoulder and waved me forward. Henry ignored me as I got out of the car; his sharp eyes were centered on his brother's ripped britches and bloody hands.

"Man, what happened?"

"Got bushwhacked," Jazz answered.

"Shit, you okay? I shoulda stayed to help you out."

"Naw. You did right. You know, getting Lando outa there."

Concern turned to friendly joshing when Henry realized his brother was okay. Jazz admitting he'd thought I was the car on his tail set Henry to chuckling, his version of gales of laughter. Then Henry turned to me.

"Good to see you, Mr. Vinson."

"It's about time you started calling me BJ, okay? And it's good to see you too. I was worried."

"No need. That guy wasn't gonna get us. Not even if Jazz hadn't started honking his horn. I'd been watching them for at least five minutes. You can hear a car coming a mile away out here."

"Where's Lando?"

"Inside. Man, he's screwed-up. I've got him primed, but he's still not too keen about facing you."

"Has he mentioned Dana?"

"Uh-uh, and we haven't either."

"Good. Screwed-up how?"

"He's not here. You know, not facing up to things. Either he doesn't remember anything or else he's being sneaky. Seems scared of his shadow one minute and feisty as hell the next. You know, screwed-up."

"I guess I would be too, if I'd gone through what he has. Are you okay?"

"Yeah. Not even a skinned nose, unlike somebody else I know." Henry cut his eyes at his brother. Jazz grinned but kept quiet.

"Where'd you get the rifle? I didn't see a scabbard on the bike."

"No, but there's one in the Wrangler. This is Jazz's. How we gonna do this?"

"I'd like to talk to Lando alone if there's someplace you guys can wait."

"Sure." Henry motioned with his head. "A hogan's always got a brush shelter. Not much brush left to this one, but it throws off some shade. We'll be okay."

"Good. You and Jazz introduce me to Lando, and then go wait there."

"You're the boss." Jazz turned and led the way into the cabin.

As my eyes adjusted to the dim interior, I was impressed again at how roomy these traditional hogans were on the inside. The log walls and thick roof beams topped by a layer of sod kept the temperature cool—relatively speaking. As my sight gradually returned, I concentrated on a figure pressed against the rear wall to the left of a window with its glass punched out. Dust motes floated through a shaft of bright sunlight.

"Hey, man." Jazz walked over to Lando. "This is the guy we told you about. You know, Mr. Vinson, but he just asked us to call him BJ, so I guess that's what he wants you to call him too." Jazz rattled on about his recent experience, probably intending to put Lando at ease, but he could have picked a better topic.

"Mr. Vinson. Uh, BJ, this is Lando Alfano."

I stepped forward slowly. Afraid of spooking the kid, I didn't offer to shake hands. "Good to meet you. Can you tell me your name?"

"Jazz just told you." The tone was closed, hostile.

"Yes, but I want to hear it from you."

"Lando." His light baritone made him sound almost as macho as Henry.

"Lando what?"

"Orlando," he said, as if it were an effort to remember. His voice strengthened. "Orlando Alfano. They call me Lando for short."

"Good to meet you," I repeated. "You have no idea how long I've been looking for you. Your brother says to say hello."

Lando, who had been studying something on the dirt floor, glanced up at the mention of his brother. "Aggie? You talked to Aggie?"

"Couple of hours ago."

Jazz spoke up again. "Look, me 'n' Henry gotta go take a leak. Then we're gonna find some shade and bullshit a little. You need us, you let out a yell, and we'll come running, okay?"

The kid started to protest, but Jazz and Henry swept through the doorway chattering like—well, like brothers.

"It's okay, Lando. I'm here to help. Let's sit down and talk for a minute." The hogan was completely bare, so I moved over beside him and sat in the dirt with my back against the wall. He slowly slid down beside me.

The Orlando Alfano of two months ago would have been horrified by his appearance and condition. He gave off the odor of something old and moldy. His face, silhouetted in the light streaming through the broken window, seemed mottled—dirt, probably—but the teeth were white and strong, and the bone structure, although blurred by facial hair, was good. Dirt, ratty clothing, wild uncombed hair, straggly whiskers—none of that could hide his good looks. Lando would clean up as handsome as the picture on the poster I'd had made up. He'd probably lost weight but wasn't emaciated.

"You want to tell me about it, Lando?"

"Who are you?"

"I'm the man your brother asked to find you."

"Aggie asked you to find me?"

"Yes." Lando hadn't panicked at the mention of Aggie's name, so I chose that lie. "Hired me, actually. And I've been busy at it. Found your room at the Sheraton in Albuquerque. Traced you to Chesty Westey's out at the Continental Divide." I smiled. "You and Dana made quite an impression. They remembered you weeks after you danced for them."

"D… Dana?" The word was tentative but oddly hopeful.

"That's okay, Lando. I know what happened to Dana, but before we talk about that—"

"What? What happened to him? Been looking for him. Everywhere. Where's Dana?"

Aw hell. The kid didn't *know*. And I couldn't risk telling him, not until I got all I could out of him. So I changed the subject.

"Did you know your car was stolen?"

He rubbed his face with a grimy, trembling paw. "Had to leave it. Man was chasing me. Shot at me. Followed me after—" He broke off, and the look on his face scared the hell out of me. He scrambled to get away. I caught his arm and pulled him back to a sitting position. He was beginning to remember something. If I pressed him, he might freak out. I stayed on the subject of the Porsche.

"Yeah, a couple of kids boosted it out on Halmstead Road where you left it. I hate to tell you this, but they took it back home to Taos and drove it over the Rio Grande Gorge. That beautiful orange Boxster is nothing but a pile of junk now."

"Dana! It wasn't Dana, was it? I mean, he didn't—"

"No, it was two local kids." I twisted around to face him. "When did you realize someone was following you?"

For a moment I thought I'd pushed the wrong button, but after a lengthy pause, he began talking, his words hesitant, as if he was recalling some of it as he spoke.

Neither he nor Dana had any idea they were being followed until the day they went to the Bisti badlands, but something went wrong in the relationship before that fateful side trip.

As he paused to lick his lips, trying to work some saliva into a dry mouth, I asked a risky question.

"Was Dana getting together with Jazz the problem?"

He froze for a moment and then faced me, his dark, hollow eyes full of questions, his face flushed. "They got together? Dana and Jazz?"

"Everyone says you and Dana had a fight over it."

He leaned against the wall again. "We did? I don't remember." He shook his head to clear it. "Maybe we did. I came back from somewhere—an art gallery, I think—and saw Jazz leave the motel. Yeah, we argued about it. We did. And I was pissed. Really mad. But…."

I waited out the silence as he struggled to clear the cobwebs from his mind. His limbs spasmed in agitation. Apparently, Lando didn't find what he was looking for because he returned to Jazz and Dana.

"That hurt. Hurt a lot, but I kinda understood it. Jazz is sexy." His voice lost volume.

Deciding not to press, I tried to take him back to Bisti. "Okay, so you went to Bisti the next day. How were things between you and Dana then?"

"Kinda strained, but it got better when we walked through that weird place. It was wonderful, you know—eerie wonderful. We got caught up in it and forgot everything else. It got easy again. We were okay." He hid his face in his palms. "Except things had changed."

"Changed how, Lando?"

He shook his head. "I don't know."

"Because Dana was buying drugs?"

"What?" He sat up straight, and some of the Alfano steel showed briefly. "Dana didn't buy drugs. He hated drugs as much as I did. He just… we just smoked a little pot now and then. But we wouldn't touch the other stuff. That's part of why we got together."

He cut his eyes over at me, probably to judge my reaction to his relationship. It surprised me he was sensitive about it. He'd acknowledged who he was, and he struck me as the kind of guy willing to pay the piper for his decisions. Still, it was understandable in a way because of his father's strong reaction to his homosexuality.

"What do you mean?" I asked.

"The guy he'd been with was on drugs. Started out smoking joints but graduated to crack and Ecstasy and worse—meth. Dana couldn't stand being around the heavy stuff, so he left. I guess I caught him on the rebound."

"Okay, did it have anything to do with Dana trying to talk you into supporting the De Falco buyout?"

His eyes widened and flashed dangerously. "You know about that? Who sent you? Papa?"

"I told you, I'm here on behalf of Aggie. Didn't Dana try to talk you into financing the deal with your mother's trust? Or maybe he was trying to talk you out of it."

"No, he never did that. At least, I don't think he did." Lando shook his head again. "No, he never tried to talk me into it. Or out of it, either. He's not very interested in our family's affairs."

"But he knew about the pending deal, didn't he?"

"Sure. I told him all about it." Then Lando came back to the question I didn't want to talk about until I knew what had happened at Bisti that day. "Where's Dana? I need to see Dana."

"Later. Right now tell me a little more about Bisti."

"That's where I first saw the man. Down there."

"Who? What man."

"I don't know who he was, but he knew who we were. He called us by name."

"What did he look like?"

"Just a man. Middle-aged, I guess. He was losing his hair, and he had this big forehead."

Santillanes. The LA investigator had most likely approached them at Bisti because the two young men were isolated and vulnerable.

"Was he alone?" I asked.

"I guess so. He just walked up and said he had to talk to me. Said it was family business and asked Dana to leave us alone for a minute. I thought Papa had sent him, so I told Dana to take a walk."

"Dana left?"

"Yeah. He went back over the hill to look at a big petrified log we'd passed."

"And then?"

"And then he—the man—tried to take me with him. I thought maybe he was a closet queen or something, but that wasn't it."

"How do you know?"

"He pulled a gun on me and ordered me to go with him."

Lando, even with a gun in his face, had refused. The stranger lost patience and threatened to kill Dana. When Lando yelled a warning, the man slammed him on the head with the barrel of his pistol. Stunned, but still conscious, Lando managed to stay on his feet. When his assailant whirled to see if Dana had come running, Lando shoved him into the dirt and took off to draw the nut job away from his friend. He managed to elude his pursuer, but upon reaching the Porsche, he found the man had anticipated him. Lando barely got the motor started before the PI fired at the car. Praying Dana would hide until he could lose the madman on his tail, Lando peeled out onto the road, watching in the rearview mirror as his pursuer recovered his own car and raced after him.

"But the Ford was no match for the Porsche," he finished wearily. "I was halfway to Farmington before he got out on the highway."

"Did you go to the police?" I asked. He shook his head. "Why not?"

"I needed to find out what was going on? I had to call somebody first. But… but I couldn't." That puzzled look was back on his face again.

"Why not?"

"I don't know. I just couldn't. Something…." His voice died away, and he shrugged in resignation. "I'd been hit on the head, man. I wasn't thinking straight. But I remember something else. There was another car in the Bisti parking lot when I left."

"Besides the one Santillanes was driving?"

"Santillanes?"

"The man who was chasing you."

"You know who he is?"

I nodded. "Was. He's dead. Shot."

"Shot? Who did it?"

"The FBI thinks you did."

The shock on Lando's face was genuine—I'd have bet on it. Outrage gave way to despair, and worse, to fear.

"But I know that's not true," I said. "You didn't shoot Santillanes."

"Dana?"

"Dana didn't either. He couldn't have."

He lifted his haunted eyes to meet my gaze. "How do you know?"

"Because Dana was already dead by the time Santillanes was shot."

He wobbled like he was swooning. "Dead. Dana's dead? How?" The whites of his eyes showed; the pupils contracted. He slammed his head against the wall.

"Strangled down at Bisti. On that same day."

I lost him then. He slumped forward. "My fault! My fault. I shouldn't have left him. Oh, God! Oh, God!"

Chapter 29

As Lando collapsed, I grabbed his shoulder and pressed him against the wall. Slack, lifeless, he was like an empty bag of skin until his anguish came pouring out in wracking sobs. I took a moment to bring my own emotions under control at finding Lando alive before speaking. Besides, he needed time to absorb the worst body blow of his life.

"I need your help."

No response.

"I intend to find out who killed your friend… your lover. He must have been quite a man to deserve your devotion. You could have given that love to anyone, but you chose him. So that makes him a worthy person."

He straightened his spine and seemed to grab on to some inner strength. His brown eyes glowed. "He is… was a good guy. A great guy." Lando gulped air and met my gaze for the first time. "If he was killed because he was gay, I want you to find the bigoted son of a bitch who did it. If he was killed because"—his voice caught in his throat—"because of me, I want someone to pay. What do you want me to do?"

We sat in the dirt in that hogan for another hour while I probed his family relationships, friendships, his homosexuality, everything and anything in the hope something would kick-start a thought process that would tell me what I really wanted to know: Why he hadn't reached out to his family when he got into trouble. I learned little I didn't already know or suspect except that his first gay experience with a soccer mate on a team trip to Sacramento was more an act of defiance than desire, but when he met Dana Norville at an immigration rights meeting on the UCLA campus, the pump was already primed, and he overflowed. It was the first solid connection he experienced where he did not feel someone was currying favor because of the Alfano money.

He avoided involving himself in the family business beyond working for Tom Scavo in the lab during his high school years, but that changed with the De Falco proposal. When his mother expressed her reluctance to use the Sabelito Trust to finance the buyout and Aggie opposed it outright, Lando plucked up the courage to place himself between his frail mother and his demanding father.

What Aggie had neglected to tell me—or perhaps did not know—was that Mona had given Lando a written power of attorney to act for her in the matter. As a consequence, Alfano turned his considerable pressure on his younger son, who simply walked away, taking Dana with him on a visit to the southwest to isolate himself until the De Falco matter fell of its own weight.

I now understood why he would not accept calls from his father on the trip, but I was not completely convinced that was the reason Lando did not turn to Alfano when things went wrong. Although Lando would not admit it, it was obvious he considered Santillanes was sent by his father to bring him home. He was probably right.

None of that mattered at the moment. The task now was to decide what to do with Lando. He should be handed over to the FBI or the sheriff, but his emotional condition gave me pause. Besides, I wanted to talk to Del Dahlman first. It was after six, so he should have arrived in Farmington by now. Maybe he would have some lawyer's trick up his sleeve to justify a delay in handing over the kid without getting us all into trouble.

Henry agreed to stay with Lando at the hogan while Jazz and I returned to Farmington. Jazz insisted he didn't need to be checked out at the hospital, but he wanted to make arrangements to recover his Jeep. I promised to rent another vehicle so Jazz could bring water and other supplies, including sleeping bags, since they would be remaining overnight. Actually, that wasn't a bad idea for another reason. If we decided to hide Lando a little longer, a clean vehicle no one else knew about might come in handy.

DEL DAHLMAN smiled as he sat across the small table from me in my motel room and took in the faded, thirty-year-old wallpaper, two laminated walnut headboards bolted to the wall, and the fifties-style gooseneck double lamp on a table between the two beds.

"Reminds me of the days we used to prowl the state back when… we were younger," he said, hedging more than just a little. He was referring to the time he was a brand-new lawyer and I was a city cop.

There had been a strong attraction between us from the day we met, and when we discovered a shared passion for small, historic towns in remote corners of the state, we believed we would share a long and wonderful life together. A fugitive's bullet in my thigh—helped along by a handsome hustler who captured Del's fancy—put an end to our four-year relationship.

"It's not the Four Seasons, but this is where Alfano and his buddy were staying at the time Norville was murdered. I came here to be close to the scene."

He cleared his throat and got down to business. "So what's the status?"

After I brought Del up to date, he leaned back in the chair. "You have to turn him over to the FBI. They have a fugitive warrant out for him."

"I understand that, but I want a little more time with him before I do it. Maybe I can turn him over to Sheriff's Detective Lonzo Joe. He might be a little more accommodating. Give me better access to his prisoner."

Del shook his head. "The FBI will claim Lando, and the sheriff will give him up. He'll let the feds stand the cost. The county can always try him later."

"Then figure out how to buy me a few days—hell, a few hours—without getting our tails in a crack. It's not just me. Jazz Penrod and Henry Secatero have also put themselves at risk."

"I wouldn't worry about them too much, but I can't say the same for you. You could lose your license by abetting a fugitive—at the very least."

"Not if a smart lawyer runs interference." I looked straight at him.

"You know I'm not a criminal attorney."

"You're not totally ignorant of that side of the law, either."

"Do you know how many things I had to juggle to make the time to come up here?" Apparently recalling I had dropped everything to come to his aid last year when he was blackmailed, he stopped. "That's not important. Let's see what we can figure out."

The only thing we came up with was for Del to contact Gaines the next morning and arrange for me to surrender Lando at an agreed time and place. It didn't buy me much, but at least it should keep the feds off my back. He would also inform Lonzo of our intent in order to protect us from that jurisdiction too. Gaines wouldn't be entirely happy about the way this was playing out, but he would go along with it. Plainer was the wild card. Fortunately he and the BLM played second fiddle to the San Juan County Sheriff in the Bisti killing.

My phone burbled. It was Jazz letting me know he'd successfully arrived back at the hogan with supplies and sleeping bags. He swore he was feeling fit as a fiddle and that everything was under control on that end.

Hard on the heels of that call, Aggie rang to let me know he was back in his room. Back from where? Probably a late dinner. I didn't ask; I merely invited him to join us.

The two men had met briefly when Aggie showed up at the airport, but Del decided to rent his own transportation, so they had done little more than exchange names. Now I watched each take the measure of the other.

Del would first see Aggie as a handsome, desirable man before regarding him as someone involved in the case. Aggie, for his part, treated Del as a potential lifeline, someone to help his brother in a time of trouble. I doubt he even recognized the attorney was gay.

Now that I'd figured out how to handle things, it was time to let Aggie in on the news. "We found him, Aggie."

He popped up from his seat on the bed. "What? When? Where is he? Is he all right?"

I held up a hand. "He's okay. A little banged up and a bit confused, but he'll be fine. Those vets I told you about located him and sat on him until we could pick him up. As to when? Well, early this morning."

"Early this morning? *Before* we had brunch?"

I nodded and braced for the explosion.

Flushed from the neck up, he let loose. "Why the hell didn't you tell me about it this morning? What kind of professional are you? You owed me that much, Vinson. We're not paying you to keep secrets from us." His nostrils flared in outrage. His dark eyes went flat. "Where is he? You turned him over to the FBI, didn't you?"

"No, I didn't. Not yet. I didn't tell you this morning because, first of all, I hadn't seen Lando at the time, which meant I only knew they'd located somebody who resembled him. I wasn't going to get your hopes up until I knew for certain. Secondly, I genuinely needed your help in slipping that tail. If you thought we'd located Lando, would you have gone along with me on that?"

Aggie gave me a look of exasperation. "No way in hell. Not then and not now. I want to see my brother. Now, Vinson. Now!" Something moved behind his eyes. "That's why all the questions this morning. You were thinking about keeping me away from him, weren't you?"

"You'll have to forgive me if I'm paranoid, but I was afraid you would alter your pattern of behavior and let whoever is so damned interested in Lando know something was up."

"Bullshit, you just wanted to keep me away until you talked to him."

He made a conscious and very obvious effort to bring himself under control as I told them both about the incident at the hogan, although I made it seem as if it happened at a cabin in the mountains near Aztec. I still hadn't done a bug sweep of the room, and the man who assaulted Jazz this afternoon wasn't necessarily the same party who bugged my car.

"Someone shot at Jazz and chased Henry and Lando? So much for using me to mislead a tail," Aggie said. "In case you hadn't noticed, it didn't work."

"You're making an assumption."

He blinked; his attitude eased. "What assumption?"

"That there's only one of them."

"Well…." He faltered. "You mean there's more than one?"

I shrugged. "I don't know for certain, but it makes sense. I assume one is your father's man. You said he likes to cover his bets. But if Santillanes was his PI, Lando thinks the man intended him harm. And Santillanes did put two shots into the Porsche when Lando tore out of the Bisti parking area."

"The Martinez kid said that happened while the car was parked down there," Aggie said.

"He said he heard shots close to the house, but he also admitted people were always shooting rabbits and squirrels down there."

"What did Lando say about it?"

"We haven't covered that yet. I only got as far as him leaving Bisti and going back to look for Dana later. When I told him about Dana's murder, he fell apart. That's why Del has to buy me some more time. I need to know what happened after that. I promised him I'd find out who killed his friend, and I intend to keep that promise."

The phone rang. It was Jazz again. "Got a problem," he announced. "Lando got hold of my rifle and tried to shoot himself. He didn't do any damage except for a bullet through the roof before Henry got it away from him. Nobody's hurt."

"Watch him. Close. You guys up for that?"

"Yeah, sure."

Aggie went ballistic when I reported what had happened. "Take me to him now."

"No way. It's too dangerous. Nobody's going near him tonight."

"Now wait a minute. I have a right. You work for me, you know."

Still playing it safe, I snatched a page from my pocket notebook, scribbled on it quickly, and stuck the note under his nose. It told Aggie to storm out of here in anger, take his own rental unit west on 64 to Fruitland. If I hadn't caught up with him by that time, he was to wait for me at the edge of town.

He nodded and got to his feet. I handed over the keys to his Jag, and he pitched mine to me. Then he stormed out of the place threatening to fire me, and if that didn't work, he promised to whip my ass. As soon as he was gone, I gave the note to Del and signed that I needed his keys. I did not want to remove the bug on my vehicle even though it had probably fooled no one this morning.

Thirty minutes later I found Aggie parked at the turnoff to Fruitland. There had been no sign of another vehicle on his tail. In fact, most of the traffic seemed to be going in the other direction, toward Farmington. I had taken a chance in revealing we'd found Lando, but any electronic listener would have been misdirected by my Aztec reference, provided, of course, he didn't already know it was a lie. That town lay in the opposite direction from the reservation. Of course, if Aggie was not to be trusted, he was aware of the deception and had had the last half hour to make arrangements for help. I would have to keep a careful eye out for a tail.

I must have startled him when I whipped a strange automobile in front of his parked Jag. He was slow to lower the window, even when I got out of the car with a flashlight. Ignoring him, I spent a good ten minutes searching the outside of the rental for a bug. I found nothing. That was only partial relief. The device could be on the inside if the bulldog was Aggie's.

Still without speaking, I got back in my car and pulled away. Aggie followed me south. After a quarter of an hour drive over a bumpy track through a surreal nighttime environment, we arrived at the small log shelter. Mindful that Jazz and Henry had a loaded rifle, I gave four short beeps on the horn—our agreed signal—before stopping the car. I checked my watch by the dome light as I got out and waited for Aggie to join me. It was almost midnight.

"Who's there?" a voice called from the darkened interior of the hogan.

"It's me, Jazz. Aggie Alfano is with me. Okay?"

"Yeah. Come on in."

As I followed Aggie inside, the panicked look on Lando's face made me grab for the Smith and Wesson tucked into my belt.

Chapter 30

"LANDO!" AGGIE cried. He started forward but halted when I grabbed his arm. My revolver was out of sight at my side. He shook me off and called to his brother. "Hey, man, it's me."

"Aggie?" Lando said. His face cleared. He scrambled to his feet from the lotus position and hopped across the small fire laid in the center of the hogan, showing more animation than I had witnessed thus far. "Aggie!"

Heart hammering, I eased the weapon into my belt and covered it with my jacket. The affection between the Alfano brothers was obvious, easing the fear that I'd made a huge mistake in bringing Aggie to the hideout. Nonetheless, while the two Alfanos greeted one another, I motioned Henry over and asked him to go outside and watch for unwelcome visitors.

"Dana," Lando said in a raspy voice. "Dana's dead, Aggie."

"I know. I was there when they found him."

"F… found him?" The kid's eyes began to glaze.

I took over the conversation before we lost Lando again. "Aggie and I made sure he was handled with dignity."

With a hand on his shoulder, I led Lando around the fire and gently pushed him onto the sleeping bag where he'd been sitting when we arrived. Despite this momentary setback, he appeared considerably calmer than this morning—well, technically yesterday morning—and certainly more rational than when he had grabbed the rifle. The brothers had done a good job settling him down. Perhaps it was only a trick of the campfire, but his coloring seemed better, more robust. A couple of discarded paper bags and Styrofoam cartons revealed Jazz had treated them to a meal, probably burgers and fries. Nonetheless, Lando's movements were still a little jerky.

"You feel up to talking some more?" I asked.

He stared at me without focusing for a moment. "If it'll help Dana," he said at length. "You'll find out who did that to him, won't you? You promised."

"I'm going to do my best, and so is Aggie. He's helped a lot in the investigation."

Lando picked up a stick and concentrated on stirring the fire before abruptly losing interest in the flames. "What do you want from me?"

I sank down beside Jazz, not directly across the fire from Lando, but obliquely so I could see his facial expressions and body language as he spoke.

"This afternoon, you told me you left Bisti with Santillanes trying to follow you."

"Santillanes? Oh. The fellow who pulled a gun on me down in the Badlands."

"That's right. After you lost him in Farmington, what did you do?"

"I drove around, you know, until I thought it was safe to go back for Dana."

"How long was that?"

"I don't—" Lando's voice started to rise, but he caught himself and calmed down. "I don't know. I started back that same day, but when I turned off the highway onto the dirt road, I saw that car. That Santillanes fellow."

"Did he see you?"

Lando nodded. "He turned around and chased me."

"He turned around? He was ahead of you on the road? Headed for Bisti?"

"Yes." Lando's attention was beginning to wander. What terrible thing sent his mind off-kilter when he got too close to it?

"But you outraced him again, right? And then what happened."

"I drove around some more, but I thought I saw him on the street near the motel, so I headed out of town—south but not back to Bisti."

"Out toward Halmstead Road?"

"I don't know where that is."

"That's about four miles south of the Trail's End. That's where you left the Porsche, remember?"

"Oh. The place where I parked and slept. The place with the trees and the white horse."

"You went to sleep while Dana was stranded out on the desert somewhere?" Aggie said.

I shot him a look. "Lando didn't go to sleep. He passed out. I'm surprised the cops didn't pull him over for drunk driving. He had a concussion from that blow on the head Santillanes gave him."

"Concussion," Lando parroted. His expression lightened. He'd probably been struggling with the same guilty thought Aggie had blurted aloud. "I had a concussion. A concussion."

"That's right. It wasn't your fault, Lando."

That raised the question of whether the kid was still concussed. Should we get him to a hospital? I eyed Aggie. I knew what his response would be. Throw Lando into the Mitsu and get him home to the family doctor. I mentally shook my head and resumed my questioning. But I'd keep a sharp eye on Lando. "What time did you go back to Bisti again?"

"Dunno. It was dark, but it was getting light by the time I got there."

"Was that third car, the one you told me about, still there?"

"Uh-uh. There wasn't anybody there. I spent hours looking all over that spooky place. Calling Dana. Looking for him. He wasn't anywhere." Lando put both fists to his head and rocked back and forth. Then he fixed his gaze on me, and for the first time, I got a sense of the real Lando Alfano. "Where did you find him?"

"It wasn't anywhere you would have looked, and we had help finding him. The important thing now is to tell us the rest of the story. What did you do next?"

"Drove. I went back to the motel but was afraid to check in. I figured that's where that man… uh, Santillanes would be waiting."

"Why not go to a different motel?" The question earned me another shrug. "You filled up your gas tank that day, didn't you?"

"How did you know?"

"I located the Giant station where you bought gas."

"You found the station?" He sounded like a child reacting to a magician's trick.

"Yes. And so did Santillanes."

"How?"

"Canvassed both sides of Main a mile in either direction. It was your car that gave you away. Everyone remembered your orange Boxster. What did you do next?"

"I called the motel a couple of times to see if Dana had left a message. He hadn't."

Melissa had neglected to mention that. Or perhaps she wasn't on duty at the time.

"Mostly I just drove around looking. I went back to Bisti twice. I didn't know what else to do, so I just kept driving around—everywhere."

Out of the corner of my eye, I saw Aggie open his mouth. I shook my head. It wasn't the time to ask the question I knew was on his lips. We needed to stay on neutral ground until we had everything Lando could remember. Then we'd ask the hard questions.

"You went back out on Halmstead Road the next afternoon, didn't you?"

"Yeah, I guess. To that same place, anyway, if that's Halmstead Road."

"Why?"

"I thought maybe Dana'd show up there. We'd been there before. It was a nice place we found by accident one day. You know, big, shady trees. A turnout on a curve that was sorta private, and it had a green meadow across the road. We sat for an hour one day watching that white horse running in the meadow."

"So you went back there hoping Dana would remember it. Then what happened?"

"There was an arroyo that ran off to the south we'd explored one day. Dana said it would make a good hiding place. A whole army could hide in there, is the way he put it. So… so I thought maybe he was there. I walked clear down to where it goes under the highway bridge. There was no sign of him. When I got back to the Porsche, Santillanes's car was parked behind mine, and he was going through my glove box. I sneaked back into the gully, but when I heard him following my footprints, I panicked and ran down the arroyo. He stumbled around looking for me, but I found a rocky place that didn't leave prints, so he didn't find me. After he passed, I went back to the car. But I couldn't find my keys. He must have taken them because I'm sure I left them in the ignition."

Taken them and then replaced them later. Petey Martinez had said they were in the ignition. Had the PI been watching from concealment when the Cruz brothers stole the Porsche? One thing was clear. Santillanes had Lando and Dana in his sights for quite a while because he knew about their special place on Halmstead Road.

"Why didn't you hot-wire the ignition?" Jazz asked. "That's what I'd have done."

"That guy came back too soon and spotted me. All I had time to do was grab my backpack and run. He was blocking the arroyo, so I jumped the fence and took off through the field. I managed to lose him, but I guess I lost me too. When it got dark, I didn't have any idea where I was.

I wasn't feeling so good. My head hurt, and I was hungry and thirsty. I finally fell asleep in some bushes."

"And in the morning, you swiped a pie from a house in the neighborhood," I said.

His mouth dropped. "I didn't swipe it. I left a twenty-dollar bill. I paid for it."

Apparently Widow Ingfield had neglected that part of the story when she titillated the neighbors.

"Why did you take the time to grab your bag?" I asked.

"It had my billfold in it. All my money. I'd brought a lot of money along in case… in case—"

"In case you wanted to stop using credit cards and drop off the radar," I finished for him.

"Yeah, that's right."

"Why didn't you go back for your car?" Aggie asked as I dialed Del on my cell to see if he'd come up with a better strategy for dealing with the FBI. The call went to his voice mail.

"I tried," I heard Lando say. "But I couldn't find it. I got all mixed up."

I hung up and led him through the rest of his story. He had hiked back into Farmington and ended up out on the reservation when he went to a truck stop, intending to take a shower before hitchhiking or catching a bus west. But he saw Santillanes's car cruising the street and slipped into the back of a pickup parked nearby, covering himself with a tarp. Still at the stage where he fell asleep easily—the head wound again plus the fact that he hadn't had any decent rest in days—he dropped off and didn't wake until the pickup began moving. Trapped, he stayed hidden and went wherever the pickup took him. He knew from the chatter coming through the open back window that the driver and passenger were Navajos. After a long time on the road, they stopped to open a gate, and that was when he slipped out of the bed of the pickup and hid in a gully.

Finally realizing he was about to be stuck in the middle of nowhere, Lando popped out of his hiding place, but by then the truck was bouncing down the dusty road, and he couldn't make himself seen or heard. He'd tried to walk out but didn't have the strength. Thirst was getting to him, further sapping his energy. He spent that night in the bottom of a sandy arroyo. Baking before the sun went down, he froze during the night, so he took all of his clothing from his travel bag and tried to cover himself.

He finally dozed but woke when he heard someone above him on the lip of the gully. Panicked, he ran, abandoning everything except his billfold, now in his hip pocket, and his toilet kit. He'd held on to that, hoping something in it would provide moisture—his aftershave, his deodorant, anything.

"Why did you run?" Aggie asked. "Why didn't you wait for whoever it was to help you?"

"Like I said, I panicked."

"That was probably old One-Eye you heard," Jazz said.

"Yes, Lando was the old man's shape-changer," I agreed.

Jazz pressed him. "But how did your shaving kit end up over by the Hernandez place?"

"The aftershave lotion made me dizzy and sick to my stomach. I couldn't stand the taste of anything in there, so I dumped the kit when I got tired of lugging it around."

"And somebody stumbled over it and traded it to Crespido Hernandez," Jazz said. "Everybody's a trader out on the reservation. Then Hernandez hocked it in Shiprock. What happened next?" He was caught up in Lando's story.

"I finally found the highway and waved a pickup down. I gave the driver twenty dollars for a ride and some water. He threw in a thermos of mutton stew."

Lando had blundered into one of the homeless hangouts by accident and slept in one hobo junction or the other for a few nights. Some men came asking questions about him, but nobody gave him up. Then Santillanes came, and he got scared and slipped away. He avoided the homeless places until he got rolled in the alley in downtown Farmington. After that, everything was sort of fuzzy. I understood; he'd been kicked in the head and injured again.

Further prodding failed to bring out anything else pertinent, so it was time for that hard question. The one Aggie had been itching to ask.

"There's something I don't understand. Presumably, you still had your cell phone and some money, so—"

"Not my cell phone. I lost it somewhere."

"Okay, but you had money, at least until you were rolled. And you had your credit cards. Why didn't you call your family for help?"

Lando tensed. In the uncertain light of the small campfire and the glow of a lantern near the far wall, he looked like an adolescent asked a trick question on a pop quiz. Bewilderment shone through the grime matting his face and clinging to straggly whiskers.

"Why didn't you?" Aggie prompted. "I would have come for you in the Mitsu."

"I… I don't know." The words were anguished and sounded true, but his body language said otherwise. His frame folded in upon itself. The squared shoulders rounded, the slender neck sagged. He lowered his head until his eyes were no longer visible. His fists clenched the filthy fabric of his trousers. After a moment's silence, he roused himself, sitting up straight to eye us defiantly. "I… don't… know!"

The interview was effectively over, but Aggie wasn't satisfied. He asked the same question two or three different ways, but Lando, his eyes shifting wildly, clung stubbornly to his story.

I watched the interplay for a moment before slipping outside to huddle with Henry. He nearly scared me out of my wits as he rose up off the desert floor right beside me when I softly called his name.

"Jesus!" I exclaimed, jumping sideways.

"Sorry, didn't mean to scare you."

"Anything?" I scanned the darkness blindly. The only light came from a couple of billion stars sparkling overhead. There was no sign of a moon.

"All quiet."

"Okay, you can go back inside now. And thanks."

I didn't know he had left until I caught the glow of the lantern as he slipped past the blanket to enter the hogan.

It was almost two in the morning when I headed back to the Trail's End. Despite the fact that there were not enough sleeping bags for everyone, Aggie insisted on remaining with his brother. Henry solved the problem when he decided everyone should take turns standing guard. After all, someone had already shot at both Jazz and Lando. And, of course, Lando had made an attempt to harm himself, although I felt that was behind him now. The challenges we threw at him in the session tonight had actually helped stabilize him.

I mulled over Lando's story as I drove back to Farmington. Not everything made complete sense, but that could be rationalized away by a couple of thumps to the head. There was no question he'd suffered a concussion, probably a second time when Shirttail Bob Hawkins kicked him in the head. But it would take a powerful shock to the system to keep someone like Lando—who was one of the protected rich kids despite his admirable penchant for independence—from heading straight for the nest when he got into trouble.

He had not done what was natural, and that bothered me. Lando wasn't on the best of terms with his father, but he could have called on Aggie. Why hadn't he? Was the fox guarding the henhouse tonight?

I passed no suspicious cars. Nor was there a shadow on my tail unless he was driving in the darkness without lights. When I hit Main, the street lamps showed several blocks behind me totally clear of traffic. Of course, if someone had been tailing me in the darkness, he would know where I was headed and could have dropped back out of sight. My rumbling stomach reminded me I hadn't eaten since Aggie and I had breakfast yesterday morning. I was tired and hungry and frankly not functioning at the top of my game. I stopped at a mini-mart and picked up a tuna on rye. Not my favorite, but at least it shouldn't be dried out like some of those prepackaged meat sandwiches were. After a quick snack, I planned to head for bed—for a few hours, anyway.

There was no convenient parking space at the Trail's End, but I took the closest one to the room and remained in the car to see if anybody showed up behind me. No one did. As I sat there, I suddenly missed Paul so badly it was almost physical. I yearned to pick up the phone and wake him but resisted the urge.

Instead I got out and walked to the door of my room, alert for any sign of a threat. The world was muted. Even the traffic on Main was slow. Rap music drifted up from the all-night convenience store down the street. Otherwise, everything was peaceful. A bank of fast-moving clouds partially obscured a newly risen moon lying low on the horizon. The effect was disconcerting; even stationary objects appeared to move in the darkness. I put my key to the lock, took a final look around, and slipped into my room. As I turned to fasten the chain, something bit into my neck.

My body went rigid. My head exploded, and I dropped helplessly to the floor, fighting to keep control of my bodily functions. The old bullet wound in my thigh burned unbearably.

Chapter 31

A NARROW beam of blinding light pierced my eyes, kicking off a splitting headache. But it was the light that focused me, brought me back from the edge of nowhere.

"He's coming around," the man behind the beam said.

A drawl. A south Texas drawl. Grappling for a sense of reality, I managed to snare that thought and hold on to it. Someone else mumbled, and I tried to turn toward the source of the sound.

"Hold it right there, partner," the first voice said. "Just lay there like a good little puppy dog. Ain't nothing over there for y'all to see. Let's get down to business. Where's the kid?"

"What you… do to me?" I rasped through a parched throat.

"Just a little old stun gun. Ain't hurt you none. I answered you. Now you answer me."

"What kid?"

Something touched the back of my hand, and my body arched. A powerful electric charge pulled a groan from deep inside me.

"Ain't gonna be none of that, fella. Where is he?"

I tried to think, but the sinister black gadget with the big bite in the man's left hand commanded all of my attention. The glare, I finally realized, was a penlight focused right between my eyes. I wanted to put up a hand to block it, but the effort was too much. I was exhausted. Beat.

"Tell me who," I struggled to form a rational sentence. "Maybe tell you… where."

"Fair enough. Orlando Alfano. Where is he?"

"FBI has—ungh." I grunted as he zapped me again. "Damn it, stop. Can't help if they—"

He touched me again, longer this time, and my body danced to the charge. I was growing weaker.

"We know they ain't got the kid. They still looking for him."

"Tonight." I labored to get the word out. "Turned him over tonight. Where I was… coming from…." I sighed, unable to muster the energy to finish.

Far off, as though in a dream, I heard mumbling. It took a moment to realize the second man in the room was speaking. The thug with the stun gun reached for me. My flesh crawled, but he merely hauled my limp, boneless body erect.

"Okay, fella, y'all's coming with me."

"Where?"

"Wherever the hell I say, partner. Come on."

As he spun me around, my knees buckled. I would have flopped on the floor had he not held on to me. A vague, amorphous thought floating around in my addled head gradually gelled into an old adage. Never, *never* get in a car with a kidnapper. You won't come out alive. My hand reacted automatically, grasping the edge of the table near the window. The effort used up all of my remaining strength, but it moved. I strained against the man pushing me toward the door.

"Aw, fella, don't be like that."

The terrible pain came again. My muscles spasmed. I felt my mouth gape in rictus. I was vaguely aware of a loud crash as the table went over, banging against the wall. That was important. Something about the room next door.

"Fucking asshole," my attacker mumbled.

Imagining that pernicious little box reaching for me, I attempted to roll to the side and reach for the gun in my waistband, but lacking control of my muscles, I sagged backward against him. Caught by surprise, he fell across the mattress, taking me with him. My flailing hand slammed against the lamp stand between the two beds. The telephone crashed to the floor. The lamp struck the wall and broke, eliciting a cry from the other room.

That was it. The room next door was Del's. Still mentally floating in limbo, I laughed aloud at the realization.

I heard a muffled yell—in a familiar voice—and the door to my room suddenly banged open. A shadowy form fled into the night. It wasn't the bozo with the electric charger; he was still pinned by my legs. But not for long. I sailed into the air as he literally threw me off and scrambled to his feet. As I flopped to the floor between the beds, he hesitated a moment before running after his companion, brushing past Del as he came charging into the room.

"Vince!" Del yelled, flipping on the light.

"Chase," I squawked, flapping a hand that didn't seem to belong to me. "Catch 'em."

Del spun on his heels and scrambled out of the door, returning moments later. "Lost them. Two cars tore out of here at the end of the building, but I couldn't see enough to identify them. What happened? Are you all right?"

"Think so." He pulled me from the floor and dumped me on one of the beds. "Two men. Stun gun."

As I fought for breath and my nerves began to settle, my fried brain cells struggled to assess the damage. Stun guns are not lethal. Powerful, but nonlethal. The electricity turned blood sugar into lactic acid, slowing and confusing muscle movement. Charges to my torso were the most debilitating; those on my arm and hand, while painful, were less severe. I was partially paralyzed but would be okay if I could just rest a little.

"I'm calling the police," Del said.

I'd forgotten he was standing beside the bed. I nodded, and he picked up the telephone from the floor where it had fallen.

At that moment a voice shouted from the doorway. "Hold it. Don't move a muscle."

A youngster who looked all of seventeen stood in the open doorway holding a big, black semiautomatic pistol that wavered uncertainly back and forth between Del and me. He was dressed in a dark blue uniform with a "Four Corners Security" patch on the shoulder. The kid's eyes, whites showing, roved all over the place as he tried to assess the situation.

"It's 'kay," I wheezed. "My room."

Del took over. "His name is Vinson. This is his room. I'm Dahlman from next door. He was attacked by two men with a stun gun. You need to call the police."

It took a minute for the security guard to act, but he finally reached for his radio and called in the situation. Then we all stood, or in my case lay, without moving, as if something would explode if we did. And it might have been the pistol the kiddie guard waved around. He relaxed only when sirens announced the approach of one of FPD's Patrol Division units. *I* didn't relax until a seasoned police officer came into the room and cajoled the kid into holstering his gun. I managed to get my body to cooperate enough to turn over and reveal my own revolver in the belt at my back. The cop confiscated it.

Del righted the table and put the telephone and broken lamp back on the lamp stand before he and the patrol cop dumped me into one of the room's two padded chairs. Then I stumbled over my tongue while trying to relate what had happened. I finished just as the room phone rang. At a nod from the policeman, a barrel-chested veteran of about forty who wore a nametag reading Harrison, Del answered and a second later brought it over to me. My hand shook like a Parkinson's victim as I brought the receiver to my ear. I mumbled a hello and then listened.

"How long ago?" I asked, and then told Jazz to hold.

"Del, Aggie took his brother. Need to… call FBI."

Without questioning my conclusion, he turned to the policeman and asked him to contact FBI Agent Gaines. "Tell him the fugitive, Orlando Alfano, is in the company of his brother, Aggie. They're probably heading for the Four Corners airport where Alfano has a Mitsubishi on tie-down. Detective Lonzo Joe of the County Sheriff's Office should be informed as well."

"They're… coming from reservation. Jaguar rental. Green," I managed to add.

As soon as Harrison was on his radio, I put the phone back to my mouth.

"You get that, Jazz? Did good, guys." I took a deep breath and steadied my voice. "Now… go out to Black Hole. Take Henry. Be careful. If there's a plane there and no guard, keep it on the ground. Let air… out of tires, okay?"

When Jazz said that was cool and hung up, my befuddled mind closed on something. Jazz had said his car was out of commission and Henry's tires slashed. How would they get to Black Hole? He was a resourceful kid, so I assumed he had a plan. But why had he called on the motel phone? Why hadn't he dialed my cell? I handed the receiver back to Del. "Find my cell."

He located it on the floor beside a squashed tuna sandwich near the table I'd overturned. The phone was smashed, but the search for it produced more positive results. The thug who attacked me had hesitated because he'd lost his stun gun when I fell against him. It lay not two feet from my broken cell phone.

Harrison picked it up by the strap. "Glad he wasn't wearing this around his wrist like the book says to. Otherwise he wouldn't've dropped it. Oughta be able to get some good prints off this unless he was wearing gloves."

"Not too clear… don't think so."

"That means he'll run for the border. Leastways, that's what I'd do," the cop said.

I more or less returned to normal over the next few minutes as we gave a formal statement to the officer, but my stomach was giving me fits. We needed to get out to the airport—fast. I asked Harrison to escort us as soon as he finished asking questions and allowed Del to go back to his room to change out of his dressing robe.

THE FAR side of the airfield was abuzz with activity when we arrived. The two black SUVs probably belonged to Gaines and Plainer, but they'd also called on the local police for assistance. A squad car was parked directly in front of Aggie's Mitsu. A sheriff's unit sat below the left wingtip. Lonzo Joe was there as well. They all clustered on the ground near the open hatch where Aggie was engaged in a heated discussion with Gaines.

"Go do your thing, Del," I said as he braked beside Harrison's unit.

"Who do we represent?"

"Orlando Alfano. Scruffy character between those two policemen. Hadn't had time to give him a bath."

"I'll stand downwind." Del started across the tarmac, yelling in a loud voice, "My name is Dahlman, and I'm Mr. Alfano's attorney."

Smart. Make them take a few minutes to sort out which Alfano he represented.

As I approached at a more deliberate and wobbly pace, Plainer moved to intercept me.

"He's with me," Del snapped. "He's my investigator. I want him here." Gaines nodded. "Mr. Alfano, don't say another word," Del continued after dealing with Plainer.

I think Gaines was surprised when he addressed Lando rather than Aggie. The advice was, however, intended for both.

"I need a few minutes with my client," Del said to the senior agent.

"You can see him after he's processed over at the San Juan County Adult Detention Center."

"Fine, I'll meet you there. In the meantime, remember, Mr. Alfano. You give them only your name, ID information, and address. Nothing else. Do you understand?"

Lando, looking pretty well out of it, nodded mutely. Gaines signaled the officers, and they hustled the prisoner to Lonzo's Crown Victoria.

Gaines faced Aggie. "Now, what do we do about you?"

"What do you mean? I was just trying to take my brother home. Our lawyer—our California lawyer—would have called you tomorrow and arranged for us to turn him over to you. In the meantime, we'd have cleaned him up and explained his rights to him."

"I think the detention center will take care of the former, and Mr.… uh, Dahlman will accomplish the latter. But you were aiding and abetting a federal fugitive. That's a crime."

"You can't be serious," Aggie protested.

"What's the range of that plane, Mr. Alfano? It would probably make it to Canada without much trouble. How do I know you were taking him to California?"

"Because that's where his home is, where all his support is. And that support is considerable," Aggie added rashly.

"Yes, I know all about the Alfano money and the Sabelito Trust and the muscle your family has in that state. But you aren't in California now. This is New Mexico. All of which is irrelevant since the crime was committed on federal trust lands."

Aggie had the good sense to shut his mouth.

"I'm going to withhold judgment on charging you for the moment, but I don't know how Detective Joe feels about it."

"I'm okay with that," Lonzo said. "At least he flushed the fugitive for us." The words were benign, but Lonzo's dark eyes were fixed on me as he spoke.

"Very well, you're free to go for the moment," Gaines said. "But be warned, I may change my mind before this is all over."

"Don't worry. I'm going to the detention center with you."

"You won't be able to talk to your brother tonight. Might as well go get some rest. I'll make arrangements for you to visit him tomorrow."

"I—"

"Go home, Mr. Alfano. Or rather, go to your hotel or motel or wherever you're staying. Where are you staying, anyway?"

"The Trail's End."

"Glad to see all the eggs are in one basket," Gaines said. "Same goes for you, Mr. Vinson. Mr. Dahlman can have access to his client, but nobody else—at least until tomorrow."

I touched Del's arm and gave him a questioning look. He nodded.

"Before you go, there's something you should know," I said.

Gaines contained his impatience as I stumbled over my tongue relating the events of the attack on me at the motel. Then he turned to Officer Harrison, who had escorted us to the airport, and made certain the evidence—namely the stun gun—had been handled properly.

"We'll sort out jurisdictions later," he said before he allowed Del to drive me back to the motel.

When we arrived at the motel, a crime scene unit was working over my room. They permitted me to get my shaving kit and a clean pair of clothes before handing over a key to a new room. Mine would be off-limits until they were finished. Del advised me to go to bed before he headed out to the detention center to see his client.

"You look like hell, Vince. Get some rest."

There was nothing I wanted more than to fall into bed, but first I had to talk to Aggie Alfano.

Chapter 32

Aggie's room was directly on the other side of Del's. He opened the door at my knock and scowled at me. "What do *you* want?"

"We need to talk."

"You turned us in, Vinson. Why should I talk to you?"

"Yes, I did. And we need to talk about that too."

Curiosity apparently got the better of him. He stood back and allowed me to enter. "Why'd you do it?"

"For Lando's sake."

"The hell you say. Lando's better off in jail than with his family?"

I entered and sat down next to a table identical to the one I'd upended earlier in my room. He sat on the edge of the bed, facing me.

"Look at it from my perspective. Somebody was trailing your brother and Dana. Santillanes tried to kidnap Lando. Someone killed Dana. And it all ties back to your family somehow."

"I don't know why you are so hung up on that theory."

"And then you take off in the middle of the night with your brother, disabling Jazz's car and puncturing the tires on Henry's bike."

"I didn't puncture them. I just let the air out."

"Whatever. But right about the same time somebody assaulted me in my own room demanding to know where your brother was."

"That ought to let me off the hook. I was out on the desert driving like hell for the airport. The first time I heard about the attack was when you told Gaines tonight. I'll swear to that. It was probably the same guy who tried to bushwhack Jazz out on the reservation."

"Yes, it probably was, but that begs the question. Why did you take Lando?"

"Why do you think? There was someone out there with a gun looking for him. And you were going to turn him over to the FBI."

"That's what had to happen—for his own sake. Before some nervous rookie put a bullet or two in him."

"That's why I needed to get him home. The old man's got contacts there. He could have arranged to turn Lando over and have him released into our custody." He shrugged. "I saw an opportunity and took it."

"And you see the results. That's why your father hired me, Aggie. I've had more experience in dealing with the law than you have. Besides, your father can still throw his weight around if he's got that much juice."

"Yeah, but right now Lando's sitting in jail. How do you think he's going to handle that?"

"He'll be fine. Gaines is no fool. He knows your family has money and influence. He'll put Lando in isolation. Besides, Gaines was right; you could have taken him to Canada and made him a fugitive for the rest of his life."

"You think I'd do that to my brother?"

"To be honest, I don't know what to think. But I'll say it one more time. Somebody in or close to your family—or at least to the De Falco acquisition—is mixed up in this. Nothing else makes sense. There's no evidence either Lando or Dana got into trouble—serious trouble—along the way. So there's no reason for perfect strangers to be after them. And we all agree they weren't dealing drugs—well, except for Gaines—so what else is left? It's the buyout."

"You told me this place has a bad civil rights rep. Maybe it's somebody who hates gays."

"A possibility. But in my experience, if a bigot gets in his licks, he struts away and brags about it to his buddies. This started in Albuquerque and has continued halfway across the state. It doesn't fit the pattern."

"So you're looking for a killer in my family." Aggie ran a hand through his hair. "Maybe Santillanes went overboard and killed Dana when Lando got away from him."

"There was someone else at Bisti. I'm sure you picked Lando's brain and know there was a third car down at the Wilderness the day Santillanes chased him. And then Santillanes winds up dead. Do you really think Lando did either one of those killings?"

He sighed. His body slumped with fatigue. "No, I don't. Lando didn't kill anyone." He gave me a look. "So I'm a suspect? Okay, tell me why I would kill Dana. What's my motive? He's—" Aggie licked his lips and started over. "He was a good kid. In fact, I think he was good for Lando."

"I can't think of a reason for you to strangle him right off the bat, but that doesn't mean there isn't one. You've got to admit this thing runs deeper than it seemed at first."

"This conversation is over. I'm wiped out. I need to get some rest."

"Good idea. Have you let your father know what's happened?"

"Yeah, I called him earlier. I didn't talk to him directly, but I left word."

"You didn't speak to him?"

"He's down in LA on business. I left a detailed message on his cell."

"He hasn't called you back?"

"Not yet. That's probably the next thing that'll come along to cost me sleep. It makes a guy envy Lando in isolation."

With hair bristling and my back puckering uncontrollably, I went to my new room and unlocked the door with the key the crime scene supervisor had given me. I reached through to flip on the light before throwing the door wide. Officer Harrison had returned my pistol, but no assailants waited in ambush this time. Still a little enervated from the zapping, I collapsed on the side of the bed and seriously considered turning in without bothering to clean up. But the blinking red light on the telephone revived me. Impressed that the night clerk had been on the ball enough to have rerouted the call, I retrieved the message from the motel's old-fashioned communications system and listened to Jazz's disembodied, clearly frustrated voice.

"This is you-know-who. Where are you, man? I've been trying to reach you."

Shit, I'd forgotten to give him Del's cell number until I could pick up a replacement phone.

From the guarded way he spoke, it was obvious Jazz was getting into this private investigator thing. "We went to the assigned spot. Guess what? There was this little airplane sitting there. Don't know what kind, but it has some big numbers painted on the side—N-5642. Maybe that can ID it for you. Anyway, there's nobody standing guard, so Hen—uh, my buddy and I followed your suggestion, if you know what I mean."

He meant they'd punched holes in the tires. Was Henry getting as big a kick out of this caper as his brother?

"That sucker's not going anywhere for a while. Do you want us to stay here or go home? I got my phone on vibrate so it won't wake the neighborhood if you call when you get this message. We need instructions, okay?"

I punched in his number on the room phone. He must have been asleep because the cell rang for quite a while before his voice came over the wire.

"BJ?"

"Yeah. Sorry, but I've been tied up with the FBI. They stopped Aggie before he could get in the air. Took Lando to the detention center."

"So you really turned them in?"

"You heard me on the phone talking to the cop. I had to, Jazz. If we'd helped Lando escape, we could all have been in big trouble. I didn't want that for any of us. Besides, I'm not sure why Aggie ran with him, so Lando might be safer in jail."

"You think Aggie could be in on this? He seems like a pretty square dude to me."

"With 'pretty' being the operative word." I couldn't resist yanking his chain a little.

"He's sure that, okay. A dude'd have trouble picking out the best-looking brother in that family. But seriously, he seemed all right."

"There's money involved, and when money's involved, things get complicated. He might have simply been trying to protect his brother like he said, but even if that's true, helping him get away wasn't the best way of doing it."

"So now what? What do you want Henry and me to do?"

"If it's not too much trouble, stay there the rest of the night. I was assaulted in my room just before you called about Aggie running with Lando. Chances are the two men who did it might try to leave the area. Which reminds me, how did you get to Black Hole? I thought Aggie put your car and Henry's bike out of commission."

"He let the air out of the bike's tires and yanked out the distributor off the rental car. It's probably out there in the desert near the hogan, but it was too dark to look for it. Henry carries a tube he rigged up, so we used the air in the car's tires to inflate the bike. It's a neat contraption."

"So you're on the bike? That's good. You can hide it easier. Look, if anybody shows up at the plane tonight, you stay out of the way. Don't let them see you. Do you understand?"

"Loud and clear. Stay out of their way. You want me to call you at the motel if they show?"

"No, they'd be long gone before I could get there."

"Okay, then we'll follow them."

"No!" Crap, that was exactly what those two would do. "No," I repeated less stridently. "It makes more sense to stay on the scene. They might go for help to repair the craft, so I want you to stay there and warn me if that happens."

Disappointment was evident in the junior PI's voice as he agreed. I could have found worse local help in this matter—lots worse. Next I woke Charlie and asked him to find out all he could about a plane with tail number N-5642.

DEL HAD paved the way, so I had no trouble interviewing Lando in the detention center early the next morning—actually, later that same morning. Del, looking like something out of *GQ*, despite the fact that he'd had less sleep than I had, led the way to where the young man was waiting in a small cinder-block interview room that probably resembled one of the detention cells. We took seats opposite a freshly scrubbed and barbered but still bewildered Lando. I led him through his story again just to be certain I hadn't missed anything of significance the first time around. He recited details he hadn't remembered last night, but they merely fleshed out things without changing the basics. They did, however, show his mental condition had improved. Then I posed the question I came there to ask.

"Lando, why did you oppose the purchase of De Falco Fine Wines by your father's company?"

The question seemed to catch him by surprise, and for a moment I was afraid it had sent him back into limbo. But after a brief clouding of his eyes, he answered. "At first, I was against it because Aggie was. But when Mama started stressing out over it, it hit me that Papa was using her money to finance something that was half the size of his own net worth. That didn't seem fair."

"So you supported her. Opposed the buyout, I mean."

"Using her money? You bet. He didn't have any right to do that. That's when the trouble started."

"What do you mean?" I listened to his voice carefully. There was nothing in his syntax or his inflections to suggest he was gay. Orlando Alfano was better looking than most men his age and perhaps a little more graceful, but a fellow would need pretty good gaydar to pick up on anything more. Unless Lando wanted him to, that is.

"It ended up with me pulling her one way and Papa pulling her the other," he said. "And Victoria too. She wanted the buyout to go through."

"Your sister? Was that for her husband's sake?"

"Partly, but she wanted to run that division herself and build her own little empire inside the company. She'd put William—that's her husband, William Vitrillo—in as her second and hire her own kids when they got old enough. And, of course, William was brokering the deal, so he'd get a couple of million bucks out of it right up-front."

"Was Aggie pulling at your mother from the other side?"

He paused, tilting his head slightly as he considered the question. "No, I don't suppose he was. Thinking back on it, he was relying on me for that. My mom and I are close."

"I see." I put my palms on the table and prepared to rise.

"That's why I changed my mind."

"What?" I dropped back into my chair.

"Well, Papa was still coming at her hard—real hard. Victoria too. Sis is as much a bulldog as Papa when she sets her mind on something. Mama's not strong. She gets colds and bronchitis real easy, and stress makes it worse. And she had cancer, but I guess they got that. Anyway, that's why I asked her for that power of attorney to act in the De Falco matter. I thought that would take the pressure off her."

"Did it work?"

"Sorta. Right after she gave it to me, Dana and I took off on vacation. It got me out of the line of fire, but a power of attorney isn't irrevocable. Once I got out of his reach, Papa started putting pressure on Mama again."

"So you changed your mind and decided to support the purchase?" That was the first time Del spoke since we started the interview. "I'm not certain I understand your reasoning, Lando."

"Fifty million is a small part of my great-grandpapa's trust, so I decided it would be easier on her to go along with Papa. Aggie is stronger than Mama. If he was dead set on stopping the deal, he'd have to do it on his own. He can take the pressure better than she can."

"Did you tell Aggie about your decision?"

Lando nodded, and my gut clenched. Why had Aggie denied any knowledge of it?

"Yeah, he said he understood, but he asked me to think it over some more before I told anyone else."

"When was that?"

"About halfway through the trip. Before we came up to the Four Corners area."

"So Aggie was the only one who knew you were switching your position?"

"Dana knew."

"I suspect there weren't many secrets between the two of you."

That comment kicked off the law of unintended consequences. Lando's jaw dropped as if he'd been slapped. His facial muscles spasmed. Tears sprang to his eyes. He brushed them away with the back of his hand and cursed.

"What is it, Lando?"

He met my eye squarely—except he didn't. The pupils were directed at me, but there was nothing behind them. Lando's mind had gone somewhere else. I glanced at Del. He was as perplexed as I was. Maybe I'd been wrong. Perhaps he and Dana *had* had a falling-out, and Lando killed his lover. I discarded that idea and pressed the issue.

"Lando. What is it? Why did you react when I asked that question?"

He blinked. "What question?"

"It wasn't really a question. I just said I thought you two were close enough so there weren't many secrets between you."

"I'm tired now," Lando said, his slender shoulders drooping. "Can I go back to my room… my cell?"

"Your attorney needs to talk to you a little longer, but I have to leave now. I'll talk to you later, okay?"

"Yeah… sure."

Del leaned forward on the table and prepared to make like a lawyer. As soon as I got out of the center, I took a moment to consider the risk before phoning Gaines. He agreed to see me right away, so I drove over to the FBI building with my head spinning. I spoke before our handshake was finished.

"Agent Gaines, I really hope you'll cooperate with me on a couple of things. I just left Orlando Alfano, and he seems to be recovering." That, of course, ignored the fact I'd said something that sent him into orbit again.

"I'm still trying to figure out your role in all of this, Vinson." He lowered his long frame into a high-backed black executive chair, the one item in the room that did not fit the government-issue appearance of the place. "But I'll do what I can."

"I need to see the log of calls to and from Dana Norville's cell phone."

"What are you looking for?"

I slid a scrap of paper across the desk to him. "That's Aggie Alfano's cell number. I want to see how often it shows up."

It showed up five times as both sent and received calls. Dana had been in intermittent contact with Lando's brother from the time they left for New Mexico almost until the day Dana died. There were also calls from an unidentified number, which the FBI confirmed as a cell phone but hadn't yet traced.

I deflected Gaines's questions, promising to explain as soon as I filled in a few holes. He wasn't happy, but he didn't arrest me for impeding an ongoing investigation or for withholding evidence. Nor did he ask what role I'd played in finding Lando and stashing him away on the reservation, but sooner or later, he would get around to it.

I went to the crime lab at FPD to see if they had identified my attacker from fingerprints on the stun gun. It was a little early yet, but maybe we'd get lucky. We did; our man was in the system. Lonzo Joe was out, but since the assault happened within the city limits, the police had jurisdiction. Dix Lee showed me a mug shot of a thug named Joe Kinkaid, minor muscle for the mob who'd gotten his wings clipped in LA a few years back and went home to San Angelo, Texas. South Texas.

The police had located his Farmington motel room at the east edge of town, but he had flown the coop in his rented automobile. There was already a bulletin out on him. At the moment the San Angelo PD was unable to provide a list of known associates. Kinkaid had come back to San Angelo with a little money and lived quietly on a small farm outside of town. Dix had no lead on the second man in my motel room—the one giving the orders.

As I left the bullpen area, I ran into Aggie, who was just entering the building.

"Just the man I want to see." I stepped in front of him.

"Get out of my way. I'm going to see my brother."

"Then you're in the wrong place. He's down at the San Juan County Adult Detention Center on Andrea Drive."

"Where's that?"

"East part of town. I can give you directions or drive you over if you want."

"No, thanks," he snapped. "I'll find my own way."

"Suit yourself. Have you talked to your father?"

A quick frown crossed his face. "No, I haven't. He's still out of the office. Gilda's trying to run him down for me."

"You need to climb down off your high horse. Sooner or later, Agent Gaines is going to come after me for the information I have, and you need a heads-up before he does. Besides, Lando's with his attorney right now."

"Your attorney, you mean. We'll retain one of our own."

Gilda's comment that Carl Brasser always delivered flashed through my mind. Why wasn't he already here? It was probably a little too soon, especially since Aggie hadn't been able to reach his father, but Brasser would be on his way quick enough.

"That's fine. Del's just holding down the fort. You know, seeing Lando's protected and trying to get him a bail hearing. I'm not sure the bail part will fly. Not with two dead bodies lying around."

"Two? Oh, you mean Santillanes. Lando didn't kill anyone."

"That's your opinion, but then you thought he was going to support your opposition to the De Falco buyout too. Maybe you were wrong *both* times."

Aggie blinked and glanced around. "Let's talk outside."

We found the shady side of the building and faced off. I threw the first verbal punch.

"You lied to me. You knew Lando was no longer opposing the buyout."

"He's been on both sides of the issue. I honestly didn't think he'd end up changing positions on me. Not after he thought it through. So I didn't lie."

"You didn't level with me either. Aggie, I know why a $100,000 deposit was made to Dana's account. But your timing was lousy. He was already dead." I cocked my head at him. "Or maybe the timing was perfect. Maybe the money was to throw everyone off track. Who would pay a hundred grand to a man he'd already killed?"

"You're crazy."

"Why do you oppose the De Falco Wines buyout?"

He shifted his weight and stood sprung-hipped on his left leg, arms folded across his chest, chin thrust forward. "We've already discussed this… at length."

"And we're going to keep discussing it until you tell me the truth. All of the truth."

"I told you. We haven't digested the last buyout. Besides, we'd be buying an organization half as big as our own—with borrowed money. And their grapes are the wrong kind for us."

"Money borrowed from a friendly source. That's not enough. It's not enough to make you go to such extremes to quash the deal. One hundred thousand isn't chicken feed—even to the Alfanos."

His face flushed. Those dark eyes bored into my own. "You want to know why, Vinson? Because I'm tired, that's why. It'll all fall on my shoulders one day, and I'm not up to the task. I'm not old school like Papa. I won't devote my entire life to the business."

He leaned back against the wall of the police building and closed his eyes. "You don't know what it's like. My family still lives in medieval times. The oldest living male is king. Patriarch. Tsar. It's one-man rule. All that power, all that responsibility rests on Papa's shoulders, and he loves it, thrives on it. Me, I want to spend time with my wife and kids. I want to go rock climbing, flying. Don't get me wrong. I'll run the business, but I won't let it consume me the way it has him." He met my eyes. "Lando's no help. He's too busy being gay."

The tone wasn't vicious, but the sentiment was sincere, making me wonder how Aggie really felt about his brother's sexual orientation.

"At least he's got the courage of his convictions," Aggie went on. "He'll take his advanced degree and end up teaching history in a prestigious college somewhere."

"There's always your sister. I hear she's cast in your old man's mold."

"She is. And if she'd been born with the right plumbing, it would all be on her back. May still end up that way, but not while Papa's alive. It's the old way with him. You know, I've often wondered what would have happened if Lando had been the elder son." He gave a half snort. "There would have been blood on the floor, and I'm not sure all of it would be Lando's."

"Haven't you ever heard of delegation, Aggie?"

"Yeah, and I've put some good people in place to move up when the time comes. I can handle what we have now. Make a good life for me and my family and still do right by the company. But not with De Falco added to the mix. I'll become a slave again when that happens. I went through that ordeal the last time we bought a business." He gave a deep sigh. "And we haven't even mentioned the Sabelito money. I'm a trustee on that too. When Mama goes, I'll be responsible for the whole shooting match. Tell me, BJ, what kind of life is that?"

"The kind men dream about, scheme for, kill to get."

"Yeah, men who don't know any better. I'm not a slacker. I'll run the business, but I won't sacrifice my wife and kids for it."

"So when Lando changed his mind and decided to finance the buyout, you saw all your plans going up in flames. Apparently Dana wasn't doing the job you hired him for."

"You don't know what you're talking about."

"Yes, I do. The FBI has his phone records. I know you spoke to him several times, including twice in the last week of his life."

"Okay, I made a deal with him when Lando called and told me he was going to support the buyout because Papa's pressure was affecting Mama's health. Lando was the cork in the genie's bottle. If he switched sides, I'd have to be the buffer." He drew a breath.

"Hell, he has Mama's power of attorney. He can make it happen all by himself. I asked him to think it through a little better, and he agreed. Then I sweet-talked Dana's cell phone number from Gilda and called him. They were at some service station west of Albuquerque, and Lando was inside paying for the gas, so we had a couple of minutes to talk. I made a deal with him—or thought I had. He was going to make sure Lando stood up to Papa, and I was going to pay him $100,000. I kept riding his back, and he kept stalling. I decided to go ahead and pay the money to pressure him to do what he'd agreed. When I called and told him that, he said he couldn't go through with it."

Aggie shook his head. "But it was too late; the wire transfer process had started. Besides, I still hoped the money would convince him." He leaned against the building again. "There was something going on. I think he and Lando already had a problem—something between them."

"Jazz Penrod?"

He shook his head. "Maybe, but I think it was deeper than that."

Remembering Lando's reaction when I mentioned secrets, I silently agreed with his assessment.

"So now," I said, "we have given the sheriff the one thing he's been missing."

"What's that?"

"A motive for Dana's murder."

"What are you talking about?"

"Think about it. Dana betrayed Lando by taking money to influence him, and that's on top of getting it on with Jazz. Lando became enraged and strangled him."

"Bullshit, that didn't happen."

"That's what Lonzo will say as soon as he traces that money back to you."

"No way. Those funds went through about three different banks before they reached his. That's why they were late getting there."

"You're forgetting one thing. I won't lie to the law. Not for you or Lando or anybody."

"You're privileged."

"Not legally. Lando's attorney didn't hire me to look into this, your father did. So there's no way to claim privilege. Of course, they might not ask me about it, but that's not something you can count on."

His cell went off at that moment, startling both of us. His expression deteriorated when he answered. "Papa's here," he announced as he closed the call.

"Here? In Farmington?"

Aggie nodded. "At the Marriott. I've got to go see him."

"I'll go with you."

"Uh-uh. He wants to talk to me first. He'll catch you later."

Chapter 33

I PICKED up a replacement cell phone, an expensive device with all the bells and whistles, including a built-in recorder, and went through the hassle of changing to my original number before heading back to the motel room where I found an exasperated message from Jazz. I didn't blame him; I'd forgotten to touch base with him again last night.

I got him on his cell phone and explained the problem I'd had with mine. "Anything happen last night?"

"Yeah. Not an hour after we talked, this car pulled up to the plane and two men got out. We were too far away to hear what they said, but they did some big-time cussing when they saw the wheels were flat. They argued a minute… well, that's not right. Wasn't much of an argument. Seemed like one guy was in charge, and the other one was taking all the guff. Anyway, they got back in the car and tore out of there. Sorry, but we couldn't see the plates on the car. All I can tell you is it was a sedan of some kind. You know, the four-door kind."

"Would you be able to identify the men if you saw them again?"

"Nah. They were just black shadows. One of them walked in front of the headlights, and I got a glimpse of him, but like I said, we were too far away. Besides, you know how it is; all you white dudes look alike." When his little joke fell flat, he went on, "Beefy guy, had a hat on, so don't know about the hair. Big nose. That's all I can tell you. Course, if we'd followed them…."

"Thank God you didn't. Tell Henry you guys did a good job. Where are you now?"

"Right where you put us, and we're hungry as hell. Also my cell battery's about gone. Henry's too. We used it to find somebody to haul my Wrangler back and fix it up."

"Okay, you guys go home now."

"Will do. How's Lando holding up?"

"Seems to be doing better. Remembering a few things. Thanks for sticking it out on the mesa last night."

"That's what we're here for."

Then I called Charlie, who said the plane stranded out on the rim of Black Hole Canyon was a restored Piper J-3 Cub, a tandem two-seater craft primarily used by the Civilian Pilot Training Program in World War II. FAA records showed the N-Number was registered to a Los Angeles company called the Pied Pipers, apparently one of the many Cub associations around the country. He hadn't had time to root out the owners, but personnel at the home field had given him a couple of names and told him the craft was regularly rented out to qualified pilots in the area.

I told him I needed to know who had it under lease, when it had departed LA, and where the flight plan indicated it was heading. Then I really dumped on him, asking him to trace Anthony Alfano's movements for the last few days. Aggie had said his father was in Los Angeles when he left the message advising that Lando was in FBI custody. Today he showed up in Farmington. That was possible, given the company had an executive jet, but I wanted to ascertain the location of the players—or potential players—in this little drama. Charlie's head must have been spinning by the time I finished listing everyone: Victoria and her husband, William Vitrillo, Bruno Wills, and the company's principal officers. This included Frank Baratta, Ariel Gonda, and Tom Scavo, who might have had "feelings" for Lando.

"BJ," he objected, "that could take months and stir up a whole lot of trouble."

"Understood. Find what you can, as quickly as you can. I have the feeling we're about to be fired from this job."

After that I stole a few minutes to dial Paul's cell and caught him walking between classes at the U. He couldn't resist tweaking my nose.

"Vinson… Vinson. I used to know a guy by that name. Don't know what happened to him. He headed north one day, and I never saw him again."

"This is the same fellow. Doing his best to wrap up this assignment and get back to you as fast as possible."

"God, I miss you, Vince."

"You don't know how good that makes me feel. But I don't think it will be long before I'm back. This case is going to break—one way or the other."

"What does that mean?"

"My client's son is in the pokey, and I think the old man is about to fire me."

"Man, I hope so. You've been gone so long, some of these guys on campus are beginning to look good to me. Hell, some of the *girls* look good to me."

"I'll catch the next flight out. Seriously, it shouldn't be long now."

There was a missed call from Aggie on my cell when I hung up. A summons, no doubt. Well, he could wait. So could his father, for that matter.

A quick run by the airport confirmed that the Alfano corporate jet was not at the field, nor had it been there recently. Dix Lee was in the station and reported there was nothing new on Kinkaid except she had located his car rental agency—agencies, in fact. Kinkaid had rented a gray Toyota Corolla and a green Ford Taurus from different agencies. Neither had been returned.

Del raised me on my cell as I left the station to tell me the court had agreed to a bail hearing. We both knew that didn't mean much; Gaines was merely dotting the i's and crossing the t's, to make sure the family couldn't find fault with Lando's treatment. It was set for four o'clock this afternoon. That gave me a little over four hours to see what additional information I could develop.

"Have you met Alfano Sr. yet? He was waiting at the detention center when I came in," Del went on without waiting for an answer. "Nobody would let him see his son, and he was raising hell. He's used to throwing his weight around."

"Did he get in?"

"Nope. The FBI won't let anyone see Lando except his attorney. As of now that's still me."

"You haven't been replaced?"

"No, and I thought I'd be back in Albuquerque by now. I don't understand why the old boy didn't bring a bevy of lawyers with him."

"I don't get it either, but I haven't seen the man yet. Maybe I'll find out something when I do. That's next on my list. Am I still cleared to speak to Lando?"

"As long as you're with me."

"Stay close, Del. I want another try at him after I see Alfano and take a reading on him."

"He's all bluff and bluster and money."

"I'm pretty sure he's not all bluff," I said.

"No, but he sure is bluster and money."

THE COURTYARD by Marriott Farmington was a hotel built in the Pueblo Revival style with a wide portico, floors stacked one upon the other, and the entire structure covered in earth-brown stucco. When Anthony Alfano opened the door to his room, I saw a heavier, older, somewhat coarser version of his two sons. He carried his fifty-five years well. At five ten and two hundred pounds, he was a strong man in decent physical condition. A peek at his medical records would probably show him to be as fit as the proverbial fiddle despite the beginnings of a roll around his middle. The veins on his nose hinted he preferred Sabelito's hard stuff to the grape he peddled. The gray in his wavy hair looked like streaks of gypsum in a seam of coal.

After I introduced myself, he invited me inside in the gravelly bass I remembered from our phone conversations.

He didn't offer his hand but stepped back from the doorway so I could enter the suite. Aggie's lanky form was sprawled in an easy chair. A snifter of white wine sat on the table beside him. Anthony's drink was red. I waved away his offer of a glass.

"Good to finally meet you in person." I tried playing the etiquette game, but he brushed aside the small talk.

"Good job finding my son, but why in the hell did you turn him over to the FBI?"

"For his own protection."

"Bullshit. Aggie could have had him home in a couple of hours. There's no place safer than that."

"Maybe, but then he'd be a fugitive, and Aggie would have been aiding and abetting. That's no life for your sons."

"That decision wasn't yours to make. You overstepped your contract."

"So fire me," I said with a smile. In his world, dismissal was the ultimate threat, and he might as well know it wouldn't work on me.

"Consider it done," he shot back. "Send me your final bill."

"Wait a minute." Aggie straightened in his chair. "For some reason Lando trusts BJ. We need to keep him around until we get a better handle on the situation."

Alfano put his own twist on Aggie's declaration. "I can have our own bodyguards here within four hours. We don't—"

"I'm not talking about bodyguards. I'm talking about someone with a little moxie. Lando was as messed up as any down-and-out hobo I've ever seen, and BJ brought him out of it."

Alfano winced at the mental image. Maybe the old bastard had a heart after all.

"Okay," he said. "You're not fired—yet. What's next?"

"Gaines, the FBI agent in charge of this case, is going to try to isolate Lando, which means he'll give you some grief about getting in to see him. Your temporary attorney successfully petitioned the court for a bail hearing. It's set for four this afternoon. He also got me access to Lando by claiming I'm his investigator. I want to talk to Lando one more time before the bail hearing. After that, regardless of the outcome, Gaines will probably give you a few minutes with your son."

"Hell, we'll take him home with us. I'll post whatever bail is necessary."

"Might not be that easy. This is a murder case. Possibly a capital case since there are two bodies. I don't expect them to grant bail." I cut off his protest. "How did you get here so fast, Alfano?"

"What's that got to do with anything? When I got Aggie's message, I was in LA. A business associate flew me over. I'll hitch a ride back with Aggie. Anything else you want to know?" His tone said he was holding on to his temper with difficulty.

"What do either of you know about the Pied Pipers?" I asked.

"Who the hell are they?" Alfano demanded. "Are we playing children's games now?"

"Aggie?"

"Never heard of them. Why?"

"Just ran across the name recently. I'm on my way to meet Mr. Dahlman now, and we're going to make certain Lando understands what's going to happen in the hearing this afternoon. Any message you want me to convey?"

"Tell him we're behind him a hundred percent. We know he didn't kill anybody," Alfano said.

"I'll also tell him he'll see you at the hearing. I assume you'll both be there."

"Certainly."

When Aggie walked me to the door, I motioned him outside.

"What?"

"I'm going to ask you a very personal question, and I need an honest answer. I think your brother's hiding something—at least his conscious mind is. There was something wrong between him and Dana, and I've got to learn what it was. It might be the key to this whole thing."

"Why would he forget something so important?"

"Because it was so traumatic."

Aggie thrust out his chin. "Okay, ask away."

"Did you have intimate—by that, I mean sexual—relations with Dana Norville?"

"What?" The word exploded from Aggie. His face darkened dangerously, giving me a glimpse of his father lurking inside him. "Of course not. Never."

"Hang on for a couple more, and they might be even rougher. Did you ever *try* to seduce Dana?"

He was in control of himself now; his mottled complexion faded. The dark eyes lost their feral glint. The answer was a flat no.

"Here comes the biggie. Did you ever have or attempt to have sexual relations with your brother?"

"You are a sick son of a bitching faggot," Aggie said in a low, even voice. "No."

"I accept your word on it, but I had to ask. I never believed you had. I'm going through a process of elimination here."

"I guess I understand." He paused as he reached for the doorknob. "Papa's got a couple of attorneys from the Brasser firm on the way. You might want to let Dahlman know."

JAIL APPARENTLY agreed with Lando, at least compared to life on the streets. He was a different man. It wasn't only the fact he was clean; he was more alert than he had been in our first interview at the detention center. He rose to shake our hands, addressing both Del and me by name. For the first time, I caught myself thinking of him as an Alfano instead of "Lando."

We were in a different room this time, one provided for attorney-client consultations, and he glanced around the small chamber with interest. A guard stood outside the steel door with a small window for observation. The place had an antiseptic smell about it. The table was metal and bolted to the floor, as were the chairs. Lando's orange jumpsuit made me think of the Porsche lying at the bottom of the Rio Grande Gorge outside of Taos.

"What's going to happen to me?" It was a straightforward question without a hint of pity.

"There's a bail hearing set for four this afternoon," Del explained. "But don't get your hopes up. You are charged with two murders, and the judge is not likely to approve a bond, no matter how much your family can put up."

"Two? Who am I supposed to have killed besides—" His voice caught. He cleared his throat. "Besides Dana?"

"Santillanes, the PI who tried to abduct you at Bisti," I said. "Did you do that?" The question earned a frown from Del.

"No, I didn't kill either one of them. I've never killed anybody."

"You look stronger, Lando. Do you feel stronger?"

"I'm okay." His piercing chocolate-brown eyes shifted away from me.

"Look at me, Lando," I ordered. Startled, he glanced up and met my gaze. "You're hiding something, and if you want me to find out who killed Dana, I need to know what it is."

"I'm not hiding anything."

"You may not know it, but you are. When we talked last time, I asked about secrets between you and Dana and you fell apart. You need to face up to whatever it is."

"Secrets? I don't know what you mean."

"I mean the relationship between the two of you was under stress, and I don't think it was because of Jazz Penrod. Something happened before Jazz came along, didn't it?"

"That's not…." His voice trailed off. "Well, things weren't as easy between us, but it was just the trip. You know, being together 24-7."

"Don't try to snow me, Lando. What was going on?"

We danced for thirty minutes. I went at him every way I knew how without getting down and dirty. Finally that was the only way left.

"Lando, who else was fucking Dana?"

His head snapped back as if I'd clipped him on the chin. His eyes went wide. A groan rolled out of him. His torso rocked back and forth. The way he glared at me, I thought he was going to come across the table. Then he dropped his head onto his arms folded on the table.

Del gave me a look. "What the hell are you doing, Vince?"

"Trying to get to the truth."

"What do you know that you haven't told me?"

"It's just a suspicion, nothing I know for certain. But I think what he's hiding—from himself more than from us, most likely—is the key to everything."

"You believe the murders were sexually motivated?"

"Not lust, if that's what you mean. But one of them had a sexual context. The other was to cover up the first."

"That third car down at Bisti?"

"Right. Santillanes was hired by someone to tail Lando and Dana. When he caught up with them, he phoned his client and kept tabs on them until his boss arrived. Then he tried to snatch Lando while his client went after Dana. And Dana ended up dead. Dead with semen inside him."

"If there was semen, then there's DNA. Surely, Gaines has taken Lando's DNA by now. It either matched, or it didn't."

"He hasn't had time to get the tests back on Lando's DNA. And when they do, it's not going to match. Unless Lando and Dana made love that morning."

"We didn't."

The low, muffled voice startled us. I had assumed Lando was so out of it he wouldn't notice us talking over him. But if he'd gone away, he was back. He lifted his head and stared me straight in the eye.

"We didn't," he repeated. "We hadn't made love since he got together with Jazz. We argued about it. And… and that's when he told me what was really wrong—what was tearing him apart. The thing that was tearing us apart."

"What was that?" Del asked.

Lando shook his head slowly. "It's too…." He shuddered.

"Was it Aggie?" I asked bluntly.

His lips tightened; his chest expanded. The rising outrage in his eyes turned cloudy. Lando dropped his gaze to the table and sagged visibly.

"No, not Aggie. Papa. Papa *raped* him!"

Chapter 34

LANDO DROPPED his head to his arms again, but a moment later, Del and I witnessed another of those amazing transformations from boy to man. Lando sat up with fire in his eyes. His voice took on timbre and strength.

"I'd been planning a vacation for a long time but put it on the back burner when this De Falco thing came up. I didn't want to leave Mama under that kind of stress." He took a deep breath. "Then out of the blue, Dana said he needed to get away. Claimed he couldn't take the pressure. You know, Papa's dislike—no, his hate. I started to argue with him until it hit me. If Mama would trust me with a power of attorney for the acquisition, I could just disappear and let nature take its course. The De Falco people wouldn't sit around and wait forever. We'd heard there was another interested party, which was why Papa was stepping up the pressure. So Dana and I packed up and took off."

"You didn't let your father know where you were going?"

"Yeah, I did. I stood right in front of him and told him to go to hell. Told him I was going to get lost somewhere in New Mexico, and I wouldn't take his calls. When I left his office, I wasn't sure if he was having a fit or a stroke. And didn't much care which one it was."

"So Dana probably didn't see your father again after the… uh, incident. And at that point you weren't aware of what had happened?"

"Nope, and it's a good thing I wasn't. The bastard didn't have to do that to Dana just to get back at me. He did it after preaching all these years about me manning up. If I had known, I'd have killed the son of a bitch. Still might."

I would have dismissed that as bravado except this was an Alfano, and I was beginning to wonder if anything was beyond any of them.

Del spoke up. "Lando, you've got to understand that rape isn't sex. It's violence, domination. It's a way to terrorize."

Lando took another deep breath, and his defiance collapsed. "I know. But he didn't have to do it that way. That… that made it my fault. It wouldn't have happened if it wasn't for me."

"Your father did it to drive Dana away," Del continued. "And it worked. If you hadn't agreed to get out of town, Dana probably would have gone by himself."

"Yeah. I figured that out. Dana got happy as hell when I agreed to go with him. We decided to make it a vacation. No cares. No worries. Just fun. And it was for a while. We had a great time, but I could tell something was bothering him. And it got worse. It started interfering with things. I tried to get him to tell me what it was. But he wouldn't. I guess I pushed too hard, because it got so he wouldn't talk much at all. Everything really fell apart when we came here."

Lando drew a deep breath like a man coming up from under water. "I thought it was because the trip was coming to an end, but I finally figured out it was the phone calls. The last week or so we were together, his phone started ringing all the time. After a while he'd just hang up without saying a word. I thought it was Bruno, you know, his ex, bugging him, but at first he claimed it was wrong numbers, and then it was a problem with his preregistration at school. A couple of times, I grabbed the phone when it rang, but whoever it was just hung up."

"Did you see the number displayed on the phone's screen?" I asked.

He shook his head. "It was restricted. There wasn't a number. Anyway, he got nervous—like he was worried. He'd shy away when I wanted to make love. But then he'd apologize and everything would be fine. But he'd changed. It was almost like he was a different guy. Otherwise he wouldn't have hooked up with Jazz. It was just us. You know, the two of us. The rest of the world didn't matter—at least for a little while. God, I miss him."

Lando shuffled his feet and thumped a fist on the metal table, making a sound like a muffled Chinese gong. "When I came back from the art gallery and saw Jazz leaving the motel that day, I was really bummed. Jazz is a natural-born flirt. I don't think he even knows he's doing it half the time, but it drove me crazy that Dana was eating it up. I accused him of two-timing me." Lando paused and swallowed hard.

"He… he said Jazz was the least of our worries. It took me an hour to get it out of him, and we almost ended up in a fistfight. But he finally admitted Papa offered him a lot of money to go away and leave me alone.

You know, break up with me. Move out of state. When Dana wouldn't do it, Papa went down to LA while I was on the way home for the weekend. He talked Dana into meeting him at a motel to 'settle things between them,' Papa said. But what he really wanted was to up the ante to get Dana to leave me. Things got kind of bad. Papa started slapping him around. Dana said it turned into something else. Papa said…. Papa said…."

That faraway look came back into his eyes. The man was retreating; the kid was coming back. I reached across the table and clasped his shoulder, hoping my touch would ground him.

"That's good. Keep on going. You need to tell us everything, Lando. Say it out loud. What did your father tell Dana?"

Lando's gaze wavered before he looked me in the eye. "Papa said he'd show him how a real man fucked. Threw him down on the bed in the motel where they were meeting and… and raped him."

"Lando, your father's a strong man, but I saw Dana's body. He was well-built. He could have put up a fight and kept it from happening."

"Yeah, that's what I said too. But that's before I found out what Papa did."

"What was that?"

"He had a stun gun. He put it to Dana's back and stripped him while he was helpless. When Dana kept trying to fight, he zapped him again. Then he raped him. He *raped* the man I loved. And all this time he'd been telling me what a sissy, what a mama's boy, what a pansy I was. He said what Dana and I did would make a real man sick to his stomach. And then he did that. Dana didn't know how to handle it. He tried to deal with it himself, but he was falling apart. I think that's why he got together with Jazz."

He expelled a breath of air. "Aw, I don't know, maybe I'm making excuses for him. But we'd always been faithful to each other… until then. Oh, God, I wish I'd handled things better. But I didn't know it was about to end. That Dana was going to die." He cradled his head in his arms again.

"Why do you think he died?" I asked.

Lando's body froze. Muscles trembled as he grappled for an answer— or a plausible evasion. Then his head rose slowly. "I don't know."

"Your father's in town. He and Aggie will be in the courtroom this afternoon."

He scrambled to his feet. "No."

I turned and waved to the guard watching through the window, signaling everything was under control.

"Sit down, Lando," Del said. "I'm sorry, but the courtroom is open to the public. Your father and brother can enter just like anyone else. But you don't have to talk to them if you don't want to."

Lando slumped back into his chair. "I don't want to talk to either one of them."

"Did Dana tell you about Aggie?" I asked.

"About trying to bribe him to influence me?" Lando's voice hardened. "Well, Dana did his job. He had to die for it, but he did his job."

"What do you mean?"

"There's no way in hell I'll let that son-of-a-bitching father of mine have De Falco now. Not after what he did to Dana." Lando stood again. "That's enough. Take me back to my cell." He smacked the table with his hand and yelled for the guard.

"Son, you need to stay a bit longer. Mr. Dahlman has to prepare you for this afternoon's hearing."

I nodded to Del and took my leave. I had lots to do before four o'clock rolled around.

I CONTACTED Jazz and had him describe once again what he and Henry had observed out on the rim of Black Hole the other night. Then I phoned Gaines and told him about my surveillance of the stranded aircraft, informing him two men had spent some time wiping down the plane after they discovered they were grounded. Gaines's opinion was they were probably drug smugglers, but he promised to send someone to check it out. He also agreed to contact the Pied Pipers and get all the information he could on whoever rented the craft. But after I went over what Lando had told me and suggested he collect DNA from the Alfano family, he balked.

"You must be crazy. Those people are connected. I've already had calls from the agents in charge of Los Angeles and San Francisco. Besides, what's my probable cause? The word of an unstable young man who's suspected of murdering two people?"

"You could expedite Lando's DNA tests. You probably already have the test results on Dana Norville's body, so compare the two. They won't match, but there will be enough markers to show the rapist was a close relative. Then you have probable cause."

"Vinson, you know that semen deteriorates rapidly. There might not even be DNA available from a body lying out on the desert for a couple of weeks."

"Dana was well protected from the elements," I argued. "And sometimes the dry desert air preserves things. At least we can try."

"I've already sent samples, but the results are not back yet. We'll just have to wait and see."

"There's one other thing. Lando said Dana got a lot of calls the last week they were together that he wouldn't explain. I recall seeing another number on Dana's cell phone record. Have you been able to trace it?"

"It's a prepaid throwaway cell. Not registered to anyone. It's going to take time to trace the calls to the source, and then we still won't know much."

"It had an LA area code, as I remember."

"Yes, and that's all we know about it."

I thought for a moment. "I assume the US attorney's going to oppose granting bail this afternoon."

"That's my recommendation—regardless of what you say." Irritation made his voice harsh.

"Good. That's what I recommend too."

"What? Why?"

"Who would Lando be released to if he made bail?"

I left him thinking that one over and touched base with Charlie back in Albuquerque. He had the name of the pilot who rented the Cub, but the name meant nothing. The description was vague and could have fit about anyone of middle years. The pilot's license cited on the rental contract was phony. That made me wonder exactly how safe we were from terrorists soaring around overhead in small aircraft.

Next I reached Dix Lee, and she agreed to have Kinkaid's stun gun examined for prints in the battery compartment and on the batteries themselves. After that, I stopped by the Bean Bowl to eat and do some thinking. Given that Alfano used a stun gun on Dana, I suspected he had supplied the weapon to Kinkaid. And I was pretty damned sure Alfano was the second man in my motel room that night. Had he intended to harm his younger son if I had delivered him up? It was a stretch, but not out of the realm of possibility.

The worst part was that Anthony Alfano might get away with it. His money and a battery of high-powered attorneys would make it difficult for Gaines to obtain his DNA—through the court system, anyway. That left me with one additional job.

Lady Luck was kind to me; Alfano and Aggie had just finished a late lunch in the Marriott's dining room. I sat down uninvited, earning a look of curiosity from Aggie and irritation from his father. I waited patiently as Alfano signed a credit card slip while a busboy cleared the table of everything except their half-empty wineglasses.

"I just left Lando." I paused to gauge Alfano's reaction. There was none. He stared at me blandly. If he was worried about what I might have learned from his son, it didn't show. Of course, he had spent a lifetime developing a poker face for his high-stakes business dealings. "There might be a problem at the hearing this afternoon."

"What?" Alfano lifted his glass and took a sip of white wine.

"He doesn't want you present. Either of you."

Alfano's eyes didn't flicker. "He's just embarrassed over the situation he's gotten himself into. That will pass. In the meantime, I'm going to be there to support my son, whether or not that support is welcome. And I imagine Aggie feels the same way."

"I don't know, Papa. That will put more pressure on him, and he's pretty fragile right now. Maybe it would be better to let the lawyer handle things. We can see him after he's calmed down."

"Nonsense, we're going to be right there so he can see he still has his family's support. I don't want him thinking we abandoned him in his time of need. Even if I did warn him about hanging around with that faggot. It invited trouble. Dana finally propositioned the wrong guy and paid the price for his perversion."

"Down at Bisti Wilderness?" I asked. "Out in the middle of nowhere."

"You're the investigator. You tell me. Right now, we need to get ready for the hearing."

His son surprised us both. "You go on. I'll be along later."

"You'll be right at my side in the courtroom, Aggie. No argument." Alfano stood, took a final sip of his wine, and stalked out of the dining room.

"He's right, you should be there."

"But—"

"You need to see Lando's reaction to him for yourself."

"What do you mean?"

"Trying to buy one half of a loving couple to influence the other half for your own personal aims was despicable. It was bound to fail, you know."

"Why? The biggest risk was I wouldn't get my $100,000's worth."

"But that was nothing compared to what your father did." Aggie said nothing. I had his full attention. "The irony of it is that because of your father, Lando's going to see he never gets De Falco Wines, at least not with your mother's money."

"What? When did he tell you that?"

"An hour ago, right after he told me your father went to see Dana in LA before they left California. He offered him money to leave, get away from Lando, and never come back. Dana refused. They had words and then started scuffling. It ended in rape, Dana's rape."

"Bullshit. That's impossible."

"Why? Because Dana was big enough to defend himself, or because Anthony Alfano wouldn't do that to another man?"

"Both. My father's not gay."

"Come on, it wasn't sex. It was a demonstration of power. To show his son's lover he could do anything he wanted to him. As to overpowering the kid, your father used a stun gun to render him helpless and then did what he wanted. Used a stun gun—does that sound familiar?"

"That's what happened to you."

"Right. And there were two people in my room that night. One I never saw clearly or heard speak. He only whispered. The police have that stun gun, and I asked Sergeant Lee to check the inside to see if there's another set of fingerprints besides Kinkaid's."

Aggie's hand trembled as he took a sip of water. He set the glass down hard, spilling some.

"And remember, Dana was raped either before or after he was strangled to death. There was DNA inside him."

"The old man's not stupid. If he did what you say—and he didn't— he wouldn't leave DNA on the body."

"Perhaps he thought the body would never be found, at least until it was too late to recover anything useful. We only found Dana because that Honcho kid had his cell phone."

Aggie shook his head. "No way. He wouldn't take a chance like that. Besides, he was in California at the time."

"Are you sure of that? I called a few times, and Gilda said he was out of town."

"He's been traveling some, that's true. But he was in touch by phone."

"Cell phone? How do you know where someone is when he calls you on one of those? He could be in Timbuktu or the room next door."

"You're wrong, BJ."

"How much do you believe what you're saying?"

"Without question."

"Are you willing to back that statement up with action?"

"What do you mean?"

I pointed to his father's wineglass. "There are fingerprints and DNA on that. We can take it to Gaines for comparison."

Aggie's nostrils flared. "Go ahead, make a fool of yourself."

"Good, but you'll have to attest it's a glass your father drank from. Are you *that* certain?"

"Fucking A."

I called a waiter and asked for a couple of bags. After he brought them, I held the stem with a napkin and used my pen, a Sharpie fine point, to initial the base of the glass, note the time, date, and restaurant. Then I asked both the waiter and Aggie to put their initials beside mine. I tore paper from the pocket notebook I carry and wrote out a brief statement for the waiter, attesting that he had served wine in this glass to Mr. Alfano. Aggie and I both signed the statement as witnesses. For good measure, I took a snapshot Aggie carried of his father and had the waiter initial that as well. Then I carefully placed the glass in one bag and the statement and photo in the other.

As we got up to leave, Aggie halted. "I don't feel right about this."

"If you're right and I'm wrong, all it will do is clear your father. If not—"

I left the rest of that thought hanging in the air as I walked away with the evidence.

Chapter 35

I SAT in my car and watched the Alfanos exit a green Ford Taurus and walk toward the courthouse entrance. If they noticed me, they didn't let on. Alfano's flat-footed gait irritated me for some reason. Damn, if only Gaines had gotten back to me with information on that blind cell phone, I might have been able to put a crimp in somebody's tail. The thought hauled me up short. Alfano was far too sharp to keep the thing on him. That's why they were called throwaway phones, but nothing ventured, nothing gained.

I got out of the rental, dialed the number of the telephone that had made so many calls to Dana's number shortly before his death, and fell in behind them, straining to hear a ring and praying the instrument had not been set on vibrate.

"Yeah?" A rough voice answered, taking me by surprise. I recognized it even though I had been in an electrical fog the last time I heard it. I halted and turned away from the two men walking in front of me.

"Hello, Kinkaid."

"Y'all got the wrong number, partner. Who's this, anyway?"

I pressed a key on my cell phone and began recording the conversation. The expensive little gadget was about to pay off.

"I have the right number, Kinkaid. This is Vinson, the guy you roughed up in the Farmington motel. I just wanted you to know Alfano gave you up."

"Dunno what y'all's talking about. Who the fuck is Alfano?"

"It's too late for that bullshit. The police have the stun gun with your prints on the outside and his on the batteries," I lied. "That puts the two of you together. If that's not enough, you didn't get all the prints wiped off the Piper Cub out on the mesa. Not only that, you rented a car for him, and I saw him in that green Taurus not five minutes ago. The police already have the lease you signed when you rented it. Both of your prints are on that too. The best thing you can do is turn yourself in to the nearest police station."

"Think y'all's scaring me? Forget it. I was hauling water for the mob before y'all was outa diapers. I know all the tricks."

"Yeah, but that's the point, Kinkaid. The mob lives by a code. They stand by their soldiers. Alfano's an outsider. He's got no moral code."

All that got me was a grunt, but it was enough. He was listening.

"Right now you're only wanted for breaking and entering and assault with a dangerous weapon. Cooperate, and I can make that all go away. Otherwise you go down as an accessory after the fact in a double homicide. He's probably plotting to set you up to take the fall for the killings as we speak. You know what big money can do."

"Yeah, it can buy me lots of protection."

"Why would he protect you?"

"Because I can put his ass in jail—lawyers or no lawyers."

"For assaulting me? That was his idea, right?"

"Yeah."

Out of the corner of my eye, I saw Dix Lee coming down the sidewalk with Lonzo Joe. The sheriff's detective was here to protect the county's interest, no doubt; Dix was probably merely curious. I waved them over and tipped the phone so they could listen.

"Let me understand this, Kinkaid. Alfano hired you to assault and kidnap me? Kidnapping's a federal offense, you know."

"Yeah, but nobody got kidnapped."

"Maybe not, but he told you to take me, didn't he?"

"So what if he did?"

"And you tried."

"I'm hanging up now. Against the law to talk on the telephone while driving in this state, y'all know that?" His bellowing laugh died abruptly as he ended the call.

"You get that?" I asked the two officers.

"Enough. Old man Alfano trying to kill his own son? Hard to believe," Lonzo said.

"Not kill his son. It was his son's lover he was after. It's a long story. I need to catch Gaines's attention. Will you back me up about the phone call?"

"Sure," Dix answered. "Right after you give us that phone number so we can get somebody to work pinning down Kinkaid's location."

"I would have headed north to Colorado. Or Utah," Lonzo suggested.

"He'd have been there by now. He's still on the road, so I'm guessing he's trying for Texas," I replied.

"Dumb."

"Nobody ever accused mob muscle of being smart. That's not what they're hired for," Dix said.

It was five of four when Lonzo went inside the courtroom and pulled Gaines out to listen to the recording of my call to Kinkaid. I took the opportunity to hand over the call and the glass from the Marriott Restaurant and explain what they were to the three of them. Although Gaines wasn't as positive about the idea as I was, he authorized Dix to deliver the items to the crime lab at FPD and start processing them.

"All you've got is speculation, Vinson," he said as Dix headed for her cruiser. "None of this is going to put a halt to the proceedings in there."

"Didn't expect it to. But at least you have a few additional things to check when you prepare for trial."

"That's the US attorney's job, not mine."

"Maybe not, but guess who'll do the grunt work."

"Point taken." He checked his watch. "I'm going back inside now. They're about to start."

"Me too. I wouldn't miss this for the world."

Lonzo merely grunted as we started for the courthouse steps.

The proceeding went as expected. The judge heard arguments and denied bail. Lando accepted the decision, but Anthony Alfano was enraged. As he left the room in shackles, Lando shuffled past his father and brother without giving them a glance, despite Alfano's loud proclamations of support over the noise of an emptying courtroom.

I walked outside with Del to update him on the morning's developments, but we had no opportunity. Alfano approached, stiff-legged, and snarled at Del.

"Is that the best you can do? What kind of shyster are you anyway?"

"You may talk to your own lackeys that way but not to me. Get a civil tongue in your head or this conversation is over." Del had a pretty well-developed sense of self and wasn't about to be bullied.

"You're fired. You hear me? Fired."

"Sorry, but you're not my client, and Lando wants me to represent him. He said so before we went into the hearing. By the way, he asked me to keep you away from him."

In his younger days, Alfano probably had put up with a lot of lip, but I doubt anyone had talked to him like that in the past ten years. He didn't take it well.

"Wait until my attorneys get here—real lawyers, not night school shysters—and we'll see who represents my son. In the meantime, I'll hold you responsible if anything happens to him."

"I can hardly wait to meet the gentlemen," Del replied.

We watched Alfano, trailed by his older son, walk toward the green Taurus. Anger radiated from the older man; despair flowed from Aggie. As soon as they pulled out of the parking lot, I filled Del in on my telephone call with Kinkaid.

"What did Gaines say about the DNA on Dana? His body was out there in the desert quite a while."

"So he reminded me, although he had already asked for tests. The results are not back yet, but he did send the wineglass to the lab for processing."

"You say Sergeant Lee heard the conversation?"

"Dix and Detective Lonzo Joe. The important part of it, anyway."

Del's broad forehead wrinkled in thought. "The FPD can probably tie Alfano to the attack on you—"

"And attempted kidnapping," I reminded him. "That's a serious felony charge."

"I'm not sure I'd go that far. To most people it would only look like an attempt to get information from you. Kinkaid sounds hard core. I'm not certain he'll back you up, but we need to find him."

"Kinkaid lives by a code, one you and I might not fully understand, but turning on a snake who's ready to give him up and who is not one of the *famiglia* won't be a problem for him."

"I hope you're right."

"Look, I want to talk with Alfano alone. When I'm ready I'll call and have you phone Aggie with some excuse for him to meet you. You can say Lando is asking for him—just him, not the old man. Will you do that?"

"Okay, sure. What strategy are you going to use with Alfano?"

"We know semen deteriorates rapidly, but I wonder if Alfano does."

I left him mulling that over. I needed to get away before his lawyer's brain started sifting through possibilities and came up with what I had in mind. He would have put his foot down hard—squarely on my toes.

Chapter 36

By the time I was prepared to face down Alfano, hours had passed, and a gibbous moon hung high in the sky. Gaines had refused to go along with my plan until he had a long session with Lando under the wary and watchful eye of Del Dahlman—thankfully without tipping my hand to Del. Technically we didn't need the FBI's help or cooperation since my assault had taken place within the city limits of Farmington; however, I'd learned it was better to have the FBI with you instead of against you, and Gaines did have a stake in the whole thing.

I parked in the Courtyard's busy lot and tucked my S&W 9mm in the belt at the small of my back before walking across the asphalt toward the porte cochere. Flickers of lightning in the southwest sky illuminated the scattered cloud cover and threatened us with more monsoon moisture. It seemed an ominous sign. Of course, all I intended was to face down a bully and listen to him try to explain his way out of assault and murder—and the rape of his younger son's boyfriend. Shouldn't be much of a problem.

I clutched the attaché case in my right hand. All it contained was a transcript of my call to Kinkaid and a hidden camera with audio—a backup in the event Alfano discovered the wire I was wearing. Given his reputation as a crafty businessman, that was a distinct possibility. I wouldn't be surprised if he'd used a few wires over the years himself.

I mounted the stairs to the second floor and headed down the hallway to the Alfano suite. The old man should be alone. Aggie had left the hotel a few minutes earlier in response to Del's call. It was a diversion but not a sham. Lando had finally agreed to talk to his brother.

Alfano answered my knock, and the sight of me at his door kindled a bright anger behind those dark eyes. If I had expected to see him in a silk smoking jacket with a cigar held in a hand with a pinkie ring, I was disappointed. He looked like a thousand other businessmen at the end of a hectic day: suit jacket off, white shirtsleeves rolled halfway up corded arms. Over his shoulder I saw a jumble of pens, keys, and pocket change littering a table beside the couch. A stogie burned in an ashtray.

"What do you want?" he growled.

"Need to talk."

"I've got nothing to say to you."

"Maybe not, but I've got plenty to say to you. Hear me out before deciding whether to talk to me or not."

"So talk."

"Not out here."

He poked his head through the door to check out the hallway and then backed inside to take a seat on the sofa. I plopped down on the chair opposite him. Pungent cigar smoke wafted between us—expensive cigar smoke. Alfano lacked the patrician features of his offspring, but he had the kind of plebeian good looks that usually coarsen with age. He had reached that stage of life.

"Well, what is it?" His eyes bored into mine; he sat hunched forward, alert.

"There are several developments I haven't told you about. But first, tell me—for my own edification—why is the De Falco acquisition so important to you?"

"It's good business."

"Not according to Aggie. He believes you need to finish imposing your corporate culture onto the last buyout. Build your team before taking on someone half your own size."

"It's not my son's judgment that built the company into a $100 million enterprise; it's mine."

Even as he spoke it hit me, and I thought I understood the urgency, the extreme measures this man was willing to take in order to ascertain the purchase went through. It made a weird kind of sense in light of the crash course I was getting in the makeup of Alfano's psyche.

"It's Mona's grandfather, isn't it? You weren't good enough for him, were you? Well, he was right. You can't walk in the man's shoes. You're jealous of an old duffer who's been dead for—what? Thirteen years? You can't even match a tenth of what he put together in his lifetime. You don't measure up. But why De Falco? That won't close the gap on the old boy." I laughed. "And worse, you'd be using Sabelito money to buy it."

"Maybe you're not as dumb as you look, Vinson. Yeah, the bastard did everything in his power to see his precious Mona didn't marry that Tuscan garbage. *Cianfrusaglia*, he used to call me—trash. But I got her anyway. Swept her off her feet. That's the only time in her life she defied the old tyrant. As for using his trust? That's the beauty of it. I use his money to beat him at his own game."

"It doesn't wash. You'd still be a piker compared to his billion."

"I guess you aren't so smart after all. Believe me, it matters. It's going to end up making Titus Sabelito look like the piker."

What did that mean? What was I missing? Whatever it was, I didn't have time to figure it out.

"The real tragedy is that Lando had decided to support you in the purchase." At the sudden gleam in his eyes, I smiled and added, "But not now. He'll see you in hell before he lets you use Sabelito money to buy De Falco."

Alfano's hand clinched involuntarily around his cigar, spilling gray ash over the front of his white shirt. He'd almost lost it, but he recovered quickly. He slowly brought the stogie to his lips and puffed, his eyes narrowing against the cloud of smoke.

"Why?" he asked in a nearly normal voice.

"Why? He has his own reasons, which he'll give you in due time. Meanwhile, you may find this of some interest."

I took the leather attaché case from my lap and placed it on the coffee table, taking care that the camera continued to point in his direction. Then I opened it and handed him the transcript of the Kinkaid telephone call.

His anger flared as he scanned the document. The flesh around his eyes seemed to contract like a camera lens when the setting is changed. The corners of his mouth turned down, and a flush touched his cheeks. Yet by the time he tossed the papers aside, he had himself under control again. His gaze was clear when he looked at me. The spot of color was gone from his face. "That means nothing."

I smiled. "You made a mistake, Alfano, one of many. You should have dumped the cell phone in the river, but I imagine you left that up to Kinkaid, and he decided to keep it. Now I have a recording of him admitting you hired him to assault and kidnap me."

"He doesn't exactly say that, now does he?"

I reached for the document. "Seems pretty clear to me. I asked him if you hired him for that purpose, and his answer was 'Yeah, but nobody got kidnapped.' That's pretty clear."

"To you, maybe. But that's not what it says to me. Besides, it's his word against mine."

"Hardly. There's forensic evidence as well. If you notice at the bottom of the transcript, Sergeant Dix Lee of the Farmington Police Department and County Sheriff's Detective Lonzo Joe testified they heard the conversation. You might be interested to learn the Dallas police picked up Kinkaid about an hour ago. He'll be back here in time to testify against you."

"You're crazy, Vinson. My lawyers will make mincemeat out of you and these hick cops, including the FBI agent. Anybody assigned to a Podunk joint like this is bound to be the bottom of the barrel. Fingerprints?" He held up both hands, palms facing me. "Take a set before you start making claims."

"Don't need to. Aggie and I got a full set from your wineglass at the restaurant this afternoon."

He froze for a second. "Aggie? So what?" It was obvious his son's cooperation shook him—more than anything so far.

"So you should have been more careful with your stun gun. Your prints were on the batteries, and they tie you to the assault and kidnap attempt."

I tensed as Alfano got up from the sofa. He eyed me a moment and then reached out and grabbed the neck of my pullover sweater. With a jerk, he ripped it to my waist, revealing the microphone taped to my chest. Without pausing, he tore off the tape, leaving me smarting from a crick in the neck and the defoliation of my chest. I managed to swallow my grunt of pain. He dropped the bug to the floor and ground it beneath the heel of his slipper.

"Now it's just you and me," he sneered. "You're trying to weave silk out of straw. You think you can take me down with shit like this? You have no idea who you're dealing with." He laughed. "I know how to pick them, don't I? I needed a queer to track down a queer. Thanks for that, by the way."

"Speaking of queers, why'd you rape Dana before you killed him?" I asked, grateful he hadn't decided to frisk me.

His face went scarlet. "What? Don't you start spreading that crap around. I'll grind you up and spit you out. I'll take everything you have. Those paltry millions your old man left you won't even cover your legal fees. You can't get away with calling me a faggot."

"It's not up to me. That wineglass from the restaurant—it's also got DNA."

That stopped him, and for one brief second the look on his fleshy face showed he knew he was losing control of the situation. The moment passed. He sneered. "Hope they got something to compare it with. When it comes up a mismatch, my civil case against you will be even stronger."

"I don't understand people like you. You put your younger son through hell because he's gay, but you're as queer as he is."

"Don't give me that shit." He hesitated and licked his lips. "Even if they find something in that Norville queen, I wouldn't be the first real man to shag a punk as payback."

Now I knew how to get to him. "I considered that possibility until I learned you fucked him before he left California."

"Same thing. *If* I did that, it was to show him he couldn't get away with debauching my son. Besides, he was big enough to fight me off—if he wanted to, that is."

"You're pathetic, Alfano. You despise your son for being what you, yourself, are."

"Anybody who knows me knows I'm not queer."

"You used a stun gun on Dana in California. Rendered him helpless, stripped him, and raped him. He confessed it all to Lando. He gave your son details Dana wouldn't have any way of knowing if you hadn't stripped for him. A rape is about power, but fucking is about lust. A rapist doesn't have to strip to do what he wants. But you undressed and challenged him to look at a real man. Begged Dana to accept you, but he laughed at you."

Alfano flinched but held on to his self-control. Was it working? Had I found a dent in his armor?

"You know what he told Lando? You did a pathetic job of it. He said he'd had high school kids better than you."

Still standing, he leaned forward, towering over me as I sat in the chair. "Laughed at me? He begged me to fuck him. Said he was tired of candy-assed kids. He wanted a real man. Wanted to know what it felt like getting it from an alpha male. Well, I showed him. I left him a quivering mass of jelly."

"Funny, he remembered it differently. Helpless, yes, because you hit him with the stun gun again before you left. Afraid he'd come after you, I guess. After being with Lando, he thought at least you'd be—"

"Shut your filthy mouth."

The man was finally rattled. It was almost too easy. Most of what I was throwing at him had come from Lando earlier this evening, but the rest was straight out of my imagination.

"Tell me about Bisti? Was Dana begging for it then too?"

"Damned right. Had his hands all over me. He—"

"You're pitiful," I said. "Why would a handsome young man in the prime of life in love with another handsome man want a gross, over-the-hill jerk like you?"

Alfano sucked air.

"We know you were in contact with him. The authorities have the records for the cell phone you gave Kinkaid. It shows a host of calls to Dana's cell. You were begging for it again, weren't you? Whining like a teenage kid. It drove you crazy imagining your son getting what you wanted. It ate you up knowing they were doing it every day. Does your wife know, Alfano? Does she know what a twisted deviant she's married to?"

"I'm warning you—"

"Dana said you were like a little kid trying to get it off. Wondered how you'd fathered three children. Wanted to know—"

Alfano took a swing but didn't get much power behind it. Still, he rang my bell. My vision blurred, but I pushed him away and tried to rise. He snatched a pen from the table. I twisted sideways, raising a hand to protect my jugular. When he touched my arm, my spine arched. I fell back against the chair, toppling it over. The damned thing wasn't a pen; it was a miniature stun gun.

He came at me again. I scrambled away on all fours, seeming to move in slow motion. He touched my neck; my nerves went crazy as electricity poured into my system. He zapped me enough to render me helpless. When the pain finally eased, I felt as if I were swimming against the tide. Every movement took great concentration.

"You fairy son of a bitch!" he screamed.

Alfano grabbed my shoulder and flipped me over on my back with one hand trapped beneath me, the other flung out. My knees were splayed. With a sense of unreality, I realized the bastard was bent on murder. Even as panic swept over me, the hand beneath me—the right one—touched cold steel. My revolver. Damn, my revolver was still in my belt. Trying to collect my frazzled wits—not an easy task with my circuits blown to hell and gone—I concentrated on the fact this was a desperate situation. Deadly.

Alfano stood astride me, making a loop of his belt, and that focused me, although it didn't restore the marrow to my bones.

"That… belt," I grunted, "strangled… Dana?" Maybe I could kick him in the crotch if my legs cooperated. They wouldn't.

Surprised, he glanced at the leather strap. "As a matter of fact, it is. You're right. I tore Norville a new one out at Bisti. Hadn't planned on killing him, just on letting him know who was boss. But he wasn't very smart. As soon as I let him up, he started yelping about telling Lando. Telling the whole goddamned world. He was going straight to the hospital and get a physical examination. Well, I couldn't let that happen. I couldn't let a little queen go around babbling about me like that."

Strength was slowly flowing back into my arms and legs. I had to keep him talking. "San… Santillanes. He figured… it out." I tried to sound weaker than I actually was.

"First the incompetent idiot let Lando get away from him. Then I find out he shot at him—shot at my kid. Then on the way to the plane out on the mesa, he was dumb enough to demand more money. It was so damned easy it was almost funny. As soon as he parked the car, I reached over and pulled out his pistol. It was right there on a holster practically under my nose. There, does that tell you everything you want to know?"

I managed to shake my head. "N… no. What… going to do with Lando if… if Santillanes caught him?"

"Reason with him. I'd have won him over. Lando's a smart boy. He's family. Family loyalty would have kicked in."

"Like now?" I asked weakly. "He told everything to… police and FBI."

"You fucking liar!" he screamed. "Lando won't betray me. He's my blood. And blood—"

"Means nothing," I said, more forcefully than intended.

He bent over me, and I saw he still held that vicious silver cylinder. It didn't carry the punch of a larger gun, but it would do the job if he held it to my flesh long enough. I batted at his hand and he drew back, giving me an evil grin.

"Oh, no. None of that."

I stalled. "Can't get away with… dead body… your room."

His laugh was more like a snarl. "Of course I can. You came up here uninvited and tried to blackmail me with lies about what Lando said to you. We argued. One thing led to another. I had to protect myself, didn't I?" He laughed again. "My lawyers won't have any trouble convincing a jury that a captain of industry's words are worth more than a queer who snoops into other people's business."

I willed my leg to move—the one with the bullet wound because the throbbing scar let me know it was still alive. It was more of a spasm than a kick. Even so, the force of the blow to his groin propelled him backward. He fell across the coffee table and went over. Still flat on my back, I fished around in my jacket pocket, jerked out my cell, punched a single digit, and yelled, "Now! Now!"

Groaning with pain, Alfano crawled to his feet and kicked the phone out of my hand. He no longer held the tiny stun gun, which was somewhere amid the wreckage of the table, but he still had his belt. He quickly swung the loop over my head, and with his foot planted on my chest, he jerked the leather strap tight, the buckle snug against my throat. I watched his cold eyes as he strangled me.

Darkness closing in fast, I tried to fight, but nothing would work properly. He batted away my ineffectual blows. I tried to twist my body, but his foot on my chest held me down. Finally I fumbled around beneath me. My hand closed over the pistol's grip. Unable to see anything but diminishing shadows, I managed to pull my gun out. With no idea where I was aiming, I pointed upward and pulled the trigger. My hearing was virtually gone, but I knew the thing went off because it jumped out of my hand. The pressure eased slightly. I managed to catch one breath before it tightened again.

But now I was able to get a couple of fingers beneath the belt buckle crushing my larynx. My eyesight partially restored, I dimly made out Alfano teetering over me. His knees began to buckle; his shoulder glistened with blood. He dropped to all fours across my chest, struggling to maintain the pressure even as his strength ebbed. He was intent on killing me if it was the last mortal act of his life.

There was a loud crash and the sound of wood splintering. Suddenly men poured into the room. Men and a woman. Dix Lee was the first person I recognized as she pulled a now unconscious Anthony Alfano off me.

"'Bout… time," I wheezed as she loosened the belt from my neck.

"Had a little trouble with the lock," she said matter-of-factly. "Had to smash in the door."

As Lonzo helped me to a sitting position, Dix took in my naked chest. "Nice."

"Thanks. How's Alfano?" I croaked.

Gaines handed me a glass of water. "He'll probably live if they get the bleeding under control. Why did he try to kill you? He must have known he couldn't get away with that."

"Because he's an arrogant SOB who thinks money can buy anything," Lonzo answered for me.

Nothing had ever tasted as sweet as that water. Dix pulled away the glass before I was through. I protested.

"Not too fast. Just wet your throat. Tell us what happened. The bug went dead. I take it from the state of the rag hanging off of you that Alfano found it."

I nodded. "But not the camera and the recorder in the attaché case. That got everything. He admitted it. Admitted he…." I coughed. "Admitted he killed them both. Norville and Santillanes."

"Well, he's got another charge to face too," Dix said. "And this time the FBI, the sheriff's office, and half the FPD saw him. And there's a good chance you've got video of it too."

Epilogue

FOUR OF us gathered in my room at the Trail's End shortly after noon the following day. My neck was badly bruised but I was able to talk so long as I kept something at hand to lubricate my pipes. At the moment, that was one of the bottles of fine Alfano Zinfandel Aggie had located in a local wine shop. He and Lando spent an hour or so with me before heading back to Napa Valley.

If either man was distressed with me for shooting his father and exposing him as a double murderer, he hid it well. I detected a certain grimness in Aggie, but I understood that was because he recognized that dreaded day had finally arrived. The whole weight of the Alfano business enterprise was now draped squarely across his shoulders.

Lando, although his metamorphosis back into a full-fledged Alfano was complete, had a cloud of sadness clinging to him. It would take a long time before he got over feeling guilty about Dana's death.

Paul had chartered Jim's Cessna as soon as he heard about the attack in the Courtyard, and Del, already studying a brief on his next case, returned to Albuquerque with Jim. Now, Paul sat on the bed beside me, sipping wine and inspecting the angry welts on my throat. The way Jazz and Henry, on the bed opposite us, eyed their drinks made it clear they were not fans of the grape. I thought of offering Henry a beer from the minifridge in the corner but didn't.

We had already watched a copy of the DVD from my surveillance tape. Much of the visual action was rendered into rubbish because the camera got tossed around during the melee, but the audio was clear and audible 95 percent of the time. I also told them my story, giving them details not contained on the DVD.

Henry shook his head. "I don't understand why he tried to kill you. The guy might have been able to weasel out from under everything if he hadn't done that."

"I get it," Jazz said. "There's nothing a macho man hates more than having his testicles questioned. And a man with an ego like his—and the bucks to match it—would think he could get away with anything. BJ kept poking at him, making fun of him, attacking his manhood until the guy snapped." Jazz flashed a brilliant smile. "But he's not gay, is he?"

"No," I admitted. "He used rape as a weapon to dominate Dana. Intimidate him. And that means he was telling the truth about one thing, at least."

"What was that?" Henry asked.

"He didn't intend to kill Dana. He would never have left his DNA in him if he had. But when Dana said he was going to the hospital, Alfano knew he couldn't permit that. The tables would have turned against him then."

"You took a hell of a chance, Vince," Paul said, a note of censure hiding in his voice.

"And almost got creamed for your trouble," Jazz added.

"My fault," I said. "I counted on Alfano being arrogant and overconfident because in his mind he was just dealing with a fairy. Even so, I ought to have realized he'd have some sort of protection within reach. And his history with stun guns should have made me suspicious."

"Well, he made a mistake," Jazz said. "He tangled with the wrong fairy. Too bad you didn't kill him. He deserved it. Dana was a nice guy."

"I'm glad I didn't. That would have been too quick. Can you imagine the humiliation of going from a Napa Valley powerhouse to a federal inmate? And when the feds are through with Alfano, the state of New Mexico wants its piece of him."

"I didn't know they caught that guy Kinkaid," Henry said. "Didn't hear a word about it on the news."

"They didn't. I lied to Alfano. But don't worry, they'll get him. Maybe those two will share a cell."

"Vince," Paul said, still eyeing my bruises, "there's something on that tape I don't understand. Why was that buyout of the other vineyard so important? Like you pointed out, it wouldn't even begin to close the gap between him and Sabelito."

"It was a big secret, but Alfano had put together a consortium to build a large commercial development on the De Falco land. He'd planned on doing that with Sabelito money as well. And he was right. The old man's money would have helped him become as big or bigger than Titus."

"How does Aggie feel about that?"

"You know, I kept asking Aggie why he opposed the De Falco buyout, and his reasons—while true—didn't quite make sense. Before he left, he admitted he'd been working with a different group to buy the land and put up a similar commercial and industrial complex. His bunch was the other interested party Lando mentioned."

"So what's the big deal?" Henry asked. "Let his old man do it, and he reaps the benefits anyway."

Again, it was Jazz who figured out the answer. "Because then it would have been his old man's accomplishment, and he wanted it to be his own. Am I right, BJ?"

"Dead on, my friend. Aggie has an ego too. If he'd pulled this off, he would have been free of his old man."

"Guess he is anyway," Paul said. "Alfano's out of the picture now—for good."

"And it couldn't happen to a nicer guy," I added.

"Aggie turned out to be sort of an okay guy, despite all that," Jazz said.

"Yeah, he did." I slid my hand beneath the pillow closest to me and pulled out two envelopes. "And he left these for you guys. Cashier's checks for $5,000 each. More important, you made a very powerful friend for life—a couple of them."

"Right on. A guy can always use friends." Jazz looked at his check and whistled. "I've never seen that much money before."

"Not of my own, anyway," Henry agreed.

"Don't spend it all in one place."

My decision not to pull out the beer proved to be prudent. The two brothers left shortly thereafter, leaving me alone with Paul. I endured the mandatory lecture on being careful—Paul's plus the one he delivered for Hazel. Then he twisted on the bed and gave me a look.

"What?" I asked.

"You didn't tell me what a looker Jazz was."

"I didn't? I was sure I—"

"I'm glad you didn't. I'd have been red-faced and green-eyed."

"You would have worried for nothing. I've got the looker I want."

"You already told me you were tempted."

"Yeah, tempted to drop the case and rush back home." I turned serious. "But that's the only battle I had to fight. You've got Jazz outclassed ten ways from Sunday."

Paul smiled. "Liar. But you get an A for effort."

"And what does an A get me?"

"Come over here, and I'll show you."

Prologue

Lazy M Ranch in the New Mexico Bootheel

THE THIEF froze as a string of sharp yips ripped the quiet night. Both big Dobermans were darted and sleeping soundly out at the fence, so this yapper must be a house pet.

A light flashed briefly as the back door opened. A furball with pointed ears bounded down the steps and made straight for him. The feisty canine latched onto his pant leg and whipped it back and forth, growling furiously. A growl was preferable to a bark, so he dragged his dog-impeded leg like a zombie in some old Hollywood movie.

As he reached the poultry pen, all hell broke loose. A single quack built into a raucous caterwauling. Someone must have flipped a switch up at the house because brilliant light suddenly flooded the enclosure. He reeled backward, stunned by a sea of white.

Ducks. Dozens of ducks. *Hundreds*. How was he going to find the right one?

The dog attached to his pant leg shifted its grip and closed painfully on his ankle. Cursing, he gave an involuntary kick, sending the pooch over the fence and into the pen. The ducks scattered, opening a circle of dark earth around the confused mutt. The pup transferred its attention to the birds and began a joyful chase, dashing this way and that, parting its panicked prey in dizzying waves of undulating white and creating a living kaleidoscope of shifting shades and shapes.

Then he saw her. In a coop all by herself. Like she was waiting to turn into a swan or something.

A clamor from the house galvanized him into action. He vaulted the fence, threw open the cage door, and dragged her out by the neck. He ignored the claws raking flesh from his forearms as he fled through a horse corral at the back of the pen. He made it to the cover of some shrubbery before the ranch came alive. Moments later a woman's agonized wail rose above everything.

Remembering he was to deliver the duck alive, he loosened his hold on the feathery neck. The bird immediately set up a loud protest that could have awakened the dead but wasn't enough to overcome the clamor of the hundred or so other birds. He turned and headed for his pickup. Best get out of there before Millicent Muldren's drovers filled him full of lead.

Chapter 1

Ten days later. Albuquerque, New Mexico

I JERKED the cell phone away from my ear and looked at it as if it had lost its mind—or its chip.

Del Dahlman, a local attorney, wanted me to drop everything and run down to the UNM Emergency Center to interview a man named Richard Martinson. When he told me why, I assumed he was kidding. He had to be.

"You want me to go question a ducknapper? There's no such thing. He's just a plain, ordinary chicken thief."

"Whatever," Del said. "BJ, I need you to catch him before he leaves the emergency room."

He always called me Vince, a carryover from the days when we were a couple. Anytime he resorted to addressing me as BJ like the rest of the world, he was pissed. But this was simply too good to let go. "Have you called in the FBI yet?"

"Don't be an ass," Del snapped.

"Donkeys, now? What is this? A menagerie run amok? Who did it? The pigs? Good Lord, it's Orwell's *Animal Farm* come to life."

"Dammit. I'm serious. *This* is serious. I need you to get over there right away."

I stared at the bright blue sky on this cloudless Saturday afternoon and considered hanging up on him. I was standing on the fourth tee of the golf course at the North Valley Country Club with Paul Barton. Although we lived together, it was a rare occasion when Paul and I could share the daylight hours. Between my confidential investigations business and Paul's schedule—UNM grad school summer courses and an aquatic director's job at the country club—we were the proverbial ships passing in the night.

I resented Del's intrusion, but he and I go back a long way—some of it sweet, some of it bittersweet, and some downright sour.

"You need to get a move on," he said. "You've got to get to him before they let him go. His name's Richard Martinson, but… but they call him Liver Lips."

Del didn't like playing the straight man.

"Liver Lips? Calves' liver or—No, don't tell me. Let me guess. Goose liver."

"You're wasting my time."

"Hey, you called me. Right in the middle of my backswing, as a matter of fact."

"You're a private investigator. Are you going to go investigate or not?"

I sighed. Del was one of my better clients. "Okay. Give me the details. There's really a lawsuit on this thing?"

"It's not actually a suit… yet."

"Then why is your firm involved? More to the point, why are you involving me?"

He went defensive. "We're New Mexico counsel for the Greater Southwest Ranchers Insurance or GSR, as they like to be called—and the VP handling their problem and I are old friends. At this point I'm simply doing this as a favor to him. At any rate, the missing bird's name is Quacky Quack the Second. This—"

"Quacky what?"

"Shut up, Vince."

I snickered through the rest of his briefing, hung up, and turned to my golfing companion. Paul got as good a laugh out of it as I had. In fact we both broke up a couple of times during the retelling.

I DO not like walking into a situation I don't understand, and I damned well didn't understand this one. But I had no trouble locating Martinson in the waiting room at the hospital. Liver Lips. The young man's nickname described him perfectly. His thick, purple-hued oral projections drew my eye like a magnet. It was only later I noticed he was skinny, seedy, and carried a generally disreputable air. Gray eyes darted here and there as if he were constantly searching for a bolt-hole. The man's scalp glistened through thin strands of frizzy blond hair. Whether talking or listening or simply idle, his dark tongue periodically snaked out to wash those heavy lips.

Seldom had I been so thoroughly repulsed by another's physical appearance.

He looked at me blankly after I handed over my card and introduced myself. Then he read the card aloud.

"B. J. Vinson, Confidential Investigations. A private eye, huh? What you want with me?"

"I need to ask you a few questions." I nodded at the bandages covering his forearms. "What happened?"

"Got in a fight with a thorn bush. Frigging bush won." He went for humor, glancing up through thin, colorless lashes to see if it worked.

I pointed to the red veins snaking up out of the white bandages just short of his elbows. "Thorn bushes didn't give you that infection. That's blood poisoning. How'd you get it?"

"Tangled with the wrong bush, I guess. Didn't get it treated, so it turned bad on me, I guess."

"Come on, and I'll give you a ride down to my office where we can talk in private."

"Ain't got time. Gotta get outa here. I been here six frigging hours."

"Okay. I'll call Lt. Eugene Enriquez down at APD, and we'll have this talk in his office."

He blinked rapidly three times. "No cops, man. Don't need no cops. I ain't done nothing, so leave me alone."

"What are you doing up here? You live down in Deming, don't you?" I drew on the thin biography Del provided.

"Ain't no law against a man visiting the city. I guess that's why they do all that advertising on TV for. You know, to get me to come up here and spend my money."

"You want to tell me about it?"

"About what?" He seemed genuinely perplexed by my question.

"About stealing a valuable… bird."

If I'd said *duck*, I'd have burst out laughing.

"Don't guess I know what you're talking about."

"You do a lot of guessing, Richard. But I don't think the sheriff of Luna County would have sicced me on you if he was just guessing."

"Hidalgo," he blurted.

"What?"

"Sheriff of Hidalgo County."

"Okay. Now that you've admitted you know all about the theft, tell *me* about it."

"Didn't admit nothing."

"You know where the abduction—uh, theft took place. Stop wasting my time. What did you want with a prize duck named…." I stopped, unable to call a bird by that ridiculous name.

"Quacky Quack the Second," he said. "That's what old Mud Hen calls her. Ain't that a hoot?"

"Mud Hen?"

"Millicent Muldren. Everbody calls her Mud Hen."

"She's the duck's owner?"

"Yeah. She's run the Lazy M Ranch since her old man died."

"Why'd you steal her duck?"

"Who says I did?"

I improvised. "About everybody in the countryside. Police chief, sheriff, Ms. Muldren. There's a warrant out for your arrest. Talk to me, and maybe I can do something about that."

Old Liver Lips wasn't as dumb as he looked. Those blood-suffused appendages quivered a couple of times before he squared his thin shoulders. "Ain't nobody gonna arrest me for nothing, I guess. Who'd press charges on something like that?"

"Mud Hen for one and the insurance company for another."

"Insurance company?"

"You didn't know the owner insured her property?"

"Shoot. I guess there ain't no insurance company in the world that'd insure a frigging duck."

I didn't know much more than he did, but I couldn't let up on him now. "Then you'd guess wrong. They'll insure soap bubbles if you pay the premiums."

Liver Lips wiggled in his chair, looking distinctly uncomfortable. "Uh, you said something about a warrant?"

I was flying totally blind. I had no idea if there was a warrant out for this character. In fact I didn't even know why he was suspected of the theft or how Del found out he'd be at the UNM Emergency Center today.

"Yes. But I can deal with that if you give me what I want."

"Like what?"

"Like what have you done with Qua—with the duck?" His eyes slid away as he opened his mouth and licked his lips. I held up a hand. "Don't bother to deny it. You're caught flat-out. Man up and admit it. Where's the duck?"

"Dunno." The word came out in a whisper.

"Why not?"

"Somebody took her."

"We've already established that. You took her. What did you do, pluck her and eat her? You like roast duck, Liver Lips?"

His thin shoulders twitched. He did that rapid blinking thing and twisted his neck to loosen it up. A bead of sweat worked its way through thin tendrils of blond hair and trickled down his forehead. It looked muddy by the time it reached the corner of his eye. "Hell, I didn't eat her. I give her to somebody."

"Who?"

His pale eyes clouded over. "Just somebody wanted to play a trick on Mud Hen."

"Who was this 'somebody'?"

"I give up his name, he'll get me in trouble. And he can do it too."

"So can I. A world of trouble. You've already given me enough to report to the insurance company. You're the chicken thief, Liver Lips. And they'll come after you hard. You have any idea how far they'd go to keep from paying out all that money?"

"How much money?" His attitude changed. If Liver Lips possessed a crafty side, this was it.

"More than you can ever repay in your lifetime." I built on the fiction I was spinning. "They'll see you prosecuted for grand theft. What does your record look like? Probably penny ante, right? Well, you made the big time with this."

"For stealing a duck?"

I stared at the raunchy-looking man and wondered if this was an act. "Answer my question. Who hired you to steal the duck?"

"Hired?"

Jeez. The guy hadn't even been paid. He'd done it as a favor. Or else someone had leverage on Richard Martinson.

"Who told you to take the duck? Who'd you give it to?"

"Her."

"Her?"

"It's a her. The duck, I mean. Quacky—"

"Who'd you give her to?"

Liver Lips crossed his arms over his chest and hugged himself tightly. "Oh shit! I hurt, man. They supposed to be getting me something for the pain. And the infection too. I gotta go check on it."

"Okay. We'll go together. Maybe I can help."

"I can do it." The words came out as a whine. "I ain't no kid that needs babysitting."

Despite his objections I trod on his heels as he walked toward a counter. They'd made some big-time changes at the UNM Emergency Center since I was here last. It was now housed in a new building called the Pavilion, but I was pretty sure this wasn't the outpatient pharmacy. Liver Lips was getting ready to make a move. He did, but it wasn't the one I expected. Probably not the one he anticipated either.

He turned a corner and bumped squarely into a burly Albuquerque cop. Backpedaling, he held out his hands in a plea. "Sir, this here guy won't leave me alone. Can you make him stop pestering me?"

The six-foot-two officer transferred his irritated look from Liver Lips to me. His shoulder unit belched static, but he ignored it. "What's going on?"

I took a quick peek at his nametag. "Corporal Hines, my name is Vinson. I'm a licensed PI. I'm going to reach for my ID, okay?"

The outside door crashed open and I whirled. A man and a woman rushed inside with a little girl nursing a bloody hand wrapped in stained towels. Hines brushed by me to see if his help was needed. When I turned back to confront Liver Lips, he was nowhere in sight. I made a quick sweep of the hallways, but he'd disappeared. Maybe Liver did have a crafty side, after all.

Muttering under my breath, I headed for the parking structure to get my Impala. On the way, I hit the speed dial on my cell.

Del wasn't pleased with the interview results, and I couldn't blame him.

"So to sum it up," he said, "you're convinced Martinson kidnapped— excuse me, *stole* the duck. You think he did it at the behest of someone else and has turned the bird over to that party. Other than that, the only thing you learned is that Millicent Muldren, the esteemed daughter of an old-line New Mexico ranching family, is called Mud Hen behind her back."

"That about covers it. What do you want me to do now?"

"Nothing. I'll let the client know Liver Lips is running, probably back to the Deming area. He doesn't seem to have personal ties anywhere else. Go back to your golf game, Vince."

"Too late for that. And thanks, by the way. Today was the first time Paul and I had any time together in a month."

"The two of you still making it okay?"

"Smooth as silk, except for our schedules. We seldom manage to meet up except at night."

"That's probably why it's still working." He hung up.

I was out of sorts, possibly for the rest of the day. Paul's schedule reclaimed him, so I left the UNM parking structure and headed west on Lomas. The office was closed, but I'd been in the field working on a case since yesterday afternoon, so my manager, Hazel Harris, likely left a pile of documents for me to review and sign. Might as well get that chore over and done with instead of waiting for Monday.

Hazel and Charlie Weeks—the retired cop who was fast becoming a full-time investigator for me—had wrapped up a couple of cases. Charlie was not only a godsend to my business, but he also kept my mothering, smothering office manager off my back. The two were becoming quite a pair around the office, although they continued to believe it was a secret.

I settled down at my desk and reviewed the reports they'd left for me. After signing off on the documents, I went through my unread mail, making a few notations and dictating an answer or two before snapping off my desk lamp.

Still vaguely disgruntled, I swiveled my chair to the windows behind my desk and allowed the vista to slowly calm my nerves as I came to grips with my ill-defined sense of unease. It was not Del's interruption of my pleasant afternoon with Paul—although that was a factor—as much as it was a sense of failure. Of leaving a job unfinished, a goal unattained. Liver Lips had outfoxed me, and that did not sit well.

A pleasant evening with Paul finally laid the thing to rest.

Until, at one fifteen in the morning, the telephone rang.

DON TRAVIS is a man totally captivated by his adopted state of New Mexico. Each of his mystery novels features some region of the state as prominently as it does his protagonist, a gay ex-Marine, ex-cop turned confidential investigator. Don never made it to the Marines (three years in the Army was all he managed) and certainly didn't join the Albuquerque Police Department. He thought he was a paint artist for a while, but ditched that for writing a few years back. A loner, he fulfills his social needs by attending SouthwestWriters meetings and teaching a weekly writing class at an Albuquerque community center.

Facebook: Don Travis
Twitter: @dontravis3

THE ZOZOBRA INCIDENT

A BJ VINSON MYSTERY

DON TRAVIS

A BJ Vinson Mystery

B. J. Vinson is a former Marine and ex-Albuquerque PD detective turned confidential investigator. Against his better judgment, BJ agrees to find the gay gigolo who was responsible for his breakup with prominent Albuquerque lawyer Del Dahlman and recover some racy photographs from the handsome bastard. The assignment should be fast and simple.

But it quickly becomes clear the hustler isn't the one making the anonymous demands, and things turn deadly with a high-profile murder at the burning of Zozobra on the first night of the Santa Fe Fiesta. BJ's search takes him through virtually every stratum of Albuquerque and Santa Fe society, both straight and gay. Before it is over, BJ is uncertain whether Paul Barton, the young man quickly insinuating himself in BJ's life, is friend or foe. But he knows he's stepped into something much more serious than a modest blackmail scheme. With Paul and BJ next on the killer's list, BJ must find a way to put a stop to the death threats once and for all.

www.dsppublications.com

9 781635 331127